FALLING

FALLING

JOHN CONNOR

First published in Great Britain in 2007 by Orion Books,
an imprint of The Orion Publishing Group Ltd
Orion House, 5 Upper Saint Martin's Lane
London, WC2H 9EA
An Hachette Livre UK Company

A CIP catalogue record for this book is
available from the British Library.

Typeset by Deltatype Ltd,
Birkenhead, Merseyside

Printed in Great Britain by
Clays Ltd, St Ives plc

The Orion Publishing Group's policy is to use papers that
are natural, renewable and recyclable products and made
from wood grown in sustainable forests. The logging and
manufacturing processes are expected to conform to the
environmental regulations of the country of origin.

www.orionbooks.co.uk

This is for Veronica and Tapio Ollila,
and for Joseph and Rachel Ball

ACKNOWLEDGEMENTS

Thanks to Thomas Alexander Winship. And to Anna, especially this time. To Yvette Goulden, Sara O'Keeffe, Melissa Weatherill, Ray Dance, Andrea Rees, Sarah Hardman and Nicola Bieliki. And to Jas Mahal, Dennis Roddy, Tony McCourt and, again, to Rachel Leyshon for excellent work on the detail.

FRIDAY, 8 JUNE

1

Steve Fleming lay in the darkness listening, holding his breath. A noise from outside had punctured his dreams, kicking him back to consciousness. He waited for his senses to catch up, then turned his head, looking towards his wife, who was sound asleep beside him. Enisa was so quiet, so still, he had to place his fingertips against her bare shoulders to reassure himself. She registered his touch and mumbled something from the depths of her sleep.

The heat from her skin was startling. Since she had fallen pregnant strange things were happening to her metabolism. At night she became so warm the quilt was always pushed away from her, bunched up as now in the space between them, leaving her naked. Before the pregnancy – in London – they had slept wrapped around each other for nearly the whole night. Now, within minutes of falling asleep, she was so hot there was a slippery sheet of perspiration between them, and he had to roll away. He could not remember it being like this with Jana, their first child.

His ears strained into the night silence. He could hear nothing. Perhaps he had dreamed it. He allowed himself to breathe, but carefully, still alert. He slept so lightly these days that almost anything could wake him. They had been in this house for six months, but the place still felt unfamiliar to him, full of unexplained night-time movements. Partly it was the entombing silence from outside that unsettled him. He wasn't used to living in the countryside. Every house he had lived in before had been near a busy road.

He tried to remember the sound. A car door gently closing? But he had heard no engine, and the nearest public road was nearly half a mile away. If a car had driven the distance to his driveway he would have heard the engine long before someone got out and closed the door.

He turned onto his side towards the open bedroom door and looked out along the short corridor towards the living room, listening for sounds from Jana's room, halfway along. Jana was six years old and slept like a log. Normally she made no noise at all. He was sure it had not been her. He could see that the light in the living room was still on, as he had left it. Nothing different.

He sighed a little. Why was he so frightened? Enisa slept like her daughter; nothing woke her. But then she was used to the countryside – the silence, the space, the blackness of a clouded night sky without electric light, the absence of neighbours. She had grown up in this kind of environment. And West Yorkshire was her home; they had returned here for precisely that reason.

He had no such comforts. He too had grown up here, but he had spent most of his adult life trying to forget that. West Yorkshire only made him nervous.

Outside – from the direction of the tall pines flanking the drive – an owl screeched, disturbing him again. Had something scared it? His eyes found the alarm clock on the bedside table: 3.33 a.m. How many times did he look at a clock and see the numbers lined up like that: 11.11; 10.10; 14.14? It had happened at least ten times in the last two days. He heard the owl call again, further away now.

In his mind he replayed the sound that had woken him. It was definitely a car door, he decided. He even had an image to go with it, implanted into his dream: men getting out of a car parked just outside the house; balaclavas, gloves, weapons. Maybe he *had* heard the engine. Had there been an engine in his dream? He started to sweat. He had fears like this almost every night. Why had he allowed Enisa to bring them back here?

He had left West Yorkshire fifteen years ago, in 1986, just after his sixteenth birthday. The circumstances of his departure still made him deeply uncomfortable. In effect, he had run away – although he had told his parents where he was going – and went to stay with an aunt who lived in Brentford, a suburb of London. His parents had then come to some kind of arrangement with the aunt to keep him there. He had told no one the reason for his departure, but somehow they had all sensed that trouble was behind it, and that had been enough.

In London things had got better for him. The aunt had encouraged him to study, and taken an interest that was lacking in his parents. His father was an unemployed textile mill worker, and through most of Steve's childhood he had seemed to be either drunk, asleep or ranting about 'pakis'. His mother had worked all hours in a variety of menial jobs, trying to support them without State help. But she had shared his father's reliance on booze and, in the end, it had unravelled her too. By the time Steve was a teenager they were both out of work and the atmosphere in the flat was a poisonous mixture of stale alcohol, racial bitterness and explosive, drunken rows. They had rarely been sober enough to control a teenage son.

The flat had been on a Bradford council estate, near Dudley Hill. Not a bad estate – at least, not as he remembered it – but certainly worlds away from where he was now. That he was living in a 'detached' house still made him want to snigger like a guilty kid getting away with something. As a child he had always had the smallest room in the flat – a space a little larger than the second toilet in this place. The flat had been in a five-storey sixties block with paper-thin walls, so he had grown accustomed to filtering out sounds. Now he was finding it difficult to sleep in the absence of noise. He had to remind himself that silence was no cause for fear. Isolation was a good thing. There was much less chance of anything happening out here than on a council estate.

Another noise, again from the front of the house.

His heart began to quicken. He sat up in bed, wide awake now, his brain running through the options. Had he heard someone whispering?

He placed his feet on the cold, rough floor. They had hired a machine for this weekend, to strip the boards. He stood up and turned towards Enisa, ready to tell her to be quiet if she woke, but all his senses focused on the silence now, on what he could detect from outside. He heard it again. *Someone was whispering.*

Enisa slept on. He walked quickly into the hall, past Jana's closed door, then crept through the living room towards the front door. There was a small window to the left of it. If there was someone out there he would see them through that. Belatedly he realized he was naked and looked absurd, but there was nothing he could do about that now. He had to see what it was.

As he brought his eye to the dusty pane of glass, he began to think of innocent explanations. The farmhouse was situated in an area of woods and fields east of Leeds, between Aberford and Barwick. To burgle this far out of town meant a deliberate targeting. The thieves would have to get a car, plan the attack. But why would they do that? The place was in the process of being renovated – the entire first floor was gutted and unusable, with flooring and old plaster piled into a skip on the drive – so the house looked shabby from the outside and was even less impressive within. Maybe it was something else. For an instant he expected to see a police car, thinking it might be some work-related issue, but as his sight adjusted he realized he could see nothing. The driveway outside the house was empty. Had he imagined it?

A slight movement in the shadows at the edge of his vision. He twisted his head sharply, trying to peer through the pane at an angle, so he could see along the front of the house. At the same time, from behind him, he thought he heard the sound of someone stepping onto the gravel outside the bedroom window, to the rear of the house. He straightened up, heart thumping loudly.

He heard the sound again: a foot crunching the gravel. It was unmistakable. They had come round the back as he had moved to the front. The bedroom he had just left was at ground level, right beside the patio. They were there – where Enisa was.

He took two quick steps back, still thinking that it couldn't be true, that he was imagining it, that this was the sort of thing that only happened in a nightmare, or a film. Then he heard the glass break.

He froze. The sound was not very loud, but it had come from the bedroom. A crack, like the pane going in (but broken carefully), then the rattle of pieces on the floor. He heard Enisa waking up, murmuring something. Desperately, he looked towards the kitchen. He was unarmed. He thought of the big bread knife, but immediately there was a louder noise – the patio door to the bedroom being kicked in.

He started to run as Enisa shouted out for him. He entered the bedroom flat out, his brain empty of everything except to get there quickly. As he came through the door he had time to see the flapping curtains, the broken glass and two shapes – huge, threatening, alien to his room and his house: one was in front of him blocking his view; the other was on the bed, *actually on the bed*, kneeling over Enisa, doing something to her. Then there was a noise like a firework going off. Something flashed in front of him, hitting his chest with an explosive force. He crashed backwards, striking the bedroom wall and sliding to the floor.

A black silence folded over him, cutting him off from everything. He slipped into a different world. He was aware of himself, floating within the silence, but for a moment could not feel, see or hear. The sense of urgency vanished.

Consciousness returned only slowly, in fits and starts, like a badly spliced film. He knew he was still in his house, but couldn't work out where, or what was happening. The sensations coming at him were ragged; one second rushing and chaotic, saturated with a pain he couldn't place, the next dead quiet, as if sinking through a deep liquid.

Time moved unevenly. He wasn't sure if he was conscious, unconscious, or somewhere in-between. He tried to fix on sounds, smells, touches, to hold onto them, but everything slid past him. He tried to pull himself to his knees. He could hear a sound like air being let out of a tyre. Around his eyes there was an intense pressure, but he could see nothing. Was that Enisa, screaming at the top of her voice? He slumped over again, curling into a ball, unable to stand. From above him he heard blows, grunts, men shouting things.

Something was wrong with him. One of them had struck him with something, but he didn't know what. He tried again to stand but couldn't get his legs to move. He was gasping for breath. The hissing noise was coming from somewhere near his chest. He tried to hold himself still, to concentrate on being able to see something, to hear what was happening.

There were two male voices, shouting and arguing, but not with Enisa. They were shouting at each other.

'No fucking violence! I told you no violence—'

'He was coming at me. I did what I was told to do.'

'We were told to *burgle* this place …'

Broad accents. One from Yorkshire, the other from Manchester. Behind them the sound of his wife, whimpering and sobbing, hysterically pleading with them. '*Please. Please. You have to let me help him …*'

They were shouting over her, infuriated with each other.

'I should fucking kill you for this—'

'*Please. He has hurt no one. Please let me go to him …*'

'I had instructions from Kershaw—'

Kershaw. The name pricked at his memories.

'You had instructions from *me …*'

The words faded from him, then returned, but sounding further away now.

'… keep hold of her, she's seen everything …'

'*Please. I have to help him. Please. I have a daughter …*'

'*You* fucking shot him. You idiot … you fucking idiot … *Keep hold of her!*'

'Not this … I can't. I can't do it …' Was the one with the Yorkshire accent crying? Something about his voice was familiar.

'This is your fault. She saw everything, you fucking arsehole …'

Suddenly he couldn't hear Enisa at all. He began to panic again. He had to move. He had to get them away from her. He reached out a hand in the darkness and found the bed, then turned his head and looked towards the smashed patio doors. His vision cleared slightly, but it felt as if one eye was closed. The room was empty. He could see no one. Outside, as if from very far away, he could hear them arguing still. They were in the garden. He began to pull himself towards the doors.

He managed to stand up, holding himself against the wardrobes, his legs shaking like jelly. He looked around the room, trying to keep focus. He remembered Jana. He couldn't hear her or see her. Where was she? He tried to look behind him, back towards her room, but began to fall as soon as his head turned that far.

Something was seriously wrong with him. He caught himself and stood still. The bed in front of him was empty, the sheets in disarray. He could feel wetness all down the front of his body. He staggered to the patio doors and looked out. The tungsten light at the side of the house had come on, like a floodlight, showing him everything.

There were two of them there. One was holding Enisa, a hand in her hair, pulling her down to his feet, dipping towards her and swinging the other arm, hitting her. She was struggling, trying to get away. The other man was trying to drag him away from her, shouting at him. Steve began really to panic, chest heaving with fright. He had to stop them.

He stumbled forward, out of the doors and into the garden. On the gravel he fell flat on his face. The hissing noise in his chest was louder now, every time he gulped at the air he could hear it. For a moment he was paralysed. He became frantic with fear, his heart thundering. What were they doing to Enisa?

But time was racing, leaving him behind. Had he lost consciousness again? He managed to get a hand to his chest. There was blood running out of him. He began to crawl across the garden, trying to shout at the men, stupidly, trying to tell them to stop, that she was pregnant. But the men were already gone …

Had there been a blade in the hand of the one standing above her? He rolled onto his back, gasping for breath. He was suffocating. Above him he could see stars through a gap in the clouds. He shouted Enisa's name, the voice rasping in his throat. The stars began to spin. He saw the man again, dipping towards her. His brain re-interpreted the image, filled in the blanks.

There had been a knife in the hand that was punching her. The man had been stabbing her.

He closed his eyes and turned over, gritting his teeth, crawling in the direction he imagined she must be. He shouted her name again. This time something bubbled into his throat, choking him. He waited until he could breathe then pushed himself to his knees. Something had happened to one of his eyes. He concentrated with the eye that could focus and picked out her shape, a few feet in front of him.

She was naked, lying in a little heap, curled up, covered in blood. He could see no movement at all. He forced himself towards her and reached out a hand to grip her leg. The skin was warm, but it felt different. She was too still, too heavy. He tried to find her ear, to whisper into it, but her hair was matted with blood, obscuring it.

His strength was leaving him. Pulling his arm around her, he could feel the holes in her stomach, where the baby was. A little boy; they had seen the images of him on the ultrasound scan machine.

He buried his face into the back of her neck and began to sob uncontrollably.

SATURDAY, 16 JUNE

2

Karen was in Leeds with Mairead when her mobile rang. It was a hot summer day – T-shirt and jeans weather – the sky above the town centre a cloudless, washed-out blue. In the streets there was enough heat and congestion to make the air smell of sweat and rubbish.

They were pushing through crowds of slow-moving shoppers on The Headrow, just coming up to Briggate. There was a shop somewhere near the Victoria Quarter Arcades that Mairead had been insisting they visit all morning, a designer 'boutique' where she was hoping to talk Karen into buying her an overpriced bikini.

Recently her daughter had been befriended by an older girl called Alexia. Karen had not met her, and knew only what Mairead had said about her. Alexia was from a wealthy family and older than Mairead by at least a couple of years. She had access to a private pool at someone's house and there was a plan to have a pool party there. That was why Mairead wanted the new bikini.

Mairead swam well, so that didn't worry Karen, but she wasn't sure whether she was being given the whole truth about the proposed party. She instinctively didn't like Mairead mixing with older kids, but there was little she could do about it. She would feel better if she actually met Alexia.

When the phone began to buzz Mairead was in the middle of telling her that Pete Bains – Karen's partner, the man they lived with – *had* met Alexia several times already. If that was true he had said nothing to Karen. It was the kind of thing that, at the moment, provoked endless, petty arguments between them.

Karen kept walking and dug into the cloth bag hanging from her shoulder, looking for the mobile. She found it and paused at the top of Briggate, calling out to her daughter to wait. The crowd pushing out of the pedestrianized street parted clumsily around her. She watched the movement warily, individual people indistinct shapes in her vision. She hated being in crowds, hated the smell of them. Someone bumped into her and she stepped sideways, towards the building line. She kept her eyes on Mairead and pressed the phone to her ear, trying to hear above the sound of traffic and shoppers.

'DC Sharpe?' A male voice, not one she recognized. 'Karen Sharpe?'

'Yes?' A few paces ahead of her, Mairead had walked over towards Borders bookshop.

'DS Thorne. I don't think we've met.'

'No. I don't think so.' She had heard of him, but nothing worth remembering.

'I'm sorry to call you when you're off duty. I hope it isn't a bad moment …'

'It isn't a good moment.' She heard him pause, not liking that. 'But go on. What do you want?'

When he spoke again she could tell he was already irritated with her. 'I'm on Bulldog,' he said. 'I have instructions to call you in. Urgently.'

She felt her spirits sink. It had taken weeks to get this outing with Mairead organized. Not because her own diary was full – for the last year she had been working a straight five-day, nine-to-five shift at Halifax CID – but because Mairead, incredibly at the age of thirteen, never seemed to have a weekend free.

'Can you get here within the hour?' Thorne said, not really asking. 'We work out of Killingbeck.'

She knew that already. She also knew all about Bulldog. News travelled fast from that kind of inquiry. In the last few days she had already picked up more detail about it than she needed or wanted from gossip, divisional briefings and the press. She looked around her and sighed. 'What's it for?'

'Family liaison. I'll tell you more when you get here.' He cut the line.

A rude fucker. He hadn't even waited for her to say she would come. She looked past Mairead to where the crowd was congealing around a couple of buskers, who were about to start playing.

Family liaison. The words grew slowly in her mind, along with the implications. For the last year there had been an unspoken understanding – in Halifax, at least – that she wouldn't be asked to do this kind of thing. She had to deal with victims all the time, of course, but family liaison usually meant the relatives of murder victims. At Halifax she had been sidelined into thefts and frauds. There were victims, but all they had lost was money or property. The cases were difficult, from an evidential point of view, but there wasn't much emotion involved. Emotion was something she needed to avoid.

She knew there was a bereaved child on Bulldog, a six-year-old. When she had been on the CPT – the Child Protection Team – she had dealt with a lot of distressed children. But that was over four years ago. Eighteen months ago things had happened to her which she still couldn't bring herself to think about. She couldn't go back to spending all her waking hours with rape victims and damaged children. Not now.

She chewed her lip and thought about it, worried. She hadn't told Thorne she would come in. Could she try saying she didn't have the training for it? It was over five years since she had dealt with a murder victim's relative, and even longer since she'd completed the family liaison course.

Looking beyond the two buskers in front of Borders she could see a news-stand selling the *Yorkshire Evening Post*. The headlines were the same as they had been every day that week. Tony Blair's second-term election victory hadn't even got a look in. At this distance, without putting on her glasses, she couldn't read all the words, but she could just pick out 'ENISA FLEMING' and below that 'RACIST FURY' ...

'Mum? Are you OK?'

She looked down. Mairead was standing next to her.

'Who was that on the phone?' Mairead asked.

'Someone who wants me in Killingbeck within an hour,' she said. She heard the buskers begin to play. There was a girl with a fiddle and a man with a drum, playing Irish folk tunes.

'Are you going? You promised you would come with me.'

'We'll still get your bikini. Don't worry.' She smiled at Mairead, but inside she was irritated with Thorne for ruining things. Matters were complicated enough between herself and her daughter, tainted by the peculiar history they shared. They rarely got on without friction, but so far today they had surprised each other. Nothing had gone wrong at all. They had enjoyed themselves. Even the wrangling about the bikini had been light-hearted. The plan had been to get the bikini then eat somewhere, a pizza, maybe. There wouldn't be time for food now, and Mairead would have to make her way home alone.

'I might not be able to eat with you afterwards,' she said. 'I'm sorry.'

She began to walk towards the buskers. They were playing something she recognized. She stood on the edge of the circle of people watching them, and tried to rationalize the worry seeping through her.

Enisa Fleming was a paediatrician who had been stabbed to death, along with her unborn child. Her husband Steve Fleming – a prosecutor from Leeds – had survived a gunshot wound; a 'miracle', the press was calling it. But that was eight days ago. Presumably they hadn't waited this long to break the news to their six-year-old child. Someone else would have already been given that shitty task. But that didn't mean they didn't want her to talk to the girl. That was what she had done best when she was on the CPT – child witness interviews.

She felt Mairead's fingers slip through her hand, gripping it, and looked down at her again. Not very far down. Mairead was only a few inches shorter than her. She didn't look thirteen years old. Her unusual height made her proportions seem more adult than many of her friends, not just because she was tall, but also because the growth had stripped her of puppy fat. She had long, straight, dark hair falling to below her shoulders, fine, arched eyebrows (very carefully plucked, Karen noted), high cheekbones and a wide mouth. Of her facial features, only her eyes spoke of youth. She had bright, green eyes, still full of childish innocence. Or so Karen liked to think.

Mairead pushed up against her, slipping her other arm around her waist and squeezing gently. 'You OK, Mum? You look worried.' She didn't have a thirteen-year-old mind, either. Already she had witnessed more horror than most people would encounter in their entire lives.

'They want me to go on that murder inquiry,' Karen said to her, not thinking. The buskers were playing a slow air she recognized from her childhood. The theme stirred an indistinct nostalgia in her.

'Which one?' Mairead asked.

'The one with the stabbed woman. The pregnant Asian woman.' She pointed to the news-stand.

3

Two hours later, at Killingbeck, Karen took a deep breath and un-folded again the sheets of paper they had given her – copies of the two statements so far made by Steve Fleming. She was sitting alone in the office of David Riggs, the Senior Investigating Officer, waiting for Tim Thorne to appear.

She had already read Fleming's statements once, but she made an effort to read them again, this time trying to think about what he had said, so she would remember. The first was made three days after the attack, when he was out of intensive care. The statement was written by a detective named Debbie Moor, a hard-headed and competent officer Karen knew from her days on the CPT.

The most harrowing part came after Fleming had been shot:

... I could see two men attacking my wife on the lawn about ten yards away from me. I could not hear anything they were saying. I could not get to them, though I tried and tried. I tried to get to Enisa and to shout at the men, to frighten them off. But I couldn't shout and couldn't walk. I couldn't do anything. I was very desperate and frightened. I could see that one of the men was holding Enisa down, holding her by the hair, but I couldn't get there to stop him. He was stabbing her, over and over again. I didn't see the knife very well, but the blade was very long and thick, not like a kitchen knife. The men were white. I cannot say what height they were, or what they looked like. They spoke with Northern accents, but I cannot be sure of the exact area ...

Even reading it for the second time she felt her heart reacting to the words. A year and a half ago she would have read it professionally. She would have looked for the details that were useful to the investigation. She would have considered everything rationally, without imagination.

17

The images wouldn't have touched her. But now the scene was running through her head as if she were *there*, watching it: a wounded man helplessly witnessing men knife his pregnant wife in the belly. Over and over again. They had told her at divisional briefings that there were thirty-four separate wounds to Enisa Fleming's torso and that the knife was probably nine inches long.

The men who had inflicted those wounds had looked into Enisa Fleming's terrified eyes when she was thirty-six weeks pregnant. She would have known where they were stabbing her. What had her eyes been like, looking up at them? Confused, vulnerable, stricken with fear, pleading and begging with them for her life? Could they really have looked into her eyes and felt nothing? Was that possible? *She* could feel Enisa's fright and panic *now*; just imagining it brought a tight knot to her chest, constricting her breathing.

This was no good. She took her eyes away from the statement and looked at the calendar hanging on the wall by the SIO's desk. She took a long, deep breath. Her pulse was so fast she could feel it beating in her neck. She forced herself to think about what she was looking at, to ignore the images behind her eyes. The picture on the calendar was of a river and a field, with trees and clouds in the background, painted, not photographed. She made herself hold it in the front of her conscious-ness, then describe it, mentally, finding words to match the pattern of shapes and colours. The more detail the better.

Long ago they had taught her how to do this. To get her mind focused and sharp, to get to a point where she could obsessively and dispassionately observe and enumerate, consciously picking out and memorizing one insignificant detail after another. Her brain was slow to get it now, but she persisted. After a few minutes her mind clicked into the groove, remembering how to do it. She filled her conscious-ness with the picture, the colours, the shapes. She began to describe them to herself, then memorize them. Her breathing settled, and the images from Steve Fleming's garden lost their emotional force.

She turned back to the first statement and tried to consider it like that, keeping her mind on the detail; conscious, observant, detached. Her pulse was still racing, but she felt calmer. She memorized every-thing she could, then turned to the second statement. It was dated a day later. But Fleming had now decided he was uncertain about what had happened:

... In a previous statement I said I thought the men who attacked my wife were white. I have thought about this and can say now that I am not sure about it. For the reasons I have previously given, I was unable to see anything very clearly. I also said they had Northern accents. But their voices sound unclear in my memory. I do not know what accents they spoke with, or what they said. I do not want to confuse anybody, or say things that will lead to the wrong people being arrested. I have tried my best to remember things, but nothing about the night is clear for me ...

'Karen Sharpe?'

She looked up. Two men had entered the office. The first was her own height but powerfully and proportionately built. He was wearing a smart, charcoal-grey two-piece suit, a pale-blue shirt and a navy-blue tie. He looked about forty years old. If he was into a sport she guessed it would be rugby, but not in some brutish position. More like a winger, or fly-half – a role in which speed would be required as well as strength.

He had an immediately commanding presence. He stood in front of her with his hand extended, and she instinctively stood to greet him. She took his hand with the expectation that her own would be crushed. But his grip was careful, surprising. They shook hands, then she stepped back from him automatically, though he was no closer to her than the other man.

'I'm Ronnie Shepherd,' he said.

He had piercing blue eyes and a bald head that was so devoid of hair she could see the fluorescent lighting shining off it. He was staring at her.

'I'm Deputy SIO,' he said. 'Thanks for joining us.' He spoke with a deep bass voice, words weighted with an accent she couldn't place. His face was clean-shaven, with a strong jaw-line and a striking, aquiline nose. But his skin had the blotchy, worn look of someone coping with too many nights without rest. There were dark circles around his eyes and, beyond the intense stare, a weariness with which she was all too familiar. For a moment he held her gaze, as if trying to make a decision of some sort. She kept her position in front of him, her eyes on his.

The other man moved slightly. 'Tim Thorne,' he said. 'We spoke earlier.'

She broke the eye-lock with Shepherd and looked at him. He was shorter and younger than his colleague, with thick brown hair and green eyes. There were old pock marks around his chin, and his lips had a pinched look. He had a younger man's aura of pent-up aggression. He was wearing a creased light-grey suit, which looked as if it might have come from M&S, and a white shirt with the top button undone, no tie.

'Yes,' she said. 'We did.' She forced her brain to relax.

She sat back down in one of two chairs in front of the SIO's desk, expecting Shepherd to move behind it. Instead he sat in the chair next to her, leaving Thorne to walk behind the desk.

'You come highly recommended,' Shepherd said to her. He sat back in the chair, carefully avoiding her personal space, but still very close to her. 'Thanks for coming in.'

'Recommended? By whom? And for what?'

'By Ricky Spencer,' Shepherd said. 'He used to be your boss in the CPT, right? He says you're good with kids.'

She swallowed and stared at him. So it *was* going to be about the child. That meant she was going to have to tell this man something about her past. There was no other way to get out of it.

'I'll try to bring you up to speed,' Shepherd said. 'What do you know so far?'

Should she try to tell him now why she was wrong for this – before he gave her the info? For some reason Thorne's presence was off-putting. Instinctively, she felt she might be able to talk to Shepherd without it getting too awkward. But not to Thorne. She would have to wait until he was gone.

'I know what I've heard at divisional briefings, on the grapevine, and in the press,' she said. 'I've just been given copies of Steve Fleming's statements ...'

'For three days we couldn't get anything from Steve,' Shepherd said. 'Then he gave us what you've seen. He's obviously shocked and confused. An officer called Debbie Moor has been assigned to him, but he doesn't seem to have warmed to her.'

'I rate her,' Thorne said. 'She's a good officer and she'll get there eventually. Fleming doesn't know what planet he's on right now.'

Shepherd didn't look at him. 'That may be, Tim,' he said. 'But at the moment Fleming doesn't want us speaking to Jana, and that's a problem we don't have time for.'

'There are ways we could work around it, to do it without his permission.'

'But we'd rather not. Until today it wasn't even possible to get medical permission to see her.'

'Jana is Fleming's daughter?' Karen asked. She knew that already, but Thorne was making her uncomfortable. Shepherd seemed calm, rational, polite; Thorne was on edge.

'Yes. Six and half years old,' Thorne said. 'She's staying with her grandmother at the moment – Varisha Hussein – up in Alwoodley.'

'Steve and Jana are the only witnesses,' Shepherd started again. 'Unless Steve regains more memories – or more clarity – then he isn't going to be much use. So it's down to Jana.'

'She saw something?' Karen asked.

'We don't know,' Shepherd said. 'We know she made the call to the emergency services. Her mother had taught her how to do it. When we got there she was out in the garden lying next to both of them, asleep. She had even taken a blanket from her room and wrapped it around her mum. At first we thought they were all dead …' He paused to clear his throat noisily. 'From the very beginning,' he continued, 'we've struggled to make sense of what happened. All of Enisa's jewellery was taken, including some very valuable items. So burglary stood out as an obvious motive, but what burglar stabs a pregnant woman to death? Why do that? They were disturbed, certainly, so maybe one of them overreacted and Steve was shot. But why go on to stab Enisa thirty-four times?' He looked at her as if he thought she might answer. 'There are only two real possibilities. One: we're dealing with a psychiatric case, a burglar with a screw loose. Two: they were professionals who killed her because she witnessed the shooting of Steve. They used a knife, instead of a gun, because she had escaped outside, where a gun might be heard.' He held his hands up helplessly. 'We need to know which it was. Steve has given us nothing. Jana *may* have seen something. More likely, she could have heard something, and might be able to tell us about it. That's top priority right now. At the moment we're getting nowhere with what we have. The SIO wants Jana spoken to before the end of today. That's why you're here.'

4

Shepherd insisted on driving her to Leeds Royal Infirmary, where Steve Fleming was being treated. The haste put pressure on her, and they walked in silence to his car, which was parked in the back yard of the station. Outside the sky was still clear, promising further heat and pollution. She was expecting him to drive something big, a four-wheel drive, perhaps; they all seemed to have big black SUVs at that rank. But it was a navy-blue Porsche Carrera, soft-top. Not very practical for a Deputy SIO. Not something you would want to take to every call.

The top was up and the space inside was restricted, intimate. She would only have to move her hand a few inches to touch him. She could smell a faint trace of aftershave on him, nothing too overpowering, but she didn't recognize it.

'Before we go anywhere I need to talk to you,' she said.

He nodded and took his hand away from the ignition. 'I thought so. I could see you were worried about something up there.' He looked across to her. 'Not enough preparation time?'

'No. Not that.'

His expression didn't change. 'What, then?' he asked. He sat twisted in the seat, hands on his knees, looking at her.

She decided to try the easy way first. 'Do you know anything about me?' she asked.

'A little. Tim spoke to Ricky Spencer about you.'

'I'm surprised Ricky recommended me for anything,' she said.

Shepherd allowed himself a very subtle smile, the first she had seen since meeting him. 'Command thinks you have the right skills,' he said. Debbie Moor is good but hard. You're more vulnerable. 'Debbie doesn't really care what happened here. That's why she hasn't clicked with the victim.'

How would he know whether she was vulnerable?

'I got your personnel file out after I knew you were coming,' he said. 'You have commendations for undercover work down in London. But not for the Met. It doesn't say who you were working for.' He paused, waiting for her to say something. She looked blankly back at him.

'That kind of work requires imagination,' he said eventually. 'Enough to be able to pretend to be someone else. People with imagination are always vulnerable. Most coppers have no imagination at all.'

'That file doesn't say much,' she said. 'I was suspended and investigated for two deaths about a year and a half ago. Did you know that?'

'I was told about it. No evidence on one, self-defence on the other.'

She was surprised. Normally that would be enough to put them off. 'You want that kind of risk on your inquiry?'

He shrugged. 'If you end up in that kind of situation, things occur. It could happen to any of us.'

That kind of situation. He didn't have a clue.

'Not *any* of us,' she said.

'I was told you shot one of them.'

'Shot *at* one of them. There was no evidence that bullet even hit him.' She was choosing her words carefully.

He made a dismissive gesture, as if she were pointing out technical differences. 'It happened to me,' he said. 'A long time ago, and not quite the same, but I was suspended and investigated. A man called Ernest Maxwell pulled a shotgun on me at a farm in Swaledale. His wife had put in an emergency call, saying he was attacking her with a knife. I was in the first car to get there. I was a uniformed constable at the time. He pointed the gun right at the car as I came through the farm gates.' He pointed his fingers at her like a gun. 'I drove into him. Didn't even think about it. The gun went off, but wide. He smacked his head off the barn wall and died twelve hours later. He was depressed, apparently, about to kill himself. His wife was unharmed. She spent fourteen months trying to get a manslaughter charge going against me. Ring any bells?'

She shook her head.

'Exactly. But at the time it was a *cause célèbre* of police brutality in North Yorkshire. Nobody has heard of Maxwell now. Nobody remembers. Except his wife, perhaps. And me. I think about him now and again.' He looked only a little sad about it.

'I wasn't around here then,' she said. It was worlds away from the sorts of things she had done. 'I'm sure it was bad for you, but it's not the same. The details against me could easily come out in court. You wouldn't want that.'

'I don't care. All I want you to do is talk to a six-year-old kid that's lost her mum, develop an empathy with her and try to find out, before the end of today ...' He paused, realizing how that sounded, '... *if possible* before the end of today, find out if she saw anything useful. Maybe she didn't. But the SIO, Riggs, wants it doing. I don't need you to give evidence about anything.'

She sighed. It wasn't working. She was going to have to tell him more.

'You have a child, right?' he asked suddenly.

'Yes. A thirteen-year-old. Why?'

'Is that what's bothering you?'

She was puzzled. 'How? How would that make a difference?'

'Ricky told Tim you were a single parent with one child ...'

She scowled. She could just imagine what Ricky Spencer had said about that.

'It wasn't a criticism,' he added quickly.

'What has it got to do with this?'

'I know what that's like,' he said, speaking softly, carefully. 'I know it's different if you have kids. That brings us – you and me – closer to Steve Fleming and his daughter. Fleming is in the same position as you now – he's a single parent. If you speak to little Jana you will probably have to stop yourself getting upset. I understand why you're like that. But it's not something to be worried about. It's normal. I'd be the same.'

'You have a child?' It was hardly a basis for his assumptions.

He grinned, a big open smile that disclosed his teeth. 'She's twenty-five now. But she's my only one. And I brought her up alone.'

'No wife?'

'I had a wife. She walked off twenty-three years ago. We haven't seen her since.'

That he was telling her this would have been clever if it were some kind of strategy to win her over, but he seemed genuine.

'Haven't missed her, either,' he added.

'You're single?'

'I am, as it happens.' Another smile, more inscrutable this time.

'And I was a single parent for a long time. But as I said, Laura is twenty-five now.'

She moved the pieces around in her head, trying to find the pattern that would fit him – single parent, rugby player, Porsche, expensive aftershave, killed a farmer, North Yorkshire, attractive voice, DI, very free with the self-revelations. It didn't work.

'Trust me, you'll be good for this,' he said. 'Debbie Moor, Tim Thorne, half of the rest of them up there,' he waved his arm, '. . . they don't really give a shit what happens to Steve or Jana Fleming. They go home at night and sleep soundly.'

'But not you?'

'Doesn't it show?' He pulled down the sun visor and looked at his eyes in the mirror. 'Look at the state of me. I look like something out of a freak show.' He rubbed his face and scalp harshly, stared at himself. Then he looked momentarily embarrassed. Was that *really* his impression of his own appearance?

'You've been very patient with me,' she said. 'I'm grateful. But it's something else.'

'What else?'

Tell him, she thought. Tell him now.

He turned from his own face in the mirror and looked at her, waiting.

'It's something more personal,' she said at last, then she looked quickly away from him and bit her lip. Even the thought of talking about it made her feel emotional. It was stupid, but she couldn't help it.

'Something to do with what happened a year and a half ago?'

Another good guess. She didn't answer. She couldn't look at him now. She just had to sit there and control it, not say anything. If she spoke he would catch it in her voice.

'If it's something serious, Karen, then you don't need to tell me. If it upsets you, I mean. You don't have to say anything more.'

She knew now she wouldn't be *able* to say anything more. She was shaking a little, and kept her head turned away from him, looking out of the window. She couldn't tell him, which meant she would have to do what he wanted.

'Maybe you're right,' she said after a while. 'Maybe I will be OK.'

5

'Let's get started, chaps. We haven't got all day.' David Riggs, the SIO, glanced around the table, waiting for them all to shut up. He didn't have to wait long. The mood was subdued. Day eight without a suspect. They were well past the immediate detection window now.

Riggs was a short, compact man, with neat, soft, jet-black hair, sharp blue eyes, a delicately pointed nose and chin, and a quirky, pencil-line moustache. Tim Thorne guessed he would be about fifty-two years old – probably average for an SIO – and suspected that both the moustache and the hair were dyed. Riggs was wearing a garish dark-green suit – no doubt something very expensive and designer made; Tim didn't have a clue how to judge these things – and, more prominently, a large, green, spotted bow-tie. That was his trademark – an endless series of bow-ties, each as loud as the other. Lord Riggs, they called him, behind his back, or His Lordship. He spoke with a very plummy, public-school accent, and Tim hated him.

'This might be a big day,' Riggs said. 'Ronnie Shepherd can't join us because the doctors have said that we can speak to Jana Fleming today, so Ronnie is trying to get Steve Fleming to consent. I'm very hopeful about that.' He held his crossed fingers in the air, then placed a pair of half-rimmed spectacles on his nose and flicked through the pages of a policy log in front of him. 'Meanwhile, I need full reports from each of you,' he said. 'Then I can decide how to progress matters. I'll start with you, Simon.' He turned towards Simon Parfitt, the DS tasked with managing forensics.

They were in the large meeting room at Killingbeck and there were seven present, all seated around a collection of desks that had been pulled together to make one big table with a large gap in the middle.

Parfitt scratched at his earlobe. He was about Riggs's age, but taller, fatter and bearded. He was wearing a cardigan over weathered brown cords and a loose cotton shirt. It was Saturday, of course, but he was still a bit too casual for Tim. He looked more like an academic than a DS – and that was his manner, too. Right now he was studiously chewing a pencil.

'Keep it quick, Simon,' Riggs suggested. 'We've a lot to get through.'

Parfitt took the pencil from his mouth. 'There are, to date, eighty-five possible forensic traces from the immediate crime scene alone.' He mumbled almost too quietly for Tim to hear him. 'Eight days in, with everything expedited, I can say that nearly everything that will be of use is processed, with virtually all results back from the lab as of this morning. Many traces are multiples – that is, originating from the same subject – and many have been eliminated already, which was a lot of work and has taken us until today. Having taken out everyone who is either a friend or family of the victim, we are left with forensic questions over twelve individuals.' He looked up momentarily, to emphasize the point. 'Of these we have to date identified eight, two through matches to a database. We had in total five sets of trace group-ings originating from the builders who were renovating the Fleming home at the time of the attack. One of them matches to the DNA database – a man called Ahmed Ibrahim. He has previous for robbery and theft, the last conviction being in nineteen ninety-five. But he has an alibi.'

Riggs took over. 'Basically, it's not the building crew. We knew that from the moment we started pulling them in. The profile for this crime points to very professional operators capable of ruthlessly silencing a witness. The builders just don't fit. You said that, didn't you, Tom?' He looked over at Tom Joyce, who nodded dutifully.

'That really would have been too simple,' Joyce said. 'And Fleming wouldn't have it, either.'

'No. Fleming won't have anyone we suggest to him,' Riggs said, with a hint of irritation. He didn't seem to like Fleming. Maybe he had come across him as a lawyer. 'What about the four non-idents?' he asked.

'One of those is the killer,' Parfitt said. 'Or most probably. As we know, the trace comes from blood beneath Enisa Fleming's fingernails, right hand. The pathologist says she must have scratched her attacker noticeably – there's bits of skin as well as blood. But there's no database match from that, nor any match to other traces from the scene. So whoever killed Enisa Fleming left *only* that trace at the scene and has never been processed before – at least, not in this country; we're still awaiting various foreign results.'

He let that sink in, glancing round the table to see if there were any questions.

'Shall I list the other three unidentified traces?' Parfitt said, when nobody asked anything.

Riggs nodded, writing in his policy log now. Parfitt counted them on his fingers, giving various details. They were a mixture of saliva, hair and fingerprint traces, corresponding to three unidentified individuals, found in various parts of the Fleming home, including one from glass coming from the broken bedroom doors.

'Moving on to the eight we *have* identified,' Parfitt continued. 'You've signed off six already, sir.' He looked to Riggs for confirmation.

Riggs smiled quickly at him. 'I have,' he said. 'Provisionally.'

Tim hadn't known about that.

'With those six out,' Parfitt said, 'it means that in terms of follow-ups there are only two outstanding now – Ian Whitfield and Andrew Lavelle. Lavelle is the estate agent who sold the house to the Flemings. He's not a high probability, but we need to track him down. He left the firm he worked for about two months ago and they think he is still in the area.'

'And Whitfield?'

'Whitfield – along with a man called Ashruff – left many finger-prints throughout the premises. Ashruff is a manager for the removal company that moved the Flemings here from London six months ago. We've had him in and he checks out OK. Whitfield comes back on both prints and DNA. He's the second database match. He has previous for theft and fraud. Last conviction was in November nineteen ninety-nine. Until March this year he was employed by Ashruff. So though we need to speak to him, he also is not a priority. He had a legit reason to leave his marks. And he doesn't match either of the profiles we're working to.'

'Don't let that slip, though,' Riggs instructed. 'I want him found and spoken to. Do we have an address for him?'

'Ashruff didn't have one. That's been the delay. We found out late yesterday that he lives with his girlfriend in Keighley. Someone is due to go there this afternoon.'

Riggs nodded. Parfitt then repeated material about the blood pattern analysis and the ballistics report. Confusion had arisen because, taken together they had been unable to determine whether the same person had fired the gun and carried out the stabbing. The National Crime Faculty had supplied a profiler who had consequently only been able to provide a series of options, instead of a single clear profile. Of the options there were two strong possibilities: either someone involved in high-level organized crime; or someone with a psychiatric illness, or a very severe drug habit with psychiatric complications. Polar opposites, in other words.

Worse, two shots had been fired, one of which hit Fleming. But only one cartridge case had been recovered, leaving it possible that two separate guns had been used (the ballistics on the bullets themselves were inconclusive). The unique marks on the single spent cartridge case had not appeared on any UK or Northern Ireland database. They were still checking with Interpol for a foreign match.

'We're sure about the cartridges now?' Riggs asked. He looked over to Josh Reynolds, who was running the team responsible for the crime scene and searches.

Josh took a breath. 'One hundred per cent,' he said.

'You're one hundred per cent certain there is no second cartridge case at the scene?'

'That's right. It must have been collected and removed.'

'Interesting.' Riggs stroked his chin, staring hard at Reynolds, as if sceptical of his abilities.

By now Tim was drifting. The mention of Ronnie Shepherd at the beginning of the meeting had made him think of Laura, Ronnie's daughter. Until the beginning of the year something had been going on between them, and now it was hard to work with Ronnie without thinking about her. They even looked alike: the same facial structure, the same hand gestures when they spoke.

He and Laura had kept the relationship secret from Ronnie because Tim had insisted upon it. Ronnie still didn't know. But that hadn't kept him out of the relationship. With Laura, everything came back to her father. She was twenty-five years old but she was practically living with him. Tim found it oppressive. He had made the mistake of telling Laura that.

'Detective Sergeant Hepworth?' Riggs called out to Vee Hepworth, moving on to the team responsible for tracing and locating the goods stolen from the burglary. It was a characteristic of Riggs that he addressed women formally, but not men, unless he disliked them. So far, Tim had managed to avoid being addressed formally. Vee Hepworth began to run through a repeat of material she had already passed on at debrief the day before. Tim listened with half an ear. Basically, they were getting nowhere locating the stolen goods. She passed out a supposedly definitive list of the missing items.

Determining what – if anything – had been stolen from the Fleming house had been difficult. They were reliant on the impressions of the victim's mother – Varisha Hussein, who had taken a look around the property – and a list of valuables (with possible locations) made by Steve Fleming from his hospital bed, which officers had then searched for. At the end of that process they had discovered that all Enisa Fleming's jewellery had gone missing from the dresser in her bedroom. That single discovery was what had led to the present disposition of forces, with twenty-one detectives examining aspects of what was being called the 'professional-burglary-gone-wrong' theory, leaving only five detectives under Tim (now that Karen Sharpe had joined him) to work on the victim's backgrounds and connections.

'That is worrying,' he heard Riggs saying, as if he were also sceptical of Hepworth's abilities. 'I can't believe that items as valuable as this would have been stolen by professional local nominals and we would hear *nothing* about it.'

Unless the theft was a cover, Tim thought, or merely incidental to the main purpose. At the start of the inquiry he had tried, without success, to convince Riggs that the *modus operandi* was too brutal for the crime to be the work of local professional burglars. And the 'psychiatric headcase' theory had never worked for him because lunatics didn't work in pairs. If Riggs was wrong about the burglary motive, then the key to the crime could *only* come from the victim's background and past. Yet Riggs had given him merely a handful of detectives to examine that angle.

6

Ronnie Shepherd sat next to Varisha Hussein on one of the fixed plastic seats in the corridor outside Steve Fleming's hospital room. He had left Sharpe in there. He checked his watch. Past two already. At 3 p.m. he had a meeting with Virginia Mason, the DS co-ordinating the local intelligence effort. It would take him half an hour to get back to Killingbeck. He would give Sharpe another fifteen minutes then leave. Meanwhile he was incommunicado. His mobile had to be switched off within the hospital, not a state of affairs he could tolerate for too long.

Already he had seen it was working well. He had introduced Sharpe as a temporary replacement for Debbie Moor, then sat in the corner of the private room and watched her. But the victim's mother had arrived shortly after that, keen to talk. So he suggested they come out into the corridor.

Varisha Hussein was behaving too normally for someone who had just lost her daughter in brutal circumstances. She had the black rings under her eyes, the wide-eyed expression (was she on sedatives or tranquilisers?), but he hadn't seen her in tears yet. She could talk perfectly lucidly, ask questions about the inquiry, keep him updated on how Jana was doing. But the speed at which she talked was unsettling. He reckoned she was teetering on the edge of a massive crash. Sooner or later your brain had to face up to these things, with or without drugs.

About ten metres further along the corridor, Steve Fleming's father was hanging unsteadily out of a window, smoking clumsily. He had first appeared at the hospital three days after the attack, so drunk and dirty that nobody had believed he could have anything to do with Fleming. The man was an objectionable shambles. Most days he could hardly stand straight, or utter a sentence without swearing. When he had first appeared Varisha had been persuaded to come and look at him, to see if he really was a relative. That had sparked an argument of unpleasant ferocity. Varisha was an educated, wealthy woman with a business of her own (a local travel agency chain). She dressed and acted the part. She was also a woman who had just lost her daughter. But within seconds of seeing her, Arthur Fleming had launched into a drunken, racist rant that led to his being ejected from the hospital. Had he not been a relative he would have been arrested.

Ronnie watched him smoking for a while, sensing Varisha's discomfort beside him, though Fleming would not come near them while she was there.

'I can't believe that man is Steve's father,' she whispered to him.

'No. They're not alike.'

'I can't stand being this close to him. He is a drunken racist. I will have to go back into the room.'

He nodded, hopelessly. That probably meant Arthur Fleming would come over to talk to him.

He stood with her and looked through the glass door as she went back in. Sharpe was still sitting close to the bed, holding Steve Fleming's hand, talking quietly to him. Very impressive. Debbie Moor wouldn't have even thought about touching him. Not that it would have made much difference. Debbie could appear hard-nosed, but that wasn't really what these things came down to. Male victims who had lost their partners were susceptible to attractive, sympathetic females. It wasn't the sort of thing Laura, his daughter, would approve of, but that was life, nature. They needed mothering, preferably by someone they would like to sleep with, all other things being equal. Debbie Moor was a little on the large side, and too close to fifty. Sharpe, on the other hand, definitely had the right sort of magnetism.

He had watched her with total fascination all morning. Partly, he supposed, it was because he already knew interesting things about her. After Tim Thorne had spoken to Ricky Spencer, he had called Brian Taylor and asked him for more info. Taylor was in charge of the CID across the county. He had known things about Sharpe's suspension eighteen months ago that Spencer had not. But he had also told him about an incident a few years earlier, which Ronnie had recalled as soon as he was given the detail.

Sharpe had entered a house on the Thorpe Edge Estate and rescued a kidnapped nine-year-old girl, the daughter of a judge. There had been three kidnappers in the flat and none had got out alive. An inquiry had fully exonerated Sharpe (so much so that she had received a Certificate of Commendation from the Chief Constable). But there had been no doubt as to who had shot whom. On that occasion Sharpe, on her own admission, had shot all three men.

She didn't look capable of it. The woman he was watching was noticeably taller than average (about his own height, in fact), slim, in proportion. She held herself with care – like someone not quite at ease with her physical capabilities and appearance (including her height). As he had shaken her hand that morning he had felt a wiry strength in her grip, but there was no obvious muscle bulk on her body, nothing to suggest she spent half her life in the gym, or obsessively watched what she ate. If he had not known the facts he would have guessed she was of average female strength – certainly not strong enough to hold and manipulate a firearm effectively for a prolonged length of time.

She was dressed in ordinary clothing – a pair of tightly fitting jeans, a black T-shirt and a short suede jacket – with dark hair gathered into a pony-tail that came down to her neck. She had long legs and wore flat leather shoes. No jewellery at all, and no perfume that he had detected.

Her face was interesting. At a distance the most notable feature – and the only thing that seemed to suggest a history – was her nose. But as soon as he stood in front of her – at close range – her eyes had completely thrown him. Piercing, intense, attentive, bright-green eyes that fixed him and held his gaze without flinching. He had found himself struggling to look directly at her. He guessed the nose had been broken some time ago because it was slightly off-line. Not so much as to make her look damaged, but enough to unbalance her features ever so slightly. The cheekbones, the lean facial structure and the thin lips were all slightly at variance with it. It didn't fit. It was the one little imperfection in her appearance, but it didn't put him off – quite the reverse. For him her attraction was really all about that slightly deviated nose.

He had realized at once – even before she had started speaking to him in the car – that she didn't want to be on the squad. He should have just accepted that then and there, asked for a replacement. That would have made Tim Thorne happy. But he didn't. And his keenness to keep her was only partly due to his judgement that Steve Fleming would go for her. That judgement was, in turn, entirely based on the fact that, given the chance, he would go for her himself. He definitely wanted to see more of Karen Sharpe, wanted to know more about her, and if she wasn't on the squad he was unlikely to be given that chance. It wasn't very professional, but then the likelihood of anything coming of his curiosity seemed non-existent. She had shown no interest in him. He could usually tell when women were attracted. There had been no such signs coming from Sharpe.

He had just sat down again when the door to the room opened. He looked back and saw Sharpe step out and signal to him. He got up and went over to her.

'Any progress?' he asked, speaking quietly and looking behind her through the door window. Varisha Hussein was putting on her coat.

'Yes. But not with Steve. I don't think he would agree to anything just yet. I spoke to Varisha instead. Legally, I would say she's *in loco parentis* at the moment. And she's more than happy for me to speak to Jana.'

He smiled broadly at her. 'Good.' It would do.

'We're going up to Alwoodley now,' she said. 'She looks out of it. I think she's on some kind of tranquiliser, so I'll drive her. My car's at Killingbeck, so maybe you can take us there now? Then I'll ring you when I've spoken to Jana. Have you a mobile number?'

He took a card out and gave it to her. She checked it, then slipped it into her pocket. She looked calm, functional. No sign of the earlier emotion.

'Come and see me when you get back to Killingbeck,' he said. 'Maybe we can get a coffee or something. I appreciate this, Karen.'

'Thanks. No coffee, though.'

'Or a quick drink tonight?'

'I've got to get back for my daughter.'

He shrugged. 'Of course.' Not interested at all. Exactly as he had guessed.

'What about *him*?' she asked, nodding towards Arthur Fleming, drunkenly edging towards them, trying to listen in.

'I'm going to call Security and have him removed,' he said.

Half an hour later, at Killingbeck, he sat in David Riggs's office and listened to DS Virginia Mason's assessment of the local intelligence. Virginia was a middle-aged mother of two with a knack for getting people to talk to her. She didn't look or act like a typical police officer. She would probably have been his second choice to speak to Jana, if

34

Sharpe had backed out. She and four other detectives had spent eight days working virtually every informant handler they had, making sure that if there was any word at ground level they were aware of it. It took her twenty minutes to talk him through the detail of their enquiries, but there was nothing to work with.

'That's it?' he asked.

'That's it,' she said.

'So nothing at all?'

She held her empty palms wide for him to see. 'Just about. I've told you everything significant. There's nothing of interest that is also reliable. It's very strange. We've been in direct or indirect contact with one hundred and fifteen registered informants and two hundred and five lower grade sources. You would think we would pick up *something*.' She looked tired. 'I don't understand it at all.'

'But if it was someone big?' he suggested. 'Too big to sing about.'

'They don't exist. If we are working to the idea of a high-value burglary perpetrated by a professional crew capable of deliberately killing the witnesses, then we are talking about six people in West Yorkshire who can run that kind of operation. It's as simple as that. Big as those six are, we have our noses in their underwear. And someone will always say something. Someone who wants their fix so much they temporarily lose the fear. If we switch to the other profile – to the druggie, or lunatic who over-reacts when things go wrong – then the chances of it coming out of the woodwork are even higher.' She shrugged helplessly. 'No one in West Yorkshire knows who did this. That's how it looks.'

'Which can only mean it wasn't someone local.' He sat back in the chair and ran his hand across his scalp.

'From London, maybe,' Mason said. 'Someone from Fleming's past down there.'

7

'This is Enisa when she was fifteen.'

Karen took the photo from Varisha Hussein and looked closely at it.

They were sitting on a long, hard, modern sofa in a spacious room. Floor-to-ceiling windows opened on to a view of a fastidiously landscaped lawn. In the distance – about a football pitch away – Karen could see a copse of cedar trees and a miniature lake. The room was cleanly and sparsely decorated, mainly filled with bookshelves, easy chairs, card tables and drinks cabinets. Three frames hung on the wall opposite the windows, forming a huge, connected triptych; some kind of modern, abstract collage of fabric and paint.

Varisha had called it 'the drawing room'. There was no TV or sound system, but there was an old valve radio. To Karen's eyes, there was nothing particularly Asian about any of it. The house was a large, detached thirties building, with security gates and walled, wooded perimeters. It was at the very edge of Alwoodley, an expensive suburb on the northern rim of Leeds, more widely known because several Premiership footballers had houses there.

The girl in the photo was wearing brightly coloured traditional dress, and was standing in front of the entrance to a marquee, on a lawn somewhere. Not the garden Karen could see through the windows.

'She's very beautiful, isn't she?' Varisha said. Her voice was emotional, but not because the person they were looking at was dead. It felt as if she might be talking with love and pride about someone still very much alive.

Karen nodded. Enisa looked quite plain, she thought, but somehow still beautiful, yes. Still alive and full of energy and spirit. Karen had not yet seen the most recent photos of her – laid out on the mortuary table – but no doubt that ordeal was somewhere down the line, waiting for her on her return to Killingbeck.

The girl in the image she was holding now looked carefree, happy, maybe even slightly tipsy. There was a champagne glass in her hand. It was hard to think that she was dead, for ever removed from contact with those who had loved and cared about her. The horror of it was partly that something so sophisticated, so slow to nourish and nurture, so full of grace and complexity as an adult – everything that this image had been in the flesh – was reduced to a lifeless assemblage of organs, bones and tissue on a mortuary slab, and all that in a matter of minutes. Because someone had repeatedly stuck a knife into her. So casual, to pass from one state to the other. She could well understand Varisha Hussein's inability to come to terms with it.

'That's her fifteenth birthday party,' Varisha said. She spoke with a southern accent, no trace of the local inflections. 'We were still in the Holmfirth house then. That was in the back garden. She's wearing a dress her father brought from Pakistan. It's a family heirloom, made over one hundred years ago. Silk, you see. It preserves very well. Especially the silk they used then. We're not a very traditional family. Usually we don't wear traditional clothes, as you see. Sammy hates religion, any sort of religion.'

Samir Hussein was Enisa's father. Ronnie Shepherd had told her that he was taking it very badly.

'We taught her to make up her own mind about these things,' Varisha said. She handed Karen another photo. 'That's her eight months ago, just before she fell pregnant again ...' This time her voice cracked. 'She's my *little* child,' she said. 'I have another daughter – Sana – but she's eleven years older. She is also a doctor. Enisa is a paediatrician at St Luke's. Did you know that?'

'Yes. I knew that.' She ignored the present tense, went along with it. 'You must be very proud of her.'

'I'm very proud of both of them. They are the only thing that makes life worth it. All the possessions ...' She looked around her, taking in the room, the view. 'The possessions are worth nothing. A child is the only thing of value you can hope for. Do you have children?'

'I have a little girl. She's thirteen.'

Her eyes lit up. 'Thirteen is a beautiful age. Full of spirit and independence. You are very lucky.'

'I am. I know that.' How would *she* react, if Mairead got to Enisa's age, travelled that distance, only to suffer something like this? The thought put ice into her blood.

'Sana will be here later today,' Varisha said. 'Maybe you can meet her. She always thinks of Enisa as her little sister, looks out for her. Enisa was a gift to all of us, long after we had given up hope for a second child.'

'I'm sure she was very loved and happy,' Karen said quietly. 'She looks like someone at peace with herself. You are right to be proud of her.' She looked down at Varisha. The need for physical contact, for basic reassurance, was palpable, poking through the drug-induced distraction. The woman was sitting so close their legs were pressed together. In the car on the way up she had told Karen she was taking some kind of tranquiliser. Karen guessed her to be in her early sixties, but had it not been for the recent stresses she would probably have looked younger.

Karen smiled at her. 'I think Enisa was happy while she was alive,' she said, very gently. 'That's all that matters.'

Varisha looked at her blankly, trying to block out the past tense, then reached for another photo. 'There are so many beautiful photos,' she said. 'Would you like a cup of tea?'

'I'd like to see Jana,' Karen said. 'Is she with your husband?'

'Sammy. Yes. Sammy isn't taking things very well.' She fell silent, looking down at the album in her hands. For a moment Karen thought she would break there and then, that she would suddenly start sobbing. She hoped not. The denial was so strong the woman would certainly need medical care, and that would delay things with Jana.

She stood up. 'Can you take me to her, please?'

Keep it functional. Keep busy.

They were in a room upstairs. Karen followed Varisha up a wide, curved, marble staircase to a landing with windows facing the front of the building.

'The house is so quiet,' Varisha said. 'We have given the maid the week off. She was so upset …'

They walked to the end of a passageway on a thick, red carpet, and came to another, smaller staircase.

'Sammy has a study up here,' Varisha told her. 'He's a bookworm.'

Karen listened for sounds of a six-year-old as they ascended. She could hear nothing. When they got to the doorway – in the attic, Karen guessed, from the sloping ceilings on either side – Varisha knocked gently and then went in, indicating she should follow.

The room was a small loft conversion, with two low skylights, so low you could look down at the rear lawn from a standing position. The roof sloped from not far above Karen's head at one end of the room to half that height at the other. There were old shelves stacked in untidy, collapsing structures along all four walls, packed messily with books and magazines and papers. In one corner there was a desk of dark, grained wood, similarly littered with paperwork. An old man in a shabby knitted cardigan was sitting hunched over it, facing away from them, the back of his head brown and bald. He held a pipe in one hand, and a frail column of smoke was rising away from him to the half-open skylight on his right. The day outside was warm and cheerful, but in the room the atmosphere was heavy with misery, and the lack of headroom was suffocating. Karen stood near the door.

The parquet floor was strewn with coloured paper and children's paint tubs. Karen glanced quickly at the images scrawled and daubed across several large sheets, but they looked no different from the efforts of any other six-year-old; houses, cats, dogs, trees and clouds, cars, matchstick people with smiley faces and yellow hair, squiggle seagulls.

Jana Fleming was sitting by herself on the wide, recessed ledge of the other skylight, face, head and shoulder pressed against the glass, staring out.

Samir Hussein turned slowly as Varisha entered, focusing milky, sentimental eyes on his wife. He had a thin, gaunt face with blotchy, light-brown skin. He looked to be on the point of tears. 'You're back already,' he said, without any enthusiasm. His eyes switched focus and found Karen. 'Who is this?'

Jana looked over at them both. Karen saw her eyes brighten slightly as she saw her grandmother, then look with a terrible expectation at herself.

Karen smiled at her. 'Hello, Jana,' she said. She saw the expectation change to disappointment, and the beginning of the smile turn into a frown.

'This is Karen,' Varisha said. 'She's come to talk to Jana.'

The child looked at her again, still not saying anything.

'Don't I get a hug, little princess?' Varisha asked. 'I've missed you.'

Jana smiled suddenly, an irrepressible six-year-old smile. She slipped off the ledge and walked over to Varisha, wrapping her arms around her as Varisha stooped to embrace her. They hugged for a long time. Samir Hussein stared over them at Karen.

Varisha went down on one knee and smoothed strands of hair away from Jana's face. The girl was about average height for her age, with very long, very black hair that ended somewhere below her waist. Her face was round, open and beautiful in the way only pre-teen faces can be, the skin a light, even tan colour, the eyes coal-black and wide. She had long, dark eyelashes and perfect white teeth. Her cheeks looked slightly flushed, but aside from that there was no sign of the tiredness or wear that affected the adults all around her. She was dressed in a pair of beige dungarees and a white cotton, long-sleeved T-shirt with rolled-up sleeves. Her feet were bare. There were paint stains all over her hands and down the front of the dungarees, with a wide streak of yellow across her cheek.

'This lady has come to talk to you,' Varisha said to her. 'She's been looking after your daddy, in the hospital. Daddy says hello and,' she leaned forward and kissed Jana on the lips, 'gives you a big kiss.'

Steve Fleming had said nothing of the sort – at least, not while Karen was with him – though he had repeatedly asked how Jana was. Karen's impression of him was of a man less incapacitated by his injuries than by a kind of mute horror. Nothing of what had happened to him was manageable through any of the cognitive means available to him. He had lain in the bed, clutching feebly at her fingers, staring at her, breath rasping through his damaged chest. She had known at once that it would be useless to try to get him to understand anything. He knew at some level that he was left alone with Jana, but not at a level that would allow decisions to be made. She had not known him as a lawyer (Ronnie Shepherd had told her he had been a 'clever, smirking' character), but couldn't see him ever going back to that world.

Varisha stood up and looked at her husband. 'Leave us for a while, Sammy,' she said. 'There's not much room in here.'

Sammy pulled his eyes away from Karen and nodded at Varisha, then pushed himself to a standing position. He looked about twenty years older than his wife. He kept his pipe with him and edged past them. Karen backed out to make room, and, as he passed her, he stopped and looked into her face from a distance of two or three inches. 'You are police, right?' he asked. He had a Bradford accent. His tone was unmistakably hostile.

'Yes, I am, Mr Hussein. DC Karen Sharpe.'

His lips twisted down slightly, as if he were on the point of saying something cutting, then he turned and walked down the stairs with a sigh. Karen stepped back into the room.

How was she going to approach this? Varisha Hussein moved to the chair and sat on it, standing Jana between her legs. Karen looked for somewhere else to sit. There wasn't anywhere. The window sill Jana had been using wasn't wide enough for her. She dropped her cloth bag at her feet and sat on the floor, cross-legged, about two feet in front of Jana, moving some of her pictures to make space.

She knew from Varisha that Jana had already been told her mother had died, but didn't know how that had been communicated, or what Jana really understood of such things. She knew David Riggs was in a hurry to get information, but she also knew from experience that there was no way you could rush it. Best just to try talking to the child first, attempt to get a relaxed atmosphere between them without mentioning anything distressing. She would do that for as long as it took. See how it panned out. If she got nothing, she got nothing.

'I've heard a lot of things about you, Jana,' she said. 'I was looking forward to meeting you.'

Jana had the edge of one hand in her mouth, eyes on her. She didn't say anything.

'This is a nice lady,' Varisha said. 'Do you want to say hello to her?'

Jana took her hand away from her mouth and frowned again. 'You're not my mummy,' she said. There were no tears in her eyes, but her voice was tiny, confused.

Karen swallowed hard.

'This lady is called Karen,' Varisha said. 'Of course she's not your mummy …' But then she stopped. She bit on her lip and looked away.

'I'm not your mummy,' Karen said. 'But I know your mummy was …' Her voice dried. There was a lump in her throat, blocking it. She tried to finish the sentence, but nothing came out.

Varisha Hussein was staring at the wall, tears in her eyes.

Karen cleared her throat and started again. 'I think your mummy was …' Again it caught, choking her. She took a gasp of breath. 'I'm sorry,' she whispered.

It was absurd, out of control. There was nothing upsetting in her head, no images, nothing to be distressed about. She was doing a job, getting on with it, approaching it functionally. She was doing so well, too. But then this lump in her throat. Immediately it made her

41

breathe faster, brought the blood to her face. She felt hot, stifled. All she wanted to tell the girl was that she thought her mummy was a lovely person. She had no idea if it was true. Probably it was true, but that didn't matter. It was just something to say. She took a deep breath. She had to get it out.

Suddenly something touched her hand. She looked up. Jana had moved away from Varisha and was standing right in front of her, reaching out a hand to take hold of hers. With total astonishment she felt the little fingers curl around her own and saw the girl was calmly smiling at her.

'Don't cry,' Jana said. 'My mummy is happy. She's in a happy place. My gran told me.'

Karen brought a hand up and wiped at her eyes. There were tears. She tried to smile back. The lump in her throat was like a tennis ball.

'You look nice,' Jana said. 'You look nice, like my mummy.'

8

It took her until just after seven o'clock. Afterwards, she sat in the car outside their house and cried until her eyes were red and swollen, not thinking about anything, just letting out everything she had held back for the last four hours. It was not like the last time she had done this kind of work.

The change was totally confusing. Everything was different. Something had been stripped away from her, a layer of protection. A year and a half ago – before Stijn – they would have said she was hard, like Debbie Moor. Now she couldn't take it at all. By the time she called Ronnie Shepherd she thought she might be ready to sit all night in a bar with him and get so drunk they would have to send her home in an ambulance.

'It's me,' she told him. 'Karen Sharpe.'

'I'm sorry, Karen. I'm in de-brief. Can I call you back in a few minutes?'

She used the time to leave the Hussein place and park up outside Alwoodley Park Golf Club. Around her, life was continuing as normal: cars passing by ; people walking their dogs; warmth from the sunlight on her skin; bone-white clouds floating through a calm sky. She suffered a momentary sensation of absurdity – as if nothing around her were real. When she had been on the CPT that feeling had come to her often.

It was as if there were two parallel tracks to life on earth – the normal and the horrific. People in the normal world lived as though it were the only possible existence. They assumed it would never stop. Thoughts of death (especially their own) rarely intruded. Life was monotonous, gentle, predictable. If you were lucky you could find love and happiness; if you weren't, life still went on, in the groove.

But all the time, alongside you, there was this other world that you never saw, though you *almost* came into contact with it each and every day. Because the people who did things like that – who stuck nine-inch knives into pregnant women, who left six-year-old kids traumatized – lived in the same physical space as the normal people. But they lived in a world with different rules, for them the only rules that made sense. They didn't feel like monsters when they raped a boy, or suffocated a two-year-old girl, or knifed a pregnant woman to death. Because that *was* their world. And every time they strayed across the boundaries, helpless, hapless, normal people were left feeling as she did now – as if she were missing the one part of the jigsaw puzzle that would bring sense to it all.

The phone rang and she answered it.

'Are you still up there?' It was Ronnie Shepherd.

'I'm finished now. It took some time.'

'Did you get anything?'

'Yes. Do you want me to tell you over the phone?'

A pause. 'Can you give me the gist of it? Sorry. I've got the SIO pestering me about it.'

'She was in her room the whole time,' she said. 'By the time she came out there was nobody around and her mummy and daddy were in the garden, asleep. That's what she told me. She woke up because she heard noises. She doesn't know what noises. She went out to her mummy and daddy, and saw that they were both bleeding and cold. She thought they must have fallen over. She got a blanket from her room and covered them. Then she called an ambulance, as her mother had taught her to. The ambulance took some time, so she lay down beside them, to keep them warm.'

'The poor kid.'

'That's not all,' she continued. 'One of them came into the room after she had woken up.' Now she could almost hear him getting excited. 'After she woke up, before she went into the garden,' she clarified. 'She was half-awake, feeling sleepy, in her bed. The door to her room opened. A man walked in and came over to her bed. He bent down and looked at her. At first she thought it was her father. It wasn't. She was awake, she says, staring at him. She says he looked at her for some time without saying anything – "a long time", she said. She didn't feel frightened but didn't say anything either. After a while he put his finger to his lips and said, "Sshh." Then he went out. He closed the door behind him.'

'Jesus Christ.'

'Yes. I should have warned you.'

'Warned me about what?'

'About doing it properly. It should have been on video.'

'Forget that. She probably wouldn't have said anything if you had been in a video suite.'

'But what she said could have gone into evidence.'

'Waste of time if she didn't say anything. Better this way. She's told us that he came in then left her. That is something significant and additional to give to the profiler. He spared her life.'

'True. And she can probably describe the man, if you get an artist to talk to her. She might not be accurate, but it might be worth something. Then we could think about putting her on video.'

He was quiet for a while, thinking about that. 'I doubt it,' he said at length. 'Did she describe him to you?'

'She said he had dark, curly hair and a "round" nose. I think she meant his nose was flat, like it was broken, maybe.'

'OK. A broken nose. My God, she did give us something.'

'That's *my* guess as to what she meant. You should get an artist to do a proper interview with her.'

'Of course. But as it is, that's good.'

'I wouldn't broadcast it yet. She might change her mind. She's six years old.'

'Anything else?'

'That's it. If you get an artist to show her facial alternatives she might give you more.'

'Anything about how he spoke?'

'He said. "Sshh".'

'Right.' She heard him sigh. 'OK, Karen. That was fantastic work. I'll tell—'

'Will you set up an artist to speak with her?' She sounded like a broken record.

'Of course. I've made a note. I'll organize it in the morning. Where are you now?'

'Outside Alwoodley Park Golf Club ... Is that drink still on offer?'

'The drink?' He sounded surprised by her change of mind. 'Sorry, but I've had to make other arrangements. There are others going into town, though.'

'Where?' she asked to conceal her disappointment, but she had no intention of going.

'A place called the Fire Station. It's Nev Hanley's retirement do.'

She hated the place and didn't have a clue who Nev Hanley was.

After she cut the connection she felt slightly ashamed. Why had she wanted to see him?

Then she realized what it was. His wife had walked out on him, leaving him to bring up a young child, yet he seemed untouched by it. He wasn't letting the past sour his whole life. That was what was drawing her to him.

Her head was pounding with tension now. She thought about what she was going back to: Pete Bains, with his special freight of misery. It wasn't his fault, and he had never been anything but kind to her, but right now he wasn't what she needed.

9

Pete was in – she could hear his music coming from the bedroom as she let herself in – but if he noticed her arrival he didn't shout out to greet her. Nor did she call up to him. Instead she walked quietly through to the kitchen and found a note on the table.

Not sure what time you were due back. I cooked for you. Was looking forward to us eating together, for once. (Though that's usually my fault, I know.) Mairead said you had been called in. Got worried when you didn't show by nine, so rang Richard Powell at Halifax. He told me they put you on Bulldog. I'm guessing that's where you are. Dinner in the oven. Wine in fridge. Enjoy. I have an early start tomorrow (another trip to Lancashire). Hope everything is OK.

She sat down at the table and placed her head in her hands. The pattern was becoming grimly familiar from other failed relationships. Presumably he had already gone to bed and wasn't expecting her to wake him. Otherwise, why leave a note?

For almost a year now she and Mairead had been living in Pete's house in Heaton. She owned no part of it, but there was no reason why that should bother her. Pete himself only owned about a third of it. The rest belonged to his father. She had sold her property north of Skipton to move in here, and still had the money from that in the bank. She could cut loose at any time. She wasn't trapped.

The house was a large Victorian mansion built for a mill owner over a hundred and fifty years ago, and had a long back garden that had once contained a small swimming pool. Nothing on the scale the Husseins enjoyed in Alwoodley, but enough to provide plenty of space for the three of them. She shouldn't have been feeling claustrophobic.

It was the second try at co-habitation with Pete. She didn't know why it wasn't working this time any more than she knew why it had failed the first time. The circumstances of her departure the first time round should have hurt him enough to make him never want to take her back again. Maybe if he *had* reacted like that (like a normal person would – someone without his history of personal grief) then she would feel less crushed by his need. But she came home to notes like this and felt, precisely, claustrophobic and trapped.

She should have called him and told him where she was.

She looked in the oven and saw that he had made lasagne. He was a great cook. The food would be good even after a couple of hours drying out in the oven. But she had no appetite at all. She decided instead to go up and speak to Mairead.

She walked normally up the stairs. There was no point in creeping. From behind the closed door of their bedroom she could hear the strains of some sixties jazz, which meant he wasn't asleep yet. The music sounded cacophonic to her. She could handle anodyne jazz, but not the stuff he liked to listen to. She got all the way to Mairead's room without him coming out.

But Mairead wasn't in her room. Karen stared at the empty bed and felt a mindless lurch of panic. She walked quickly back to their bedroom and opened the door. He was in the en suite bathroom, at the sinks with his back to her, naked – aside from the ubiquitous *kara* – and towelling himself dry from the shower.

'Where's Mairead?' she asked him, standing at the bedroom door. Inside the room the music was unbearable.

'Don't you remember?' he said. He didn't turn to look at her. 'She's at a rehearsal. Then sleeping over at Alexia's.' He had to raise his voice to be heard.

Alexia again. Mairead had told her that Alexia's mother was some kind of soap star in London. Alexia wanted to act as well, though Mairead thought she didn't have much talent for it. Presumably through her mother, she had landed a very small part in a production at the West Yorkshire Playhouse, in Leeds. Mairead had been going along with Alexia to watch her rehearse. But she had said nothing about a rehearsal this evening.

'A rehearsal?' she asked him. 'At this time of night? Are you sure?'

'I took her there,' he said, still not facing her. 'It's a dress rehearsal. On the real stage.'

The music was too much. 'Can you turn that fucking music down?' she said. 'I can't hear you.'

He picked up a remote and switched it off. Then he turned to face her.

'I didn't give her permission to stay over at Alexia's,' she said. 'She didn't even ask me about it.'

'You weren't here. Alexia called and Mairead asked me.'

As if he were her father. 'Are you sure she's going to Alexia's afterwards?'

He was frowning now, getting annoyed with her. 'Why would she lie?' he asked. 'She's been before. Nothing has ever happened, so why are you worrying now? She asked me and I said yes. Sorry. If you don't want me to let her stay out …'

No. She didn't. And she wanted Mairead to ask *her*, not him. He was the one who had given her permission to stay at Alexia's the very first time, without even meeting the girl, without checking out her parents or where she lived. Karen would never have done that.

'How will she get back there?' she asked him.

'The theatre pays for them to get a taxi back. She's done it before. Have you forgotten?'

Forgotten? Did he think she was some kind of idiot? She frowned, then stepped back out of the room.

'Hello to you, too,' he called out to her.

She ignored him.

Back in Mairead's room she found what had caught her eye moments before. Lying on the bed (in full view, of course) was a brightly coloured kanga. She picked it up and inspected it. The label showed it was the exact type Mairead had pointed out to her in a shop that morning. She had refused to buy it for her because it was too expensive. In fact, it looked like exactly the same article Mairead had picked up. She took it and walked back through to Pete.

He was still in the bathroom, and looked at her in the mirrors. 'Did you get the food?' he asked.

She shook her head. 'No. I'm not hungry.' She could hear her own voice – a sulky, moody bitch. Why couldn't she be nice to him? 'Thanks for cooking it, though. I'll eat it tomorrow.'

'You should eat tonight,' he said.

And drink, she thought. She wondered if she would sleep.

'Have you met this Alexia?' she asked him. She placed the kanga on the chair in the bedroom, just outside the bathroom. She saw him glance at it.

'No,' he said. 'I've seen her, though. A couple of times when I've dropped Mairead off.'

So Mairead had lied to her. 'Mairead told me you had met her.'

'That probably counts as "meeting" in Mairead's eyes.'

Of course. He always understood her better than she did.

'She seems rich,' he said. 'I mean *really* wealthy.'

'That doesn't mean she's safe,' Karen said.

'Her family have a house on the way to Pateley Bridge, with stables,' Pete said. 'I think that's the attraction – the horses …'

'Her new little friend. She's only known her a couple of weeks and already can't talk about anything else …'

'A couple of months, maybe.'

'She's too obsessive …'

'She's just a kid. That's what kids do.'

'I know. That's what worries me.' She had done the same as a child – formed attachments so strong she had ended up being hurt by a girl long before ever being dumped by a boy.

'I found that in her room,' she said, pointing to the kanga. He was dry now, squeezing toothpaste on to a toothbrush. 'Have you seen it before?'

'I think so. What's the problem?'

'I need to ask her about it. I didn't buy it for her. Did you?'

He shrugged. 'I don't think so.'

'You didn't,' she said. He wouldn't spend £150 on a sheet of cotton. 'She stole it,' she said. 'Probably today, while I was with her.'

He looked at her, toothbrush in his mouth, the expression on his face clearly saying she must be stark raving mad to think Mairead would do that.

As if the kid hasn't been through enough to make her steal, she thought. 'We don't watch her enough,' she said. 'We don't know what she's doing when she's with this Alexia.'

'She doesn't steal,' he said. 'You're worrying unnecessarily. Just ask her about it. She'll tell you where she got it.'

'Yeah. She'll tell me a lie.' She knew only too well how proficiently Mairead could lie.

She sat down on the bed, waiting for him to finish, watching him through the open bathroom door as he brushed his teeth.

Pete Bains. Forty-two years old. He was still fit, still attractive. No beer belly or paunch, dark skin, very short, black hair (flecked with visible white and grey if he let it grow) and always neatly shaved these days. A strong facial structure, too. There was never a time, it seemed, when he was not prepared to sleep with her. ('Make love', he would say.) Was that what she needed now? She was very tense.

She thought about going down to the kitchen and bringing back the bottle of wine, plus two glasses. Try again from scratch. But he didn't drink. He was a Sikh, hence the ridged metal bangle on his wrist, the *kara*. But that wasn't why he avoided booze. Pete believed in what was there in front of him – touchable, provable, visible. The *kara* was only a pride thing, she thought, not a mark of religious belief. He was proud to be Sikh, even though he didn't believe any of it, didn't wear the turban, cut his hair, hadn't stepped inside a *gurdwara* since being forced to as a child. She wished half-heartedly that there was something in her own past that she could be proud of like that.

There were aspects to him that were far from sorted, though. Alcohol and food, for example. He ate so little she had once thought he might be anorexic. That was about control. As if you could hold your life together by being in control of how much you ate or drank. He had more need of control than almost any other man she had met. Given his past, that was unsurprising.

When he was finished he moved back into the bedroom. He had a towel wrapped around his waist now.

'Why are you going to Lancashire?' she asked him. He was a DS at Milgarth usually.

'For Squire. You know that already.'

'Squire?' The Inquiry name rang no bells.

'I've told you already, Karen. I'm on a proactive squad looking at skinheads – white, right-wing racists. The BNP, Combat 18, that sort of thing. They're going to start a riot this summer, if they can get away with it …'

'Oh.' She remembered now. There had been news coverage about it, but not in Bradford. Over in Lancashire somewhere the BNP was stirring things up. Hadn't they already had a mini-race-riot in Oldham or Burnley?

'You finished in the bathroom?' she asked.

'It's all yours. But you should eat first. You look trashed.'

Thanks, she thought. She stood and began to undress. This was another aspect of domestic bliss she didn't like. She could sit with him naked in front of her and hardly notice him. When she took her clothes off now he probably wouldn't even look at her.

She pulled her T-shirt back on and walked to the bathroom, closing the door behind her.

10

DC Clare Isles stepped up to the front door of 15, Lesley Terrace in Keighley and pressed the bell. Nothing happened, so she knocked instead, then stood back and tried to look through the net curtains of the front room window, just to the right of the door. At 9.30 p.m. the night was still too bright for her to see through. There were no lights on within.

Behind her, DC Alan Bundy was looking at the upstairs window of the house. The evening was calm and clear. Not much traffic. Not even many parked cars on the street. Some kids were playing football further down. It was on routine enquiries like this, Clare thought, that things were likely to pop out at you. It had happened to her before.

She knocked again, louder this time, then looked down the street. They were not that far from Keighley Police Station. All the houses in these streets, west of the town centre, looked the same to her. Endless, identical, back-to-back brick terraces with tiny, walled front yards. Sometimes there were still cobbles in the narrower streets, but not this one. The bricks were still stained a dirty brown, though, from the days when you wouldn't have been able to breathe for mill smog and chimney smoke.

She heard someone moving in the hallway behind the door and stepped back as a precaution. A year ago she had been on a standard call like this and the occupant had set a dog on her. She had been standing so close to the door she had had no time to react. Her right arm was still painful from the injury.

The door opened slowly. A young woman's face peered out at her through the gap.

'Nadine?' Clare asked. Ian Whitfield's girlfriend was called Nadine Askwith.

'Yes. What is it?'

Clare held her ID up. 'DC Isles. West Yorkshire Police. Is Ian in?'

She didn't introduce Bundy. He was built like a bouncer and tended to put people off. Best to try the nice way first.

The door opened fully. The woman looked about twenty-eight (which would make her older than Whitfield), with dark hair and a hard, unattractive face. She had greasy skin and dark rims under her eyes. She was shorter than Clare, but larger around the hips and chest. She looked harassed.

'No,' she said. 'Why do you want him?'

'Just a routine enquiry. Can I come in?'

Askwith looked reluctant, but stood aside. Clare stepped past her and Bundy followed.

The door opened directly on to the front room. They went in and stood there. There were three shabby sofas and a TV; a door opened on to a kitchen.

Askwith didn't offer them a seat. She held a finger to her lips and pointed to the ceiling. 'The baby's asleep,' she said. 'I've only just got him off.' She was speaking very quietly.

Clare lowered her own voice. 'This is DC Bundy,' she said.

Askwith looked at him in silence, arms folded, chest out.

'Is it OK if I have a quick look upstairs?' Clare asked.

'He's not here. I told you.'

'I know that, but—'

'You don't believe me?'

'It's not that. It's just the way we have to do things—'

'What's it about? Why are you looking for him?'

'We're on a murder Inquiry,' Bundy said, his big, deep voice not so quiet. 'The killing of Enisa Fleming.'

Askwith almost flinched. 'I've a baby sleeping,' she said. 'Can you keep your voice down?'

Bundy shrugged.

'Just a quick look?' Clare repeated.

'Ian has nothing to do with any murder,' Askwith said. 'He's been out of trouble for years.'

'I'm sure he has,' Clare replied. 'But I need to check with my own eyes that he's not here, otherwise I get into trouble with my boss. It's just standard. I'll be very quiet. DC Bundy can stay down here.' She shot him a watch-my-back look.

They walked into the kitchen. It was the only other room on the ground floor. Stairs led off from it to the top floor. The sink was full of dirty dishes and baby feeding equipment. There was an odour of rotting rubbish from a black plastic bag next to the sink. Clare let Askwith go up the stairs first.

Off a small landing there were three rooms and a bathroom. Two of the rooms were tiny and filled with cardboard boxes, junk and spare beds. The other was their bedroom. There was space for a cot at the end of the bed, but only just. Clare stood at the door and looked at the baby lying there. It was tiny and asleep. She could hear it breathing peacefully, but she could smell cigarette smoke in the room. There was an ashtray on the floor to one side of the unmade bed.

'See. I told you,' Askwith muttered.

Immediately the baby flicked its head quickly from side to side and let out a long, strangled wail. It was so loud Clare was surprised. Askwith didn't react.

'I hope I haven't woken him,' Clare whispered.

'He does it in his sleep,' Askwith replied.

Clare nodded, as if she understood. She didn't have kids of her own.

She stepped back out of the room and looked at the loft hatch, above the landing.

'I haven't even been up there,' Askwith said, noticing. 'We rent this place.'

She could probably get up if she had a chair, but there were no signs – either from the position of the hatch itself, the walls around it, or the look in Askwith's eyes – to suggest she was lying and her boyfriend was up there.

They went back down and stood in the front room, all three of them. Clare asked questions and Bundy took notes.

'Ian Whitfield is your boyfriend, right?' she started.

'Yes. He's Danny's dad.'

'Danny's your baby.'

'Yes.' She looked very tired.

'Does Ian live with you?' Clare asked.

'Yes. But he's away at the moment.'

'Does he have his own place?'

'This is his place.'

'You've been together a while?'

'Six years.'

Whitfield was only twenty-one, according to the information gathered from his employment with the removal company. 'How old are you, Nadine?' Clare asked.

'Twenty-one. What's that got to do with anything?

'Nothing.' Clare smiled at her. Keep it sweet. Beside her, Bundy had his head down and was noting everything in his pocket book.

'You say Ian's away – do you know where?'

'He's abroad. He left on the first of June. For Holland. You could check with the airport?'

If he left on 1 June, it would probably give him an alibi for the eighth.

'He flew with British Airways, from Manchester. I took him to the airport.'

'Is he on holiday, then?'

Askwith scowled at her. 'Are you taking the piss? We can't afford holidays.' She dug around in the sofa and extracted a packet of cigarettes from behind the cushion.

'He's working,' she said.

'He works abroad now?'

'Sometimes. He does what he can. Danny is expensive.'

'What kind of work does he do?'

'Anything he can.'

'Do you know what kind of work he's doing in Holland?'

She shrugged, as if that didn't matter. 'Building, probably.'

'Do you know who he works for there?'

'I haven't a clue.'

'Does he get in contact with you?'

'Not much.'

'But sometimes?'

'Yeah. He uses a payphone in some guesthouse he stays in.'

Very convenient. 'He has no mobile, then?'

'We can't afford two mobiles.'

'Do you know the name of the guesthouse, the address?'

She shook her head. Clare thought she caught a glint of something in her eyes.

'And you've been with him six years?'

'Long enough, eh?'

Long enough to know where he was staying if he went abroad to work.

'But you're sure you don't know where he is?' Bundy asked, voicing her thought with obvious suspicion.

'Somewhere in Holland,' Askwith said. 'I don't really care. I haven't much time to think about that sort of thing.' As if on cue the baby started to cry. Askwith ignored it.

'Do you know when he's coming back?' Clare asked her.

'A couple of weeks, he says.'

'When did he last call you?' Bundy asked.

Askwith frowned, thinking about that. 'I don't recall,' she said. 'Why are you so keen to find him?'

'His name came up,' Clare said. 'Nothing to worry about.'

'Because of that theft thing? That was ages ago.' The crying upstairs got louder, but still she didn't react.

'You mean his theft *conviction*?' Bundy said. 'That was in nineteen ninety-nine. Hardly ages ago.'

'And theft is *hardly* murder.'

'No,' Clare agreed. Askwith was quick enough. Whitfield's last conviction was for theft of cigarettes, for which he had received a probation order. He had been a minor part in a much larger scam to divert lorry-loads of smuggled cigarettes from France to the UK. Probably that was what he was up to now, in Holland. Probably that was why Askwith wasn't being very helpful. But it didn't matter really, because, as she said, theft wasn't murder, and if he was in Holland he had an alibi.

'We need to speak to him when he returns,' Clare said. 'Or sooner. If we could speak to him in Holland that would be better. When will he call you again?'

Bundy didn't let her answer. 'Shouldn't you go to the baby?' he asked Askwith. 'He sounds distressed.' The crying had reached a higher pitch now.

'He's always distressed,' Askwith said, speaking loudly now. She placed a cigarette in her mouth and lit it. 'That's what they're like.'

11

Karen felt cold; not on the surface, but deep inside, in her stomach. Along with it she felt an encroaching dread, exactly as the text books said you would if you were about to have a heart attack. But this wasn't a heart attack. This was something more familiar, a chilling numbness she hadn't felt for months.

She stood in the shower, leaning against the tiled wall, and let the hot water course freely over her head and shoulders. She shifted her head so that the water ran into her ears, then closed her eyes and waited for her mind to slow. If she could stop the thoughts the chill would go away. Behind her, in the bedroom, she could hear Pete putting lighter music on.

She had a pain in her chest. It had been with her, on and off, for several months now. A stress symptom. She massaged the area gently, prying with her fingers to see if she could feel anything beneath the skin. Then she let herself slide down the wall of the shower into a squatting position, the water splashing on to her head like hot rain. She let the minutes wash over her. Her eyes closed, her breathing slowed. She had to forget about Jana Hussein, get all that pain out of her head, otherwise she would never sleep.

She wished Pete had not let Mairead go out tonight. She needed to see her, to hold her. She needed to know for certain that she was safe. She thought about ringing her at Alexia's – assuming Pete had the number – or on her mobile. But she was being silly, selfish. Her concern would only embarrass Mairead. She had to get through this without her.

She tried to concentrate only on the sensations coming from her skin – the pattern of water, the rivulets streaming off her shoulders, down between her breasts. She tried to lose track of time.

After a while she heard Pete calling to her from the bedroom, but couldn't make out what he was saying. She forced herself to stand up. Had she fallen asleep a little? The coldness was still there, deep inside her. It hadn't gone away. It wouldn't go away now until it had run its course.

What was the matter with her? We have a nice life, she told herself. Domestic bliss. A teenage daughter, not by Pete, but never mind that ... good jobs, a big house, which would even have a swimming pool if Pete hadn't filled it in ... Pete's ghosts. She let them float through her head to the sound of the water. His drowned child and overdosed wife.

The story was horrific, a trauma she did not need so close to her life. Pete had been married, with a child, a toddler called Millie. But the child had fallen into the pool they had at the end of the garden, right here, in this house. He had been in charge of her at the time. A month later his wife had taken an overdose and killed herself. It was remarkable he hadn't followed her. Maybe he had tried. He didn't talk about it much, but she knew how essential a part of him it all was – the burden of guilt and horror. It was what made him Pete Bains. That was why he still lived here. He had filled in the pool but he couldn't leave the house. He needed to be reminded of his sin each and every day. When she had first met him it had seemed almost heroic that he was still alive, that he had survived something so tragic. It had been a point of attraction between them. But now she wasn't sure he *had* survived. He had gone on living, but a part of him had died as surely as if he *had* taken an overdose. He would never be free of it. Worse, he didn't want to be.

'Are you OK, Karen?' He had opened the bathroom door.

She moved out of the stream of water and looked round. 'Fine,' she said, irritation in her voice.

He caught the tone at once. 'Sorry,' he said. 'I just couldn't hear you. You've been in there for nearly half an hour.' He left quickly, closing the door behind him. She felt guilty.

She stepped out, dried herself quickly, then used the hair-dryer on her hair. By the time she was done he was in bed already, reading a book. He had put some soft jazz on. Long notes and saxophones, a slow beat. Something to sleep to.

'I'm sorry, Pete,' she said. She was shivering properly now. She sat on the edge of the bed, back to him, holding her muscles tight. She had dried herself thoroughly but the cold wouldn't go away. 'It's not you,' she said. 'I'm not feeling too bright, that's all. I had a very rough day.'

He half-turned to look at her. 'I was going to ask you about it,' he said. 'They put you on Bulldog?'

'Yes.'

'Can't you talk to someone about it? You shouldn't be doing things like that.'

'Shouldn't I?' She arched her back and felt again for the pain in her chest. The shivers made her teeth chatter.

'Get into bed, Karen,' he said. 'For God's sake, you're shivering.'

She pulled the quilt back and moved in beside him. She felt numb.

'Is your chest OK?' he asked. He was almost facing her now. He was so good at reading the library of her symptoms.

'It's fine,' she said. 'Nothing to worry about.'

'Maybe you should go to the doctor if the pains start again,' he said.

'I will,' she replied.

Her father had been a doctor, but he had still died of lung cancer. You went to a doctor, consented to a test; next thing you knew you couldn't get out of hospital.

She turned to face him, wanting him to help her, to hold her, but he had his back to her again. Had he wanted something tonight? Was that what the meal was about, the soft music now? Why had she never just told him that she hated his jazz? She pushed herself against him, desperate for intimacy, but knowing already what was going to happen, where it was going to end.

He let her slide a hand underneath him, then around his chest, through the hairs, feeling for his nipples. The other she placed flat against his stomach, pulling her hips into his buttocks and pressing her breasts against his back, giving him the chance to respond or show no interest. But when wasn't he interested?

He started to respond at once and turned to face her, at the same time dimming the light. They began to kiss with wide open mouths, his relief and desire obvious, but she was doing it on autopilot. His hands moved to her breasts, to her nipples, then between her legs. She took hold of him and began to push against him, rhythmically, wanting an urgency to it, wanting him to be inside her now, quickly, before it started properly, before it spoiled everything.

But she could see the images already, as if they were behind his head, already waiting to come through. Nothing definite or clear – just fast-moving blurs, like something waved in front of her eyes; a piece of cloth, or plastic sheeting, something someone would push into her mouth, to suffocate her. It was in her head, in her eyes, flashing at her like a jerky film. But for a while she thought she was into the act, that she could keep her concentration on Pete, forget it all. 'Get in me now,' she hissed. 'Get inside me ...' But by the time he had moved on top of her she was lost, brain racing with it. She struggled to see him as Pete Bains, a man she had once loved, with her there in the bed, a person. He was breaking apart on top of her, becoming his limbs, his eyes, his head – different pieces of muscle and tissue moving above her like an automaton. She could feel the weight of him, pressing into her. Not Stijn, crushing her. Please, not Stijn. But not Pete Bains, either. Flesh and blood, pieces of gristle and sinew, panting and grunting, his sweat dripping on to her as Stijn's had. She could smell every part of him – his armpits, the crack between his buttocks, his groin, the breath coming out of his mouth. Everything about him was disgusting. She forced herself to keep her eyes open and look at his face, but it didn't stop. It was out of control.

'Keep going,' she whispered. 'For God's sake, keep going ...'

But he was already motionless, looking down at her, face creased with worry. She realized she was crying, silently, the tears soaking her face.

He moved off her. 'I'm sorry, Karen,' he said.

She turned away from him, jamming her knuckles into her mouth. She had to get control of it. 'No,' she said, the words hardly clear. 'It's not you, Pete. It's not you ...'

'I know it's not,' he said. His fingertips touched the bare flesh at her shoulder. She jerked away, compulsively.

Stijn, she thought. *That fucking cunt. What he has done to me*. He was dead, she had killed him eighteen months ago, but the fury was still there, wracking her ...

She started to count. How often in her life had she counted like this, fending off one rage or another?

After a while the tears stopped. But her body felt red-hot now. It was the same every time. From freezing cold to boiling hot. It made her shiver, as though she had a fever. She pulled the quilt back over herself and curled into a ball. 'It will pass,' she muttered.

He didn't say anything. She lay still, measuring her breathing, waiting for the images to recede into the darkness of her brain. She tried to think about other things, tried to remember happy thoughts. But it was difficult.

After ten minutes or so her breathing began to return to normal, the shivering subsiding as the flush across her chest and upper arms faded. The buzzing behind her eyes – like white noise – continued for a little longer, but eventually it too began to stop. She had been through the process so many times she could time it.

When she was sure it was gone she turned to face him.

He was propped up on one elbow, worried eyes on her, waiting. 'It's OK,' he said. 'You know it's OK?'

She nodded.

He reached his hand out and took hold of hers, squeezing it gently. 'All right now?'

'Yes.'

He nodded with approval – 'supporting her', he would have said – then shifted closer to her. She didn't react.

'You will tell the shrink about this?'

They had given her a therapist. He hadn't helped so she had stopped going, months ago. Pete thought she was still seeing him each week.

'Yes. I'll tell him,' she said.

SUNDAY, 17 JUNE

12

Ronnie Shepherd spread butter carefully across a piece of toast. Behind him, at the table in the conservatory, his daughter Laura sat in a loose T-shirt and shorts, reading the papers, sipping from a mug of tea, feet up on the chair next to her. Her hair was messed up and unbrushed, a strawberry-blonde in the early-morning sunlight, exactly as he remembered her mother's hair. He wondered idly – and without any kind of feeling at all – whether Sharon's hair would be grey by now, and where she was. It was over twenty-three years since either of them had set eyes on Sharon Craven.

He walked over with his toast and tea, and sat down opposite Laura. He had got to bed at midnight last night – the first time he had managed that in seven days – but it had made little difference. He slept fitfully at the beginning of major inquiries, waking often to the same preoccupations that beset him by day. He was dog tired.

'Any news?' he asked. He rubbed a hand over his face, feeling the dry skin, the stubble, the pouches under his eyes. He took a drink of the tea.

'The usual,' she said, without looking up. 'Nothing happy. They're killing each other all over the world because of religion, racism or some other madness.' She paused and turned a page. 'Fourteen National Front skinheads arrested in Oldham last night amid more race rioting. Burnley and Bradford next in line.'

He took a mouthful of toast and watched her. She was beautiful, a gift to him. He had a thing about red hair and freckles, which was why he had ended up with her mother. Laura was the same. She had been out in the sun, he thought, because the freckles on her face, across the tops of her shoulders, arms and upper chest, were a dense pattern that took his breath away. *Thank God for you, Laura*, he thought, then laughed to himself. She wouldn't like him bringing God into it. 'Religion' was a good argument to have with her, one of the few things that could really get her going. Somehow she had ended up an evangelical atheist. She hadn't got that from him.

'What you laughing at?' she asked, still not looking at him.

'I wasn't.'

'I saw you smile.'

'You didn't. You had your head in the papers.'

'I felt it.'

Felt it. Was that possible?

Her house was in Whitby, a small cottage perched on the edge of cliffs to the south of the town, with fantastic sea views from the terrace and garden. It was the house they had both moved to about twenty years ago. Four years ago – when she had reached twenty-one and was still studying – he had transferred from North Yorkshire Police to neighbouring West Yorkshire, chasing a promotion. At the same time he had taken the opportunity to transfer ownership of the Whitby cottage to Laura. For himself he had rented a small flat in Dewsbury, just south of Leeds and Bradford, in the heart of his new working area, but within minutes of the motorway network that would bring him back out here. There had been no spoken arrangement between them, but one way or another he had ended up staying with her nearly every weekend since then.

She had been through several boyfriends in the time since his transfer – about the same as the number of women he had met, dated and left. They shared an inability to settle, and he was sure their close relationship didn't help. He worried often about how strange it must seem to boyfriends that their new girlfriend's father stayed with her for three nights out of every seven.

You should kick me out, he thought. He said it to her so often it was a ritual. She usually didn't even reply.

'What are you up to today?' he asked her, mouth full.

'Working from here. Nothing strenuous.' She taught politics at York University. It made him proud to think about it. Her brain was quick, surprising. He felt stupid and slow by comparison. Often he ran cases by her, things he was stuck with. She was nearly always helpful. Already they had talked about Bulldog.

Bulldog. The word darkened his day. He wished he could get rid of it somehow.

'What about you?' she asked. She looked at him for the first time, saw his eyes and frowned. 'You look whacked, Dad.'

'I am whacked.' It came with the job; no point in complaining about it. 'I have a list of about a hundred things to do,' he said, answering her question. 'Top of the list is set up an artist's interview with Jana Fleming, give new information to the psychiatric profiler, then have a meeting with Tim Thorne about the London angle.'

He looked out through the windows, following the slope of the garden towards the thin strip of distant dirty green. He was fascinated by the sea, even the North Sea, the coldest, roughest and least romantic of all seas. It looked like good sailing weather. If it weren't for Bulldog he could be out in the boat today.

'I was looking at that as you slept,' she said. She pointed to a clear plastic folder he had left lying on the table. It was a report from Josh Reynolds, prepared for the supervisors' meeting he had missed yesterday, listing and analysing all the CCTV and door-to-door evidence his team had managed to seize and scrutinize. He had looked quickly through it, then brought it home to read in detail.

'Thrilling stuff,' she said. 'Maybe you would sleep better if you didn't read material like that last thing at night.'

It made depressing reading. Five days of door-to-door enquiries and public appeals involving more than thirty officers had turned up nothing useful. The area was too rural. There was only one possible CCTV source, but it was from a farm nearly two miles from Fleming's place. The farmer had, in the past, farmed mink on the other side of the county and had suffered repeat attacks from animal rights activists, including a serious petrol bomb attack on his home. He had given it up in the end and had a normal dairy herd now, but the security fears had lingered enough to make him install a camera system covering his house, barn and outbuildings.

By chance, one of the three cameras also had a good angle on a local road that *could* lead to Fleming's house, depending on which turn you took. Traffic caught on the camera might therefore be destined for the Flemings, but also might not. Plus, there were three other ways to get to the Flemings which didn't pass the camera. The system was state of the art, with storage on DVD going back four months.

Reynolds's team had analysed hundreds of hours of footage, searching for movements from 8 June, but also for repeat sightings of vehicles going much further back, on the theory that there might have been some level of reconnaissance prior to the attack. From 8 June they had assembled a list of fifteen vehicles, all of which had been checked and none of which had proved suspicious. They had then been able to eliminate repeat sightings of local vehicles over a longer period (they had got as far as three months back, to date). That had left them with only one vehicle with a significant and unexplained repeat occurrence – a van registered to a London haulage company. They had sent a request to the Met to chase that up.

Ronnie bit into the toast, savouring the contrast between the hot crispy bread and cold melting butter, then checked his watch. Time to get going.

'Shall I send your love to Tim?' he asked, face straight.

She smirked. 'A meeting with Timmy Thorne. How boring for you.'

'Tut, tut,' he said. 'It's not so very long ago that—'

'I'd rather not remember,' she said, cutting him short.

He smiled, standing up. 'Am I still not meant to know about you two?' he asked.

'It seems so,' she said. 'Little Timmy got very flustered when you answered the phone last week. I assume he still believes you don't know anything.'

Laura had had what she described as a 'fling' with Tim Thorne last year. But for some reason Thorne hadn't wanted him to know, so Laura had pretended she had told him nothing about it, while for the better part of six months, Thorne had paid 'secret' visits to her in Whitby. It had caused them much amusement at the time, but Ronnie still didn't understand Thorne's problem.

'I don't like lying to him,' he said.

'It wasn't my choice,' she said. 'It's Timmy who thinks you would disapprove. He knows you don't like him.'

'That wouldn't make me object to you shagging him once in a while.'

She looked up, a pained expression on her face. 'Please, Dad. Do you have to talk about it like that? We're not in a locker room.'

He smiled again, then walked over to the sink with his empty mug. It was funny how she was often more prudish than he was. 'What's happening with Mark, then – the teacher?' he asked, not looking at her.

'Nothing at all.'

'I prefer him to Tim Thorne.'

'Nothing is going on with Tim Thorne. Or with Mark. And you don't have to worry about any of that. Or whether it's time for me to be kicking you out and getting a man in. Et cetera, et cetera. I can make these choices for myself. I'm a big girl now.'

13

Karen was determined to pick up Mairead from Alexia's so she could see the girl for herself, but Ronnie Shepherd called her before ten to inform her that he had already set up the interview between the police artist and Jana Fleming. He wanted her to meet the artist at the Hussein house within an hour. His tone was friendly, apologetic, professional. So much for that.

Technically, she was off duty until Monday morning, but that wasn't the way it worked on murder Inquiries. And he was polite enough to ask her, not tell her. By then Pete was long gone on his trip to Lancashire and she had already arranged with him the night before that she would collect Mairead just after midday. So even before she arrived at the Hussein place she was in a rush.

She drove to Alwoodley with the incident between Pete and herself weighing her down. She had not had an episode like that for many months. It could not have been a coincidence that her thoughts had run out of control only hours after getting so upset about Jana Fleming. This kind of reaction was why they had moved her to Halifax. This was why they had agreed she should not get involved in this kind of work.

As she rang the Hussein's doorbell she was calculating how long she had before she would have to leave to get Mairead. But the people she was about to deal with were devastated with grief. She tried to pull her concentration together as she waited for someone to answer the door.

No one appeared. She rang the bell again. There were cars on the drive, but no sounds from within. She tried knocking, quite hard. After a couple of minutes she heard footsteps on the marble floor to the other side. Varisha Hussein opened the door, but it took a moment for Karen to recognize her. Things had caught up with Varisha overnight, it seemed.

She was dressed in a towel dressing gown that was too short for her, loosely pulled around her waist and not tied, so that if she moved too quickly it flapped open, showing Karen more of her than she wanted to see. There was something that might have been vomit staining the front of it. Her hair was unkempt, with strands stuck across her face, her skin shiny and pallid. She must have been crying for a long time because her eyes were so puffed up and red she was having to squint at Karen as if she needed glasses. She didn't appear to recognize her.

'DC Karen Sharpe, Mrs Hussein. We met yesterday. I think DI Shepherd told you I was coming out again?'

The name brought no change of expression. 'Yes. Of course,' Varisha murmured. 'Please come in.' She looked down at herself, as if realizing how she looked. 'I'm sorry,' she said quietly. 'I slept very badly last night.' Her lip quivered a little as she spoke.

Karen stepped into the hallway. Inside, the air was impregnated with grief.

'Are you all right, Varisha? Have you had any sleep at all?

'No. No sleep. I was up with Sammy all night. He has been very unwell. You will have to forgive me. But something terrible …' She looked as if she was about to explain what had happened to them.

'I know,' Karen said. She placed her bag on the floor and stepped closer to her, lowering her voice.

'I was here yesterday, speaking to Jana. Do you remember?' She reached out a hand and squeezed her arm, very gently. The stain *was* vomit, she thought. Varisha had been sick down the robe and had made a poor effort to sponge it off. 'I've come to speak to Jana again,' she said. She looked around for some sign that the artist might already be there. 'Has anyone else arrived?' she asked.

'Nobody but us.' Varisha was staring at her now. 'There is nobody here but us.'

'Has Sana gone home again?' She had met Sana – Varisha's other daughter – as she was leaving the day before. Of all the family members she had seemed most functional. Maybe she could get her to sit in on the interview instead of Varisha.

Varisha shook her head. 'Sana is still here …' She frowned. 'Do you want to see her?'

'Maybe. I have to speak to Jana again, if that's OK. But I'm waiting for a police artist to arrive as well. We want Jana to describe some things to her. Did Mr Shepherd call you to arrange things?' She was beginning to doubt it.

'Yes. He told us. But there is no one else here.' Her eyes had a vacant expression. She was speaking as if she understood the words, but her facial expressions said something else. There was something broken beneath the surface.

Karen knew what she had to do to cope with it. She should sit down with the woman now and speak to her gently and at length about the whole thing. She should comfort her. But that would take too long. She had her own daughter to think about. She secretly cursed Ronnie Shepherd for bringing her anywhere near this.

'Is Jana out of bed yet?'

'She is with her aunt. With Sana.'

That was good. 'Can I see her?' She could start getting Jana into the mood for things now, before the artist got here.

Varisha nodded. 'Yes. You can see her. But I need to show you something first.'

Karen frowned. Was it going to be more photos of the dead woman? The tone of voice suggested something like that. Karen opened her mouth to start explaining her scheduling problems, but Varisha was already walking away from her. 'Please come with me,' she called back. 'This is important.'

Karen walked after her, following her up the same staircase they had used the day before. This time, however, they turned in the other direction once they reached the landing. They passed into what Karen assumed was another wing of the building. As she walked, Varisha held the gown clumsily to her body. She had bare feet.

'This is where the bedrooms are,' Varisha said to her. 'I want to show you Enisa's room.'

Karen heard a faint noise from further along, from behind one of the closed doors. It was the sound of someone sobbing. Not a child. As they neared it, Varisha paused. 'It's Sammy,' she said, not looking at Karen. 'I don't know what to do to help him ...'

Karen nodded, trying not to think about the noise, trying to ignore it. 'Is Jana in Enisa's room?' she asked.

Varisha shook her head. 'She is with Sana.' She said it as if Karen had suggested something absurd. 'I already told you that. Why would she be in Enisa's room? I would not let her in there. Not now ...' Her lip started trembling again.

'Is there any reason why you want me to see Enisa's old room?' Karen asked quietly.

'Yes. Of course there is.' A trace of her old self flickered in the irritation. She started walking again. 'No one has been in there, you see. A policeman came and asked me if there were any items belonging to Enisa that he should see. I told him there were not.' She stopped outside another door. 'This is it,' she said. Her face began to twitch, and tears began to spill from her eyes. 'It's not her "old" room, as you said – that was in the house in Holmfirth. This is the room she used when she visited us.'

'You don't need to show me it, Varisha. Not if—'

'I *have* to show you. You see, I hadn't been in there when the policeman asked me. I hadn't dared to go in ...' She was looking at the floor, holding the handle to the door, but not turning it. Just standing there, shoulders shaking. 'But I went in this morning ...' She pushed the door open and stepped sideways, to allow Karen to walk past her. 'I hope I haven't done wrong. But I couldn't go in,' she said. She wiped her eyes with the sleeve of the dressing gown. 'I couldn't go in at all. Not until this morning. Then I remembered ...'

Karen looked past her. It was a large room with pine wardrobes and a double bed. An open door at the far end led to an *en suite* bathroom. There were pictures on the walls – more of the modern art they had downstairs – but nothing that would suggest whose room it was. The décor was clean and simple, in light colours. It looked like a purely functional guest room. On the bed was a suitcase.

Karen looked back at Varisha. She clearly felt differently about it because she couldn't even bring herself to look.

'What did you remember?' Karen asked her, puzzled.

'The suitcase,' Varisha spluttered. 'I remembered the suitcase.'

Karen looked back into the room. She had an idea what was coming now. 'Is it Enisa's suitcase?'

'Yes. She brought it when they started the building works at her house. I remember she told me that it was because she didn't trust the builders. They let them work there during the day, you know, while they were away at work.'

'She brought the suitcase here because she was worried they might steal it?'

'Not the suitcase. But what is inside it. It's all her most valuable things. I saw them this morning ...' She really started to sob. 'Even her wedding rings are there ...'

Karen stepped into the room and walked over to the suitcase. It was

73

unlocked. She lifted the lid and looked inside. There were four shoe boxes within. Two were stuffed with papers, letters and documents. The other two were filled with jewellery.

'When I looked round their house ...' Varisha was saying behind her, '... when they – the police – asked me to tell them if anything was missing, I thought all this was missing. I thought it must have been stolen. That's what I told them. I didn't remember it was here ... I didn't remember ...'

MONDAY, 18 JUNE

14

Tim Thorne sat at the rear of the briefing room and watched Ronnie Shepherd moving around at the front. There was a buzz in the air that had been absent from Bulldog briefings for a few days now. The room was packed, every chair taken, thirty-five detectives present and waiting, talking amongst themselves in hushed tones, as Ronnie prepared to speak to them. The rumour mill had gone into overdrive.

Only SIO David Riggs was absent. He had a press call on one of his other jobs. No doubt the excuse was genuine, but it was still poor that he had landed the policy U-turn on his deputy.

Ronnie finished writing lists of names on the whiteboards, then turned to face the room.

'OK, can I have your attention?' he said.

He spoke quietly, but got silence almost at once. He was like Laura in that respect. Tim had once watched her lecture at York University. She had been addressing a hall of nearly two hundred teenage students and they had shut up as soon as she walked in.

Ronnie sat back against the desk at the front.

'There has been a major development,' he said after a few seconds. 'I'll tell you about it and then we'll discuss the consequences.' He sounded tired but alert, conscious of how important the information was. 'Most of you probably know by now what has happened. Yesterday Varisha Hussein remembered that her daughter had left a suitcase of jewellery at her house – for safe keeping. When we examined it we found all the jewellery previously thought to have been stolen during the attack.'

Some people obviously hadn't heard because a shocked murmur arose at once. Ronnie waited for the excitement to subside.

When we examined it. No public glory for Sharpe, then. Tim looked around for her and found her also in the back row, but right in the corner of the room, squeezed low in her seat. Trying to be inconspicuous. She was so tall that was difficult. Could he find her attractive enough to shag? he wondered. She was living with a Sikh DS called Bains. He wondered if Ronnie knew that.

'As of yesterday,' Ronnie continued, 'there is no evidence that anything was stolen during the attack on the Flemings, no evidence that any searches of the property were made. No evidence, in fact, that this was a burglary.'

The murmur of voices started again. He saw a few faces looking for Josh Reynolds, who was sitting near the front. He had been in charge of the property search at Varisha Hussein's place, and had apparently taken the distressed mother's word for it that there was nothing of interest there. In the emergency supervisors' meeting – held just before this – Ronnie had tried to stop him taking the blame for the cock-up. Tim would have let him stew. The mistake was fundamental and had serious consequences. The entire team had been looking the wrong way for ten days. Riggs should have been here now to admit that.

'These things happen,' Ronnie said. He sounded calm about it. 'The important thing now is to shift focus. The profiler has confirmed what is now obvious. If this isn't a burglary then it has to be something personal. The main purpose of the attack must have been to inflict extreme violence on the Flemings, probably to kill both of them. The motive for such an attack can only arise out of a connection between one or both victims and the attackers. Until now we have mainly looked at high-grade professional local nominals capable of this kind of burglary; now we have to turn everything round. We have to start looking at revenge and grudge theories. We have to assume this wasn't anything to do with burglary. This was a deliberate, targeted attack on the Flemings.' He looked round their faces, all tense and quiet, then sighed. 'That means we have to start from scratch,' he said. 'We have to find the connection between the victims and their attackers.'

He stood up and walked back to the whiteboards. He pointed to them. 'Hence,' he said, 'new dispositions, as of today.'

He gave them a moment to look down the list of names and find their own.

Uncapping a black marker, he continued, 'There will be three teams only, in order to keep things flexible. There will thus be two sergeants on each team and I expect them to organize their groups into subdivisions to cover the work.' He started writing areas of responsibility on the boards, beneath the lists of names. 'Team one will cover

78

Yorkshire. The Flemings have been up here for six months. We have to know everything they've been up to, concentrating initially on their working environments. Team two will cover London …' That caused a stir. He paused, pen in the air, back to the room. The noise continued. He turned. 'From all the enquiries we've made so far it seems possible that this attack was not the work of local criminals. The Flemings came here from London, so London is the place to start looking. Tim Thorne has already done a bit of that. We had two officers down there last week. But so far we've relied mainly on assistance from the Met. Now we will need our own team working with the Met. I intend to use over half the squad to do that.' He turned back to the board. 'I've put names up on the basis of my best guess as to who would be up for an extended spell away from home, but I want those people to volunteer, if possible. If someone has a good reason not to go then we'll try to honour that.'

'I have a major issue with that, sir—' Mark Slattery, speaking from the front. Normally he was a first-rate arse-licker.

'Not now, Mark,' Ronnie said, cutting him off. 'You can speak to Tim Thorne about it later.' He wrote in the heads of the teams, then turned back to face them. 'Tim will co-ordinate the London team, under me. Vee Hepworth will co-ordinate the Yorkshire team under Tom Joyce. For the next ten days these two teams are to focus exclusively on Steve Fleming's past. Team three will cover HOLMES, the indexing, family liaison, all lines that we have been previously running – all of them – *and* put together a sub-team to continue residual enquiries into Enisa Fleming's character and lifestyle.'

Tim saw that Sharpe had been moved off the family liaison role and was now on his London team. She had requested that, apparently. After finding the stolen jewellery she had spent half of yesterday trying to get an artist's impression from Jana Fleming. According to Ronnie, things hadn't gone well. Jana had ended up hysterical and the artist came away with a blank page. Sharpe had taken it badly, though Ronnie hadn't told him precisely how she had reacted. 'Better if we move her,' was all he had said.

Tim looked over to her again. She didn't look like the sort to get upset by a hysterical kid.

'The priority is Steve Fleming,' he heard Ronnie say. 'I want to know every major criminal he has prosecuted in the last year. This will involve close co-ordination with the Met and the National Crime Squad.'

Sharpe wouldn't do it for him, Tim decided – not unless he was very drunk. It wasn't just her age (she must be six or seven years older than him), it was that broken nose. How could Ronnie go for that? It would be like shagging a prop forward.

'Do you want to tell us why, Tim?' Ronnie asked, cueing him in.

He stood up. He had already known that he would be 'co-ordinating' the London team, from the supervisors' meeting. Co-ordinating was just a tactful word for 'in charge of.' He waited until most of their heads had turned to face him.

'Until now,' he said, 'because I only had four detectives, I had to keep the field of interest narrow. The most shocking and extreme violence was inflicted on Enisa, so we have so far concentrated on unearthing and cataloguing her working past, lifestyle and associations. We have done that in London and up here. We already know enough to say that it is unlikely Enisa was the primary target here, despite the ferocity of the attack. She worked as a paediatrician both up here and down in London. We've found nothing – absolutely nothing – from her working life that would yield a motive for this kind of attack.' He stopped for a second to let that sink in. 'That's why we're going to be looking intensively at Steve,' he continued. 'We think it likely that something from Steve Fleming's recent past has triggered this. Our enquiries with West Yorkshire Crown Prosecution Service have revealed nothing. He's only been up here for six months and doesn't seem to have had his hands on anything dangerous. Those enquiries need to continue, but the London angle is really the big change here. We've discovered that down in London Fleming worked extensively with the National Crime Squad. He was given cases which the CPS here say he was probably too junior to handle. They were big, proactive cases. The NCS have told us that any number of them could yield a motive for his attempted murder.'

'What does Fleming say about this?' A DC from the front asked the question. Tim didn't know his name. He was on Simon Parfitt's team, and although he addressed the question to Tim, he was looking at Parfitt.

'Fleming thinks the idea is ridiculous,' Ronnie said, answering quickly for him.

'Fleming doesn't think criminals would think of taking revenge on lawyers,' Tim added. 'We know he's wrong about that, of course.'

'Can't he assist, though? Can't he come up with names of cases?' This time it was Mark Slattery again. 'Just to help focus it.'

'I've already spent many hours going over this sort of thing with him.' A voice from the middle, again answering for him. Debbie Moor, cheeky cow. But fair enough – she had dealt with Fleming. 'I was in with him again this morning,' she said. 'He's not in brilliant shape. He was able to provide us with a list of cases he had dealt with in Yorkshire, but, as Tim says, there's not much there worth looking at. The biggest villain he dealt with up here was a fraudster who conned several women into loaning him cash. When it came to trying to remember things from London he found it much more difficult. Remember he suffered a head injury as well. He has given us *some* info, though. Mr Shepherd will take that to London with him.'

'I'm going this afternoon,' Ronnie said, still leaning back against the desks. 'Tim will stay up here and handle the admin for the deployment. I have a meeting with the Met and the NCS to finalize the necessary co-operation. I anticipate we will be able start operations down there by Wednesday.'

15

Caroline Philips knew her life was finally about to change. Perhaps it wouldn't happen at once – she might have to do more catalogues and suchlike – but even so, it would mean she could leave this job at Boots within a few months. Certainly she could get out before the time came to make the decision about the pharmacy course in Sunderland. She felt sure of it. How could your picture be published in a two-page spread in *Marie Claire* without everything changing?

That morning she had woken up with butterflies in her stomach. They persisted right through to lunchtime, when she had the chance to walk to WH Smith, next door to Boots, to check whether it was there yet. An assistant told her it would probably be Wednesday before *Marie Claire* was out. That brought her down to earth a bit.

She went back and sat in the lunch room with two of the sales assistants she had been working with that morning. She tried to get some of her ham sandwich down, chatting to them as if nothing were different. But she was too nervous. She couldn't eat a thing, could hardly focus on what they were saying.

'You get a late night, then?' Jane asked her.

'Sorry?'

'A late night, was it?'

'How do you mean?'

'You seem a bit ... well, vacant.'

'Bit more vacant than usual,' the other put in. She was called Antonia. 'Sometimes it's difficult to tell if you're awake at all,' she said. They both laughed at her.

Caroline was meant to be a management trainee, in charge of them.

'We had to stop you bumping into things this morning,' Jane said. 'The lights were all on ...'

Was it a joke about her appearance, because she was skinny and blonde, when they were both overweight, with dyed brown hair? A dumb blonde joke? She assumed they made this kind of joke about her all the time, behind her back. But she was far from dumb. She had a plan to get out of this place while they were stuck here. Probably they would work here for the rest of their lives.

'I think you have a more exciting night life than you let on,' Jane said.

'Probably Brian's a bit frisky,' Antonia suggested. 'Maybe it's his time of month.'

'Ber-why-ann ...' Jane said, her mouth twisting in a parody of his name.

Caroline looked blankly at them. It was like being back in the school yard. It had been a mistake to tell them her boyfriend was called Brian, a mistake to tell them anything about herself.

'I didn't sleep too well,' she lied. 'I'm tired.'

Any one of them could have done her job without thinking about it, and better, too. Because you had to be stupid to do this job, you had to be capable of absorbing more boredom than she could ever take. That old woman this morning, for example, shouting at her about her heart drugs. What would Jane and Antonia have done? Taken the woman aside, given her a cup of tea, sat her down on the 'wobblies chair' until she got her senses back, spoken firmly to her, maybe have a laugh about it afterwards. Instead they had stood back and watched Caroline messing it up. But then, her mind had been on the photos since she had woken up. All she could think about was *Marie Claire*.

They wouldn't have taken the piss out of Mr Smith, the manager. They were frightened of him. But he was above them all, distant; he didn't sit down and take his coffee breaks with them. That was what she should be like, if she had to take this job seriously, if it was all she had. They had taught her that on the induction course in Nottingham. *Keep your distance.* Jane was already capable of ignoring the instructions she gave her. Like the time she had refused to sweep up the spillage when old Phyllis Davis had dropped a bottle of cough medicine. 'Why should I?' she had demanded. 'I wasn't the idiot that dropped it.'

'Because Phyllis is on pharmacy now – otherwise she would do it.'

'She spilt it, she wipes it,' she had retorted. 'Didn't they teach you that on your course?' And she had simply walked off.

In the end Caroline had cleaned the spillage herself.

She wouldn't have to put up with it for much longer, though. She looked over at them, sitting in the tiny room in slightly soiled, unflattering uniforms, stuffing their faces with tuna mayonnaise sandwiches. She watched crumbs of bread dropping on to Jane's stomach. Jane already had two kids at home and was pregnant again. How old was she? Three, four years older than her? Twenty-three or twenty-four at most. She was probably OK, if you didn't have to manage her. Not that Caroline had ever gone in for the kind of things Jane and Antonia enjoyed – out on the town every Friday and Saturday night, snogging and getting trashed. Well, not so much Jane, not with the kids. But that was all Antonia talked about. Who she had 'copped off' with, how pissed she had been and how little money she had spent (because a staggering variety of men had all bought her pints of lager).

Lying on the chair next to Jane was her magazine – last month's edition of *Marie Claire*. She would finish her sandwich, get a coffee and read it for fifteen minutes. She did the same every day. If she bought the new edition on Wednesday she would be looking at Caroline's photo shoot over lunch, slurping her coffee and gazing at it as if it were something from another world.

It *was* another world. The world of celebrities, wealth, publicity. Miles away from the shit they had to deal with in Boots. Jane probably wouldn't even recognize her. No one except her flatmate Debs knew about the modelling – not even Brian or her mum and dad. Sitting there on her lunch break, looking through the magazine, Jane just wouldn't expect to come across a set of pictures of Caroline Philips, trainee manager, looking like *part* of that world.

Would they treat her differently then? Would they still think she was stupid? She had to suppress an urge to laugh aloud when she thought about it.

16

Karen was waiting for him to start something from the moment they left Leeds. At first, all he talked about was the case. She didn't mind that, but she knew that there was going to be more, because there was no good work reason to have picked her for this trip. Which meant that at some point he was going to start something other than a discussion about his working life.

When Shepherd asked her to accompany him – after the morning briefing – she had said yes immediately. He had looked to be on the point of saying something to explain his choice, but he closed his mouth at once. Best not tell an unconvincing lie if you didn't have to.

'Good,' he said, instead. 'You can have a lift if you want. I'll be driving down.'

She accepted that immediately as well. He looked equivocal then (as if she *should* ask, 'Why me?') but he still said nothing. So now the issue was between them, an unspoken question: why did you pick *me* for this?

They got as far as the Nottingham turn-off before he asked her anything personal. That meant he had talked about Bulldog for over an hour. Throughout, he kept the Porsche at a steady ninety miles per hour in the fast lane. The day was hot and the Porsche, it turned out, was old ('vintage', he said). So no air conditioning. They both took their jackets off and rolled their shirt-sleeves up. He wore a suit similar to the one he had been wearing on Saturday. She had chosen a light, cotton jacket and matching skirt, with a plain pale-blue blouse. With the jacket off she could see more of him. He was in good shape. They both wore shades, and hers were reflective, so if she sat a little to the side he couldn't see whether she was looking at him or not.

'You managed to sort out childcare OK?'

It was the first personal question he had asked her, and a tricky one. She looked out of the window and watched the sign for Nottingham flash by, then she turned to him and said, 'Yes. I have a friend who helps out.' The implication was that the friend was female and that Karen was therefore single.

He didn't react to her answer. For a few minutes he drove on without looking at her, concentrating on the road. He seemed comfortable driving the Porsche at speed, looked as if he could easily drive it much faster, in fact. Mostly he kept only one hand on the wheel, controlling it with a light touch. Behind the glasses she could see his eyes flicking regularly to the mirrors.

Getting away had been as easy as telling Pete that she had to spend two, possibly three nights in London. He knew the rules, he was in the job. She should have felt lucky about it, but didn't. She wondered briefly how it would be without him, with just Mairead and herself. Most of all, she worried about how Mairead would deal with that.

'You frown a lot,' he said.

She looked over to him, surprised.

'I like it,' he said quickly. 'It was almost the first thing I noticed about you.'

'I frown too much,' she said. She felt almost embarrassed, now he had dipped his toe in the water.

'You get on well with your kid? She's a teenager, right?' he asked next, as if he had tuned into her thoughts.

'She's thirteen. We have our moments.'

'Moments when you get on, you mean? I remember it well.' He laughed.

She wished she could join in, but didn't even want to think about the sorts of horrors that might account for Mairead's behaviour. Everything Mairead was, every problem she had, *she*, Karen, was responsible for it.

'I bet your daughter is beautiful,' she said, quietly.

He looked surprised now. 'She is. She's very beautiful. She must have it from her mother, I think ...' He gestured lazily with his free hand, indicating his own features, as if his ugliness were self-apparent.

'I didn't mean physically,' she said. 'What does that matter? I meant her personality. Growing up with someone like you ... without problems ...' *He* was frowning now, waiting for her to finish the thought. 'Someone calm like you,' she explained. 'You must have looked after her well.'

You're mistaken,' he said. 'I'm like a duck. Calm on the surface, legs paddling frantically below.'

She shook her head, not looking at him. 'You're not like that at all,' she said.

'What am I like, then?'

She smiled at him. 'Not like a duck,' she said. 'And certainly not an ugly duck.'

And so it starts, she thought. He started to ask more questions, he was keen to know things about her. The interest was mildly exciting – now that she felt sure something was going on – but dangerous. She answered questions about her working life and Mairead easily enough, but it wasn't long before he was turning to more difficult areas. He seemed very interested in what she had been doing prior to the move to West Yorkshire.

Over coffee at services near Leicester, she decided to turn it round by asking him questions about himself. The more he talked the less she would have to say. Surprisingly, he seemed eager to disclose. She kept it going like that as they returned to the car, asking him follow-ups if he paused.

In the end she had his entire life story before they reached Watford Gap.

The national crime squad meeting was in the crime manager's office at Ealing Police Station, which was where the satellite incident room was going to be, mainly because there was space available, and because the first batch of cases they wanted to focus on had been handled by the NCS, working out of an office in Slough and using the charging facilities at Ealing Police Station. Fleming had worked out of CPS offices in Harrow, covering Ealing and Hounslow boroughs.

The Met were meant to send a DI to sit in, but he didn't show up, so they were left with five officers from the NCS, all crammed into a room not much bigger than a large cupboard. The superintendent who had run the teams Fleming had worked with sat behind the single desk. Her name was Sarah Hall. She was a compact, very blonde, fair-skinned woman, dressed in a black trouser suit and white shirt. She ran the meeting with a crisp, efficient manner. Her officers spoke only when asked and respectfully called her 'Ma'am.'

They were in there for almost two hours, but didn't get further than arguing about admin and resources. The door and window were open, but it still became so airless and hot that Karen began to wilt. Both Ronnie and the man who had worked with Fleming – a very young, very black DS called Andy Barnes – seemed impatient to talk about evidence and leads, but didn't get the chance.

About halfway through, Hall stepped into the corridor to answer her mobile and Barnes quietly invited Ronnie for a drink when they were done. The implication from his tone was that he didn't want Sarah Hall to know about it. Ronnie seemed keen and accepted at once, but Karen was disappointed. After their long trip down, the idea of drinking with Ronnie Shepherd was appealing, but not a standard male booze-up with the NCS.

As the meeting finished she made her excuses and left them to it.

She didn't know Ealing well. In the six or so years she had lived in London she had been twice: once as a probationer PC, on the way back from a public order incident in Southall, and once, four years later, with Mairead's father, James Martin. Luckily, their hotel was only a twenty-minute walk from the police station, on the same road.

It was nearly seven o'clock. London was bright, warm, full of people and traffic. There were probably still three hours of light left. She passed restaurants and bars with tables on the pavements and people milling around as if they were on the Continent and the pollution didn't matter. Exactly as she remembered it. Coming here from Bradford was like coming to a different world. A world of which she had once been a part. Standing there she realized she wanted to talk to Ronnie Shepherd about that, tell him what it had felt like to be so young and to be here.

Nineteen years old. She felt a flood of nostalgia for it all. She had been in love with James Martin then, *really* in love with him. But would that have happened without the danger of being undercover? Her feelings for him had lasted many years after they had been branded illicit. What would Shepherd say about that?

She checked in, went up to her room, phoned for a sandwich and called Mairead. Pete answered.

'It's me,' she said. 'Is Mairead there?'

'No. You in London?'

'Yes. Just got in to the hotel.' She felt suddenly shattered. Or was it just talking to Pete?

'Can you give me the details and number?'

'Of course.' She read them out from a slip of hotel notepaper on the table by the bed.

'Mairead is with Alexia,' he said, when she was finished.

'At Alexia's?'

'No. They're at another rehearsal, in town.'

'Doesn't she have homework?'

'She's done it.'

Silence. She didn't know what to say to him. 'I wanted to speak to her,' she said, feeling a little lost somehow.

'Call her mobile.'

'You know I can't do that. She doesn't like it. You picking her up later?'

'At nine-thirty. Call back at ten, maybe?'

'I'll be asleep by then. I'm knackered. Just tell her I love her.'

'I will. Are you OK?'

'Fine. Yes.'

She waited for him to say something, but he didn't.

I'd better go,' she said. She felt heavy. 'Got to shower—'

'We miss you, Karen. You know that?'

'I do.'

'Me as well,' he said, to emphasize it.

'I know that, too. I miss you, Pete. And Mairead. But I'll be back on Wednesday.'

'Don't worry about her.'

'No.'

They said goodbye, then she hung up and thought about why she felt so bad. She felt she was lying to him all the time now, even when she didn't tell obvious lies – like saying she missed him.

She pulled Mairead's mobile number from the memory in her own mobile and looked at it, tempted. The last thing Mairead ever wanted was for her to call her on the mobile, as if she were checking up on her. Irritatingly, she didn't seem to mind when Pete called her. Karen had met Alexia now, and though the girl had been polite to her, she hadn't liked her. There was something far too adult about her, far too cheeky. She hadn't said any of that to Mairead, of course. Nor had she yet found the time to ask her about the kanga she had found.

She had eaten her sandwich, showered and changed by the time the phone rang. It was Ronnie Shepherd, calling from the downstairs bar.

'I've escaped,' he said. 'Finally they've gone.'

She laughed. '*You* wanted to drink with them,' she said.

'I wanted to drink with *you*. But you buggered off and left me to them.'

He sounded animated, but not drunk.

'I'm available now,' she said.

'So come down.'

17

The bar was virtually empty when she got there. They sat in low, comfortable chairs, pulled around a coffee table, and ordered a bottle of red wine.

'I hope I didn't give the wrong impression earlier,' he said. 'I talked a lot about myself, asked a lot of nosy questions. I'm sorry. It was probably all too personal. I didn't mean it to be.'

She frowned at him. He was looking into his wine glass, not at her, thinking about what he was saying. She had the feeling he might have planned the words earlier, that he had been brooding over it.

'I liked it,' she said. 'I'm interested. There's nothing to apologize for. I asked you to tell me, remember?'

'I thought you were just being polite. Because you said nothing about yourself. Nothing at all. I felt a bit foolish afterwards – going on about me. I thought maybe you were uncomfortable with it.'

Was he serious? She sat forward in the seat, nearer to him. 'That's not it,' she said. 'I wish I could talk about myself so easily. But I can't. It's not a problem with you. There are things I would like to tell you. It's just I don't have so unproblematic a relationship with my own past.'

'You're from here, right? From London?'

She looked steadily at him, then shook her head. 'No. Is that what you thought?'

'From your accent,' he said. 'I thought it was a London accent.'

'I lived here for about six years,' she said. 'In two batches. First time in nineteen eighty-three, then later in eighty-seven. I worked hard at the accent. I suppose it stuck.'

He was frowning now.

'I'm from Northern Ireland,' she said, then sat back and sighed. 'You don't know how hard it is to tell people that. When I was down here I was with SO13.'

He raised his eyebrows.

SO13 was the anti-terrorist branch of the Met. Her secondment into it had been a training deployment on the way to other units – all military, all under cover. She was sure Ronnie Shepherd would never have heard of them.

'Not behind a desk, you mean?' he asked.

'I was never behind a desk.'

She watched him digest it, saw him clicking up the possibilities.

'So you know London well?' he asked, going for something harmless.

'Parts of it. Not Ealing. So we're OK.' She smiled at him. She could feel the wine in her blood now. She filled her glass again.

'So is Sharpe a Catholic or Protestant name?' he asked.

'Sharpe wasn't my name then.'

He looked surprised.

'I've had a lot of names,' she said. She pushed a strand of hair from her eyes. 'I was christened Helen Young. Young could be Catholic or Protestant, over there.' *Helen Young.* The words sounded peculiar on her lips. 'That's who I was when I was with SO13.'

'And when Mairead was born?'

Good guess, but wrong. He was trying to fit the pieces together, make a whole picture out of it. She'd been trying to do the same all her life. 'No. I was someone else then,' she said. 'Sinead Collins. *That's* a Catholic name. Those were bad times.' Was she going to go that far? Was she going to tell him about that? She took another mouthful of wine and looked around. The bar was about twenty feet away, the barman talking quietly to a waitress from the restaurant. There were two customers there, on stools, then another group who looked to be Asian businessmen at a table nearer the bar, all out of earshot. To the other side of them there were open panelled doors on to the street (still busy with traffic at past ten o'clock) and tables on the pavement, under an awning. Several couples out there.

'I'd like to tell you something,' she started, then stopped. She looked down at her feet, under the coffee table. 'Something I don't tell many people. I want to tell you so you know me better. Because I like you.' She looked up at him. His eyes were fixed on her, waiting. 'I don't want you to get any nasty surprises,' she said.

'Tell me,' he said.

'It's about Mairead and about me.' She felt a little tremble in her legs. 'When Mairead was born I was a bit … messed up. I was doing undercover stuff. Deep postings. There's a long, detailed explanation for it, but it doesn't really work, from her point of view, so I won't tell you about it.' She took a gulp of wine and swallowed carefully. 'I walked out on Mairead,' she said. She didn't dare look at him now. Why had she started this? 'I left her with her father, near here, in Shepherd's Bush.' She rubbed the tops of her knees, then put her face in her hands. 'I was ill, apparently. I can't even remember her birth. Can you believe that?' He didn't reply. She could *just* hear him breathing, beside her. 'I didn't see her again until five years ago, when she was eight. That's another long story – how I got her back. But for all the time before that she was with her father. He was an IRA volunteer, the person I was meant to be targetting.'

She forced herself to sit back on the chair and remove her hands from her face, then looked at him. He was staring intensely at her, but not with hatred or disgust. She let out a breath, slowly. 'I'm a terrible mother,' she said. 'Really terrible. I've totally fucked her up.'

'I doubt that's true.' He spoke very quickly. 'If you were terrible you wouldn't care about it at all. You've dealt with terrible mothers. You know what they can do to their kids. You're not like that.'

She shook her head. 'Not like that, no. But there's more than one way to skin a cat.'

Silence. The metaphor was inappropriate.

'I'm glad I told you,' she said. 'Now you know a little of what I am.' She said it with distaste.

'I don't know enough,' he said. He shifted forward in his seat. 'I would like to know more.'

'Before you decide?'

He frowned. 'Decide what?'

'Whether I'm worth your interest.'

He smiled at her. 'Don't be silly, Karen. We all have a past. The trick is to survive it, move on, keep going. You've done that. We both have.' He reached forward and put a hand on her leg. 'Thanks,' he said. 'I feel better now *you've* said something. I feel less of an idiot for going on and on about me.' He seemed genuinely relieved.

She looked down at his hand, resting on her leg, just above her knee. She smiled back at him, feeling comfortable with it. 'Well, thank God for that,' she said. She felt more relief than she would want to admit to. She moved her own hand over and took hold of his, squeezed it quickly, then let go. He took it back. 'Or thank you,' she said.

He smiled again. 'I *would* like to know more, though. I meant it.'

She sat forward and picked up the wine glass. 'There's a lot more to know,' she said. 'But maybe we can ration the heavy stuff. There'll be other times ...'

He grinned at her. 'I hope so.'

They talked until nearly two in the morning, sitting there in the bar. They talked about lighter things, even laughed a bit. Then the bar closed. He asked her back to his room – to raid his mini-bar for a nightcap they certainly didn't need. By that stage she was too drunk to think things through. She said yes, knowing where it was going and wanting it to go there. She could worry about the consequences later.

In his room he poured them two gin and tonics and then sat too far away from her, on the single armchair. She sat on the edge of the bed. She looked over at him and sensed his awkwardness.

'You're very far away,' she said. Was he having second thoughts?

'You want me to move closer?'

'Of course.'

He stood up and walked over to her. He looked very serious, and slightly unsteady.

'And I want you to smile,' she said. 'What we're doing is not so serious.'

'Isn't it?'

He sat down on the bed, next to her, not touching her, about three inches between their bodies. 'I think it's the most serious thing you can do,' he said. 'This is where everything starts. From here on you don't know where it will lead.'

'*Nothing* has started yet. There's still time for you to back out.'

He smiled at that.

'I'll start something now,' she said. She put her drink down and leaned over towards him, shifting closer on the bed. He brought his head down to meet her and slipped an arm over her shoulders.

They kissed. She got excited straight away, feeling the warmth spreading through her. Then she tried to slow down, in case he got frightened. He was still only using one arm, holding the drink with the other. She could taste the gin in his mouth, and another taste that was peculiar to him, the taste of his saliva. She could feel the stubble above his lip rubbing her skin. She tried to be delicate about it, to control what she wanted to do, but it was difficult. She looped both arms around his neck and pushed her tongue deep into his mouth. He started making a light groaning noise, in his throat. That was interesting.

She kept kissing him like that, moving her tongue around his teeth, exploring his mouth, feeling herself getting more and more eager. He broke away first, gently. She held on to him and waited. He took a breath and set the glass down on the floor beside the bed.

'I hope you weren't thinking of stopping,' she said.

He laughed. 'So what happens now?'

'We kiss again like that, only longer. Then we go to bed and do the business.'

He stared at her. For a moment she thought it might be too much for him.

'That sound OK?' she asked. 'I need your consent.'

He nodded, trying to stop himself from laughing. 'That sounds perfect,' he said.

Only afterwards, when they were lying there, wrapped around each other, he almost asleep, did she remember what might have happened, what had happened every other time she had done this for the last year.

But this time it hadn't even started. No panics, no memories, no grotesque visions. Until this moment Stijn hadn't even entered her head. She knew why: there had been none of the usual triggers. This was a different man, a different place, a different pattern to the contact. That was all it took. Pete couldn't deliver that.

And it had worked. For both of them. She began to feel delirious thinking about it.

'What are you laughing about?' he asked, the words muffled because his head was pushed up against her breast.

'I'm not laughing.'

'I heard you. I heard you start inside your chest.'

'You heard nothing.'

'I felt it then. I felt you laughing at me …' He paused. 'Are you laughing at me, Helen Young?'

That made her take a breath. She ran a hand across his scalp, fingers still alive with the sensations from his bare skin. She wanted to say, '*Don't call me that.*' But she didn't.

'I wasn't laughing at you,' she said instead. 'I was laughing because I'm happy. Because I feel great. Because I feel more relaxed with you than I've felt with anyone in over four years.' *Because there was no panic.*

'That long?' He shifted his head to look up at her.

'Yes. That long.'

'Good.' He smiled at her, then moved his head back to her breast. She felt his tongue flick across the nipple. He closed his mouth over it.

'Helen Young,' he said, with her nipple in his mouth. 'That's what I'm going to call you. That's what you are to me. Karen is too sad, now that I know her. I like you *now*, as you are. I like you happy.'

TUESDAY, 19 JUNE

18

She awoke from a deep dream. A flying dream. She had enjoyed them all her life, since she was very little. Sometimes she had wings (or just floated through the air), sometimes she was underwater, but the dizzying, joyous sensation of freedom was the same. This time she was actually in an airplane, flying it. The plane was separate from her, but part of her. The wings were part of her arms, the tail an extension of her legs. She dipped through clouds and hurtled down towards a deep lake, the wind stripping through her hair. The sun was high in a perfect azure sky. She had a tremendous rush of excitement as she skimmed inches above the unruffled surface of the water.

She awoke because a telephone was ringing. Coming out of sleep, she put her hand on it automatically before another hand closed over hers, stopping her. Her eyesight cleared to Ronnie Shepherd, standing above her, dripping wet, a towel wrapped around his waist. She frowned at him, remembered everything, then smiled. He winked and put the phone to his ear.

'Morning, Tim,' he said. 'Yes. Of course. I was just in the shower. Give me ten minutes.' Silence as Tim said something. Ronnie shrugged, then winked at her again. 'Maybe she's in the shower. How would I know?' He hung up and stood looking at her.

'Timmy Thorne,' he said. 'He's downstairs, waiting for us. We're late. He couldn't get you in your room.'

'Timmy?' She pushed herself up in bed a little, letting the quilt slip.

'That's what Laura calls him,' he said. 'She was shagging him last year. For fun, I think.'

She couldn't imagine that.

He bent over and kissed her quickly on the lips. 'I'd like to do more than that,' he said. No awkwardness, no embarrassment, no regrets. 'You look gorgeous.'

She blushed at once, feeling herself colour down to her chest.

She went back to her own room to shower and dress. He was ready before her and came to her room to wait, so they could go down together. She felt slightly hungover, but he didn't look to be feeling any ill-effects. He was energetic, cheerful, talkative. There wasn't any room to think about what it all meant.

'I think you should go with Timmy today,' he said.

'Why?'

'Because it would be too much for me to have you that near to me all day. I wouldn't be able to concentrate. Besides, it will make us look forward to the evening more.'

'I don't need to look forward to it more.'

'Nor me. What are you doing Friday, back home?'

'Friday?' She frowned. He was quick.

'Yes. Friday. This Friday. I don't want this to be a London thing. I don't want to get back North and you to forget about me.'

She walked over and sat down beside him, on the edge of her un-touched bed. She was towelling her hair dry. 'That won't happen,' she said.

He put a hand on her arm. 'All the same. Come out to Whitby, if you can. Friday would be good.'

'Your daughter's place?'

'She won't be there. And it's very beautiful. You'll like it.'

She nodded, looking into his eyes. 'I'll see what I can do.'

In the lift he grabbed and held her hand for a moment, just before the doors opened on to the lobby.

'Thank you, Ronnie,' she said to him. 'Thanks for being normal.'

Then Tim Thorne was walking towards them, with his nipped, pock-marked face and greasy hair. 'Morning, sir,' he said, to Ronnie.

'Morning, Tim.'

'You have a good night? Both of you, I mean?'

He was insinuating something, she thought. He hadn't even both-ered to say hello to her. She ignored him.

They had breakfast together in the hotel restaurant, all three of them. Thorne had apparently driven down that morning. He looked tired enough. Ronnie went over everything that had happened the day before.

'I want you to go to the CPS in Harrow today,' he said to Tim, at the end of his account. 'Take Karen with you. Make sure you get a definitive list of all Fleming's cases from the last year he was working here.'

Thorne nodded assent. 'I've already done that,' he said. 'But I'll double-check.'

'Good. There's no point in coming with me,' Ronnie said. He had another meeting with Sarah Hall first, then more senior officers, to get the resources up and running. 'We can meet up for lunch, to exchange notes.'

The three of them walked to the hotel car park. Karen kept her distance from Ronnie, trying to keep Thorne between them. It was automatic – covering their tracks, keeping it secret – but it was hard. She could smell his aftershave all the way through breakfast and down to the cars, feel his mouth on her body, his arms around her, the movement of him inside her. She felt something close to an ecstatic contentment. And it was going to repeat. They were going to do it again tonight.

She knew it was juvenile. As an adult you weren't supposed to value such floods of superficial sexual feeling, but that didn't stop it happening. All through breakfast she had wanted to reach out and touch him. The need for tactile connection was so powerful she had to keep her eyes off him and stare at her food. Every now and then their eyes would meet across the table and that silent message of confirmation, desire and complicity would flash between them. Visible only to them, she hoped.

In the car park, almost as soon as Ronnie began to split away from them, Thorne began to talk to her. 'So. You OK, Karen? Sleep well?'

'Well enough.'

'How's Pete these days?'

She felt her neck tingle. Was Ronnie still within earshot? 'Pete?' she asked, and immediately felt guilty, as if the betrayal of pretending not to know who Thorne was talking about was worse than what she had done to him last night.

'Pete Bains,' Thorne said.

She glanced behind her. Ronnie was walking away from them, showing no reaction. She doubted he could hear. She looked back to Thorne, spinning his car keys through his fingers, a twisted little grin on his ugly features. 'That's none of your fucking business,' she said quietly.

But he had achieved his aim. He had put Pete in her mind, broken the spell, reminded her that what she was doing would have consequences.

They drove in silence from Ealing to Harrow, Thorne apparently no longer seeing much point in pretending he liked her, now that Shepherd was gone. She wouldn't have had anything to say to him anyway.

It took an hour and a half to get to Harrow, a distance of about seven miles. Thorne parked on a street five minutes from the Crown Prosecution Service offices, and they walked to the building.

'I've already done this twice,' Thorne grumbled, as they signed for visitors' passes.

They sat for five minutes in the Branch Crown Prosecutor's office, in an extremely untidy litter of files and papers, while the BCP herself made them coffees. Karen counted 238 files as they waited. They were bound in thick buff jackets or white card, held together with tape and elastic bands, stacked in messy piles behind the desk, against the walls, all over the desk itself, spilling out of two large filing cabinets on to the floor. On the desk there was hardly a clear space to work in.

'What a fucking tip,' Thorne said. 'No wonder they keep losing files.'

The BCP was called Nita Patel. She was a neat woman in her early forties, wearing the usual lawyer black and whites. 'Last time I was here she cried on me,' was all Thorne could say about her. She came back into the office with coffees, accompanied by another woman, slightly younger, also in standard lawyer clothes, but Caucasian, with blonde hair pulled into a pony-tail and escaping over her forehead and ears in untidy straggles. She had a slightly dreamy air about her. The BCP introduced her as Fleming's previous Team Leader, Lizzie Harnden. They were both extremely polite and concerned. They had worked with Steve Fleming for a number of years.

Karen spent some time answering questions about Fleming's health. They had neither of them known or even met his dead wife, it seemed. Then Thorne apologized, produced a few sheets of paper from the briefcase he was carrying and started to ask his questions again.

It soon became clear that the boss – Patel – knew nothing of Fleming's individual cases because, at the time he had been working there, she had been the same grade as him, not his manager. She had only just been promoted to run the branch (she apologized profusely for her predecessor's mess). She referred all questions Thorne asked to Harnden, who had been responsible for allocating Fleming's work. But Lizzie wasn't very clear about what Fleming had been doing, either.

'But you would have known about any high-profile cases?' Thorne asked.

Karen noted a sickly little sparkle in his eye as he spoke to the woman. Presumably she was his type – blonde, posh, slightly vague, friendly in an off-hand way.

'That's the list I've already given you,' Harnden said. 'We can't really do better than that.'

'Do you have these files?' Thorne asked her, pointing to one of his sheets of paper. 'The high-profile files.'

'Somewhere, maybe.' She looked to Patel, who shrugged helplessly.

'I've already obtained the police files for these,' Thorne explained. 'But we should have yours as well. Especially if he worked on them.'

'They might be in archiving,' Patel said. 'You can look now if you want.' She stood up.

'Can you go with her, Karen?' Thorne asked. He handed her the slip of paper. 'These are the reference numbers and names. I have some more questions for Lizzie.'

'Of course.' She stood up, only too glad to leave him to it.

They took a lift to the floor above, walked through a large open-plan office full of desks but very few people, and came to a store room.

'It's awful,' Patel said, as she opened the door. 'I can't think about it without getting upset.'

The room was small but full of ceiling-high open racks, stuffed to overflowing with thick brown jacketed files. There must have been more than a thousand. Patel explained the system to her. There wasn't one. The list Thorne had given Karen had about fifteen file numbers.

'I'll get some admin staff to help you,' Patel said. She walked to the door, then turned back. 'Did anyone tell you about Myers?' she asked.

'Is it a case?'

'No. I can't remember what the case was called. But Steve will re-member, if you ask him. Myers was the name of the main witness – Freddy Myers. It attracted some media attention. I was working with Steve then. I remember he was shocked by it all. This wasn't from his last year here, though. Probably it's from around spring of nineteen ninety-nine, a bit before.'

'That doesn't matter. What happened?'

'He died in court. Not actually in court, giving evidence, but in the witness room during an adjournment. He had a heart attack.'

'Freddy Myers?'

'Yes. He wasn't very old. Not old enough to have a heart attack, anyway. Steve thought it was his fault, I think. Myers hadn't wanted to give evidence and Steve had got a witness summons to force him. The judge was threatening to lock him up if he didn't speak.'

'What was the case about?'

She shook her head, trying to remember. 'I can't recall exactly. Nothing very big. A pub brawl of some sort. It was one of the first cases Steve prosecuted himself at Crown Court. That's why he felt responsible. I just remembered because I worked with him then. Sorry.' She looked to be on the point of leaving.

'Why did you think it might have been important?' Karen asked her.

'I'm sure it isn't. But Myers had a son who was very angry about it. He had written letters to Steve beforehand warning that his father wasn't up to it and shouldn't be forced to give evidence. If I remember rightly there was never anything medical mentioned, so Steve just pressed on. Afterwards the son sent Steve a letter, more or less threatening to kill him and the judge. The police here – in Hounslow, because this was all at Isleworth Crown Court – arrested the son, ran an inquiry and put a file up for advice. But the judge wasn't interested and Steve felt bad enough anyway.'

'So no charges?'

'No. The man had just lost his father, and there wasn't sufficient evidence. A BCP from another office reviewed it. I'll try to get you the file.' She was standing by the door, thinking about it. 'I met the son once,' she said, after a moment. 'I think he was called Thomas. He came here in person to try to persuade Steve not to use his father as a witness. He seemed very weird to me. I'm not saying he looked dangerous, or that he might have been capable of doing something like this, but he didn't look normal.'

Karen waited for her to explain. But instead she shook her head.

'It was nothing I could put my finger on,' she said. 'I shouldn't mention it really. Maybe his eyes were just too close together.'

WEDNESDAY, 20 JUNE

19

Today was the day. At 1 p.m. Caroline couldn't wait to take off the white overall they made her wear and walk next door to WH Smith, to see whether it was in.

It was. Middle shelf, halfway along. *Marie Claire* magazine. There were about ten copies stacked on the shelves. There was a sales assistant further along the racks stacking more magazines into spaces. The shop was crowded, all of Halifax browsing on its lunch break.

A woman about her own age, dressed in a nurse's uniform, was standing right in front of the magazines, blocking her way. As Caroline came up behind her she saw her take a copy from the shelves and begin to look through it. Caroline paused, holding her breath, waiting for her to come to the page. But the woman started reading an article instead.

'Excuse me,' Caroline said quietly. She felt as if everybody in the shop might be looking at her, as if they knew who she was. It was a ridiculous thought. The woman moved slightly, letting her slip an arm through and take a copy.

She opened it carefully, enjoying the moment. The cover photo was a model she recognized from other shoots, but whose name she didn't know. Not from her own agency. She flicked carefully through the centre pages, hardly taking in the content. She found the shoot with the front-page model quite quickly – a summer bikini thing, shot on location somewhere. That would come to her one day – location shoots in the sun, although the secretaries at the agency had said they were nothing but hard work.

Then she had them – her own two pages.

She had seen the photos already – but that wasn't the same. Now they were published, real, and, in the middle of the magazine, they looked completely different. For a moment she felt stunned. She felt herself turning a bright pink and actually had to stop to make sure that no one was looking at her. She even held the magazine slightly closed as she viewed it, so that it would be difficult for someone to peek at it over her shoulder.

Was it her? For a second she thought it couldn't have been. *She* was skinny, awkward, clumsy. When she looked in the mirror she saw only someone ugly. Well, maybe not completely ugly, but not attractive – not like this. She had never liked her appearance. But this woman was beautiful. She could see that clearly because it felt as if she were not looking at herself. And it wasn't the clothes, the Sugoni & Briar label that she was, in effect, advertising. The clothes were special, as was the Carelli jewellery and the Franchini-Stappo shoes, the setting on some country estate in Kent was high-class, refined, expensive, but it was the model that stopped you turning the pages and moving on.

The photos were fantastic. Marcus (they had been on first-name terms for the four hours of the shoot, so why not call him that?) had caught the essence of her, and brought it out. Not *her*, not the *real* Caroline Philips, but this mysterious, poised and proud woman she was looking at now. The woman even looked six inches taller than her.

In front of her the nurse replaced her magazine and turned round. Caroline saw her look at her, saw something flicker in her eyes – recognition?

'Caroline?' she asked.

Caroline closed the magazine quickly. Had they printed her name? They assured her that never happened. 'No,' she stammered. 'I mean … yes …'

'I'm Trudy. A friend of Brian's. We met at Eric's christening, remember? At St Peter's?'

That afternoon she could hardly work. She hid the magazine in her locker and tried to appear normal, but she felt light-headed. At the coffee break she looked with something bordering on paranoia to see if the magazine supply in the staff room had been restocked. It hadn't, thank God. In the toilets she stood in front of the mirror and tried to see herself as the person in the pictures, but it was impossible. It was like some kind of magic trick.

As usual, Mr Smith gave her a lift to the top of Saville Park at the end of the day. He drove a BMW and lived in a big house up in

Ripponden, but he was usually OK. In the store they said that his wife had some kind of progressive illness – maybe MS – and was confined to a wheelchair. The staff found it a mark of courage that he had 'stuck by her'. He gave Caroline a lift home almost every night. For some reason he had taken a fatherly kind of interest in her career. He had no kids himself.

'Listen to anything new?' he asked. He had an interest in classical music and ever since he had found out she played piano he had seen it as their main point of connection. In fact, it was virtually the only thing they could talk about that wasn't work-related.

'I bought an old Sibelius recording at the weekend,' she said. She found it hard to talk at the same level as him. For her, one CD was the same as another. It was the music she was trying to listen to. But his obsession seemed to be with different recordings of the same piece, or even with the technical details of the recording process.

'Good recording?' he asked, on cue.

'It's old,' she said, wondering how he would take this. 'It's conducted by Sibelius himself.'

'Digitally remastered, though?'

She shook her head. 'I don't know.'

She was relieved when he let her out.

She hurried across Saville Park because she was dying to get back to show Debs the pictures. Normally she took her time. The park was a wide area of grassland, crisscrossed by pathways and intersected by roads. At the top end most of it was in full view of Crossley Heath school. Further down the old Victorian houses bordering it were nearly always visible. There were trees in long avenues, bordering some of the paths. She knew that one of the Yorkshire Ripper's attacks had taken place somewhere on Saville Park, many years ago, but still found it hard to believe that someone could be murdered in a place so wide open to public view. Maybe if there were a thick fog, or if it were dark. She never took this route home in winter. Now, as ever, there were people walking dogs, out for a stroll, or walking home, like herself.

It was at a bus stop not too far from here that all this had begun. Life was unfair. Every Saturday for some weeks now she and Debs had been watching a TV reality show where a dozen desperate teenagers competed against each other for the chance to be a fashion model in one shoot. Almost every week the judges stressed how difficult it was to get anywhere in the modelling world, how thousands of hopefuls ended up disappointed. Even for the successful, the road was long, slow and hard.

But she had experienced none of that. She hadn't even wanted to be a model. A Halifax photographer, Jeff Gant, had seen her at a bus stop on Skircoat Road when she was in her last year at school. He had stopped, spoken to her, asked her if she was interested in doing a photo shoot. She had thought he was joking, but he had been so enthusiastic she had given him her home address and phone number.

She had not thought he was trying to get her clothes off. But that was what her father had said immediately. It had taken two phone calls and three meetings with Jeff Gant before Dad had decided he was genuine and shouldn't be reported to the police. Gant thought she 'had the face for it'. That was how he described it – never in terms such as 'beautiful' or 'sexy' or anything that would embarrass her or her parents. Nevertheless, it had come to nothing. Her parents had absolutely forbidden any photos while she was still at school. In any case, her dad had said, Jeff Gant was nothing but a Halifax wedding photographer, a hack.

What they didn't know was that he had secretly taken a photo of her already, before he had even spoken to her, and had sent that photo to a London agency called XI, which was apparently famous. They had then sent a younger photographer called Nico Kummert to speak to her father. But once again her father had refused everything, though even then the money offered had been significant. She had no say in the matter. When her father had spoken to Nico she had sat in her bedroom, ostensibly studying for her A-levels, but in fact listening to their discussions. Her father had been like a stuck record: she would do nothing before she had finished her exams and education.

So she had waited until the day after her last A-level and then called Nico herself. The following month he had come up – without her parents knowing – and had spent three hours taking photos of her in Jeff Gant's studio. Jeff Gant – twenty years her senior – had got nothing out of it except a fee for the use of his studio space.

The agency had taken her at once and the assignment with *Marie Claire* had followed within a year and a half, without her doing anything. So life really was unfair. But then, the hopefuls she and Debs watched in the TV show were the most pretentious and conceited idiots she had ever come across. They didn't deserve it.

Debs was already in when she got back. As soon as Caroline fitted her key into the latch she could hear her screaming with excitement. She hardly had the door open before Debs was running down the hallway towards her, arms wide, a copy of the magazine in each hand. 'Caroline Philips! I can't believe it's you! I can't believe it!'

They danced around the hall, hugging each other, giving in finally to a kind of childish frenzy she had been forced to bottle up all week.

'You've done it! You've done it!' Debs was shouting. 'I'm so proud of you!'

Caroline put her bag down and started laughing.

'I can't believe it!' Debs shouted. She was jabbing her finger into the open page of one of the magazines. 'You are so *gorgeous*! I can't believe I share a flat with you!'

'I don't think it's me,' Caroline said. 'I think they must have computer-enhanced it.'

Debs stopped in front of her. She was a large woman, obsessed with her weight. By day she had a job as a security guard at the Nestlé factory. They had been best friends for as long as either of them could remember.

'Don't be so stupid, Caroline,' she said. Her face was suddenly serious. She stepped up to Caroline and took hold of both her hands. 'You *are* that person,' she said. 'You are *that* beautiful and you always have been. Maybe now you will begin to realize it.'

FRIDAY, 22 JUNE

20

DC Chris Broadley stopped his car by the chain fence ringing Gates Haulage, and watched a commuter train rattle noisily over the railway arches backing the property. He checked the address on the message sent through from West Yorkshire Police a few days ago: 110, Woodside Road, Southall. Gates Haulage. This was the place.

It was, he guessed, a place to park trucks overnight. He couldn't see anyone moving around. He read the message again. A white Toyota van, registration SXG 85L, was registered to this company at this address. The van had been picked up on CCTV footage from a site near a murder scene in a place called Barwick-in-Elmet, which was somewhere near Leeds. He had never been to that part of the country. The van had been sighted four times in a three-month period. West Yorkshire Police had sent the exact dates and times, along with a request to identify the driver. He had been given the action three days ago and had only just found time to get round to it.

He got out of the car. The main gates to the yard were closed, but there was a narrow, low gateway cut into the chain linking. He pushed it open. He was a tall man, so stepped through it with care; his suit was new and he didn't want to snag it. The yard was empty except for two vans parked up against the arches, neither with the registration number he was looking for. He walked with distaste through puddles of oil spillage and grime to a doorway under one of the arches, which he assumed was the office. He checked the time. Nearly 6 p.m. Maybe he was too late for them.

There was no response to his knock on the office door, but it was open. He stepped inside a cramped room (with a flat false ceiling) and surveyed an untidy desk, littered with paperwork, walls covered with nude female pin-ups, a small table and four chairs in a corner, coffee cups and plates left on the surface. The place smelled unpleasantly of engine grease. He stepped back out.

He walked along the arches, knocking on the doors until someone called out to him from within one. Inside he found a garage space with another white van up on ramps. He checked the registration on his piece of paper. Not the one. Someone was underneath it, in dark grey overalls. He slid himself out on a dolly and looked up at Chris.

'DC Broadley,' Chris said. 'Southall Police. Are you the manager?'

'I'm Gates, yeah. What's the problem?' His face was almost completely black with oil, dirt and grease stains, but he was unmistakably white. In this bit of Southall everyone was white, just as everyone was Sikh a few hundred metres up the road. The whole place was an elaborate series of ghettos. Chris had been moved here only a few weeks ago, from Hampstead. He was still getting used to it.

'No problem,' he said. 'I just need a word with you.'

Gates pulled himself to his feet and dropped a tool in amongst a rack of other tools. The floor and walls were strewn with tools, tyres, and cartons containing oil and gunk. Chris stood so that it was clear they shouldn't shake hands.

'Has there been an accident?' Gates asked him. 'One of my vans?'

'No. But I'm trying to get information on one.'

'Has it been involved in something?' Gates dipped his fingers in a bumper tub of Swarfega, rinsed them in a grimy sink and wiped them on a rag.

'Not sure,' Chris said. 'It's a request from West Yorkshire Police. Do you have work up there?'

'Loads. We deliver ready-cooked curries to Leeds and Bradford. It's half the business.'

'Curries to Leeds and Bradford?'

'Coals to Newcastle, right? But it's straight up. They cook 'em down here and ship 'em up there. We cover the whole of the North of England.'

They walked back to the office. On the way, Chris discovered that Gates had a fleet of fifteen vans and fifteen full-time drivers. Mostly the vans did back-to-back trips, if they could organize it, picking up a variety of freight from the North to cover the return trip. 'They'll start getting back in at about eight or nine,' he said.

'And they left from here when?'

'Five or six in the morning.'

'Long day.'

'Yeah. Because of the tachos and the regulations. You know that.'
He sat down behind the untidy desk and offered Chris a seat opposite
him. Chris looked at it and decided against it. 'They spend half their
day asleep,' Gates said. 'Which van you interested in?'

'SXG 85L.'

'That's one of mine. It's out now. What's the interest?'

Chris read him the four dates. 'I need to know who was driving it
on those days,' he said.

Gates looked worried now. 'You don't want to tell me what it's
about?'

'It's a murder inquiry,' Chris said. 'They're running through everything picked up on a CCTV camera near Leeds. This van comes up
four times, on those days. It doesn't mean anything.'

'I see.'

He opened a drawer and pulled out a huge leather-bound book, be-
smirched with black oil stains, bound with huge elastic bands, stuffed
full of paperwork and used tachographs. He opened it on the desk and
leafed laboriously through the pages. 'Give me the first date again?'

Chris read it out.

'No. Shouldn't have been up there then. He was on a run to
Nottingham. Next?'

The same thing. Gates shook his head. 'Cheeky bugger's been
moonlighting,' he said. 'He should have been in Carlisle.'

The next two dates were better. 'That's OK,' he said. 'That van was
on the Leeds run both those days.'

Chris nodded. He would have to take all the paperwork with him.
'Who were the drivers?' he asked.

'Same driver each time. Chap who left us a month ago. Thomas
Myers. Mean anything to you?'

Chris shook his head. 'Not to me.'

21

It was late evening – nine-thirty – but still warm. Karen sat at a table in the garden sipping a drink, as Ronnie paced around on the mobile, taking a call from London. He had only arrived back from the capital an hour and a half ago, just in time to meet her here. They had spent Tuesday night together in Ealing, then she had returned north on Wednesday, leaving him there.

The call didn't look positive. Ronnie had been hassled when she arrived and looked hassled again now. When he finished the call he sat down and bent forward, leaning his elbows on his knees. From what she had overheard he was having problems keeping NCS co-operation at the level he wanted.

They were on the lower terrace of Laura's place in Whitby, sitting at a wooden table tinged pink by the evening sunlight. The garden ended abruptly, crumbling over the edge of steep sandstone cliffs, which fell directly into the water a couple of hundred feet below. Out across the North Sea, Karen could see the shadow of the land lengthening as the sun went down.

'I need to make another call,' Ronnie said.

She nodded and settled back into her chair. The smell of wave-battered rocks and seaweed drifted up to her on the back of the incessant crying of gulls. She drew the air deep into her lungs, enjoying a kind of illicit holiday feeling.

It wouldn't last. She had not been able to think up a foolproof lie to tell Pete, so would have to drive back tonight. But worse than that, she had decided she would tell Ronnie why she was going. It wasn't just guilt. Tim Thorne knew she was with Pete, so probably many other people did, too. That meant it was only a matter of time before both Pete and Ronnie found out from someone else. She didn't want that. She didn't want Pete to get hurt like that. And if it was possible, she wanted something to come of this – which meant she needed to be honest about Pete with Ronnie, too. So she was going to tell them both. Starting tonight, with Ronnie.

He started to key a number into the mobile again, then stopped as a voice called from behind them, from the house.

'Dad? Are you out there, Dad?'

Ronnie looked over to her, eyes wide. 'Shit,' he said. 'That's Laura.' He stood up quickly.

Karen was wearing a dressing gown he had loaned her; he was in shorts and a T-shirt. She pulled the dressing gown around her, then realized it was probably Laura's. 'I thought you said she was away,' she said. She stood up, too.

'I thought she was.' For the first time since she had met him he looked panicked.

'What do you want me to do?' she asked.

He looked unsure.

'Dad?'

'Shall I jump over the cliff?' Karen asked.

'Shit. You're in her dressing gown,' he said, then called up the garden. 'I'm down here. I'm with a friend.'

Karen sat down again. A friend. No need for her to panic, then. She took another sip from the very light cocktail he had mixed her. She wanted to say something to him – something scathing perhaps, because he was, after all, a grown man – but she kept her mouth shut. She looked up towards the house and saw a young woman walking towards them down the gravel path. Ronnie was still standing by his chair, but she could see him trying to compose himself now.

'God, it's gorgeous out here,' Laura said, as she neared. She looked over to Karen, then back to Ronnie. Karen saw a faint smile at the corners of her mouth. 'Hello, Dad. Sorry I had to come back ...' They kissed each other on the cheek, twice, like a French greeting.

'That's OK,' Ronnie said. 'It's nice to see you.' He looked over to Karen uncertainly. His face was bright red. For a moment it looked as if he wasn't going to introduce her. She stood up again. 'This is Karen Sharpe,' he said. 'Karen, this is Laura, my daughter.'

'So *this* is Karen,' Laura said, eyes flickering with mischief. 'I've heard about you already.' She came towards her as if to do the continental kissing thing, but Karen held her hand out. They shook hands and Karen sat down again. Laura had a strong grip.

'I was meant to be at a friend's tonight,' Laura said, looking at Karen. She sat down next to her, in the chair Ronnie had been using. 'Up in Newcastle. Sorry. We had a long meeting at work and things ran over. I'll go up there tomorrow now.' She looked over to Ronnie. 'You can sit down, Dad,' she said.

He sat.

'I tried ringing to warn you,' Laura said. 'Nobody answered.'

In the end it wasn't so bad. Ronnie made his calls, then Laura forced him to cook cheese on toast for all of them and mix more drinks. As the sun sank, he brought warmer clothes from the house, and they all sat there until after eleven, talking. Ronnie even began to relax. Mostly they talked about neutral subjects, nothing too personal. Laura was good at it.

Karen had to resist the urge to ask her morbid questions about what it had been like to be 'abandoned' by her mother. She found herself staring at her almost as much as she looked at Ronnie. Would Mairead turn out like that? Could it be that simple?

But Mairead was different. She had done things to Mairead *since* leaving her. It wasn't just the walking out on her. It was what she had exposed her to since then.

At half past eleven Laura stood up to go to bed. Karen watched her disappear into the house then looked back to Ronnie. He looked pleased now, as if something nerve-racking and unexpected had gone well. Pity she was about to spoil it all.

It was dark by the time she started telling him. He was sitting close to her then, holding her hand, half-lit by the light coming down to them from the house.

'I've something I need to tell you,' she said. 'I'm a little frightened to say it.'

'Something about your past?'

'No. It's about now.'

She sat still, looking at him. He waited. The gulls must have settled down somewhere, because all she could hear from the darkness beyond the cliff edge was the lash of waves.

'Are you going to say it?' he asked, finally. His eyes were very wide. She thought the pause had made him frightened, too.

'It's nothing so bad,' she said. 'Nothing important really. Not to me.'

She paused, feeling guilty at dismissing Pete so glibly. It wasn't true, either. 'I hope you can see it that way.'

He moved then, releasing her hand and sitting back in the chair a little. 'What is it?' he asked, voice a bit harder.

She swallowed, took a breath. 'I live with someone at the moment,' she said. 'That's why I have to go back tonight.'

'Live with someone?' He repeated the words as though he didn't understand them. 'Like who?'

'Like a man. He's called Pete Bains—'

'The DS? Pete Bains, the DS who works out of Milgarth, the Sikh?'

'Yes. That's him.'

'You *live* with him?' He was frowning, his voice still confused. 'You mean … like you're in a relationship with him?'

'Yes. That's right. A tired, dull relationship. One that's over already, in effect. We both know that, I think. I just need to—'

'Jesus Christ. Why didn't you tell me this?' He had moved back even further now, so that he was in shadow and she couldn't see his expression. He sounded angry.

'There hasn't really been a chance,' she said. 'Until today I didn't know whether there was anything more to us than what happened in London. Besides, it's between me and Pete. It has nothing to do with you—'

'Nothing to do with me?' His voice was slightly louder.

'Not like that. I meant nothing to do with you in the sense it was already over before I met you. You and I haven't known each other very long, Ronnie – only a few days. This is the earliest opportunity I've had to tell you this.'

'That's not true. I asked you. I asked you when I first met you—'

'You asked about childcare. I told you a friend looked after Mairead. That was the truth. That's how I see him now – as a friend.'

'Don't tell more lies, Karen. Does *he* know that's all he is?'

She chewed her lip. It wasn't going as she had thought.

'Does he?' His voice had gone very quiet now.

'No. Not explicitly. As I said, I need to tell him. I should have told him before telling you.'

'Fucking hell.' She heard him shift in the seat.

For a long time neither of them said anything. She tried to think what else she could say to salvage things.

'I told you other things about me,' she said at last. 'Things that were more important—'

'You said you didn't want to give me any nasty surprises. What do you call this?' His voice was very low, very soft. There was no anger in it now, but something worse – disappointment, or betrayal. As if they had been seeing each other for months and she had slept with someone else. It was silly.

'It's not important to us, Ronnie. It's something I have to deal with. That's all.'

'I don't see it like that. Who is looking after Mairead right now?'

She didn't reply.

'Right now?' he repeated. 'As we are sitting here, discussing his lack of importance, he is looking after your child. Am I right?'

'You know you are. But it's not that simple—'

'I've met the guy, for Christ's sake. I've worked with him.' He sounded hurt. 'You should have told me, Karen. That wasn't fair.'

'We've only known each other a week, Ronnie. You're being too severe about this.'

'I'm not being severe at all.' He spoke very calmly, as if he had already made a decision about it. 'I'm reacting as any normal person would. Sorry about that. But I don't know what to do now.'

'You don't know what to do?'

'No.' She could just see him shaking his head.

She felt a tremble inside her. Then, very quickly, a spark of anger. Was he going to *dump* her? She stood up. He was expecting things of her when it was way too soon for all that. He had no right to expect anything, and there was certainly no need for her to sit here and grovel. 'Fine,' she said. 'I have to go now.'

He didn't move, didn't say anything. As if he *wanted* her to go.

Fuck you, she thought.

She moved the chair that Laura had been sitting on, and stepped around him. 'I can get my own stuff,' she said. 'There's no need for you to disturb yourself.' She started to walk up the path. He didn't follow. *What a wanker*. She stopped and turned round. He was sitting in the same place with his head in his hands. 'When you think about this,' she said, 'focus on the fact that we have met maybe three times and known each other for a week. You have no fucking right to be like this with me.' She turned and walked away, not expecting a reply. There wasn't one.

In the house she stumbled around collecting her clothes. She felt shaky, angry, full of a destructive energy. She made no effort to be quiet. When she had changed and found her bag she let herself out of the front door and closed it with a bang. She got into the car and started it. Still he didn't appear.

That's that, then, she told herself.

THURSDAY, 28 JUNE

22

As Mr Smith dropped her off at the top of Saville Park, Caroline felt miserable. She had been the same all day. There should have been everything to feel happy about. That morning Antonia had recognized her from the photos, and had confronted her in the back corridor on the way back from the ladies, the magazine open at her images.

'Is that you?' she had asked, almost aggressively.

Caroline had blushed, suddenly, as if it were something to be embarrassed about, then nodded. 'Yes. But please don't tell anyone. I haven't spoken about it yet.'

She expected her plea to be in vain, that Antonia would come up with some catty comment, but instead had the pleasure of watching her eyes widen in stunned appreciation. 'My God!' she whispered, glancing around to make sure nobody else was within earshot. 'You look so beautiful, Caroline. I told Jane it was you, but she wouldn't believe me ...'

The photos had been out only eight days and already the agency had new bookings. She was planning to hand her notice in next week because she would not be able to do everything they could give her for July without quitting Boots. The money she was due to earn was the equivalent of nearly a year's salary with Boots, so there were no difficult choices there.

But both Brian and her father were spoiling things. Last night she had rowed terribly with Brian. The evening before it had been her father. Only Debs seemed pleased for her. Her father had been annoyed because she had lied to him – or at least, not told him the full truth. She could cope with that. But the strength of Brian's reaction had taken her by surprise.

'You think *this* is something to be proud of?' he had asked her, jabbing his fingers at the photos. He was speaking in that deliberate, quiet way that usually meant he would end up shouting at her.

She had been in the kitchen with Debs when he had arrived. She had told him she had something interesting to show him, hoping to surprise him. But he had not reacted at all when she had laid the magazine in front of him. At first she had thought he hadn't recognized her. 'It's me,' she had said then, explaining. 'I've got a modelling contract.'

'I can see that,' he said, voice cold. 'You want me to be pleased about it?'

Debs had stood up. 'You're such a tosser, Brain,' she had said. 'I don't know why Caroline's with you.'

He had glanced at her as she walked out, but hadn't replied.

'I thought you would be happy for me,' Caroline said, as the kitchen door closed on them.

'About *this*?' He held up the magazine, gripping it between thumb and forefinger as if it were something dirty. 'Quite apart from you lying to me—'

'I haven't lied—'

'Keeping it from me. It's the same thing. Apart from that, you ought to be able to see that this is little more than pornography. What on earth were you thinking of?'

She was speechless.

'Look at you. Either you are hardly wearing anything, or the shots are deliberately provocative. And for what? To sell these clothes? You think that's clever? You think that's a good way to depict women? As sex objects, for hire to the highest bidder? It disgusts me to look at this. I can't believe you have done it. It betrays everything I have ever believed in.'

It had gone from bad to worse. The money she was getting paid made no difference at all – if anything, it proved his point. Which basically – when it was reduced to essentials – seemed to be that she was a slut.

She realized now that she should have anticipated it. The key difference between Brian and herself had always been religion. To think of her as some kind of 'sinner' because she had modelled for a very well known, respectable magazine could only come from a religious mindset she didn't understand.

So why was she with him? She glanced towards the big, Victorian building that was Crossley Heath school and then ahead of her, along the narrow pathway leading diagonally downhill across the park, away from the main road. It was a warm evening, the sun still high in the sky, casting long bands of light through the leaves of the trees flanking the road. She expected to see the usual number of people walking through the park, but noticed that for once she was almost alone. She slowed down a little, not wanting to get home too quickly. Probably Brian would already be there, waiting for her.

They had met at a party she had been invited to by her brother. She had been in the lower sixth form then, her brother – a year older than her – in the upper sixth. The party had been in a church hall in Northowram, but her brother had told her it was the eighteenth birthday party of a friend of his and the hall was hired out, so she hadn't expected it to have anything to do with religion. Very quickly, however, she had realized that the friend in question was some kind of happy clapper at the church, and that most of the people there, though only her own age, were religious. There hadn't even been any alcohol to drink. Within half an hour she had shrunk into a corner of the place and was contemplating leaving. Brian had stopped her.

In a way *he* had lied to *her*. Almost the first question she had asked him was whether he was also a member of that church. (It was some variety of Baptist church.) He had told her he wasn't and after that she had relaxed a little with him. They had even poked fun at the group, who started playing guitars and singing some kind of 'walk in the light' hymn, beatific smiles on their faces.

So it had come as a surprise to learn a few weeks later that Brian was a regular attender at *another* church. By then she had met him perhaps seven times and had thought she knew him quite well. Indeed, religion had not intruded into their relationship even once. He had kissed her, had his hands all over her breasts (under her T-shirt, but above the bra – she would have happily taken the bra off and gone the whole way, but he hadn't asked for that). So he had seemed normal enough, if a little slow. Was that what she thought now, that he *wasn't* normal? Some of the things he said were very definitely not normal.

She heard footsteps some way behind her, someone catching her up on the path.

But at least Brian was good-looking, she thought. Even Debs thought he was physically attractive. Perhaps that was all there was to it. In which case maybe it was time to get rid of him. She would meet a lot of interested, good-looking guys now.

The person behind her was beginning to run. She stepped slightly sideways, off the line of the path, to let him or her past.

Then, out of nowhere, a massive blow struck her in the back, a blow so powerful it snapped her head back and catapulted her forward.

Her legs collapsed beneath her at once. The surface of the path slammed against the front of her body, driving the air from her lungs and bringing a black cloud to her eyes, blinding her.

She had hit the concrete head first. She felt herself skidding, her knees and legs stripped by the gravelly surface, then her face bouncing off it. She tried to take a breath, to get a scream out, but almost at once a massive weight landed on her back, pinning her. She began to squirm, struggling desperately to free herself. Her first thought was that a tree had come down, crushing her. But there were no trees in this part of the park. She had her mouth open and was trying to scream, but all she could hear was a roaring noise in her ears.

Then she felt the weight shift and realized what was happening. It was a *person*, sitting on her back, striking her. She felt hands in her hair, dragging her head back, then a hand closing over her mouth. She tried to move her head to twist it away from him. At the same time the thought flashed through her head that he could not be trying to rape her, not here, not in Saville Park, at seven in the evening in broad daylight ...

She found her voice and tried to scream, summoning all her strength and twisting under him at the same time. Abruptly the weight came off her. She rolled quickly, gasping for air, but only in time to feel him throw himself at her again. This time his knees hit her chest, his arms moving above her face, trying to pin her arms to the ground. For the first time in her life she felt a rush of real terror.

She tried to make out what he was saying, but couldn't. She tried to see him, but everything was blurred. Something was running into her eyes. It was happening too quickly for her to understand. Her handbag must be somewhere near her. Why wasn't he just taking it? His hand caught hold of her throat, then moved to her jaw, squeezing again, forcing her mouth open. She brought her hands up and flayed at where his face must be, trying uselessly to reach for his eyes. He moved his free arm around hers, then down towards her mouth. She saw something flash, something metallic, then felt it in her mouth.

He had pushed something into her mouth. He was screaming and shouting at her, but there were no words to it, just a continuous, unintelligible, jabbering noise. She felt liquid welling in her mouth and realized the thing he was holding there must be a blade. Blind panic flooded through her. It was blood she could feel pouring down her throat. He had cut her inside her mouth. She began to scream, the noise a frantic gargle. His voice changed, the noise still charged with fury, but for a split second she thought she could recognize it, understand what he was saying. Then she felt him pull the thing from her mouth, still holding her jaw open with his other hand.

He stabbed down towards her face – once, twice, three times – massive, punching movements. She felt nothing, could not even feel it stabbing into her. He kept going, moving the thing rapidly in and out of her mouth. She began to choke on her own blood ...

23

Ronnie hadn't liked Steve Fleming as a lawyer. Before this case he had come across him on two jobs, both murders. On both occasions Fleming had happened to be the lawyer on duty in court when the defendant had first appeared to be remanded in custody, and that had been the limit of his involvement. Though Fleming had reviewed many murders in London, the West Yorkshire CPS didn't rate him as experienced enough to do theirs. As it turned out, Fleming had done his bit competently enough and the defendants had ended up in custody, as requested, but his personal style had led to friction. His whole manner had radiated distrust of the police and a desire to make clear who was boss. It wasn't what Ronnie was used to from West Yorkshire prosecutors, and he had been relieved to learn that the files would not be staying with Fleming after court.

Even now, with Fleming confined to a hospital bed and surrounded by an array of drips and monitors, barely able to speak without gasping for breath or bursting into tears, his attitude to Ronnie was still suspicious and defensive.

'Yes, I'm sorry we couldn't warn you we were coming,' Ronnie said, in answer to Fleming's objections to their presence. 'But we've only just received the information that brings us here – and it's urgent we speak to you about it.'

The information in question was the news that Thomas Myers had been arrested in London and was on his way north in police custody.

'What if Jana had been here?' Fleming muttered. 'I don't want her to see any more strangers or uniforms … it's too upsetting for her …'

'We're not wearing uniforms, Steve,' Debbie Moor said, standing opposite Ronnie at the other side of the bed, and speaking far too loudly for the hushed room. 'And Jana knows both of us already.'

Fleming let out a heavy, irritated breath, but didn't look at her. 'What do you want?' he asked, eyes on Ronnie.

Ronnie wished he had Karen Sharpe with him. She knew how to handle Fleming; Debbie Moor knew only how to annoy him. But Karen was gone, dropped from the inquiry four days ago. Riggs, the SIO, had made that decision, not he. He had merely passed on the instruction so Tim Thorne could speak to Karen and release her. The squad was losing resources every week now, the lack of results leading to a routine re-assessment and scaling back. If they were digging in for the long haul they couldn't afford nearly forty detectives. Officers had to be released back to their divisions. Riggs had identified duplicate family liaison capacity and preferred to keep Debbie Moor on this case. Ronnie had tried gently to steer him in the other direction, but hadn't wanted to push too much. Gossip had its own life in a police force and he wasn't sure how much might have already got round about Karen and him.

Thinking about her brought an unwanted turbulence to his thoughts. She wasn't just off his inquiry, she was out of his life. The strength of his reaction to the news that she was living with Pete Bains had taken him by surprise, and he still didn't know whether getting her to walk out on him was what he had wanted. Over the weekend she had called his mobile twice, but left no message, so he had not called her back. But the last few days had felt unsatisfactory. He was missing something he hadn't properly noticed until it was gone – an intensity that had spilled out of the encounter and coloured much more than his time in her presence.

'I have to ask you about a line of enquiry that has arisen from London,' he said to Fleming. 'We've arrested someone down there and we'll be interviewing him this afternoon.'

'You've arrested somebody in London?' Fleming looked sceptical.

'Yes. Just this morning. He's on his way up here now.'

The Met had detained Thomas Myers at his mother's house in Feltham. Enquiries at the haulage company he had worked for had revealed that he had left their employment a month previously. The only address the company had for him was his mother's place, but preliminary enquiries with her had drawn a blank. She had told the Met that Myers hadn't lived there since after his father's death. But he *had* lived there before then – in the same house as his parents up to the age of fifty-three. For Ronnie, that alone made him suspicious. A loner, possibly dysfunctional. It wasn't normal to live with your parents that long; yet wasn't that practically what Laura was doing, what he was *forcing* Laura to do?

Myers's mother was in her eighties and had insisted she had no idea where her son was. The Met had nevertheless thought she was lying and would have arrested her, if someone hadn't decided it would be a better idea to leave her and see if Myers showed up to visit. Sure enough, that morning he had appeared and been arrested without incident, before he even got to the door.

'We managed to identify a van which featured repeatedly on a CCTV camera positioned on Watkin Farm, about a mile from your house,' Ronnie continued. 'It was registered to a haulage company in London. From them we've found out who the driver was—'

'What do you mean – "featured repeatedly"?' Fleming asked, interrupting. 'You mean it was at my house repeatedly? When was this? I've seen no van at the house—'

'Not *at* your house. A little further down the road. So it *could* have gone on to pass your house. This was during the two months leading up to the attack.'

'A van from London?'

'Yes.'

'Why? Why would it do that?'

'To scout the premises. As preparation for an attack.'

'An attack? You mean the burglary?'

Ronnie shrugged. 'If this *was* an attempted burglary. You know we're looking at a much wider series of motives now.'

Fleming frowned and looked away. He had already made his views clear about the grudge motive. 'So who is it?' he asked.

Ronnie waited for him to look back at him. He wanted to see Fleming's reaction to the name. 'A man called Thomas Myers,' he said, when he had eye contact. 'Ring any bells?'

Fleming seemed to relax slightly. Or was Ronnie imagining that? A slight movement in the shoulders, like a sigh. The gesture was almost imperceptible, but it came a split second before the frown which said the name didn't ring bells.

'Thomas Myers.' Fleming repeated the name, trying to recall it. 'I don't think so,' he said. He rubbed a hand across his face. 'Who is he?'

'He was the relative of a witness in a case you prosecuted.'

'Of course. *Myers.*' His expression changed at once. 'The loony whose father died in court. I do remember him. Sorry. So much has happened …' He looked away again, his lower lip trembling.

Debbie Moor moved to say something, but Ronnie caught her attention and silenced her. He didn't want any prompting. He waited for Fleming to continue.

'I met him,' Fleming said eventually. 'He came in once to the office in Harrow. But he didn't do this.'

'Why do you say that?'

'Have you seen him?' Fleming asked.

'Not yet.'

'You'll know when you see him. He's pathetic. He couldn't kill anyone. Let alone like this …'

Something about Fleming's response was pulling at the back of Ronnie's mind. 'What happened when you met him?' he asked.

Fleming shook his head. 'Nothing much. He wanted me to give an undertaking not to call his father as a witness. Because he was ill. I thanked him and told him his father had to make that request, not him. He seemed to understand. He went away. I heard nothing from the father. We pressed on.' He shrugged. 'You know the rest of the story, I assume?'

'I think so. Was Myers aggressive with you at all?'

'Not then, no. But he wrote a few stupid letters after his father died.'

'I've seen copies. He made threats.'

'It wasn't him. He's not a killer. The letters were rash. He was distraught …' His voice trailed off. 'I know how he felt.'

'There was an investigation—' Ronnie started.

'Yes. But this wasn't him.' Fleming almost raised his voice now. 'Are you listening to me? Thomas Myers didn't do this.'

'We understand that's what you think, Steve,' Moore said. 'But we have to follow every line. You know that.'

'You're wasting your time going after him.' He looked up towards the clock hanging on the wall opposite him. 'Jana will be here soon,' he said. 'If this is all you wanted to talk about then you have to leave. This is futile.'

Ronnie looked over to Debbie Moor. She raised her eyebrows. Fleming wasn't looking at either of them now. Ronnie took a step away from the bed.

'*Is* that all you came for?' Fleming asked.

'Yes. That's all. I had to ask you because there was a chance that once you heard the name you might remember something relevant. Something we didn't know.'

'It wasn't him. That's all you need to know.'

FRIDAY, 29 JUNE

24

Karen sat in a small office within the intensive care ward, waiting for the consultant to call for her. She was trying hard to keep her emotions under control, but there were too many things going wrong too quickly.

When Tim Thorne contacted her on Monday morning to tell her she was off Bulldog and was to return to Halifax after her rest days she had been stunned.

'On whose instructions?' she had demanded.

'The boss.'

'David Riggs?'

'Don't be silly. Ronnie Shepherd.'

'Ronnie told you to move me back to Halifax?'

'We're being scaled back the whole time. You know how it is. It's nothing personal.' She thought she detected a hint of smugness in his tone. Was her reaction *that* obvious?

She had heard nothing from Ronnie Shepherd since she had left his daughter's place in Whitby the preceding Friday. Walking out on him had seemed easy enough at the time – she had been angry. But over the weekend she had felt increasingly miserable and confused about it. By Monday she had called his mobile number twice, intending to ask him what was happening. But both times she had been too frightened of his reaction and had cut the connection before he could answer. Probably that had irritated him. He would have seen her number, known it was her and felt pestered. Then told Thorne to get rid of her.

She sat in the garden for most of Monday afternoon brooding about that, feeling her mood plummet. She had to admit to herself that she had been looking forward to seeing him on Bulldog. Now it felt as though he had dumped her after all. She was assaulted by a welter of stupid teenage emotions that she had no idea how to handle. That evening she had felt relieved she hadn't already burned her bridges and spoken to Pete about the situation. Not because that was no longer necessary – it was – but because things were miserable enough without having to cope with that as well.

Then this morning, on her first day back at Halifax, they had landed her with this. She had turned up at ten and found a CID room frantic with activity. A young girl had been attacked in Saville Park, a possible attempted rape. She had survived but was in intensive care. They had put together a seven-man team the night before and worked through the night trying to get somewhere. The operation had been given the codename Scythe. But the team was literally seven men. She reported to DI Richard Powell and was informed that she was number eight, the only woman on the squad.

'I need a woman to speak to the victim,' he had said.

She'd only just escaped the Bulldog victims. 'But I came to Halifax on the understanding that I wouldn't be given this kind of tasking.'

'That was a year ago. I've been told that no longer applies. You were doing family liaison on Bulldog until earlier this week. This is easier than that.'

Easier? For the fourth time that morning she read through the two main statements in the case file and felt her legs beginning to shake. The first was the statement that had somehow been leaked to the press yesterday evening, sparking an explosion of overnight racist attacks in the town centre. (Twenty-five had been reported in the last seventy-two hours; most were minor, but there were three major incidents and one attempted murder). The statement had been taken by DC Andrew Lewis. The witness was a fifty-eight-year-old man with a long list of previous convictions for petty thefts (all committed in the 1970s) who had nevertheless managed to secure work as a part-time caretaker at Crossley Heath school. His name was Ian Hogg:

... I was on the third floor of the school, about 150 yards from where it happened. I had a clear view of everything. At the time I was smoking a cigarette, which we are not permitted to do within the school, so I was leaning out of the window of an office on that floor. I was already looking at the pathway across Saville Park when the young girl began to walk across it. This was at about 7.15 in the evening. It was a warm, clear summer night. The street lighting had not yet come on because, at that time, it is still broad daylight at this time of year. I have good eyesight.

She walked from my left to my right, coming from the direction of Free School Lane, so that, as she came past the school, her back was to me. Her head was down, I think, and she appeared to be walking very slowly. I heard a man shout from behind her, but I could not understand the words. When he shouted he was not in view, but the girl must have heard him because she glanced back towards Free School Lane, then continued walking. She did not appear concerned.

The next thing I saw was the man run into view, coming past the school on the same path the girl was using, moving in the same direction as her, from behind her. I do not remember seeing anything in his hands. He appeared to be dressed normally, in trousers and a shirt. He was not wearing a jacket. I don't think I could recognize him again. From his skin colour, facial features and the language he spoke (which I did not understand), I concluded that he was foreign. He was light-skinned, possibly Mediterranean in appearance. His height was about five feet nine inches. He looked to be aged between twenty-five and thirty years old.

He was running very fast. When he reached the girl on the path I knew something was going to happen. He did not collide with her by accident. There was plenty of room for him to step around her. Instead he ran straight into her back, arms outstretched. He struck her with such force that she was knocked from her feet and sent sprawling on to her chest and face. Before she could get up the man sat on top of her back and, holding her hair with both hands, began to bang her face on the ground. I could hear her screaming, and immediately I began to shout back into the school for my colleague, Derek Kelters, who I knew was working on the same floor. I did not want to lose sight of the man on top of the girl. I also shouted out of the window at the man, but he did not react.

He may have banged the girl's head three or four times. I cannot recall exactly. He then turned her over. It did not seem difficult for him to turn her over, and I thought she must be unconscious, or at least dazed. When she was lying on her back he began to undo her trousers. He was standing above her trying to do this. I formed the opinion at this time that he was going to rape or sexually assault her. The girl had been holding a handbag, which was lying on the path next to her. He did not try to take this.

When she began to shout again her voice was feeble. The man sat on top of her. I saw him pull a knife from the rear pocket of his trousers. The trousers were ordinary blue jeans. The blade was already visible as he took the knife out. I think it must have measured about six inches. I saw him stab the girl eleven times. I counted them, and all the time I was screaming at him to stop. He was stabbing her in the head using his right hand. With his left hand he was holding her down. At first she was trying to struggle, but as the attack went on she appeared to be just lying there, without moving.

After he had stabbed her he stood up and again tried to get her trousers off. Then I think he heard me shouting, looked up towards me and walked off. He did not run, but walked, back in the direction he had come from, leaving the girl lying on the ground. He looked very calm. At that point the girl was not moving at all and I was very afraid for her. When he was out of sight I ran back through the building and called the police. I did not go out to help the girl because I had seen a woman approaching her from nearer. I was also frightened that the attacker might return and I knew that he had seen me.

I have been asked whether the man I have described was saying anything throughout this incident. I can say that all the time he was on top of the girl he was shouting at her, even as he was stabbing her. I could not, however, understand the words. They were not in a language I understood. He seemed to be very angry with her ...

The account left her physically sick each time she read it. The victim had been young and beautiful; seriously beautiful in a clear, incontestable way. She had been on the verge of some kind of break-through in the modelling world. In the case file was a copy of *Marie Claire* magazine, which had published photos of her. These were the details the press had picked up, along with the words from Hogg's leaked statement (leaked by one of the other seven detectives on the inquiry, she assumed), stating the suspect to be 'foreign'. That had already invited columns of comment on the 'disproportionate' numbers of asylum-seekers in Halifax and West Yorkshire. The national papers had all reproduced the *Marie Claire* photos next to accounts of Caroline's horrific ordeal at the hands of a foreign suspect.

Overnight they had managed to get only two direct witness statements. Hogg was the first, and it seemed to Karen that he was clear about two things: the man had been trying to sexually assault Caroline Philips and he was foreign. The other witness, however, was less sure. She was a middle-aged teacher called June Shaw:

... *I was walking home as usual, through Saville Park, passing from north to south, roughly, between Free School Lane and Skircoat Moor Road,* walking directly across the heath. This will have been just after seven in the evening. It was a bright, sunny evening. I heard a woman shout something, and looked up towards Crossley Heath school. About one hundred yards away from me I saw movement on the path to the west, which runs diagonally down towards Saville Park and the chip shop. At first I could not make out what was happening, but I could hear a man shouting as well, so began to walk in that direction. It will have taken me perhaps thirty more seconds to get a clear view and all that time I could hear both a man's voice and a woman's. The woman sounded desperate, frightened, distressed. The man sounded aggressive. I could not make out what he was saying. I am not sure now what language he was using, as I couldn't hear well enough to make out the words.

As they came into view I saw that the man was seated astride the woman and they were struggling. She was on her back and trying to fight him off. At first I was shocked, then I thought it might be a domestic quarrel. But as I watched the man took an object from one of his pockets. I saw him do something to it with both hands then it looked to me like he began to punch the girl in the face. He punched her about five times, then stood up and walked away from her. He was still shouting as he punched her. When he stood up he simply turned round and walked back up towards the school. He didn't run. He didn't look frightened. But the girl was then very still on the ground and very quiet. I was extremely shocked and distressed by what I had seen, and frightened for the girl.

I ran up to her. When I got to her I could see that there was blood pouring from her mouth, but I still thought that the man had only punched her there. It was only when I bent down and tried to help her that I realized what he had done. I could not believe it then. Her injuries were horrific. I feared the girl wasn't conscious, and I could see that she was choking on her own blood, from terrible injuries to her face and mouth. I didn't know how to resuscitate her. I was very fearful and desperate. I did my best to help her, turning her over and trying to keep her airways clear. An ambulance arrived very quickly, so I assume someone else must have seen what had happened and made an emergency call.

The man I have described was of normal height – perhaps five feet eight or nine inches. He was probably in his early twenties. He was wearing black trousers and a T-shirt. He was clean-shaven and had light skin. I do not know whether he was white or black, in ethnic terms. I could not see him that clearly. When I got to the girl her clothing was disarranged, as if she had been in a fight, but her trousers were not undone. I did not see the *man attempt to sexually assault the girl, or try to rob her. Her handbag was still lying beside her. I don't know what he was doing. At first it looked as if they were arguing and that they might have known each other. It did not look like he was trying to sexually assault her, or rob her, simply that he wanted to attack her. Then I saw that he had not been punching her, that the thing in his hand must have been a knife …*

The first time she had read the account she had felt weak and had to sit down. The casual and devastating nature of the violence felt suddenly overwhelming. To sit on top of a helpless twenty-year-old woman and deliberately stab her, repeatedly, *in the mouth*. That was the image she couldn't get rid of – the blade going into her mouth. What was he trying to do?

She sat back in the plastic seat and ran her hand frantically through her hair. As with Jana Fleming, her reaction to the case was confusing. She had taken for granted a professional, protective detachment from the horror thrown at her by her working life. Prolonged exposure had cauterized her imagination, cutting it off from the detail. This intense, visual reaction – making the injuries and suffering run before her mind's eye like a jerky film reel – was new and disorientating, punching through the carapace that kept her stable. One stabbed woman after another.

The door next to her opened and a man stepped out. She looked up at him. It was the consultant she had met earlier, the man who had given her the sterile gown she was wearing. He was Nigerian, in his fifties, with very dark skin and an erect way of walking. She pushed the statements back into the file and stood up, her legs still trembling. He looked at her with obvious irritation. 'Is this absolutely necessary?' he asked.

'At some point it will be,' she replied. Her voice sounded too high. 'As I told you an hour ago,' she checked her watch, 'in fact, an hour and a half ago, it's up to you to decide when it is safe to speak to her.'

'We will try it now,' he said. 'Then perhaps you will leave her alone.'

He thought she was doing something frivolous, unnecessary. Only the injuries mattered to him, not the story behind them. But Karen had to know the story.

'You are not permitted to say anything,' he said. 'I will ask the questions. Is that understood?'

'The questions I give you,' she said. 'We have written them out.'

'And I can promise you nothing,' he added. 'Probably she won't even understand what *I* am saying. She is very confused and unwell. She will go to surgery later today if she is stable enough. You should stand near the door, I think, and keep silent.'

She followed him towards the door, her heart already beginning to speed up. She did not want to look at Caroline Philips's face. She fumbled with the sheet of paper on which Richard Powell had written out their questions. The doctor turned just before he entered, took the paper off her without looking at it, then said, 'I should warn you. Her appearance is quite shocking. She does not look like the woman in the magazine, if you have seen those photos ...'

'I'm used to dealing with victims,' she said, snapping at him, too nervous to react calmly. 'You don't need to give me warnings.'

'I tell you just in case,' he said, looking closely at her. 'You look frightened of what you might see. I do not want your reaction to alarm her.'

'I'm not frightened,' she said, trying to sound normal. She stepped through the door after him, closed it behind her, then looked towards the bed.

Almost at once she lost it. She barely had time to take in the bandages and tubing before her heart was hammering at her ribs, blood rushing to her cheeks. She took a sharp breath, trying to stop herself from gasping. It was ridiculous. There were already tears springing to her eyes.

25

The man did have eyes that were too close together, exactly as Nita Patel had said. Karen had told him about the BCP's comment. Ronnie sat across the table from Thomas Myers and knew in his gut that Steve Fleming was right – this wasn't their killer. He had known that since he had watched him being booked in to the cells yesterday afternoon.

'I'm going to go through the main exhibits once again, Tom,' he said. 'To give you one more chance—'

'My name is not Tom.'

'Sorry. Thomas. Do you understand what I'm going to do now?'

No response. Ronnie sighed. He couldn't believe he had come in here to help this man. Myers had done nothing but try to irritate and obstruct him, while denying none of their key allegations. He wasn't doing himself any favours.

They were in one of the cramped, stuffy, neon-lit interview rooms at Killingbeck – Ronnie, DC Mike Appleyard (one of the squad's designated interviewers) and Thomas Myers. Myers had repeatedly refused a solicitor, so forcefully that Ronnie had slowed everything down yesterday to arrange a psychiatric assessment. He didn't want to interview him without legal representation only to be later accused of oppression because the man was unhinged. The man *was* unhinged, he thought, but the doctor hadn't agreed. So here they were. An hour and a half into the fifth interview session since he had been taken into custody.

'This first exhibit—'

'I've already seen it.'

'This first exhibit is a letter.'

Mike Appleyard dug into the brown paper exhibit bag at his feet and extracted 'JBA37'. He placed it on the table between Ronnie and Myers, still in its clear plastic wrapping. It had come from the advice file that the Met had put up to the CPS to determine whether Myers should be charged with Threats to Kill.

'Can you read the writing through the sealed packet, Thomas?' Ronnie asked him. 'If you can't I'll take the letter out for you.'

Myers didn't look at it.

'For the benefit of the tape recording I'll point out that you are not looking at the exhibit, but this is the same exhibit – JBA37 – that you earlier told DC Appleyard was a letter written by yourself. Is that right?'

Myers was behaving like a petulant kid, sticking out his lower lip, avoiding eye contact, shifting backwards and forwards on the little plastic chair as if he were in the headmaster's office being accused of some breach of the school code. And there *was* something juvenile and underdeveloped about him – Ronnie had seen that at once. The man was in his mid-fifties but even his face looked boyish. Not in a simple way. You wouldn't have thought him younger than his years. It was more like the effect Ronnie had seen on people with dwarfism, so that Myers looked both old and young at once.

He was wearing a standard prisoner jumpsuit now, a lurid light-blue overall made from squeaky nylon, but when they had brought him in he had been dressed in what Tim Thorne had called 'old men's clothes' – a tattered cardigan, a linen shirt that was threadbare around the collar and cuffs, a dirty brown tie, huge, thick brown cords held up by braces, scuffed black brogues. All this, plus the eyes that were too close together. Ronnie could understand why half the squad just wanted to charge the man and get it over with.

But he couldn't see it. He tried again – as he read out the letter – to see the man as a killer, as someone capable of that level of brutality. Not personally, because they knew already that the blood under Enisa Fleming's fingernails wasn't his (he was already on the database for minor public order offences in London and Kent). But could he have become so angry that he had hired people to do it for him?

'"… my father was a great man …"' Ronnie read out. '"For what you have done to him you both deserve to die …"' That was it. Even the so-called threat hadn't turned out to be much. More juvenile foot-stamping. 'Those are your words, Thomas. Is that right?'

No response.

He pushed the letter to one side and asked Mike Appleyard for the diary. Appleyard dug in the bag and passed it out to him, again in a sealed, see-through plastic bag. Ronnie looked at it. It had been found in Myers's jacket pocket on his arrest. It was for the year 1998, full of pencil scribblings they couldn't yet decipher. They were sending it to a handwriting expert after this. But at the back was his address book. In amongst a variety of other entries were the addresses of both the Flemings – their previous London address and the new Yorkshire home – and the judge in the case involving his father, HHJ Salmond. In previous interviews with Appleyard, Myers had reluctantly conceded that he had deliberately hunted out the Flemings, in London and in Yorkshire, by using an internet facility called 192.com. He had then 'visited' them on at least one occasion to check he had the correct address. The judge had been easier – he had simply followed his Jag home from court one day.

'Tell me why you wanted to know where Steve Fleming lived?' Ronnie asked him again.

'I've already told you.'

'Tell me again.'

'This is stupid. You know why I wanted to find him. That's why I'm here.'

'Because of your father?'

'Be careful.'

Ronnie frowned at him. 'Be careful about what?'

'Be careful what you say about my father.'

'Of course.'

'I won't tolerate you slandering him. You understand that?' He glanced darkly at Ronnie from under furrowed brows and Ronnie could see the anger starting again. They had already had two demonstrations of it. He didn't want another.

'I'm not sure you understand how serious your position is—' Mike Appleyard started.

'I didn't kill anyone.'

Ronnie looked at Appleyard, eyebrows raised. It was the first time Myers had actually denied it.

'In that case, can you tell us where you were on the eighth of this month, Thomas?' Appleyard said.

So far, Myers had given nothing that would count as an alibi, though, given the absence of linking forensics, they were less interested in that than in getting details of his associates. Appleyard and his colleagues had spent four interviews trying to tease detail from Myers, knowing that any case would depend upon trying to find a link between Myers and someone capable of committing the actual act. To do that they needed to know much more about Myers and his lifestyle than he had so far been prepared to give them. It had taken three interviews to get out of him that he was now living in cheap bed and breakfast accommodation in Ramsgate. Kent police were meant to be verifying that.

'I don't remember where I was,' he said, as if it were unimportant. 'I don't remember at all.'

'The problem I have,' Ronnie said, 'is that I can't see why you would go to all that trouble – to follow Judge Salmond to his home address, to track down the Flemings four times – if you weren't intending to do something with the knowledge you gained. Why would you drive all the way to Yorkshire on four occasions in a two-month period—'

'That was my job. I was working as a driver.'

'We've checked with Gates Haulage and they say you had only two trips to Yorkshire during that period.'

'I don't recall going four times.'

'We have the van on tape—'

'It doesn't mean I was driving it.'

Ronnie stopped and sat back in the chair. 'It looks as if you were scouting the premises, Thomas. That's what a jury will think.'

Myers laughed, quietly, still looking away from Ronnie.

'You think that's funny?' Appleyard asked.

'Very funny.'

'Why is that funny?' Ronnie asked.

Myers shrugged and looked at him again. 'It's a joke, isn't it? *That's what a jury will think*. It sounds like something off the telly.'

Ronnie shook his head hopelessly.

'I didn't kill anyone,' Myers repeated. 'I want to see Fleming and Salmond pay for what they did to my father. I found out where they lived because I couldn't stand the thought that they had done that but were protected. They were faces in a courtroom. They came in to work by day and ruined people's lives, then they went home anonymously to some posh little country house where nobody knew what they had done. I wanted to expose them, to tell people where they were, who they were, what they had done. Maybe I would have, if I'd had been stronger. But I didn't want to kill them. I don't kill people. That's what *they* do.'

Ronnie ran his hands across his face wearily. It was going from bad to worse. He felt sure Myers was not responsible. But if it went on like this there was going to be enough evidence to charge him anyway.

'Your father wouldn't have liked to hear you say things like that,' Appleyard said, pushing the button.

'Don't you dare speak about my father.'

Appleyard shrugged. 'Would your father have wanted you to hurt Steve Fleming?'

'My father was a good, kind man. You leave him out of this—'

'Good kind men don't want their sons to be involved in—'

'Leave him out of it!' He sat up suddenly and leaned across the table towards them. He could be menacing, when he wanted to. 'You leave my father out of it! You hear me?' His voice was hard now, the words hissed at them through gritted teeth. If Appleyard continued this line, he would start pointing at them, jabbing his finger in the air, eyes full of hatred. Then he would be on his feet, shouting. Great stuff for the jury, but Ronnie had already seen it. He stood up.

'OK. We don't need any more of that,' he said. 'I'm ending this interview now. The time is 3.12 p.m.' He bent over and switched off the tape. 'You take him back to his cell,' he said to Appleyard. 'Then come up to Riggs's office and we'll talk.'

SATURDAY, 30 JUNE

26

Karen stood and walked to the window. Outside it was a bright, warm morning, but she registered that only vaguely. She had hardly slept at all. Too many images in her brain, too many tugging, insistent fears. Caroline Philips and Enisa Fleming were just the tip of it, lighting the fuse on a long trail of horrific associations in her memory. She was going downhill fast. At the end of it all was the truth she had buried eighteen months ago. She had to keep the lid on that, stop it from blowing up in her face.

'Will you be able to take Mairead to the stables?' Pete asked, from somewhere behind her in the room.

'Stables?' She frowned. 'Doesn't she have school?'

'It's Saturday. And term ended yesterday.'

Of course. Saturday. Over a week since she had spoken to Ronnie Shepherd.

'I'll take her,' she said. 'No problem.'

She heard him pulling a shirt on, then leaving the room. 'No problem,' she heard him mutter. 'She is, after all, your daughter.'

Recently it might have been an excuse for her to go after him and shout. Without any justification, though. He was right.

'I'll make breakfast,' he called out on the way down the stairs, speaking to Mairead, she assumed.

Summer. Last day of term yesterday. That meant there would be a lot of riding, a lot of exposure to Alexia. She had to speak to Mairead about it. She forced herself off the bed and into the bathroom, used the toilet, showered, cleaned her teeth, dried herself. Then she dressed in jeans and a light cotton shirt. She had to speak to Mairead about the kanga, too. Pete already had and said he was happy with her replies. She wasn't.

Mairead was inside her room, getting ready. The door was a little ajar. Karen knocked and pushed it open.

'Can I come in?'

Mairead looked round, raising her eyebrows. She was brushing her hair. 'You're up early,' she said. 'I thought you were starting late.'

Karen sat down on the edge of her bed. 'I want to speak to you,' she said. It sounded very formal.

'Yeah?'

'Yes.' Karen looked around the room. It looked different. 'Have you changed things in here?'

'I took down all the stupid posters.'

The boy-band posters, Karen remembered. The walls were bare now. 'Are you going to put anything up instead?'

'No. I like the clean space. What do you want to speak to me about?'

Karen stood up and took the brush from her daughter's hand. 'I'll do that for you,' she said.

Mairead smiled. It was something she liked too much to object to.

Karen began to brush her hair. It was past her shoulders now. 'I wish I had hair like yours,' Karen said. 'It's beautiful.'

Mairead leaned back against her, ever so slightly. 'You always say that.'

Karen ran her hand over her head, following the brush. 'Because it's true,' she said. 'Everything about you is beautiful, Mairead. Don't ever forget that.'

Karen looked at both of them in the mirror above the dressing table. Mairead was looking at her, still smiling slightly, the expression in her eyes one of rare childish contentment. It was funny how she could switch from angry teenager to innocent child in an instant. Karen winked at her, then concentrated on the hair, using both hands to brush through the knots lower down, without pulling at it painfully. It would take a while to get through it all.

'My skin's not so beautiful,' Mairead said. She brought a hand up and picked at her chin. On the dressing table was a line of products meant to cure dry skin, some of which Karen had bought for her. Others she had bought herself.

'Your skin is fine,' Karen said. 'Not a spot in sight.'

'I don't get spots. I get dry skin. You know that.'

'Dry skin is nothing. I can't even see it.'

'Dry skin is as bad as spots. After a while it turns red and flakes off. If it gets very bad it can turn into eczema. Alexia says it looks unsightly.'

Karen bit her tongue, suppressing her first response. 'Alexia said that about you?'

'Not about me. She has the same problem. I think she said it about herself. She gets eczema around her nose. It's because her parents split up, she says.'

Karen thought about that as she brushed. Had Mairead intended it as a criticism? Her expression hadn't changed at all as she said it.

When she was finished she placed the brush on the dressing table and sat down on the bed. 'Come and sit here,' she said.

Mairead finished buttoning her shirt then came and sat next to her on the bed. Karen slipped an arm across her shoulders. 'You have beautiful skin, Mairead,' she said. 'But even if you were covered in spots and eczema that wouldn't matter.'

Mairead shrugged, tensing, no doubt expecting a moral lecture.

'No matter what happens to you,' Karen said, speaking slowly, deliberately, making sure Mairead heard and understood every word, 'no matter what problems you have to deal with, I will always think that you are incredible. Without you I don't know what I would have done. You've made my life worth living, Mairead. Maybe I don't tell you that enough.'

'You tell me loads, Mum.' Mairead moved an arm around her waist and squeezed it gently, but Karen could see other thoughts running behind her eyes now. There was too much between them for a simple expression of love to be taken at face value. Or maybe Mairead was just getting older, more discerning. After all, there *had* been a purpose to Karen coming in here, and it hadn't been simply to tell Mairead she loved her.

'What did you want to speak about?' Mairead asked, voicing her suspicion.

From downstairs Karen could smell bacon and eggs.

'That kanga,' Karen said, with a sigh. She didn't want to mention it now. She could predict Mairead's response. 'Pete's spoken to you about it already.'

'Yes?'

'You told him Alexia gave it to you.'

'Yes?'

'Was that true?'

Mairead stood up at once, angry. She walked over to the wardrobe without saying anything.

'I'm worried about you and Alexia—' Karen started.

'For God's sake, Mum! What *is* the problem?' Voice raised now, speaking through half-gritted teeth.

'*Did* she give you the kanga?'

'Yes.'

'Look at me when you answer.'

She took a step back and stared straight into Karen's eyes. 'Yes. Yes. Yes.' No sign that she was lying at all. But then, Karen had taught her very carefully how to lie convincingly.

'Why? Don't you have enough clothes of your own?'

'Jesus Christ, Mum! What's the fucking harm?'

'Don't swear like that. And stop getting dressed for a moment. Come over here. I want to talk to you about this.'

Mairead ignored her.

'I'm not trying to be nasty,' Karen said. 'I'm just worrying about you.'

'I don't see why.'

'Because this girl is much older than you, because she wears clothes like that – older, more expensive things – because you feel you have to keep up with her, because she might lead you into all sorts of things you shouldn't do, because you seem to worship the ground she walks on ...'

'That's all total rubbish.'

'... because I did all this myself, when I was your age. Because I was exactly the same as you. And I got hurt.'

Mairead had been about to shout at her, but she paused now, looking curious instead. 'You got hurt? By who?'

'By a girl.'

'An older girl?'

'She was my age, as it happens. But she felt older. She knew things I didn't.'

She could see Mairead thinking about it. She let her, waiting to see if she would thaw a little.

'When was this?' Mairead asked, after a while. Her voice was calmer now.

'When I was your age. In Northern Ireland. She was called Sara Collins. I was in love with her, I think.'

'In *love* with her?' Mairead tried to inject some surprise into the tone, but Karen could see already that she knew exactly what she was talking about.

'Yes. In the silly way you can love someone – boy or girl – when you're that age.'

Mairead stepped towards the bed.

'I hero-worshipped her,' Karen said, looking at her knees, remembering. 'I thought she could do nothing wrong, that she was incredible, that we would always be best friends. That kind of thing.' She felt Mairead sitting down on the bed beside her. 'I got into a lot of trouble because of her,' she continued. 'I ended up fighting with people—'

'Real fights?'

'Yes. Real fights. With real weapons and real injuries. Sara knew how to defend herself. She knew a lot of things like that. She was a tomboy. That's what we called it them. I wasn't really, but I copied her. I thought so little of myself I copied everything she did. She was a Catholic, too. That was problematic. My mother hated Catholics. Her father was the local IRA head-case. So everyone was frightened of her. Except me. I just thought she was fantastic.' She smiled at the thought.

'Did you ever kiss her?'

Karen looked up at her, shocked. 'Kiss her?' Was that what was going on with Alexia? 'No. She didn't go in for that sort of thing—'

'Only joking, Mum.' Mairead grinned at her, then placed her hand on her leg, reassuringly.

Karen sighed. 'I probably would have kissed her,' she said, 'if she had been into that. I didn't know too much about those things then …'

They sat in silence for a moment, pondering that.

'How did she hurt you?' Mairead asked. 'Did she dump you?' She said the word 'dump' with irony, with a hint of cruelty even. It brought thoughts of Ronnie to mind.

'You could say that,' Karen said. 'I went to boarding school in Belfast when I was thirteen. I wrote her letters and she never replied. I didn't miss my mother or father. I was glad to get away from them. But I missed Sara. I missed her so badly I cried every night. The first time I got back I tried to find her …' She broke off. Even now the memories stung.

'Yes?'

'But she found me first.'

Mairead waited.

'She attacked me with a broken bottle,' Karen said. Her voice sounded matter-of-fact. 'She wasn't the only one. There were a group of ten of them. I was from a Protestant family, remember. I didn't believe in anything myself, but to them I was Protestant. They were Catholic. Religion does that kind of thing.'

'Were you hurt?'

'I lost two teeth, got a big scar in the hairline, went to hospital, got into a depression, took an overdose.'

Mairead looked horrified.

'I was in love with her,' Karen said. 'I told you. It can do that to you. You end up as if you are under a magic spell. You believe that people who are nothing are incredible. She was nothing. I can see that now. It was all in my head. I invented her, gave her that power over me. Strong people are easy to get attracted to, especially if you can't fight, if you're always being picked on. But they don't do any good in the world. It's the people who are full of doubt we should be attracted to ...'

She stopped. Mairead had moved so close to her that her head was resting against her shoulder. Karen reached a hand up and stroked her face. Mairead closed her arms around her chest, hugging her tightly. She was shaking. After a while Karen realized she was crying as well. 'Don't cry, Mairead,' she said. 'There's nothing to cry about. What have I said? Why are you crying?' She stroked her daughter's head, feeling helpless.

'I didn't steal it, Mum,' Mairead said, voice muffled. 'I didn't steal the kanga.'

Karen nodded. 'That's OK,' she said.

'You have to believe me. I don't steal.'

'I do believe you. Don't worry. Is that what you're crying for?'

For a moment Mairead said nothing, then: 'I'm worried, Mum. I'm worried for you.'

'For me? Don't be silly.'

'I was there, Mum. I know what happened to you ...'

'You were where?'

'*There.* A year and a half ago. I was there, remember? I heard everything ...'

'Don't talk about that,' she said, quickly.

'I know what he did to you, Mum—'

'*Don't talk about it.*' She couldn't go there, couldn't even think about it.

Mairead pushed herself away. 'Promise me you won't do anything stupid,' she said, voice suddenly firm.

Karen was confused. 'Like what?'

'Like kill yourself.'

'Kill myself?'

'Yes, Mum. I'm worried about you. We both are – Pete and me. You're so miserable at the moment. We're frightened you might kill yourself or something ...'

Karen felt shocked, as if she had hit her face.

'I'm not going to kill myself,' she said. She had come in to talk about her daughter's problems and ended up with this. She had to get a grip on things, think about what she was saying before she opened her mouth. Brooding about her and Pete, or her and Ronnie Shepherd – even obsessing about Caroline Philips and Enisa Fleming – it was all beside the point. Mairead was all that mattered.

27

It was the first time Jana had been to see her dad without her gran staying in the room with them. Her dad was getting better now. He could get up out of the bed if he moved very, very slowly. Once on his feet he was wobbly and could only walk one step at a time, thinking about each step before he took it. Also, he had to push around a tall metal thing wherever he went. It looked like a coat hanger, or hat stand, on wheels. There were bags of liquid hanging off it, with tubes going into his arms and side. Instead of his real clothes he had to wear a hospital gown that looked like a green dress. It stopped above his knees, and Jana could see his hairy legs. It would have been funny, if she was allowed to laugh when she visited him, but the room was always too miserable for her to laugh. When she visited, everything had to be quiet and slow, or Daddy started getting a bad headache and they had to leave. Sometimes she saw that he was crying about things, and trying to hide it from her.

She sat now on the end of the bed and he asked her questions about what she had been doing at Gran's house. He always asked her questions. She didn't mind, but she wished Gran hadn't left her here alone. What if something happened to her dad's tubes while she was alone with him? One of them might fall out of his hand, or a bag might slip off the hat stand and burst on the floor. She wasn't sure what she should do then. She thought she should probably run out into the corridor and shout for the nurse.

'I've been doing drawing and painting,' she said. 'Sometimes with Grandad, sometimes with Gran.'

'That's good. What have you been drawing? Did you bring me any pictures?'

'I forgot,' she said. She felt bad about that. 'I could do you one now, though.' She had paper and pencils in her satchel.

She got down off the bed and sat on the floor with her satchel. Above her, on the bed, she could hear Daddy wheezing – that was what they called it when you made a whistling sound as you breathed.

'Have you remembered what I told you last time?' he asked her.

She took her paper and coloured pencils out.

'Jana. Have you remembered what I told you last time about looking out for suspicious men?'

'Yes,' she said, though she hadn't really remembered, not once they had left the hospital.

'You have to watch things that are happening around you, Jana. Watch to see if there are the same strange men looking at you more than once. If you see anyone you don't know watching you, you must tell Gran and me straight away. It's really important. And never talk to anyone you don't know. You must listen to me, Jana. This is important. Look at me.'

She looked up at him.

'Will you do this for me, please?' he asked.

'Yes.' She wasn't sure what he meant really. It made her worried when he spoke like that and she didn't understand. She had told Gran about it, and Gran had told her just to say yes to everything and not to worry because Daddy was still very poorly.

'Good. That's a good girl.' He tried to smile at her, she thought, but there was a tube going into his nose, with some sticking tape holding it to his chin. It meant she couldn't see his mouth properly. She smiled back at him anyway.

She drew him a picture of Mummy. The woman who had come from the doctor to visit her had told her she should draw as many pictures of her as she wanted to. Gran said her mum was with the Angel Gabriel – who was an angel for Christians and Muslims. He was the highest and most important angel. Mummy was happy with him. That didn't make *her* happy, but the woman from the doctor said that was OK, too. It was OK for her to be unhappy.

She knew her mum was dead. They had explained all that to her. It meant she had gone to a happier place and wouldn't come back, ever.

She drew her mum with long, black hair, as she remembered her, and big, brown eyes. She put little light blue shoes on her feet, because her mum had a pair like that, but she didn't do the high heels because Daddy was always telling Mummy they were bad for her legs. She didn't want to annoy Daddy when he was still so weak.

When she got up and showed it to him he asked her who it was.

'It's Mummy,' she said, smiling. She thought he would be pleased. But his face turned red and he closed his eyes tightly. She watched him, wanting him to say something nice about it, but he looked away from her. She thought she must have done something wrong. 'I didn't do the high heels,' she said, thinking that might be it, but he didn't reply. 'That's the Angel Gabriel,' she tried, pointing to the figure behind her mum, higher up. He opened his eyes and looked, but still didn't speak. He must have known that it was Gabriel already, from the wings.

What she wanted to say to him was that she didn't want Mummy to be with Gabriel. She wanted her to come back here. But she hadn't told anyone that and didn't dare. Her mum had died because she had covered her with a blanket, thinking she had fallen over and was cold. A blanket was the first thing she had found in the bedroom. She knew now that her mum had been too cold with just a blanket and she should have brought out a quilt from her own bed. If her mum had been warmer then she might not have went away to be with Gabriel.

'What are you doing?' Daddy asked.

She looked up at him, wondering what he meant. He had asked her the question very quietly.

'Do you know what you're doing?'

She knew what he meant now, because she could see what he was looking at. He was watching her head. It was moving rapidly from side to side. 'Twitching' was what Gran had called it to Granddad, thinking she hadn't been listening. She could feel the movement only slightly. It didn't bother her. She didn't know why it was happening. It had started a few days ago.

'Don't frown like that, Jana. Please. I'm not angry with you. I just want to know if you know what you're doing with your head.'

She bit her bottom lip and tried to nod, but instead the twitches got worse.

'It doesn't matter,' her dad said. He pointed to the picture. 'It is very beautiful. Mummy would love it.' His voice went funny then, like he was going to cry again. 'What's this at her feet?' he asked instead.

'That's the blanket I put on her,' she said. 'I put it over you, too. It was meant to keep you warm but it wasn't warm enough for Mummy. So she died.' She shrugged.

'That's not why she died,' Daddy said. 'It had nothing to do with anything you did, darling.' He started to say something else, then stopped and started burbling, spitting words through his lips that she couldn't understand. Suddenly, there were tears pouring out of his eyes and his chest was shaking. She watched him, frightened something would go wrong with the tubes, or the machines plugged in around him. His skin turned blue, like he was straining, or holding his breath. Then he started banging his forehead with his fist, not saying anything, just banging his fist against it.

'Please don't cry, Daddy,' she said. 'You might have a relapse. Gran says you have to be calm or you will have a relapse.'

'Jesus!' He shouted the word, then banged his fist into his face, hard. 'I have done this! I killed her. I killed her!' He began to sob out loud. She didn't know what to do.

'Mummy is happy,' she tried to say, but he was crying too loud and couldn't hear her. 'Please don't cry.' She was crying herself now. She moved closer to him and he reached an arm out to her. She climbed up on a chair next to him and let him pull her into his side, crushing her against him. The tubes going into his side pressed up against her uncomfortably. 'This is all my fault,' he was saying. 'This has nothing to do with you, Jana. This is all my fault.'

28

In the Ladies at Richmond Close Karen closed the cubicle door and leaned against it. The pain in her chest was back, this time so bad she felt as if she had a stitch. Except the pain was bang in the centre of her chest. When she inhaled deeply it actually felt like a lump, obstructing her breathing.

She sat down on the toilet seat and checked her watch. She was late already. DI Richard Powell had booked the first-floor conference room for midday, to brief them about overnight developments. Andy Lewis had found a new witness the day before, someone who had apparently given a clear enough description to build a computer image, and had worked through the night on it. It was 12.05 now; she had to get up and go in.

She stood and opened the door. The toilets were empty. She walked over to the sinks and looked at herself in the mirrors. Her face looked drawn, and dark patches were developing under her eyes.

For the first time in over three years she had taken the time to check her car that morning before getting into it. Many years ago they had given her a mirror, angled on a rod, so she could check beneath the chassis for devices. She had dug it out of Pete's cellar that morning before taking Mairead to the stables. She didn't really know why.

She turned away from herself and walked to the exit. Richard Powell was passing the Ladies just as she stepped out.

'Karen?'

'Yes, sir.' She stopped. If *he* was late then she was OK.

Powell cleared his throat. Was that a nervous habit? If so, why hadn't she noticed it before? 'When we start just now could you say something about Caroline?' he asked. 'Since you're the only one who has actually seen her.'

'What do you mean? Say what about her?'

'Tell them about her injuries, what she looks like. Just to make it clear. So we know what we're dealing with.'

She could feel her facial muscles working as she looked at him. She nodded. 'OK. If you want me to.'

She followed him into the room, the pain in her chest still there. She was the last in and the only woman. She had barely sat down before he was starting things, hushing them all, telling them he had important new developments. She looked quickly round their faces. There were nine men now. Five were from Halifax and four had been pulled in from elsewhere because of the racial tensions brewing as a result of the case. They were listening to what Powell was saying. She saw them look at her and realized with a start that Powell had already asked her to speak. She wanted to flinch. Or stand up and run away. She could feel her face colouring with embarrassment.

'I saw Caroline yesterday …' she started. Her voice sounded rough. She cleared her throat and started again. 'I saw Caroline yesterday, but wasn't able to speak to her. She wasn't aware of what was going on. She's still heavily sedated.' She stopped, trying to think of something useful to say. In the silence she saw them watching her, all their eyes focused on her, waiting. Did she look emotional? Did she look how she felt? 'Maybe it would have been better if he *had* killed her,' she blurted out at last. She saw some of them frown at her. 'She will never be young again, never be that person in the magazine. I got upset looking at her. That doesn't normally happen to me. I don't know why …' She faltered, listening to the awkward silence in the room. 'The mess her face in …' What was she meant to tell them?

She took a breath and cleared her throat once more. 'Sorry,' she said. 'I'll start again. With the facts.' She looked over to Richard Powell. Did he want her to do that? He nodded at her. She turned back to them. 'Caroline was stabbed six times. Three thrusts penetrated deep inside her mouth, severing her tongue then piercing the back of her throat and the roof of her mouth.' She tried to speak automatically, with a dead-pan voice, but it was an effort. 'Two entered through her right cheek, causing three-inch lacerations and cutting deep nerve structures. Her jaw was broken in two places, and eight teeth were knocked out or broken. One thrust slashed her left cheek, in a line from the corner of her mouth almost to her ear.' She pointed to the places on her face. 'The whole cheek was cut wide open so that the flesh was, they told me, hanging down from her jaw, exposing all her teeth, the bones …

she must have looked like a skull. Everything opened up. You could see what was underneath the skin, what she is, what she *really* is …'

Frowns. They didn't understand that. She heard Richard Powell cough politely behind her, but didn't look at him. She started again.

'She has a total of three hundred and twelve stitches, over half of them internal. There is a great deal of surgery still to do. Many operations. She will never speak properly again because about a third of her tongue was severed and could not be re-attached …' Her voice was breaking up now. She couldn't help it. She started to speak more quietly to keep it from cracking. 'The nerve damage means she will look like she has had a stroke for the rest of her life – one side of her face sagging, the other side, where she was cut from the lip to the ear, scarring into a …' She stopped. Why were they not reacting? Why were they staring at her like that? 'Scarring into a permanent lop-sided grin.' One or two of them averted their eyes, embarrassed. 'And all this for what?' Behind her Richard Powell cleared his throat again. He was trying to shut her up now, finally. They looked slightly frightened of her. Or frightened *for* her? 'It's not what Caroline was expecting, of course,' she said, finishing. 'Not what she thought would happen when she went out to work that day.'

'Are you all right, Karen?' Powell's voice.

She looked over at him. 'I promised her we would get this bastard,' she said. It was true, but Caroline didn't know that. She had said nothing aloud to Caroline, only in her head. 'I made that promise for all of us. That we would find out why this happened.'

'That's OK, Karen,' Powell said, voice gentle. 'We *will* get the bastard. Do you want to take a break?'

Why was he speaking to her like that? She took a deep, deep breath, the pain stabbing right through the middle of her chest. 'I'm fine,' she whispered. Powell stared at her for a moment, clearly concerned, then stood up, moving back to the whiteboard.

'Right,' he said, 'Karen took Caroline a number of questions.' He wasn't looking at her now. In her peripheral vision she saw heads turn from her, focusing on him instead. She felt relief. 'We wanted to know, obviously, what she thought her attacker looked like, what he had said. But, as you've heard, in the end Caroline could barely understand where she was. We're still waiting for DNA from the scene. We have traces from at least three individuals and the analysis has been expedited. Most promisingly, we have blood under Caroline's fingernails. There are some good shed hair samples, too. The results should be back on Monday.' He coughed, then wrote two names on to the whiteboard: Ian Hogg and June Shaw.

'Until last night these were our only useful witnesses, and they gave a confused picture.' He quickly wrote the essence of the descriptions they had given underneath their names. 'As you see, they are not much use. Shaw says she doesn't even know whether the man was white or black. Hogg says he was foreign. Reliant upon these two we were stuffed. But things are different now. He wrote up another name: Colin Norton.

'Do you want to tell us about Colin Norton, Andy?'

Andy Lewis stood up, and Richard Powell moved away from the whiteboard, sitting next to Karen and immediately leaning towards her 'You sure you're all right, Karen?' he whispered. He placed a hand on her shoulder.

She gritted her teeth. 'I'm fine,' she said.

Powell held her eyes for a moment, as if she were lying, then looked at Andy Lewis.

'I took a statement late yesterday,' Lewis said, 'from a man called Colin Norton. I haven't had a chance to check out his antecedents yet, but he seemed straight enough, if a little rough-cut. He gave a very accurate description of a man he saw walking at the top of Saville Park towards King Cross around about seven-fifteen on the day of the attack. He says the man was walking, not running, which ties in, and that he was wearing a grey, heavily blood-stained T-shirt. There was blood also on the man's face and hands, he says. I won't write up the description he gave just yet because it seemed obvious we could get a computer image or an artist's impression from him. I got both produced independently; both were very similar. The artist and the ID team worked through the night with Norton and myself.' He unrolled a small A4 size sheet of heavy paper and fixed it to the whiteboard under Colin Norton's name. When he stepped back Karen saw that it was a black and white drawing of a roughly Semitic face, with heavy stubble and distinct bulging eyes.

'It's very clear,' Lewis said. 'So clear I recognized this man immediately.'

'I did, too,' Richard Powell said. 'Anyone else know who it is?'

There was a buzz in the room now, a palpable increase in excitement. Karen scanned their faces. *She* didn't have a clue who it was.

'It's almost certainly Akil Al-Talehi,' Richard Powell said.

Lewis stepped back beside his picture, obviously pleased with himself. 'Al-Talehi has a flat in Gibbet Street,' he said. 'I can see the Halifax officers here know him well.' *Not me*, Karen thought. 'He's also well known in Bradford, because he is the man who was exposed two months ago by a journalist for recruiting Palestinian suicide bombers out of a mosque in Manningham. Anyone remember that?'

Murmurs of assent. Karen had not heard about it.

'He's a lunatic,' Lewis said. 'Certifiable. I knew him before the BBC made him famous because he could regularly be found in the town centre ranting about Jews and calling for jihad against Israel. Until now he's just been a nuisance.'

'We put up with him because he's an asylum-seeker,' Richard Powell said. 'A Saudi dissident. At first he was in the hostel on Hanson Lane, then he was given the flat in Gibbet Street. He has a history of mental illness. He's been in and out of the cells for all sorts of things. Sometimes he wears a long white Arab shift. Sometimes he has a beard. I suppose we would have said he was just a bit sad – until now.'

'Now we need to find him quickly,' Lewis said.

Richard Powell stood up. 'I've struggled with motive on this one,' he said. 'It didn't really fit for an attempted rape, despite Hogg's evidence. Caroline's underwear wasn't disarranged and, despite what happened on Saville Park with the Ripper and all, it really isn't a private enough scene to get away with a rape at this time of year and at that time of evening. But then it clearly wasn't a robbery, either, as nothing was taken. So when you rule out rape and robbery, what are you left with? Either a grudge or a madman.' He cleared his throat again.

Should she speak to him about that? Karen thought. It could be a habit, but it could be a sign of something else, too. Throat cancer could start with such symptoms.

'As soon as Andy told me he had a picture of Akil Al-Talehi I knew where we were,' Powell said. 'We're dealing with a lunatic here, a straightforward mental health case.' Now he was looking directly at Karen, as if his words were providing the explanation she had asked for. 'It's a senseless attack. Someone's life has been ruined by a violent madman. That's all it is. When we track down Al-Talehi he's probably going to tell us Allah told him to do it.'

29

This was the problem with David Riggs. If you hadn't worked with him before you might assume from first contact that he was haughty, autocratic and not interested in anybody else's views. But when it came to the crunch, when a decision had to be made, you ended up with this mess.

Ronnie had been sitting in the meeting room at Killingbeck for nearly an hour and a half now, while everybody put in their bit and Riggs listened, discussed, went this way and that, made a decision, changed his mind, canvassed more views, weighed the pros and cons. It could go on for ever. The man couldn't make a decision to save his life.

They were meant to be deciding whether to charge Thomas Myers or get an extension to hold him longer. When Kent Police had finally done their work they had discovered that Myers had the perfect alibi for 8 June: he was locked up in their cells on a drunkeness charge. They had no evidence to suggest Myers had hired someone else to attack the Flemings, but that wasn't stopping the discussion.

Ronnie was only half-listening. His mind kept stumbling across thoughts of Karen Sharpe. He knew he was going to have to call her. Laura had thought him mad when he had told her what had happened. It was just a matter of trying to work out what to say. For some reason the idea of calling her with no excuse at all, just to speak to her, seemed terrifying. Like the first time he had asked a girl out, but worse.

He looked up. Riggs was addressing him. Had he been trying to get his attention for a while? He stopped doodling and put the pen down.

'Yes, David?'

'Did you hear what I said?'

'Sorry, no.' How embarrassing. 'Could you repeat, please?'

Riggs sighed elaborately. 'What's your view?' he said. He had pushed his chair out to peer around Tom Joyce. Everybody at the table was looking at Ronnie now. 'You still think we should be pursuing the London angle?'

On the table Ronnie's phone began to ring. He placed his hand over it, grateful for the excuse to get out of the room.

'I don't think it's any of the NCS cases,' he said. 'We've got nowhere with them. But we still have ten detectives working flat out down there to try to bottom six possible cases where …' The phone was getting louder. He stood up. 'Sorry,' he said. 'But I'll have to take this.'

Riggs glowered at him.

He closed the door behind him and stood in the corridor. It was Richard Powell, a DI at Halifax. Would that make him Karen's supervisor? Ronnie listened as he told him about a distressing case they were working on. In fact, Ronnie had already heard about it. A young girl had been stabbed in the mouth.

'We're looking for a man called Akil Al-Talehi,' Powell said. 'I'm not sure how reliable it all is, but thought you should know.'

Ronnie paced up and down as he listened, thinking about it. The MO was similar, but not very.

'Frenzied knife attacks on women?' he said, thinking aloud. The frenzied element was significant. Maybe he had missed that.

'I was thinking of Al-Talehi's profile, too,' Powell said. He cleared his throat. 'He's a psychiatric case, with a history of psychiatric disturbances. I thought you had a profile going along those lines?'

'We did. At one point.' He needed to think about it. They had moved off the madman theory, maybe too quickly. 'But is Al-Talehi on the database?' he asked.

'Yes. And we have blood under our victim's fingernails. We're still waiting for a DNA comparison.'

Blood under the fingernails. A superficial similarity. 'He's not our attacker, then,' Ronnie said. 'We have blood, too. He would have come back to us already if he's on the database.'

'OK. Just thought you ought to have some of the detail.'

Ronnie closed the phone and stood with it against his lips, pondering. Out of the corner of his eye, through the meeting room window, he could see Riggs straightening his bow tie.

Akil Al-Talehi. Where had he heard the name before?

*

He walked quickly down to the incident room and found a HOLMES terminal. There was one indexer in, trying to catch up on the backlog. He sat down opposite her and ran a search for Akil Al-Talehi. The program would be able to tell him if the name had come up anywhere in the statements or documentation for Bulldog. Provided his name had been indexed in.

The search drew a blank. He sat back and tried to remember. He was sure he had heard it somewhere. The indexer opposite him was watching.

'Anything I can help with, sir?' Her name was Linda Kemp, he remembered.

'The name Akil Al-Talehi ring any bells?'

She took off her glasses and rested her chin on her hands. 'He's not in there?'

'No. But I've heard the name. Just can't place it.'

'I think I remember him, too,' she said. She was still thinking about it, frowning, trying to get it.

Maybe something to do with the builders, Ronnie thought. Linda held a finger up. 'What about Ahmed Ibrahim, the builder who was on the DNA database?'

'Snap. That's what I was thinking.'

She pushed her chair back and looked on the shelving behind her. There were two large fireproof cabinets filled with indexed ring-binders containing the actions, documents and statements. Already there were more than eighty folders of material, sorted chronologically. She selected one from near the bottom of the shelf and placed it on the desk.

'What are you looking for?' he asked.

'Early actions involving Ahmed Ibrahim. Someone will have been tasked with checking his associates.'

She put her glasses back on and leafed through the action slips.

'You think Al-Talehi is an associate of Ibrahim?'

'Maybe not an associate. We would have indexed him if he was an associate ...' She broke off, concentrating.

He waited. She turned a page, then smiled.

'Here you are,' she said. She passed him the ring-binder, open at the right place.

He stood up, took it, placed it on the desk in front of him. 'That's pretty impressive,' he said. 'How did you do that?'

'I have the memory for it,' she said. 'I remember the spacial position of things, like where they are on a page or in a book.'

He looked at the action and found Al-Talehi's name at once. He wasn't an associate of Ibrahim, not strictly speaking, but they had discovered, while doing the background on Ibrahim, that he regularly attended an 'Islamic prayer group'. They had met in a mosque in Bradford, until the regular worshippers had discovered what they were discussing and had excluded them. From then on they had met in a house in Harehills. The group was interesting enough to have attracted the attention of Special Branch, who had designated it as a group dedicated to the promotion of a 'pan-Islamic state'. Akil Al-Talehi was listed as the leader.

Ronnie looked up from the report. Linda was watching him.

'Any use?' she asked.

Not Al-Talehi, he thought, because he hadn't come back as a match to the trace from Enisa's fingernails. So not as a trigger man, or blade-wielder, anyway. But Ibrahim and one other, perhaps, incited by Al-Talehi? No. Not Ibrahim. He had an alibi. But had they checked his alibi closely enough? Or maybe it was someone else from the same group. It depended what sort of things this group was proposing. It would need looking at.

'Maybe,' he said. 'Just maybe.'

SUNDAY, 1 JULY

30

For eight years she had been happy, living as Karen Sharpe, doing this job. She watched Richard Powell's lips moving as he spoke to her, his face a picture of paternal concern, worried about her mental state, no doubt. Then the IRA had sent someone to kill her. That was when it had all started to unravel. She was still living with the effects of that now. One thing led to another, then everything led to Stijn.

Stijn.

She suppressed a shudder. She had to close her mind to him, concentrate on the present. Sometimes she thought he might not be dead. She had nightmares about that.

'Sometimes it can get to you, Karen,' Powell said. 'It can get to all of us. And you've been through a lot in the last couple of years.'

If only he knew. What would he do if she told him everything? Told him about all the people she had killed or seen killed.

'Perhaps I should have listened to you,' he said. 'You tried to tell me yesterday that you were having problems with the idea of speaking to Caroline, but I thought you could handle it. Then I watched you talking yesterday. I was worried for you. You looked as though you were going to crack up.'

Ronnie Shepherd wasn't going to help with all this. How could anyone help her? *It was what she was.*

'I'm fine,' she said to Powell. It was getting to be a refrain. 'I just want to know why you've put me on to background checks.' She had come in that morning to find her tasking changed. 'You've taken me off finding Al-Talehi, off the main task.'

Powell stood up and came from behind his desk. 'Sit down, Karen,' he said. She sat. He closed the door to the CID room. 'I've not taken you off anything,' he said. 'The tasking has nothing to do with my concern for you. I've got nine male detectives out there who think that this was a crime committed by an Asian.' A pause for that throat-clearing again. 'Apparently all Halifax wants to think the same thing. They *want* this to be some kind of ethnic issue. It doesn't help that the BNP are milking it for all its worth. Someone out there, one of my detectives, is even helping them by leaking information.' He looked disgusted. 'Of course, the attacker *might* be Asian, or Arab. Until yesterday I thought we had Akil Al-Talehi in the frame. But this morning I started asking questions about our star witness – Colin Norton. I found out he has previous for assault.'

She shrugged. 'Doesn't mean he's a liar.'

'It was a racially aggravated assault,' he added. 'I'm annoyed with Andy Lewis – he should have checked that out earlier.' He sat down again, facing her. 'So I need to know more about Norton,' he said. 'That's why I've given you the background.'

'OK. So I look at Norton. But that will only take me half a day. Why do I have to—'

'If he turns out to be dirty, unreliable, then we need to know we have covered all the angles on this. The grudge theory is the only one we haven't put resources into so far.'

'Yes, but the idea of—'

'So if you are OK, as you *say* you are ...' He raised his voice, talking over her, then stopped, waiting for her to correct him, giving her another chance. '*Are* you OK?'

'Yes. I am.'

'Then get out there and do what I have asked you to do. Check out Norton, then do Caroline Philips's friends, family and boyfriend. Understood?'

She nodded. He wasn't going to budge.

Caroline's flatmate was called Deborah Hemmings. Karen interviewed her in a security office at the Nestlé factory where she worked. It was slow because Hemmings couldn't stop crying. Karen attempted to ignore that. There was a knack to checking out the bereaved – you assumed they were faking their grief and tried to get the alibi details out of them without causing offence. Then you asked the supplementaries, pretending all the time that you were sympathizing with them. For Karen, that morning, it was like swimming in an emotional whirlpool. She hated it.

Hemmings didn't have an immediately verifiable alibi. She had been shopping alone in Leeds at the relevant time. It could be checked, but since all descriptions involved a male attacker Karen simply noted the details down and moved on. Hemmings was a strong, capable-looking woman, but she wouldn't be mistaken for a man.

She was unable to name anyone who might hold a grudge against Caroline. She did, however, make some interesting comments about the boyfriend, Brian Johnson. 'He's got a screw loose,' she said. 'I don't know why Caroline is with him.'

Karen asked the usual questions about Caroline and Brian's relationship, whether they argued, whether there was any violence. It seemed there was not.

'They shouted and screamed at each other – well, mainly Caroline shouted and screamed. Brian didn't do that. He was more sinister, kept his voice low when he was threatening her. But she never told me about him hitting her, or anything like that.'

'But you say he's a bit strange?' Karen persisted.

'I think he's mad.'

'*Mad*? Or just different?'

'Mad. Not quite there. One brick short of the full load. He thinks the Lord Jesus talks to him. Caroline told me that. He has conversations with God.'

Caroline's father was more forceful about it.

'Brian Johnson's a freak. I don't know why she started seeing him.'

Karen sat in the front room of their home in Greetland, and listened patiently as he listed all the things that had been wrong with his daughter's life. As if, taken together, all her 'wrong turns' would somehow explain what had been inflicted upon her.

He was a short, sour-looking man with lank, thinning hair and a habit of running his hands through what was left of it. He kept blinking compulsively. He didn't like Johnson, didn't like the modelling contract, didn't like her job at Boots. He thought Debs Hemmings was probably a lesbian, and that it was reckless for Caroline to have moved in with her. If she had stayed with them she wouldn't have been walking alone across Saville Park.

He didn't like the police, either. Why did he need to say all this again when somebody had already spoken to him? In the end his rant ran out and he broke down and cried. His wife and son sat meekly on the other two chairs in the room and watched it all. They had all been about to go to the hospital when Karen arrived, and still had their coats on.

They were struggling to take in what had happened, each of them in their own way. The father was eaten with anger, the mother in shock, the brother numb. They all had the same alibi because they had all been in the house together when it had happened.

No one said anything until the father started crying, then Caroline's mother apologized for him, gently. 'He loves her so much,' she said. 'We can't take this in ...' Her lip started to tremble.

'I don't know anybody who would hurt her,' her brother said. 'Why would they?'

She was on her way to Brian Johnson's when her mobile rang. By then she had absorbed enough misery and pent-up anger to make her feel saturated with it. She answered without looking at the number, pulling the car over at the same time.

'Yes?'

'Karen?'

'Yes?'

'Ronnie Shepherd.'

She switched the engine off and waited.

'I've been told you're on Scythe,' he said, inserting a tiny germ of confusion into her mood.

'Yes. That's right,' she said. 'Is that why you're calling me?'

'Well ...' he said. He almost stammered. 'No. I suppose it's not. I just felt I had to say that, otherwise I might not have had the courage to call at all.'

She felt something relax inside her. She sank further back into the seat. 'So why are you calling?'

'To apologize for last Friday. You were right, of course. We hardly know each other. I had no right to get into a sulk because you were already with someone.'

'That's OK,' she said, quickly. 'I shouldn't have reacted so angrily.'

He didn't say anything. Was that all he was going to do – apologize then say goodbye? Like signing it off.

'I'd like to see more of you,' he said finally.

She felt a surge of relief. 'I'd like to see more of you, too,' she said.

She heard him sigh. 'Thank God for that. I thought you might have written me off. I was so stupid ...'

She could feel her spirits picking up already. 'You shouldn't have moved me off Bulldog,' she said.

'I didn't. Riggs moved you. I tried to talk him out of it.'

'Timmy Thorne told me it was your decision. I thought you wanted rid of me.'

'Tim Thorne can be a twat sometimes. I didn't want rid of you. I've sorely missed your personal skills.'

She laughed at that.

'It wasn't a joke,' he said. 'I've missed your touch with Fleming.' A pause. 'And with me.'

'We should meet up, then,' she said.

'Tonight?'

'The sooner the better.'

Maybe they could get back to where they had been the week before last. She had felt almost happy then.

31

Ronnie drove to a meeting in Rochdale feeling as if the clouds had lifted. For the first time he noticed it was a beautiful, hot, clear day. He stopped at the Hartshead Moor services, lowered the top of the Porsche and put his shades on. Then, coming over Saddleworth on the M62, he played a CD Laura had given him last year for his birthday, which he still hadn't listened to. She was on a mission to educate him, musically, without much hope of success. This one was a jazz pianist Ronnie had never heard of, playing a solo improvised piano concert in Cologne in 1975. The wind rush was too great to hear it properly, though. He switched it off and thought instead about playing it for Karen tonight. Would she like that sort of thing? Creating a soft, romantic atmosphere wasn't something he had done much of in his life. He doubted she had, either.

It was nearly one o'clock by the time he got to Rochdale. His meeting was with a DI called Alex Woolrych who worked on the Rochdale division of Greater Manchester Police. Ronnie skipped lunch and they met at Rochdale Police Station, in an office adjacent to the CID room.

'Sorry to get you out on a Sunday,' Ronnie started. He sat down on a shabby, plastic chair and accepted the coffee Woolrych held out to him.

'No. It's our own fault. Don't worry.' Woolrych waved his hand dismissively. 'We should have done the follow-up by now. Sorry.' He was a bald man, probably in his mid-forties, dressed in a suit that was cheap and creased, long overdue a trip to the dry cleaners. He looked hassled and overworked, his jowls showing signs of a three-day growth. He sat down opposite Ronnie, at the other side of a desk that probably wasn't his, judging by the way he disapprovingly viewed a surface littered with paperwork and used coffee cups, before carefully moving things to make room for his own paper cup.

'I know how it is,' Ronnie said, trying to be diplomatic. 'We marked it low priority so it's not surprising you didn't find time yet.'

Aside from finally persuading David Riggs that there wasn't enough evidence to charge Thomas Myers – Myers had been bailed yesterday at the expiry of his detention limit – Ronnie had spent the last twenty-four working hours searching for lines they might have overlooked or written off too early. To get to that point wasn't necessarily a sign of desperation – it was a standard part of major inquiry methodology to review and re-review – but it felt frustrating to Ronnie. Essentially he was double-checking ground that had already been covered.

The checks had led to him compiling a long list of still-open actions that had been graded very low priority. One of the first concerned a piece of information that had come in from GMP within the first seven days of the inquiry.

'You want to know about Aidan Kershaw,' Woolrych said.

'If possible. I've had someone look through the IT already. I just want to make sure we have the complete picture.'

The information from GMP had been no more useful than a suggestion that someone called Aidan Kershaw – a local drugs nominal – had been 'involved' somehow in Enisa Fleming's death. The item was graded E4, meaning it was from an unknown source and was considered unreliable. The inquiry had sent a follow-up request to GMP, but hadn't prioritized it. On killings like this they had to sort the wheat from the chaff. Every undetected killing presented a chance for drug dealers to gain ground by making false allegations against their rivals. There had in fact been six such low-level snitchings sent to the inquiry from various neighbouring forces. The follow-up requests were standard, but GMP were alone in not having actioned theirs.

'I've put this together for you,' Woolrych said, handing a thin, buff file across the desk. 'It's mostly local intelligence stuff I got the collator to copy. Some of it comes from the Drugs Squad.'

Ronnie took it from him and scrutinized the contents, which included a photo of Kershaw. He started to read. 'Tell me about him,' he said. 'I'll read this and listen at the same time.'

'Not much to tell. He's one of many at that level. Low-level local operation running out of a health club between here and Heywood. The information we originally sent you was phoned in anonymously, so there wasn't much we could do about following it up.'

They could have worked other informants for information, Ronnie thought. That was what he would have done with the request. He could still ask them to do that now. But was it worth it? In a way it felt like a waste of time coming out here in person. He looked up from the file and stared out of the window, not seeing anything but his thoughts.

'Is there any reason why you are chasing this up?' Woolrych asked, as if reading them. 'I mean – why you *personally* are chasing it up. The info seemed snide to us.'

'Snide?'

'False. A stitch-up job. That's why we haven't really done anything with it. We didn't expect the Deputy SIO to be interested.'

Was there a reason he was interested? It was Sunday, a dead day – most of the squad was resting. He knew that ultimately the only way to get a response if GMP weren't playing the game was by pulling rank in person. That was a good enough reason. Nevertheless, he did have a vague, nagging hunch, something that had started with Steve Fleming showing relief at the name Thomas Myers. That relief had ruled out Myers before Fleming had even remembered who Myers was. Had Fleming ruled out other leads like that? That was the question he was asking himself. That was why he had started looking at other dead lines. But he didn't want to tell anyone about that just yet, let alone a stranger from GMP.

'Just being sure,' he said, smiling. 'Go on, please. Tell me what you know.'

'Kershaw works with a man called Micky Rawson. They get their supply from Raheesh Khan. At least, that's what we're told. No one has ever pinned anything on Khan, of course. Or Rawson. On paper they're clean. Rawson has a military background—'

'Is Khan big time?'

'Top drawer. A large-scale importer, direct from Pakistan and Afghanistan. Strictly off limits for us. NCS territory. He's a pillar of the local community in Altrincham. He's another reason we thought the information was snide. Khan is a very wealthy, very powerful, very dangerous man. He spends a fortune making sure everything around him is bleached white. He wouldn't tolerate anyone connected to him stabbing a pregnant Asian woman to death during a botched burglary.'

'If that's what it was.'

'Whatever it was. If people linked to Khan were in on it they would have vanished by now. It's happened before.'

Ronnie looked down at the file again.

'Rawson has no convictions,' Woolrych said. 'So he really is clean. Kershaw has a long string of them, going back to your patch when he was a kid.'

'I see that,' Ronnie said, reading the list of convictions. 'He started out in Yorkshire then moved.' Most were for minor offences, but he had also done time for supplying – three short stretches, the last for eighteen months in 1996–7. 'He owns a health club?' he asked.

'Khan owns it. Kershaw manages it. Rawson is his assistant. That's the official story. Khan would claim not to know anything about Kershaw's past, I assume.' He laughed a little. 'Khan is so dug in they invite him to open things – you know, like he's some kind of local dignitary.'

As Ronnie read on, Woolrych continued talking, mostly about Khan. Ronnie tuned out and concentrated on the paperwork. Khan didn't really interest him. He read down the list of aliases used by Kershaw, then moved on to his known associates. The list was long. His eyes scanned for any names he knew. He had got almost to the end before he came across the name Ian Whitfield.

'Ian Whitfield,' he said, aloud, silencing Woolrych, then looking up at him.

Woolrych shrugged. 'Who is it? Someone we've listed as an associate?'

'Yes. Can I find out more about him? An Ian Whitfield came up on the inquiry – as a trace, in fact, from the scene.'

Whitfield was one of the men who had worked for the removal company that had moved Fleming from London. Fleming had been asked about Whitfield, too, Ronnie recalled. The response had been the same as when asked about Myers. He had ruled him out at once.

Woolrych took the folder back and looked for the name. 'You can check him from the details here,' he said. 'What does your Whitfield have previous for? You could get an ID that way. This one has previous for theft and assault. Last conviction in November nineteen ninety-nine. Is that your guy?'

'He has precons, but I don't recall what,' Ronnie said. 'I'd have to check.' He looked out of the window again, then took a sip of the coffee. The Ian Whitfield who had moved the Flemings still hadn't been spoken to. It could be a coincidence, of course, that his name arose in connection with a Manchester drugs dealer about whom there had been a fairly insignificant piece of low-level intelligence. That's what Woolrych would think. But if it *was* the same Ian Whitfield then it was an interesting coincidence. Too interesting to ignore. Certainly worth upping the ante on finding Whitfield. 'What's his connection to Kershaw?' he asked.

Woolrych looked at the paperwork again. 'He's related,' he said. 'Cousin on the mother's side. That's what it says here.' He looked up. 'And he occasionally does donkey work for Kershaw. Running small quantities of Class B from Holland, we think. Test buys. That sort of thing.'

32

Brian Johnson lived with his parents in Lightcliffe, so it didn't take Karen long to drive there. The day felt better now. Warm and calm, the sky very blue, the trees a kind of washed-out green. She drove with the windows down, enjoying the heat. She hadn't even noticed the weather until Ronnie had called.

Johnson had previously told the inquiry he was available for interview at any time, but she called anyway to warn him she was coming. It was a Sunday, after all. The Lord's day. Johnson was a history student at Leeds University, but he was on holiday.

The house, when she got there, turned out to be a large Edwardian semi, in a quiet cul-de-sac of similar properties. Solid, middle-class appearance. She walked up the path (borders full of neatly tended flowers and shrubs, a small but flawless lawn) and knocked on the door. She felt awake, alert, free of the dragging sensation that had infected her all morning. All week, even. She got a little kick out of pushing the knowledge that she would see Ronnie later – with all the excitement it raised in her – to the back of her mind. Not that the pleasure was unalloyed; if things were starting again with Ronnie then she was going to have to be honest with Pete very soon.

Johnson himself opened the door to her.

'DC Sharpe,' she said, not bothering to show her ID. 'Are you Brian Johnson?'

'Yes.' He smiled feebly. He seemed puzzled by her presence.

'I called you fifteen minutes ago,' she said.

He frowned, as if remembering. 'Of course. Please come in.'

She followed him into a living room, quickly noting the details: a sofa, two chairs, green painted walls, a grandfather clock, a piano, scores of pictures on the walls of all shapes and sizes, but all about the same thing (steam railways), an intricate scale model of the *Flying Scotsman* on the mantelpiece (gas fire replacing the hearth, big mirror on the chimney breast), another couple of scale models on the window-sill, net curtains across the windows, heavy drapes, no TV. No crucifix in sight.

'My parents are out at church,' he said. 'Please sit down.'

She sat on one of the single chairs, sinking too far into it and having to move to the very edge of it to stay upright. Why wasn't he with them at church? she wondered. He sat on the sofa.

'Are you the one interested in trains?' she asked, pointing to the model above the gas fire.

He looked embarrassed. 'No. That's my father. Would you like a coffee?'

'No. Thanks. I'm very sorry to bother you again, Brian. I know you already spoke to a colleague.'

He had been given a more comprehensive interview than the family members. A DS had spoken to him and pressed for an alibi on day one. At the time of the attack he had been in Sainsbury's, shopping, he said. No one had verified that yet because he wasn't a priority line.

'I know this must be a trying time for you,' she continued.

He stood up abruptly, looking anxious. 'No. Not particularly. Not trying. Things happen. Things like this.' He spoke in short, quick sentences, chopping at the words. She frowned, not understanding his attitude. 'We endure it,' he continued. 'Caroline and I will survive. Survive and move on.'

She nodded, hoping she looked sympathetic. 'Of course,' she said. 'And she's in very good hands.'

He paced in front of her. He wasn't dressed like a student, she thought. Far too neat. His face was clean-shaven and he had on what she would consider a 'work' shirt, with a starched collar, top button undone, no tie. The shirt was beautifully pressed; not a crease in sight. She suppressed the desire to ask if he had done it himself. 'Work' trousers, too – the bottom half of a suit perhaps, And shiny, black shoes. No jewellery, including no (visible) religious jewellery. His hair was neatly trimmed and – if she wasn't mistaken – combed. What youth his age combed his hair these days? Deborah Hemmings had told her he was attractive (and she could see that he was well built, especially in the upper body where there was evidence of some weight-training), but she couldn't see anything appealing in him.

He turned to face her. 'Everything happens for a purpose,' he said. *Right*, she thought. *Now we're coming to it.* 'We can live through these things if we have faith.'

She nodded again, waiting for him to stop and sit down. He didn't. 'Faith in the purpose?' she asked, politely.

'Faith in God.'

'I see.'

She saw him heave his shoulders up, as if he had finally said something he had been frightened to say to her. He sat down heavily and let out a long breath of air. 'I am praying for Caroline,' he said. 'I pray for her every hour.' He looked suddenly tearful.

Was this what he had been like with Caroline? Karen could understand Debs's confusion as to why they were together. 'Are you going to see Caroline?' she asked him, trying to be gentle, to understand. Caroline hadn't asked for him. But she hadn't asked for anyone yet.

He shook his head. 'I can't go. Not yet.'

'How long have you two been together?'

'A year and a half.'

A year and a half, and he still hadn't visited her in hospital.

'Do you know anyone who might have disliked Caroline?'

The question seemed to agitate him. He shifted from side to side in the chair, but didn't answer.

'That's why I'm here,' she explained. 'We have to try to work out why this happened.'

'It happened for a purpose.' He stood up again, voice slightly raised. 'Everything has a purpose.'

'Yes. But we need to find out who did it before we can work out why—'

'I don't know anyone who disliked Caroline. She was liked by everybody. As far as I am aware, that is. As far as I knew her.'

'You knew her very well, I assume?'

He smiled superciliously. 'Not quite, officer. I knew a side of her. I knew the woman who lived and worked in Halifax. The woman I met a year and a half ago.'

She was lost now. What was he talking about?

He sat down again, apparently calmer. 'However, there was another side to her,' he said.

'Another side?'

'She was deceitful in many ways. Very deceitful.' She noted the peculiar use of the past tense, as if Caroline had died. 'Do you know about her magazine photos?' he asked.

Was that what he was going on about? 'Yes. I've seen them,' she said. 'She looks very beautiful. It's a terrible, terrible thing that—'

'She looks like a slut!' He spat the words out suddenly. She stared at him, taken aback. Before she could think how to respond, he stood up again and walked over to the piano.

'She told no one she was doing that,' he said. 'So you see, I didn't know her that well. Nor did her family. None of us – except *Debs*, of course.' He made no effort to disguise his contempt for Debs. 'None of us who loved her had a clue what she was doing. And in *that* world, in the world that produced those photos, Caroline might have known any number of people who despised her. There is hatred of women written all over those photos.' He pressed at one of the piano keys, sounding a single, repeated, staccato note. The rage seeping out of him was like heat. But that wasn't necessarily unusual. Not as a response to this kind of trauma. She had felt rage herself, as she had looked at Caroline's hacked-up face. But he hadn't seen that yet.

'You think she was wrong to do the photoshoot?' she asked.

'It was sinful,' he replied evenly, not turning from the piano.

'You think that might be why this has happened?'

'Perhaps.' He turned his head down, lowering his voice. '*That* Caroline is certainly dead now – the Caroline we didn't know. The one who took her clothes off in cheap commercial magazines. That won't happen again, at least. The attack has certainly served that purpose, thank God.'

She was so dumbstruck she could do nothing but stare at his back. She could feel the hairs on her neck standing on end.

'But I will stick by her,' he said. '*That* Caroline was never the one I knew anyway.'

Karen stood up. From seeming merely strange he had slid seamlessly into something thoroughly frightening. Alarm bells were ringing now.

'Is that all?' he asked her, turning from the piano. 'Is that all you wanted to ask me?' She saw him move the sleeve of his shirt across his eyes, trying to disguise the action. She saw now that his face was wet. He had been crying as he was speaking and she hadn't noticed.

'If it's allright with you,' she said, 'I'd just like to have a look at your bedroom.'

He stood up straight, surprised.

'Just a routine thing,' she said.

For a moment she thought he might refuse. But he was too controlled for that. 'Of course,' he said. 'I'll show you.'

She followed him up a set of stairs and waited for him to open the door to a room in the rear of the building.

He stood for a moment beside the door, hand on the handle.

Then he turned abruptly. 'Do you believe in Jesus, officer?'

She took a step back and looked into his eyes. 'I don't believe in anything,' she said.

He nodded, as if that were what he had expected. 'In that case, you might not really understand what you are about to see.' He opened the door and stepped in ahead of her. She stepped quickly after him and looked.

He was right.

He has conversations with God. That was what Debs had told her. Now she saw the significance of it.

The room was tiny, with just enough space for a single bed and a small study desk and chair. In that sense it was normal. But that was it. Around the four walls almost every inch of space was taken up with pictures and photographs. All of them were of Caroline. Some of them were drawn (by him?), with small symbols like angels or crosses circling her head. Others had things written across them. 'The Lord saves' was one scribbled message she could read. There was even the two-page spread from *Marie Claire* with something daubed across it in black ink.

Karen stepped further into the room, her skin prickling. He had been so determined to cover every inch of wall space that many pictures were copies. One – of Caroline standing in a park somewhere, hand in hand with him – had been copied perhaps twenty times and tacked up. She could barely believe it. There was hardly an inch of wall space left uncovered.

Her eyes came down, following the smell her nose was picking up, past the carefully made bed and the writing desk. Then over to the furthest corner of the room. On a small stool there was a collection of candles, three or four still burning. Above them on the wall an enlarged image of Caroline's face, as it had been. And above that a crucifix.

She took a deep breath and looked at him. He was staring at her, his eyes quite dry now, the expression in them not one of fear, but some kind of aggression. Standing so close to him, Karen felt unsafe. She stepped back to the door.

'Does Caroline know about this?' she asked.

He shook his head. 'She wouldn't understand.'

'No.'

He looked around the walls, a smile coming to his lips, a different light in his eyes, proud of it all. 'I told you I was praying for her,' he said. 'This is where I do it.'

She waited until his eyes came back to her, then slowly, carefully, she said, 'Did anyone speak to you about elimination DNA samples, Brian?'

He frowned at her. 'What do you mean?'

'It's routine,' she said. 'We take blood samples from everyone Caroline knew, so that we can eliminate them from swabs we took from Caroline's hands.'

'You want a blood sample from me?' He almost smiled. 'That's out of the question.'

33

Ronnie had a cleaner – Sophia, a Pole – who came to the Dewsbury house every Monday morning. Which meant that by late afternoon on Sunday the place was a tip. His normal approach to keeping it tidy during the week was not to bother. He didn't even wash his dishes, but either stacked them into the dishwasher or just left them for Sophia. Now he had to get back from Rochdale in time to tidy the place before Karen arrived. He had to get some food, too – something to cook for her. If they got that far.

He was too late for the supermarkets so he went out to a corner shop and looked for ingredients that might be easily turned into something edible. In the tiny shop, bent wire basket in hand, his eyes moved over the selection of wilting 'fresh' vegetables; most of them were rotting, right there, fruit flies floating around all over the place. This is why people shop in supermarkets, he thought.

He moved on to the tinned section and selected two tins of ratatouille, two tins of chick peas and a box of couscous. He could mix the tins together and add some curry powder, call it couscous sauce. That would do. It even sounded slightly exotic, if not comical – couscous in Dewsbury. He already had some frozen Walls sausages to go with it. And there was plenty of wine. Anyway, they weren't really interested in the food.

They didn't eat any of it. He opened his front door to her just after six. She was wearing a summer dress that came to just above her knees. It was pastel-coloured, light and cotton, something he just had time to see as she stepped quickly up to embrace him. His arms closed around her and he could feel the thin dress slipping across her back, her bare skin beneath it.

He thought it would be a quick hug, to get things going again, but as he pulled away she clung on to him, her chin pressed tightly against his neck. He kept his arm in place and waited. She didn't break. She was just standing there, pressed against him, so close his nose was filled with her scent – not just a perfume smell, but also the warmth coming off her skin.

Where her arms were clasped behind his back he could feel her fingers digging into him. She was strong. Much stronger than she looked. He had to push back a bit to get her to let go. But then immediately her face was right next to his and there was no option but to start kissing. He turned her round, in his arms, backing her against the hall wall and keeping his mouth on hers, then tried to find the door with his foot.

The way she kissed was intense, full-on, no room for anything else in her consciousness. He could remember that – the focus she brought to bear on him, everything immediate, without any kind of build-up.

He found the door with his foot and kicked it shut. It slammed and she broke from him at once. She was grinning at him, looking relaxed, happy. They stared at each other then began to laugh at the same time.

'So *this* is your place in West Yorkshire?' She stepped away, turning her back on him and walking into the hallway as if she owned it. She was full of energy.

She strolled into his living room. She had such long legs, such a confident way of moving. Had she always been like that? He hadn't noticed, or couldn't remember. Most of time it had seemed as if she were embarrassed about her height – standing and walking in ways that would hide it. But she was standing straight now, fully occupying the space around her. She wasn't even dressed as he imagined she would dress when off duty. He followed her, trying to take his eyes off the backs of her legs. He could still feel the effects of the kiss.

She came back to him, put her arms around his neck and stood in front of him, staring at him. 'What's the carpet like?' she asked.

'The one we're standing on?'

'Is it soft enough for you?' He felt her knee pressing against his leg, rubbing it. She wanted to do it now, he realized, right here, in the front room. Thank God he had hoovered.

'It's clean enough,' he said.

She started kissing him again.

She *was* different, he thought. More confident, more direct. She was taking the lead now, and it hadn't been like that before. He tried to regain a little of the initiative by bringing his arms further down her body, feeling for her legs under the dress. But immediately her hands slipped down further and started to unbuckle his trousers. Let go, he thought. *Let* her lead it.

He took a mental breath.

They were at it for over an hour, on the carpet in his front room. Afterwards he rolled on to his back and laughed. She pushed herself against him and laughed as well.

'How old are we?' she asked, whispering into his ear.

'Younger than we were a few weeks ago?'

He worried a little about the carpet – about what Sophia would think – then laughed again just thinking about it. What did that matter?

'You were different today,' he said. He propped his head up and stared at her.

Her eyes flickered with amusement. 'In a good way or a bad way?'

'Good. More confident, happier.'

'You should have seen me earlier.'

Had she been *missing* him?

'But I'm Helen Young now,' she said.

'Maybe Helen suits you better. You seem happier as her.'

'Wasn't I happy before?'

'I didn't know you before.'

'You don't know me now.'

He looked hard at her. 'I know you well enough. People aren't that complicated. Not even you. A couple of weeks is usually enough to lose interest.' He smiled, to show her it was a joke.

'Is that right?'

'You don't agree?'

'Depends on the person,' she said. 'Depends how many secrets they have.'

'You keeping anything else from me?' He smoothed her hair away from her face.

She looked away from him. 'I'm keeping lots of things from you,' she said quietly. 'You wouldn't be lying there if you knew me properly.'

She was serious. He hoped she wasn't talking about any other relationship secrets. He had made a mental pact with himself not even to try taking the shocked, moral line again, not to ask her about Pete Bains.

They were both adults. That was her problem. His past reactions had done no good at all. He waited for her to smile again, but her mood had changed. He'd lost her already.

'The past?' he asked, guessing. But she was thinking about something else. Remembering?

'Do the scars come under that heading?' he asked, trying another tack. She had old scars on her back and thigh that he had first noticed in London.

'What heading?' She frowned at him.

'Things you don't want to tell me about.'

'The scars come from another world,' she said. 'A world I keep falling into.'

'Which world is that, then?' Already he wished he hadn't asked.

'A world where if people think you are the enemy,' she said, 'they hang you from the ceiling and use a blow-torch on you.'

MONDAY, 2 JULY

34

Colin Norton – the man who had allegedly seen a blood-spattered male resembling Akil Al-Talehi – lived in a council house on an estate in Mixenden. It was a white, working-class area, a place where life was regularly ruined for the majority by a handful of dysfunctional and violent families. Fewer than fifteen to twenty people had given the area a reputation that always seemed out of place to Karen. Nestling at the end of a steep valley, with hills, open space and woodland on all sides, it seemed incongruous to think of Mixenden as one of the Division's highest crime areas, even if most of the housing was what would be classed as low grade and public. Karen could think of worse places to live. But Mixenden always topped the Divisional league tables for household burglaries and assaults.

Racism normally went hand in hand with crime, so it was natural enough to think that Colin Norton would be one of Mixenden's racists. But Karen had already asked someone on Pete's 'skinhead' inquiry (not Pete) if they had turned up anything on Norton. They hadn't. So aside from his conviction for racially aggravated common assault two years ago, Karen knew nothing about him.

She had looked up the assault on the system. Norton had received a fine for the offence, which, though heavy for a financial penalty (at £600, his low income considered), was still a light sentence for that kind of offence. Judges were meant to give stiffer sentences for racially aggravated crimes, but rarely did. The details on OIS – the computerized information system – told her that Norton had been involved in a fight in a pub in the centre of town, had wandered out of the pub drunk and, for no apparent reason, punched a middle-aged Asian who just happened to be passing. The punch had been accompanied by the words 'fucking paki cunt', from which the prosecutor had proved a racial motivation.

Norton had told Andy Lewis that he worked at a meat-packing factory in Thornton, but that his wife had a better job, at the Halifax building society. Karen had no idea which of them would be in, but guessed one of them would be, because they had a six-year-old boy who would now be off school for the summer. She didn't mind who she met. If it was Norton's wife, that would give her the chance to get the feel of his background without him being around.

She pushed open a small, rusting garden gate and followed a short path through an overgrown lawn strewn with children's toys. The house was a good size, three-bedroom council house (owned now by Norton, he had told them) with a worn and dirty pebbledash facing. It was Norton himself who opened the door to her.

'Colin?'

'Yes?' A frown and a yawn. She had caught him early. It was nearly midday, and he was dressed in nothing but a pair of shorts. Behind him she could hear a TV.

'I'm DC Sharpe. Can I come in, please?'

He looked back. His son was standing in a further doorway, watching. A short, overweight boy with spiky blond hair. Norton didn't move. 'What's it about?' he asked.

'Just routine. About your evidence in the Caroline Philips case. Just a few more questions.'

'Have you got ID?'

She took it from her pocket, looking at him as he inspected it. Pete Bains's inquiry might not have heard of him, but he certainly looked like a skinhead; short, packed with muscle, hair so cropped it looked at first as if he were bald. She could see at least two tattoos, one on each bicep – the left one a British bulldog, the right a Yorkshire rose with the words 'Born and Bred' arching above it. He had an ugly skull – bony, large, full of asymmetrical indentations and bumps. There was more hair on his chin than on the top of his head. She looked at that instead. The statement details gave his age as twenty-nine.

'You'll have to be quick,' he told her, handing back the ID. 'My wife's at work and I'm looking after the kid. We were going out.'

'I'll be as quick as I can,' she said.

She walked after him, through a hallway and into a living room knocked through into the dining room, with a door off to the kitchen. As with the garden, there were kids' toys strewn all over the floor and furniture. The furniture consisted of two threadbare sofas with cigarette burns on the armrests. She spotted at least three ashtrays, full of used butts and ash, lying amongst the toys. The house smelled of poverty to her; a mixture of stale cigarette smoke, boiled vegetables and damp. The TV she had heard had pride of place, with everything else arranged around it. It was tuned to a day-time show along Jerry Springer lines, with couples denouncing each other in public. The volume was very loud. Since both parents were working she assumed that they chose to live this way, because they were certainly not poor in any conventional sense. She looked again at the overweight kid. He was pushing something sticky into his mouth, watching her.

'What do you want to know?' Norton asked. He lit a cigarette and sat down on one of the sofas.

She sat carefully on the other and took his statement from her briefcase. She placed the briefcase flat across her knees and the statement on top of it.

'Just a few things,' she said.

'Fire away.'

She looked at the boy. 'Do you want the child to listen?' she asked. She also wanted him to turn the TV off, but guessed there was no chance of that.

'It won't hurt him,' Norton replied. 'Besides, there's nowhere else for him to go.'

'OK.' She pretended to be looking through his statement. She heard him laugh at something on the TV show. 'Can I just ask you about why you were up in King Cross that night?' she said. She kept her voice friendly.

'I already said. I was out drinking.'

'Do you usually drink up in that part of town?' King Cross was on the edge of an area mainly populated by Asians.

He shrugged. 'We move around. The George is OK up there.'

'You were with friends?'

'Yeah. Didn't I say that before?'

'No. But maybe we didn't ask. Obviously your friends weren't with you when you saw the man covered in blood?'

'No.'

'Were you walking home by then?'

'No … yes …' For the first time he ran into a snag. She watched him thinking it through and saw at once, without a shadow of a doubt, that he was inventing.

'This was quite early,' she reminded him. 'Just after seven.'

'Yes. I think I was heading into town by then.'

'By yourself?'

'Yes.'

'How long had you been out?'

He appeared to consider that. 'Since lunch-time.'

'Drinking all that time?'

'It's not that long.'

'How much do you think you drank?'

'I don't know. I don't drink much these days. We haven't the money for it …' He seemed about to add something else, but stopped himself.

'You were sober when you saw the man?'

'Not sober. But nowhere near drunk.'

She took out her notebook and wrote that down.

'Were you intending to continue drinking?'

'No. I was coming into town to get a bus back home by then.'

'What pub had you been in at King Cross?'

He frowned suddenly. 'Why are you asking me all this? It sounds like you think I've done something wrong.'

'Just routine questions. The sort of things we need to know before we get to court. Which pub did you say it was?'

He stared at her, expression changing slowly from one of mild irritation to annoyance. '*Probably* the George.'

'And which friends were you with?'

He sat back in the chair. 'Just a few mates. Why? Why do you need to know?'

'In case they saw anything.'

'They didn't.'

'You've spoken to them since?'

'They weren't with me at the time. I told you.'

He didn't want to give their names. She turned a page of the pocket book. 'This criminal conviction you have—'

'Fuck me! I knew that would come up! I knew it!' He stood up and walked towards the child. 'That was over four years ago,' he said. 'Isn't there meant to be some kind of rehabilitation of offenders thing? Why does that always have to keep coming into it?' He stooped and took the thing the child was eating out of his hands. A doughnut, was it? 'Stop pigging yourself,' he muttered. 'You're fat enough as it is.' The child flinched and looked for a moment as if he would break into tears, then thought better of it. Norton disappeared into the kitchen. She heard a cupboard open, then a rubbish bin.

'It was a racially aggravated assault and it happened two years ago,' she said when he returned. 'If you end up as our witness in court then the defence will ask you about it. So I need to know what you are going to say.'

'That it happened when I was pissed,' he said. He sat down again. 'That's all. I was pissed. I've paid the fine.'

'Did you use the words the prosecution said you did?' She didn't want to say them in front of the kid.

'I have no idea. That was *his* evidence. I couldn't remember it happening.'

'Do you think those things, then? Was it something you *could* have said?'

He smirked. 'You mean, am I racist?'

'Are you?'

'I'm a normal white guy, like any other. I work hard to feed my family. I see things that ...' He stopped himself. 'No. I'm not racist,' he said. 'I do not consider myself to be racist. In fact, I have friends who are ...' Another pause to think. 'Coloured. I know a lot of coloured people.'

'Are you in any political parties?'

'Like what?'

'Like the Labour Party, for instance?'

'Is that an offence now?'

'No. I'm just trying to—'

'You mean like the BNP, right? Isn't that what you mean? You have me painted as a white racist because of that stupid conviction. You're just as bad as those fucking ...' Again he pulled himself short. She waited, but he didn't complete the sentence. The kid walked further into the room and stood beside his father, staring at her.

'*Are* you in any political parties?' she asked again. 'I'm not trying to be rude. I'm not accusing you of anything. I'm just trying to build a background picture.'

He shook his head. 'No politics. I work hard to keep my family. I do what I can. We both do. We live in this shit-hole and work our arses off. I've never taken hand-outs, never had help from the State. I'm a *productive* member of society. It does not cost the tax-payer a penny to keep me here. I *pay* my taxes. I even own the house. I'm not the sort of person you should be harassing. But you wouldn't know what I'm talking about. Have you ever lived on an estate like this?'

She had. Mairead had been born while she was living with Jim Martin in an estate much worse than this, in Shepherd's Bush. She didn't answer his question. 'It took you a bit of time to come in and report what you had seen,' she said. 'Any reason?'

On the TV the midday news started. Norton didn't notice.

'I told the other guy that,' he said. 'First I didn't know anything about it, so I didn't hook the two things up. You see loads of ...' He lost the word he was looking for. 'Loads of *people* up there who have been in a bit of trouble. It didn't seem important.'

'Do you know who Akil Al-Talehi is?'

He shrugged, looking away from her. 'No idea.' Another lie.

'You told my colleague you were away the day after the incident?'

'The next day. I left early for Oldham.'

'Oldham?'

She saw his expression change slightly, wishing he hadn't said that. A little bit of truth, no doubt. She had the feeling it was the only true thing he had said to her.

'How is Oldham?' she asked.

He scowled at her.

'Why did you go there?'

'To see a mate.'

'See any trouble when you were there?'

'Trouble? Like what?'

'Like race riots. That kind of thing.'

'For fuck's sake – that was a week ago.'

She nodded, wondering whether it would be worth pushing him. In the silence he tapped ash off the cigarette, letting it fall on to the carpet at his feet.

'I feel like you don't believe me,' he said. He sucked at the cigarette and blew a cloud of smoke in her direction.

She looked across at him, considering it.

'I'm not a criminal,' he said, following her eyes. 'I'm normal. Just a normal English guy who was born here. I'm proud to be English, proud to be from Yorkshire. That doesn't make me a racist.'

'Yes. Of course, Mr Norton. I'm sorry if I've given such an impression—'

Beside him the kid said something. 'Shut up, Colin,' Norton snapped. 'You're a cheeky little bastard.' The kid had the same name as his father.

On the TV the news put up footage of a police station. She thought it might be Richard Powell appealing for help finding Al-Talehi. He was meant to be doing that today. She paused and watched. But it was about Bulldog instead. It was childish, but her heart picked up a beat, thinking Ronnie might appear. Instead there was some stock footage of Steve Fleming leaving a Crown Court building she didn't recognize (maybe Isleworth?) long before the attack. Norton muttered something about Fleming. He was half watching, twisted in his seat. The reporter was saying the police were no further forward. Norton picked up a remote from amongst a pile of discarded dishes on the coffee table and switched it off. Finally.

She stood up. She wasn't going to get anything further out of him. 'That's all been very helpful,' she said. He stood with her. She stepped towards the door and heard the boy say something to her. She looked down at him, smiling, but feeling that weight inside her again. Would the kid ever get past this, growing up here, overfed, with this man as a father?

She reached out a hand and touched his head, smoothing down the spiky hair.

The child twisted away from her, as if she were about to hit him. 'She's like a dirty *paki*,' he shouted, as if playing a harmless game with another child. 'A *paki*, a *paki*, a filthy, dirty *paki* ...'

Norton stooped and brought his hand across the back of the child's head. Karen froze. The blow was so hard the child fell flat on his face. There was a moment of stunned silence, then the child began to scream.

Norton stubbed out his cigarette and looked at her. 'He hears these things at school,' he said. 'He doesn't know what they mean.'

TUESDAY, 3 JULY

35

Ronnie was slated for Bradford Crown Court all morning, waiting to give evidence on a kidnapping case he had investigated over a year before. At ten-thirty he was told he wouldn't be needed before lunch, so he walked over to The Tyrls to get a snack and a change of scene.

He ordered a pasty and sat at a table near the windows, eating without much enthusiasm, eyes squinting against the bright sunlight, wishing he'd picked a table in the shade. He was tired, stressed and irritable. The tiredness made his eyes photosensitive – though this morning they were much worse than normal. He even had a headache.

Early that morning, before leaving for court, he had met David Riggs and offloaded his pessimism about Bulldog. Riggs had felt the same, but his solution was just to keep plugging away, teasing out the detail. Meanwhile Ronnie still had a third of his squad following lines in London that were getting nowhere.

'Are you sure Fleming is being straight with us?' Riggs had asked, not for the first time. Like Ronnie, Riggs didn't like Steve Fleming because he had run across him as a lawyer and they hadn't got on. That wasn't a good reason to suspect him of anything, though, and in the beginning Ronnie had just ignored Riggs's comments, but now they chimed with his own thoughts, forcing him to re-think the issue. Was it possible Fleming was holding out on them? The idea seemed absurd, on the face of it. But was it worth pushing Fleming a bit, just to be sure?

His mobile rang. It was DS Hepworth calling to tell him that they had tracked down Ahmed Ibrahim, the builder with a robbery conviction. They had been looking for him since Saturday in order to explore the link to Akil Al-Talehi (wanted both by Bulldog and Scythe now), but had drawn a blank at his home address. Hepworth told him that uniformed officers at Bradford had been called to a disturbance in a street off Great Horton Lane and had discovered Ibrahim in the premises. They were still there now and wanted to know whether he should be arrested.

'Great Horton Lane?' Ronnie swivelled in his seat. The canteen in Bradford Central was on the top floor and had a good view of Bradford. He could see the beginning of Great Horton Lane from where he was.

'I'm almost there,' he said. 'Give me the details and I'll go myself.'

There were two uniformed cars outside the place as he pulled up, one with blue lights still flashing. The house was a terrace on a street not far from the university. The front door was open – hanging off the hinges, in fact – and Ronnie could hear raised voices from inside. A small crowd had gathered on the kerb opposite, presumably neighbours. They were all Asian.

Ronnie walked through a narrow hallway, calling out to alert them he was coming. A uniformed PC stepped out of a door ahead of him. He was a large white officer with closely cropped hair, hat off. He looked calm, in control, speaking into his shoulder radio as Ronnie arrived. Ronnie introduced himself and looked past the man into the living room. Someone through there was still shouting, but not in a language he could understand.

'PC Bowman, sir,' the officer said, introducing himself.

'What have you got?' Ronnie asked quietly.

'Two males screaming at each other in Urdu. PC Malik is through there, trying to work out what's going on. The front door has been kicked in – that's why we got the call. We came here and found them at each other, rolling around on the floor. We pulled them apart and separated them. The one in there, the one you can hear, gave his name as Ahmed Ibrahim. The other is upstairs with Sergeant Purley. He won't give any details, won't say anything. We're trying to get Ibrahim to tell us who he is, but he's not saying. Neither of them wants to make a complaint about the other, so we don't know what they were fighting about.'

Ronnie nodded and stepped past him into the living room.

The place was in disarray. Chairs were overturned, the coffee table was broken, pictures were hanging off the walls. In the middle of the floor a large suitcase full of papers was lying open, contents scattered across the carpet. Ronnie could see thick piles of fliers bound together with elastic bands. There were pictures of raised, clenched fists and Islamic symbols in bright red, but the text was in Urdu.

On a chair in the corner of the room Ahmed Ibrahim was sitting with his hands cuffed behind his back, his face red with excitement and anger. A large Asian officer was standing, legs apart, in front of him. It looked as if Ibrahim had already been arrested.

Ronnie turned back to PC Bowman, who had come in behind him. 'Whose are the premises?' he asked.

'According to the neighbours, a man called Mohammed Shabir. We're trying to locate him. Ibrahim says Shabir is an uncle who works at the university.'

Ibrahim started to shout again, directing his wrath at the PC standing in front of him. Ronnie stepped closer. Malik looked unconcerned by the abuse. He had his arms folded and was standing in such a way as to box Ibrahim in.

'Hello, Ahmed,' Ronnie said to Ibrahim. 'Do you remember me?'

Ibrahim stared at him. Clearly not.

'Ronnie Shepherd. We had you in Killingbeck a couple of weeks ago, in connection with the Fleming murder.'

Ibrahim uttered a stream of hissing, guttural words, not loud, but obviously not polite. PC Malik started to translate.

'There's no need,' Ronnie said. 'I get the picture. Have you arrested him already?'

'We had to. He was on his way out otherwise.'

'What's he arrested for?'

'Section forty-seven. The one upstairs is pretty roughed-up.'

'But won't say anything?'

'No. But we saw them fighting as we came in. We're not sure yet whether either of them has permission to be in here. We're waiting for the householder to be found.'

That produced a torrent of invective from Ibrahim. Malik smiled at him, but then he had the stature for controlling people. Ibrahim was about half his size.

'He won't tell us what they were fighting about,' Malik said to Ronnie. 'But look at this.' He stooped and picked up a bundle of fliers from the floor at his feet. 'These are leaflets calling for a jihad against corrupt, western immorality,' he said. 'Most of them are directed at pornography and women. Pornography includes walking around in western clothes, without a veil.' He seemed to find that amusing. As if anyone who could create, print and distribute such rubbish had to be both harmless and insane.

'We should seize all this,' Ronnie said.

'They're not mine,' Ibrahim said. 'They have nothing to do with me.'

'Speaks good English,' PC Malik commented. 'When it suits.'

'This is my uncle's house. I have permission to be here.'

'If that's true you might be released,' Malik said. 'But we need to find your uncle first. Then find out why you were having a tussle with the gentleman upstairs.'

Ibrahim turned away from him.

'I need him at Killingbeck,' Ronnie said, then turned to him. 'If you're released will you come straight to Killingbeck, Mr Ibrahim?'

'Fuck you.' He didn't look at Ronnie.

'I'll have to re-arrest you if you don't.'

'Fuck you.'

Ronnie left them and walked through the mess to where Bowman was standing at the door. 'I'll have a look at the one upstairs,' he said.

He walked up the stairs and found two more officers, one a sergeant. He was squatting on the landing, searching through a cardboard box which looked to be filled with more of the same leaflets Ronnie had seen downstairs. Ronnie introduced himself and was shown into a bedroom.

Inside, a short Asian man was sat on the edge of a neatly made bed, crouched over, hands to his face. A considerable amount of blood was running out of his nose. Another officer was squatting in front of him, holding a towel to his face, trying to staunch the bleeding. Both looked up as Ronnie entered. Ronnie recognized the Asian at once. He had looked at mugshots of him only that morning. The photos had shown a bearded man and the man in front of him was clean-shaven, but the eyes were distinctive. Wide staring eyes, so bulbous he must surely suffer from a thyroid problem. Ronnie felt his mood lift. He nodded to the constable, then stepped back out and pulled the sergeant aside.

'That's Akil Al-Talehi,' he said. 'He's wanted at Halifax for stabbing a girl in the mouth.'

36

Karen awoke feeling jittery, as if she had already drunk too many coffees. She looked around and realized she was on the sofa in the living room, flat out. The door was closed and there was an empty wine glass on the floor beside her. She put her hand to her head and remembered.

To avoid another argument over why she wanted to sleep in the spare room she had tried sleeping with Pete, but it hadn't worked. Long after he was snoring she lay awake, eyes wide, staring at the ceiling, the same images churning through her brain. So she had got up and poured herself a glass of wine, then come through here to lie on the sofa. That had been at three in the morning. She looked at the clock. Eleven-thirty. She had slept in.

Through the closed door she could hear Pete and Mairead chatting in the kitchen. She pushed herself off the sofa, opened the door and stood in the hallway for a while, listening to them. They sounded happy. She walked through.

'Hey, Mum,' Mairead said. 'You're up early.' She sniggered and Pete laughed.

Karen didn't get it. 'A joke?' she asked.

Mairead ignored her. She was sitting at the kitchen table, eating something off a plate.

'No joke,' Pete said. 'We didn't expect you up. Wasn't that what you said last night, that you had a late start?'

'Not this late. I slept in. What's funny about that?'

He looked blankly at her, as if he hadn't laughed at all. 'Nothing,' he said. 'Why?'

'Lighten up, Mum,' Mairead instructed her. 'We're having fun here. Pete was telling me about his father trying to fix their car.' She laughed again, thinking about it.

Karen sat down at the table and rubbed her eyes.

'You look tired,' Pete said. 'You OK?' No mention of her transfer from his bed. Not in front of Mairead.

'I'm worn out,' she said.

'You're taking me to Manny's tomorrow, Mum. Remember?' Mairead said.

'Manny' was Pete's dad, Maninder. Mairead got on well with Pete's parents, as if they were her grandparents, which was exactly how they treated her. Often they had her over for a whole week at a time during the school holidays, usually with Pete's niece, Prem, who was the same age. They were nice old people, Karen thought, but they had the same issues as their son. Mairead was as much a form of therapy for them as she was for Pete. Their new little 'Millie', to replace the drowned original.

She rested her head in her hands and closed her eyes. She felt disgusting just thinking these thoughts. Why was she being such a bitch?

'You remember?' Mairead asked her again. 'Manny's. Tomorrow. Party. Yes?' Speaking to her as if she were a kid.

'Yes. I remember,' Karen said. It was Prem's birthday and they were having a party out on the lawn. A whole troop of kids was coming over, then a few were staying for the weekend, including Mairead and Prem.

Before Alexia had appeared Mairead had been 'best friends' with Prem. Prem was Mairead's age and went to the same school. When Mairead had switched schools to start there early in 2000, Prem had befriended and looked after her. It was an all girls' school with a very high ethnic mix. Pete had persuaded her to send Mairead there because it wasn't far away and because he thought there was value in Mairead being exposed to 'other cultures'. But for the first time in her life Mairead had found herself in an ethnic minority and she hated the school. If it hadn't been for Prem she wouldn't have stayed. So much for Pete's multicultural experiments.

'I'll cook breakfast for you,' Pete said to her. 'You want it now, or you want to wait a bit?'

'I don't want it at all.'

She drove out to Brian Johnson's place feeling as if she had a stone in her gut. Things had to come to a head with Pete, soon, but the thought of hurting him so badly filled her with dread. Wednesday tomorrow, she thought. She had to keep reminding herself. Wednesday was when she had next arranged to see Ronnie. She had to force herself to speak to Pete before then. Running away from it would solve nothing.

She sat on the edge of the same chair she had used on Sunday, in the same front room with the train models. Johnson sat opposite her again, but this time his mother was in. She sat on the second chair and watched timidly. She was a small, wrinkled woman with grey hair and a frumpy dress. She looked too old to be his mother. If she was in her mid-sixties, as Karen guessed, then she would have given birth to Brian when she was over forty. Either that or she had aged very badly.

When Karen had arrived she had opened the door to her. She was wearing a linen apron then, dusted with flour. 'Sorry,' she had said. 'I'm just baking.' She had a small, frightened voice. Karen wondered what the father looked like. The apron had come off as she led Karen into the front room.

'Brian is upstairs,' she had said. 'Studying.' She went to get him.

The house was filled with the smell of freshly baked bread. Karen noticed she was the only one with shoes on. Brian was in his socks and his mother wore slippers. It was all very domestic and normal. Aside from the freaky shrine upstairs.

'It's just a couple of follow-up questions,' Karen explained.

Brian didn't say anything. He looked bothered by his mother's presence.

'They're questions for Brian really, Mrs Johnson,' Karen said. 'There's no need for you to be here.'

Mrs Johnson looked unsure about that.

'Leave us alone, Mother,' Brian said stiffly. 'This is all routine. There's nothing to worry about. That's right, isn't it, officer?'

Karen nodded. 'All routine,' she said.

His mother stood reluctantly.

Richard Powell didn't know she was here. She had written up her visit from Sunday, along with her suspicions, and left it on his desk, along with a recommendation that Johnson be arrested, so that a blood sample could be obtained to run a DNA comparison (since he wasn't giving his consent). This morning Powell had been out of the office, but he had left a note in her tray making clear that Johnson was not to be arrested. He hadn't been impressed by her arguments. In fact, he hadn't even bothered responding to them. 'Insufficient grounds', he had written. But Karen wasn't happy with that. The analysis of the trace from under Caroline's fingernails had been delayed, apparently, so as far as Karen was concerned everything was still wide open; all lines to be followed up.

'You said on Sunday that a blood sample was out of the question,' she said, once his mother had gone. 'But are you clear why we need one?'

'I don't care why you need one. You can't have one.'

That was clear, then. 'Is there any reason why?'

'I have religious beliefs which preclude the giving of blood.'

She had guessed that would be the answer. 'In that case,' she said, 'would you consent to a saliva sample, or a plucked hair sample?'

He screwed his face up and shifted nervously on the chair. He didn't like the sound of that. 'Why do you want a sample from me?' he asked. 'I don't see how it would help.'

'It's not because you're under suspicion,' she lied. 'It's so that we know which traces are yours and which are not. That's all. To allow us to focus on the right traces.'

He stood up and ran a hand through his hair, obviously worried about something. Again he walked over to the piano. As he moved, Karen tried to scrutinize his body more carefully, looking for signs of healing scratch marks. He was dressed more casually today (presumably the clothes on Sunday had been his Sunday best), but not casually enough for her to see his arms. He wore a chequered cotton shirt, with the sleeves buttoned, the collar open. Karen couldn't see any sign that he had been scratched.

'But I was told she scratched her attacker,' he said. He stood by the piano again, leaning over it with his back to her.

'That's right. We have her attacker's blood from under her fingernails.'

'So why would it help to have a sample from me? You already know that it's not my blood there, don't you?'

'There might be more than the attacker's blood there. There might be traces from yourself under her nails, too ...'

He shook his head vigorously, turning to face her, so vigorously that a lock of his hair fell across his eyes. 'No. That's out of the question. Why would bits of me be under her fingernails? We've done nothing that would make that happen.' He brushed the hair from his eyes impatiently, looking suddenly effete, then took a comb from his back pocket and ran it quickly over his head. When he had finished he saw her watching and coloured suddenly, as if caught out doing something he was ashamed of. He placed the comb aside nervously, on top of the piano. 'I don't like it,' he said. 'It makes me uneasy.'

'It's routine,' she said again.

'It makes me feel accused,' he said. 'As if I'm under suspicion. I think I would need to speak to a solicitor about it.'

That's right, she thought. You do that. The hospital had reported that he *still* had not been out to see Caroline.

She stood up and walked over to the piano, making an effort to appear casual.

'That shouldn't be necessary,' she said, smiling. He moved out of her way, frowning at her, wondering where she was headed in the room. 'You've nothing to worry about,' she said. 'As far as we're concerned, you're a victim here, too.'

For some reason that made him tut and walk away from her, irritated. She waited until his back was completely turned then reached out and pocketed the comb from the top of the piano.

37

'Have you been to see Brian Johnson again?' Powell asked her.

'Yes,' Karen said. 'I was with him only half an hour ago.'

'I asked you to check out Al-Talehi's alibi witness at two. They've been waiting an hour for you.'

'I'll do that next. Johnson was more important. I had to get to him before—'

'He's complained about you. He says you're harassing him.'

That was quick. 'We should all be harassing him. We should be looking at Johnson, not Al-Talehi.'

'I know what you think, Karen.' Powell stood up and closed his office door again. Another paternal chat? 'But I cannot arrest the victim's boyfriend just because he is some kind of religious maniac.'

'Isn't that what you've done with Al-Talehi?'

'No. We have a witness who says Al-Talehi was near the scene at the time, covered in blood. His religion has nothing to do with it.'

Al-Talehi was in the cells now. But someone had already leaked that information to the outside world, resulting in a crowd of around fifty 'citizens' gathering outside the station, baying for 'justice'; all white, all male, all looking like candidates for the attentions of the force 'skinhead squad'. Powell's nerves were frayed. He had been told there could be a further forty-eight hour delay on analysing the traces from beneath Caroline's fingernails.

'I asked you to check out Johnson,' Powell said, sighing, trying to be patient with her. 'You did that on Sunday. Thank you. Now you can forget about him and interview Al-Talehi's alibi witness. Can you do that?'

'Brian Johnson told me it was a blessing that Caroline was attacked.'

'I know. I read your report yesterday. But we have to be careful,

Karen. Technically Johnson is a victim. And Colin Norton does not say that someone fitting Brian Johnson's description was near the scene covered in blood.'

'Colin Norton is useless.' She had already told him all about Norton.

'Not completely useless,' Powell said. He looked uncomfortable about it. 'He's just not the best witness we could hope for.'

'The lawyers won't run with him. Not with that conviction.'

'I might agree with you, but let's see what the DNA result on Al-Talehi says first.'

She sat down in the chair opposite him. 'You might not like this,' she said. He was frowning at her now, waiting to see what she would come up with. She struggled to take a clear plastic zip-lock bag from her jacket pocket – the thing she had actually come in here to give him – but it wouldn't come out. She stood, took her jacket off, then sat and tried again. She got it out and placed it on the desk in front of him.

He stared at her without touching it. 'What is it?' he asked.

'It's Johnson's comb,' she said. She had transferred it to the bag once out of his house. 'It has his hairs on it. We can get his DNA from it.'

She watched his face grow crimson. He looked as if he were about to explode. He stared out of the window, then sat back in the chair and cleared his throat for a good minute. She waited. He was too angry even to speak.

'He doesn't know I took it,' she said, when the silence became uncomfortable.

'You stole it, in other words?' He cleared his throat again.

'Seized it. As evidence.'

He nodded, as if he had expected her to say something that irrelevant, then pulled the chair forward and leaned across the desk towards her. 'When you did this,' he started, 'when you stole this man's comb, what did you expect to happen?' He was speaking very slowly, very quietly, as if she would not be able to understand if he went faster.

'I wanted to try to persuade you to do a comparison. He won't consent, which in itself is suspicious, and you thought we had no grounds to arrest him. This gets round those problems.'

'He is her boyfriend. His DNA will be all over Caroline.'

'But we have blood from under her fingernails. If we get a match to that then he has to explain it. Even if he is her boyfriend his blood shouldn't be under her nails.'

He nodded, thinking it through despite his annoyance. 'Did you see scratches on him?' he asked.

'No. But I only saw his face and hands.'

He raised his eyebrows. 'I don't know why I'm even thinking about it,' he said. 'Even if we can get a profile from it, it's an illegal sample.'

'I think it's legal. I think I had grounds—'

'Did you tell him you took it?'

'No. If I had said anything—'

'Then it's illegal. Forget the grounds. You have no power to take secret samples.'

'But if we get a positive match then we could think of a legitimate reason to pull him in and get a new sample.'

'And what do we do with this one?' He stood up, sighing. She opened her mouth to reply but he held up a hand. 'Don't tell me. I don't want your answer to that.' She shut her mouth. 'It was a rhetorical question, Karen. To use a new legal sample we would have to get everyone who knew about this illegal one – including the scientists who examined it – to lie under oath.' He bent down and looked at her face. 'That doesn't happen these days. You *do* realize that?'

She looked at the desk, not saying anything. He was right. She had fucked things up. What had she been thinking? She knew as well as he that there were no legal grounds to back up what she had done. That wasn't like her, wasn't the way she normally operated. Usually she was careful. She placed her hand to her chest and could feel her heart beating too fast. Since seeing Ronnie she had thought she was OK. But something was happening still, out of sight.

Was it the worry about Pete that was getting to her? Or just the horror – the dead and mutilated women they were forcing her to deal with, the distraught kids? Her body was reacting physically as if she were frightened of something, overdosed on adrenalin. She took a deep breath.

Powell paced the tiny room behind her, then came back to the desk and sat down again. 'We have CPS lawyers in this very police station who have to review the evidence in each and every case, independently, before I get *permission* to charge anyone. One of them has *already* told us we haven't enough to keep Al-Talehi without a positive DNA match. But the lab tell me they're working to a four-day delay on our analysis. That's the world we're working in. And you want to try to direct a line of enquiry on the basis of an illegally obtained sample? How long have you been a detective? You realize what you've done, don't you? If – on the off-chance – this Brian Johnson ever does turn out to be a suspect, you have just ruined our chances of using DNA against him.' He let that sink in. When she didn't respond he said, 'Unless I forget this was ever shown to me.' He took a pen from the desk and pushed the bag back towards her. 'I didn't see it,' he said. 'You didn't take it. It doesn't exist. It's as simple as that.'

'But I think he might have—' she started.

He held his hand up again. 'Please just listen,' he said. He waited until he was sure she was listening. 'I'm *very* worried about you, Karen,' he said. 'I think you are losing your perspective. I'm this far,' he held up his thumb and forefinger about a centimetre apart, 'from telling you to take some leave.'

'The thing I need is—'

'Or worse. Be quiet and listen.' He waited again. 'This is what I want you to do. Please listen carefully. We have already interviewed Al-Talehi once. I stopped the interview because he clearly has a mental problem. He did nothing but rant at us throughout. Not much of it made rational sense. He needs an Appropriate Adult and a psychiatric assessment. That's what we're waiting for now. But already what he has said makes it look very much like Andy Lewis might be right, that he might have the psychological motive.'

'I thought Al-Talehi gave you an alibi?'

'He did. But he also said some very choice things about women, western women in particular. We can make a motive out of it.'

'But the descriptions don't even match. Al-Talehi has a thick, black beard. He wears Arab robes. How could a witness have missed that?'

Powell nodded. 'The beard is shaved. He has only stubble now. The robes aren't what he always wears. But you're right. Al-Talehi is quite distinctive. It might or might not be him. I don't know. But I don't want to let him go until we have the DNA back. That might happen today. At the latest tomorrow. Meanwhile, if we let him out he'll vanish. That is why – amongst other reasons – I tasked you,' he looked at the wall clock, 'over two hours ago to interview the woman he says he was with on the eighth of June. She has been waiting for you for over an hour. *That* is what I want you to do. *That* is what I *asked* you to do.' He stood up abruptly and opened the door to the office. 'Please let me know within the next half-hour if Al-Talehi has an alibi.'

She left his office and walked through the CID room, not meeting the eyes of any of the detectives who looked up at her. She felt as if she had just been in the headmaster's office. She felt stupid. Outside, through the open windows, she could hear indistinct chanting from the Al-Talehi reception committee. The Divisional commander had given them an hour to disperse and it was long past that now, but there had been race riots in Oldham and Burnley and they were cagey of provoking anything. What the crowd *wanted* was a fight.

She walked to the end conference room and looked out through the windows into the car park. The crowd was smaller now, but still making enough noise to attract a TV camera crew. She scanned the faces. They looked the same, each and every one of them. Even if their haircuts, clothing or facial expressions were slightly different, they still all looked the same. White trash. She felt a surprising anger.

There were two people in the interview room: a woman whose face she could not see properly because she was shrouded from head to feet in a black *burka*; and a white woman with spectacles and messy black hair, whom she assumed was the interpreter.

'Are you the interpreter?' she asked, closing the door.

'I am not,' the woman said, standing. 'I am this lady's solicitor and I wish from the outset to make it clear that—'

'You can stay if you're quiet,' Karen said. The last thing she needed was a solicitor shouting at her. She sat down. The solicitor was making some kind of protest at being kept waiting. Karen ignored her and looked across at the covered woman. *Smothered woman*, her mind said. She could see her eyes only. Dark, brown eyes. Even the whites looked slightly brown, as if the corneas had bled into them. She could read nothing from them. Not without the rest of the face to help. She might as well be looking at a robot. She would not be able to tell if the woman was lying with only her eyes to go on, not even if she did something obvious like look away. And *was* it a woman? How could you be sure, with just the eyes visible?

She looked at the solicitor, still speaking loudly, then back to the woman in the *burka*. She was perfectly still, eyes on her, hands resting on the table. Was Karen going to have to ask her to take the thing off?

Suddenly she heard what the solicitor was saying: '. . . my client would like to make it clear at once that she has no idea why Akil Al-Talehi would have given her details. She categorically denies seeing

Akil Al-Talehi on the eighth of June at any time during that day. She most definitely cannot provide him with an alibi.'

Karen let out a breath. The solicitor stopped talking.

'Can your client speak for herself?' Karen asked, looking at the woman, not the solicitor. What was her name? She looked down at the bundle of notes Powell had given her. 'Fatima Siddique.' She read it aloud, then looked at her again. 'Can you speak English, Fatima?' she asked.

'Of course I can. I was born here.' A Bradford accent. 'You assume I'm foreign because of the way I dress. That is racism.'

Karen looked at the eyes again. Were they cold, calculating, observant, frightened, amused? She had no idea. Had the woman made a joke just now, or was she serious?

'I make a lot of assumptions on account of your dress,' she said to her. 'I'm sure you do the same about mine. Don't dress like that if you don't like it.' She bit her lip. She was going to go too far here unless she did this quickly. 'All I want to know right now is whether you agree with what your solicitor has just said. Were you with Akil Al-Talehi on the eighth of June this year, at around seven in the evening?'

'I was not. I did not see him at all that day. If he has told you he was with me then he is lying.'

38

DC Clare Isles sat in a tiny, bare-walled, strip-lit office somewhere in the back corridors of Leeds/Bradford airport and looked over a virtually empty desk at the detective sitting opposite her. He was called Roger Slathe and he worked for West Yorkshire Special Branch. At the moment he was staring at a computer screen (the monitor, keyboard and mouse were the only items on the desk) while busily exploring the inside of his mouth with a plastic toothpick. He looked engrossed, but she wasn't sure whether it was the contents of the screen or his mouth that were responsible. From a bin in a corner of the room she could smell the wholesome odours of fast food leftovers. She tried to keep her mind on Slathe and off Tim Thorne, but that was difficult.

What had started this Tim Thorne thing? Three nights ago she had met up with a friend called Liz Hinkley. Liz was a DI at Bradford South who had worked with Thorne years before and still knew him socially. Clare knew Liz because they had met on their induction course and had hit it off, mainly because they had both been single for far too long. Eight years later that was still the case for Clare – she had never had a serious partner and could count her sexual encounters on two fingers – but Liz had moved on. She had a husband and two kids now, but still managed to get a night off once every couple of months to meet up with Clare and get slightly drunk.

In just that condition she had reported to Clare that Tim Thorne found her – Clare – attractive. They had both laughed pretty excessively at that, and Clare had thought nothing more of it. She suspected Liz was lying, to tease her. Nothing in her dealings with Tim Thorne had led her to believe he had even noticed her.

But this morning she had found herself looking at him differently, trying to read the subtext, if there was one. And sure enough, it had seemed possible that he liked her. Something about the way he looked at her?

'So what exactly do you need?' Slathe asked, not looking up from the screen.

She had already explained it to him once, but she tried again. 'I'm on a murder squad. We put in a request to the airline many days ago asking for details from the flight manifests to trace the movements of a man called Ian Whitfield. We've had nothing back.'

'And he flew out of Leeds/Bradford?'

'No. As I said, he flew out of Manchester. We were told by his girlfriend that he left the country for Holland on the first of June. So we contacted the airline direct—'

Slathe tutted quietly, under his breath, still not looking up. With one hand he moved the mouse and typed at the keyboard, with the other he dug around between his teeth. 'You should always come to us first,' he said. 'That's what we're here for.'

'I realize that.' In fact, if a colleague hadn't told her to try SB she wouldn't have thought of it at all. Not because she didn't know that SB had officers at every airport, but because she imagined they wouldn't take kindly to her asking them to help. Which, so far, was proving pretty accurate. She had been in the room with Slathe for over fifteen minutes and he had given her nothing. 'So *can* you help?' she asked. 'Is there an IT system you can access to get that information?' She hoped that was what he was doing already.

He laughed, took the toothpick from his mouth and looked over to her. 'An IT system? That would be nice, wouldn't it? We have an IT system that we use here at Leeds/Bradford, but we don't have anything plugged into Manchester. Manchester is a world away.' He waved his hands through the air to demonstrate the distance.

'Really?' She wasn't sure whether he was serious.

'Really.' He put the toothpick down on the desk and sat back in the swivel chair, turning it slightly to face her. 'You working on Operation Bulldog?'

'Yes.' She had already told him that. 'DS Joyce sent me. He spoke to your DI. He should have warned you.'

Slathe held his hands in the air again. 'He didn't.' He stared at her. 'But why should he? I've got nothing better to do.'

He was crumpled, fat, middle-aged, with sunken, tired eyes and thinning hair that stood at right angles to the top of his head, stiff, as if it hadn't been washed in weeks.

'Do you need to check with them, then?' she asked. There was a phone mounted on the wall to his side. She looked at it.

'I don't think so. Did you go to Tenerife in June last year?'

The question came out of left field. 'Why?'

'Because it says here that you did.' He nodded at the screen.

'Does it?' She shook her head, perplexed. She had been to Tenerife and she had passed through this airport, but so what?

'I'm just checking,' he said. 'Identity theft is rife. You know that.'

'But you know who I am. You've seen my ID.'

'Yes. I don't doubt you. I was just checking that the person who flew out last June was you.'

She sighed. 'Can you help me or not?' she asked, controlling her tone carefully.

'I can't. But I can call somebody in Manchester,' he said.

'That would be great.' Then I'll forget about you being such a prick, she thought. 'Could you do that, then?'

She waited as he sat across from her and did nothing, just stared, eyes fixed somewhere on the middle of her face. 'Will you do it now?' she asked.

He swivelled the chair and took the phone down. She watched him dial. There was something troglodytic about him, she thought. As if he were cooped up here all day and never got out. His eyes were black little things, so dark she couldn't distinguish the pupil from the iris.

She strayed into thinking about Tim Thorne's eyes instead. If he *were* interested in her she couldn't help but find it slightly exciting. She couldn't recall the colour of his eyes, couldn't recall anything about them, in fact. Before Liz's comment she hadn't thought about Tim Thorne at all, certainly hadn't found him attractive. Yet when he had spoken to her yesterday she had found herself quite enjoying the way he laughed with her about Riggs and Shepherd and all the others. It was flirtatious, to be discussing superiors with her like that. It had to be.

'Hello, David,' Slathe said into the handset. 'It's Roger. You keeping well?'

She listened as he chatted idly to 'David', showing no sign of broaching the subject of Whitfield in a hurry. That Whitfield was possibly a suspect in a murder inquiry obviously didn't matter. She learned, from one side of the conversation, that Slathe was married (that didn't surprise her at all – over the years she had got used to the idea that even misshapen, dull people like this could find some kind of life-long partner while she seldom met anyone she would even wish to cultivate a friendship with), that he supported Manchester United, that he had long ago given up all hope of promotion, and various other things. She moved noisily in her seat to remind him she was still there and waiting. Eventually he asked about Whitfield.

She waited as 'David' passed on the result. There was a moment's silence after that, then they started talking again about personal things. Finally he finished the call.

'That was the operations manager,' he said. 'You have to butter them up a bit. Tit for tat, you know.'

'Of course. Did he know anything about Whitfield?'

'Yes. Ian Whitfield flew out on the first of June and returned on the fifth. That's what the records show. Is that any help?'

'It is,' she said. 'Thank you.' She stood up at once, mildly excited now. Nadine Askwith had told them her boyfriend was still in Holland. In fact, he had already been back in the UK for three days when Enisa Fleming was attacked. Ian Whitfield had no alibi at all.

39

Karen got home just before nine, feeling exhausted, needing to sleep. Pete and Mairead were in and had already eaten. There was a pile of dishes in the sink. She went to the back room and found them sitting on the long, low sofa, watching a video on the widescreen, Mairead was leaning against Pete, his arm over her shoulders. Pete had told her he used to sit like that with Millie, on the same sofa.

The film was some kind of comedy. Mairead kept laughing. Pete stared past her at Karen. She walked over and gave Mairead a peck on the cheek.

'Stay and watch this, Mum,' Mairead said. 'It's Pete's favourite movie.'

'Favourite comedy,' Pete corrected her.

'It's a Bill Murray movie,' Mairead said, then laughed again.

Karen looked at the screen. There was a man crawling around a golf course with explosives and a detonator.

'It's called *Caddyshack*,' Mairead said. 'You'll like it.'

She felt sick looking at them, physically sick. Pete looked like he was Mairead's dad. Yet tonight she was going to put an end to all this.

'I can't,' she said. 'I have to work. I have some videos of my own to watch.'

'Yeah? What's that, then?' Pete asked. Trying to make conversation. But the knowledge of what she had to do sat between them like a physical obstruction. She couldn't even bear to make eye contact.

'Nothing interesting,' she said.

That she had been wrong about Brian Johnson was becoming obvious. Almost every idea, hunch or theory she had come up with on Scythe had been so far wide of the mark it was embarrassing. But still there was one more item she had to check before she could let it go. Brian

Johnson had told them he was in Sainsbury's Wade St branch at the time of the attack. Earlier that evening she had retrieved from the inquiry stores the Sainsbury's CCTV recording of the day of the attack.

She sat on a sofa in the living room and slotted the disc into the DVD player they had through there, hooked up to a smaller TV. She tried to close her mind to Pete and Mairead, laughing in the room next door. She needed to wait until Mairead had gone to bed, then sit down with Pete and start talking to him. The thought of it filled her with oppressive weight.

She scrolled through the timings on the DVD and found Johnson within five minutes. Immediately she felt a sensation of acute confusion, stronger than anything she normally felt when working a case. He was clearly in view entering the store at 6.52 p.m. At 7.28 p.m. she found an image of him pushing his laden trolley through the doors to the car park. He had not lied about being there. It could not have been him.

She sat back on the sofa and tried to understand the emotions she was experiencing. Akil Al-Talehi had no alibi. He had refused to say anything in interview. The psychiatric assessment had diagnosed him as schizoid. He was meant to take drugs to keep that in check, but hadn't. Colin Norton had given a good description of him near the scene at the time, his clothing stained with blood. There had been old scratch marks all over his chest, once they got his clothes off him. He was a perfect suspect. All that was missing was the delayed DNA result. But even if the DNA came back positive it didn't answer why he had attacked *this* girl, at *this* time, in *this* place. Why pick on Caroline?

Unless Caroline wasn't the first. Unless he really was unhinged, as the psychiatrist seemed to think, and had been involved in the killing of Enisa Fleming, too. The Bulldog squad were to take him to Killingbeck once Scythe was finished with him.

A random act of brutality by a madman. Could that be it? For some reason that seemed insufferable to her, so unbearable as to make her want to curl up in a ball and wait for it all to go away.

She lay back on the sofa and let her eyes close. She could hear Pete banging around in the kitchen, washing up. Did that mean the film was finished? Time to go through and bring the sky down. Or maybe she should speak to Mairead first. Should she tell her first, then think about how to break things to Pete? Did she have the mental strength for any of it?

Her brain stuttered, grinding to a halt. She let her arms drop to her sides and her head nod forward.

She heard the door to the room opening and, for a moment, was confused, unsure where she was.

'Karen?'

Her eyes snapped open. Pete was standing in the room, looking at her. He looked agitated.

'Pete. I must have dozed.'

'You've been asleep for two hours. Mairead came in and kissed you. You didn't notice.'

She checked her watch. What time had she dropped off?

'Are we going to talk, Karen? These arguments ... these patches we go through ... we have to start dealing with them.' He closed the door silently, but didn't sit down. Instead he walked over to the front window and drew the curtains.

'Did Mairead go to bed?' she asked. She rubbed her eyes.

'An hour ago.'

She took a deep breath. Her mind was still clouded with sleep. 'You should have left me sleeping,' she said.

'I want you to sleep with *me*, Karen. Not on the fucking sofa. I want us to be like a loving couple.'

She pushed herself forward and stood up. He was standing over by the window, looking at her, something like desperation in his eyes. She felt horrible. Automatically, she wanted to step over and hug him. But that wouldn't help either of them. She remembered how it used to be between them – years ago now, before the first split. It brought unexpected tears to her eyes. She turned away from him, trying to hide them, but too late. He was coming over to her, taking it as a sign of need.

'Don't,' she said gently. She put an arm up to stop him. He stopped. She wiped her eyes then turned to look at him. She had to do it now. He was standing close to her, at arm's length, a mixture of emotions in his expression. 'I'm crying because I remember how we used to be, Pete,' she said.

He nodded. 'It's not in the past,' he said. 'We still are like that. Most of the time.'

She shook her head. 'We're not,' she said. 'Not if you are honest about it.'

'It can come back. We can work these issues out.'

'We can't. Not any more. It's not you, Pete. It's the way *I* am.'

'There's nothing wrong with you.'

She shook her head again and blinked away the tears. 'I don't think you should be with me,' she said. 'I'm not good for you, Pete. I don't make you happy.'

His eyes fell to the floor and his brow creased. He could see it coming now. He waited.

'I don't think I can do this any more,' she said.

'What are you saying, Karen? Have you thought about what you are saying?'

'Yes, I've thought about it.' She took a deep breath. 'I think we have to end it, Pete. That's what I'm saying.' She looked at him, so he could see she meant it.

'You want to leave me?' he asked, very quietly.

'I don't want to. I think I have to, though.'

His lip was trembling.

'I'm so sorry,' she said.

She watched his eyes darken. 'Is there someone else?' he asked. 'Is that what's going on?'

She shrugged. She had expected the question, but couldn't bring herself to lie. 'You know that doesn't matter,' she answered. 'If we were happy the question wouldn't arise.'

'So there *is* someone else?' A little flash of anger.

'It's irrelevant. This is about me and you.'

'Is it someone I know?'

She dried her eyes. Speaking to him had brought some small relief to her, a tension easing inside her, but it was just the start, and she didn't have the strength for more, not tonight. 'I don't want to talk about it like this,' she said. 'I don't want it to be an argument.'

He was silent then, staring at the floor. She thought he might start crying. He was devastated. She could see that. It was the second time she had done this to him. In March 1998 she had taken Mairead and walked out without even leaving a note. They had started again in early 2000, but it had been wrong from the beginning.

'I should never have taken you back,' he said, quietly. 'I always knew you'd do this again.' He looked up at her, his face grey, his cheeks quivering with the effort of controlling himself.

*

When she couldn't stand it any more she left him and walked through to the kitchen. Upstairs she could hear nothing from Mairead. She hoped she was asleep. She had to speak to her fairly quickly, tell her what was happening. But not now. The atmosphere in the house was heavy; the walls felt as though they were pressing in on her. Pete didn't follow her to the kitchen and, after a while, she thought she could hear him sobbing. She had to get away from it.

She went out to her car.

She felt evil. His heart was breaking and all she wanted to do was escape. She felt disconnected, distant. The sensation was like lead, seeping along her limbs. She wanted to call Ronnie. Or sleep. Forget about it until morning, start again. She was so tired her eyes were closing again.

If you lived with someone for as long as she had lived with Pete things didn't just end in a night. Surely he knew that. There would be weeks of this now, maybe months. He wouldn't get angry at first – the feeling of being abandoned would swamp him, the horror of having to do without her – but eventually he would get angry about it. Then the arguments and recriminations would start. Then she would be able to take it a stage further and move out. But she had to wait for that. She couldn't do what she had done in 1998 and just leave him to it. Not when he was so terrified. Because that was what it was. Everyone was the same in the end – terrified of being alone.

She leaned her head back against the seat and let her eyes close. She could hardly move now. But at least it was done. She had started the process.

It felt as if she had slept for a second. Her eyes closed, then opened again. But her head wasn't clear enough for it to have been that quick. Her mobile was ringing. As she answered it she looked at the time: 2.30 a.m. She had slept for nearly two and a half hours. She struggled to wake herself.

'Hello?' She pressed the phone to her ear.

It was Richard Powell. 'Are you up, Karen?'

'I was asleep.' She looked around. She was in her car, outside a house. The lights in the house were all off. She felt disorientated.

'I'm sorry. I know we talked about this, but I'm desperate. And you said you were OK with it …'

'OK with what?'

'Dealing with Caroline. The doctor just called. She's able to communicate by writing, apparently. Distressed but lucid. She wants to talk to us. I urgently need someone to get down there and speak to her – someone trained. She might give us a description. Can you do it? If you can I'll meet you there.'

She tried to recall where she was. Outside Pete Bains's home, of course. *Her* home. The awful weight of what had occurred between them shifted and settled inside her.

'Can you be there?' Powell asked again.

'I can get there in half an hour,' she said.

WEDNESDAY, 4 JULY

40

She was asleep on the benches in the ward waiting area when the doctor woke her by gently shaking her shoulder. It was the same Nigerian she had spoken to before. He had a cup of coffee in his hands. She squinted up at him, then moved into a sitting position.

'What time is it?' she asked him.

'Just after six. This is for you.' He held the coffee towards her. 'I understand you were waiting all night.'

She took the cup gratefully. 'Yes. I must have fallen asleep. Sorry.'

'No need to apologize. Sleep is what we are meant to do at night.'

She looked around and gradually fitted together where she was. She had written Pete and Mairead a note, then driven over here. They had both been asleep when she went back into the house.

She had met Richard Powell here at just after 3 a.m., expecting to be taken in to see Caroline Philips immediately. But the medical staff on duty had changed tack and decided Caroline was still too distressed. Instead they had sedated her again. Powell had been very angry, worried that Caroline might forget everything, worried that the sedation was what was maintaining the amnesia. He still had Akil Al-Talehi in custody at Richmond Close and was still waiting for the delayed DNA result.

Powell had left Karen shortly after 3.30 a.m, both of them intending to return in the morning. But somehow she hadn't got as far as getting out of the place. She could not recall falling asleep.

'Caroline is quite calm now,' the doctor said to her. 'Awake and calm.'

'Can I see her?' she asked.

'I think so.'

'The questions might upset her.'

'They certainly will. But it has to be done. For her, too. She doesn't understand what has happened to her.' He'd changed his tune. 'She needs to understand. You will have to explain it to her, perhaps.'

She was conscious of a look of anxiety stealing into her eyes. 'I don't know whether I can,' she said. 'What do you want me to explain?'

'Not what happened. She can remember some of that. She just doesn't know *why* it happened.'

Karen stood up. 'I can't answer that. We will only know that when we find the man.'

He smiled at her. 'You will have to do your best,' he said. 'Let's try now.'

She walked a pace behind him, down to the end of a long corridor, to an area full of nurses, then into a small, private room at one end of a ward. He waited until she had stepped in before closing the door behind them.

'Good morning, Caroline,' he said. 'This is the police officer I told you about.'

Karen looked at the bed and felt a sensation of familiar dread. Caroline was propped up in a half-sitting position, staring at her. It was the first time she had seen her eyes. The same eyes she had seen in the magazine photos, but ringed black now, sunken into her head.

She stepped forward, towards the bed. 'Hello, Caroline. My name is Karen Sharpe.'

'Caroline is much better now,' the doctor said, talking over her. 'But we cannot let her speak yet.' He moved to the other side of the bed and leaned a little towards her. 'But you *will* speak, Caroline. You know that, don't you?' Her eyes flicked towards him without her head moving. 'You are going to make a full recovery,' he said. He glanced at Karen as he spoke. She had a feeling he was lying.

Her mouth now had some kind of frame fitted inside and around it, a monstrous cage thing, like a dog's muzzle, swathed in bandages, with drips extending out of it. Karen could see fluid running out over the edge of it, spit mingled with blood. And more fluid going through a tube into a huge bottle by the side of the bed. Karen couldn't tell whether the mouth was open or closed. As Caroline breathed, a slight hissing noise came from the area of her lips. There were tubes and lines attached all over her. It looked as if she had a cast fitted from the base of her neck up to just below the eyes, covering nearly all of her face, holding the muzzle thing in place and fixing her head in position. There were two holes for the nose (a tube disappearing into each), but all Karen could see of her features were the eyes. She could see no expression in them at all.

'Caroline can write things for now,' the doctor said, speaking to both of them. Karen looked down at her hands, lying on the starched, white, folded-back bed covers. There were drips going into the back of both of them, needles fitted into her veins, held in place with clear tape. The hands looked swollen. The whole room was filled with suffocating smells, the most intense one like baby sick, or slightly off milk. Then disinfectant, behind that.

'Can I ask you some questions, Caroline?' Her voice was wavering. She saw the doctor place a pad of hospital notepaper beside Caroline's right hand, then touch her fingers with a pen. The hand moved, taking the pen.

'She knows you are going to ask her questions,' he said. 'She is ready for this. She wants to do it.'

But Caroline was already writing something.

They waited. Caroline had to twist her eyes down to see the pad. The effort looked painful. Her chest began to move noticeably, her breathing heavier. The hissing sound coming from the cage became louder.

It took a long time for her to finish a few words. When she had finished the doctor took it and read: '"Why did this happen to me? Why me?"'

Karen felt a lump knotting in her throat. The doctor looked over to her, waiting. 'I was ...' Karen started. Her voice dried at once. What could she say? She reached out a hand and took hold of Caroline's left hand, carefully, just touching the ends of her fingers. The flesh was warm, as if she had a fever. She felt the fingers tighten slightly, gripping her own. It felt like a child's hand, innocent, tiny, waiting to be told the answers. She cleared her throat. 'I need you to help me with that,' she said. The eyes looking at her didn't react at all. 'We are going to find this man,' she added. 'The man who attacked you.' Still no reaction. Karen stared at her. Her legs felt weak. She searched behind her for a chair, then sat on it.

'What questions do you have, officer?' the doctor asked. She opened her mouth to start but he stopped her again. 'Caroline has to preserve her strength,' he said. 'So not many. Three or four perhaps.'

Three or four? She coughed into her hand, then looked up again. 'Can you describe the man who attacked you?' she asked.

The eyes blinked, then closed. Karen waited for them to open again but they didn't. She frowned at the doctor, but he merely held a finger to his lips.

After a minute or two she began to write. When she had finished the doctor took the pad and passed it to Karen.

She read out: '"He looked mad, with staring eyes. That's all I can remember about him. I don't know what he was wearing. His hands were very strong. I did not know him. I had not seen him before. Why would he attack me? Why would he want to do this to me? I do not understand it."'

Karen trembled as she read it. So not Johnson, the boyfriend. But maybe Al-Talehi. The description was no help for a courtroom situation, though. Richard Powell would have to wait for the DNA, still. There would be no value in organising formal identification procedures just to get a negative.

'Did he say anything to you? Do you know what he was trying to do?' she asked.

'Maybe one question at a time,' the doctor said.

'Sorry.' She reached out again and held the fingers. Once more she felt the slight response. "Sorry, Caroline. Do you know what he was trying to do to you?"

She wrote again, going through the same process, but this time it was slower. She was tiring already.

Again Karen read it aloud: '"I have no idea. He did not sexually assault me. He was not trying to sexually assault me, or take my clothes off. I thought he might be trying to rob me at first, but he took nothing. He didn't search me, didn't try to take anything. I don't know what he was doing. I need to know."'

Karen ran her hands through her hair, then rubbed at her temples. The pain in her chest was coming back, the pressure starting to build. 'I need to know, too,' she said, then repeated it. 'I need to know, too, Caroline.' The eyes held her own, hardly moving. She shifted in her seat, feeling too warm.

Last question. What was it? What had Powell written down? 'Did he say anything to you?' she asked, remembering.

It took Caroline a long time before she started writing, so long Karen thought she might have drifted off. But she hadn't.

Once more, Karen read out the answer: '" He was speaking all the time, maybe even shouting. I couldn't understand what he was saying, though. I thought that was because of the blow to my head when I fell. I still cannot hear properly. But I have thought about what he was saying and realize I could hear but not understand. I think he was speaking gibberish."'

'I think that's enough now,' the doctor said. 'Enough for all of us. If Caroline is well enough we could do more questions tomorrow.' He started to remove the pad, but Caroline knocked his hand away with surprising force and scribbled furiously.

He read out what she had written: '"Can you tell me who it was? Can you tell me why he did this to me?"'

Karen stood up. 'I can't,' she said quietly. 'Not yet. We don't know why this happened. I don't know ...' She squeezed the hand one last time, then looked at the eyes. Caroline was breathing very heavily and her eyes were brimming with tears. 'I'm sorry,' Karen said. 'I'm really sorry.'

Outside, back in the waiting area, Richard Powell was already waiting for her. She collapsed on to a seat beside him and gave him the sheets of notepaper.

'Good work, Karen,' he said.

'Read it first,' she said. 'There's nothing good about it.'

He read it then looked up at her. 'Fucking hell.'

'Maybe Al-Talehi,' she said. 'Not the boyfriend, though. And not a grudge. Someone who spoke gibberish.'

Powell let his head hang, arms resting on his knees. 'We're fucked now,' he said. 'Norton putting Al-Talehi half a mile away with blood on him won't be enough to charge him.' Searches of Al-Talehi's property had failed to recover anything blood-stained. They had sent off a whole variety of microscopic scrapings and samples from his person and his address for analysis, but it would be a few days more before the results came back. 'If the DNA doesn't come back positive for him that will be it,' Powell said. 'No lines left. We'll have to start DNA screening in the area. It's the only way. If it wasn't Al-Talehi it must have been something random.'

She looked around her. There were people arriving now, nurses moving back and forth, the ordinary life of the hospital gearing up for another day. She looked at the bunch of flowers in the vase on the reception desk (bright yellow sunflowers, with dark brown hearts), the ward sister bent over some paperwork, the doctor beside her talking on the phone. In the town the roads would be slowly filling with traffic, people sweating, swearing, chatting, listening to the radio on their way into work, laughing or crying, following the pattern, sticking to their routine; thousands of people packed up together, moving around each other, coming into contact, moving away, all the parts moving like clockwork, as if there were some order to it. As if that world was all there was.

But life wasn't like that. One minute you were walking home from work, the next you had your tongue cut out.

Something random.

41

Michael Rawson awoke in a sweat, panting. He rolled over at once and placed his feet on the floor, then pushed himself quickly into a sitting position and shook his head vigorously. He waited for his brain to clear. He was in the bedroom, on the edge of his bed. Behind him his wife said something. He took a deep breath.

'You OK, love?' he heard her repeat.

'It's OK,' he said. 'I'm fine.' He let his senses pick out the familiar household objects – the bedside table, the alarm clock, the phone. Maria's hand was on his bare back, reassuring him.

He twisted his torso to see her. She was half sitting against the pillows, her thick, dark hair falling around her face, the quilt pushed back and her chest bare. He smiled half-heartedly at her. 'Did I wake you again?' he asked. 'I'm sorry.'

'You've been tossing and turning for nearly twenty minutes. You sure you're all right?'

He nodded. He was. It was getting to be so regular he was used to it. He looked past Maria to where the cot was placed against her side of the bed. Their six-month-old daughter, Bridget, was sleeping soundly. At least he hadn't woken her.

'What time is it?' he asked. He rubbed his eyes.

'Seven.'

'I should be getting up anyway.' He had to get over to Khan's this morning.

Remembering that brought thoughts of his waking nightmare to mind, the nightmare he had been living and breathing for almost a month now. He put his hands to his face and suppressed a groan. He wasn't looking forward to today. Today, in desperation, he was going to speak to Raheesh Khan about the problem. He had tried to keep the truth from Khan for over three weeks, but it was out of hand now, and Khan was the only person he knew with the resources to provide a solution. But telling Khan the full story was out of the question. He had to give him enough to get the help, but not so much that he would be exposed if Khan didn't like what he heard.

He felt Maria stroke his back, and snapped out of it. 'Is Kevin awake?' he asked her. Kevin was their three-year-old.

'I haven't heard him yet.'

Michael pushed himself off the bed. 'I'll get ready,' he said. 'Kevin can play with me for a bit. You sleep some more.' He bent over and kissed her on the lips.

'Was it the same thing?' she asked.

He nodded.

The same thing. He stood in the bathroom with the taps running and thought about it. He had been having the nightmare for almost ten years now, but it had only recently become so bad that it woke him in distress. Maria had started asking him about it a few weeks ago. It was the first time he had ever had to admit to anyone that it was a problem.

Maria and he had grown up on the same street in Middleton and she knew him better than anyone, better than his parents, even. She had been around long before he joined the army in 1988, though they had never managed to get it together properly before he disappeared from Manchester. That had been a mistake. Maria had been keen for them to live together and marry (all her life she had been keen on him – he had no idea why), but he had held off. At nineteen he had thought himself too young to settle down with a girl he had first kissed when they were six years old and whose parents lived three houses away from his. Like most boys in his class he had standard ideas of playing the field, seeing the world, cutting loose. He had always found Maria attractive, but it didn't mean much at that age. The world was full of attractive women. So he had passed her over, left home, joined up.

Maria wouldn't have let him join the army. She hated fighting, war, aggression. If he had married her then, Kuwait and Iraq would still be something he knew about from the evening news, something distant. Instead he had the consequences to live with, every day, every hour. The nightmare was the very least of it. Everything he was doing now stemmed from his military experience. When he came out in 1994 he had been fit for none of the career options his youth had promised.

Iraq was why he was where he was now. He was fortunate Maria had still been interested when he got back, but he was certain that if she knew him as he knew himself she wouldn't even want to look him in the eye. He had explained his night-time problems to her, but not with the truth.

From the bedroom next door to the bathroom he heard Kevin beginning to wake up. He squeezed toothpaste on to a toothbrush and stared at his face in the mirror above the sink. He was thirty-three years old, but he felt and looked fifteen years older. There were wrinkles and pouches under his eyes, and at least two double chins. His nose – broken twice in amateur boxing matches in the army – had always been ugly, but ten years ago he had been able to look at his own image and see something half-attractive, some spark of an inner life that might make women look twice.

Now all he saw was a fat, tired old man. He still had all his hair – a thick, untidy mop of it – but the dark brown was so flecked through with white it looked grey in parts. His moustache was the same. He put the toothbrush down and took a pair of scissors from the cabinet behind the mirror. This was another habit he had picked up in the military, the obsessive trimming of his moustache. He had to have both sides exactly the same length or it drove him mad. He could feel when there was a difference because he fiddled with it all day. Nearly always there was a difference – one side longer or thinner. He knew the reason – his face wasn't exactly symmetrical – but that didn't stop the compulsion.

He heard a noise behind him and looked round. Kevin was standing at the open door in his pyjamas, eyes bleary, a sulky look on his face. He wasn't good at waking up.

'Hey, kid,' Michael said. He put the scissors down and turned round. 'You look happy today.'

'I want Mum.'

Michael squatted in front of him and ruffled his hair. Kevin was having a hard time coming to terms with Maria's divided attentions. Before Bridget arrived Maria would be in to pick him up and kiss him at the first sign he was waking. That had all stopped now. Bridget woke up twice each night to be fed and Maria was shattered.

'I know you do,' Michael said. 'But she's a bit tired. What about if you and me go downstairs and watch some TV, get some breakfast?'

'I don't want to watch TV.'

'OK. We'll watch a video. How about *The Iron Giant?*'

He settled Kevin in front of the widescreen, then went through to the kitchen to make himself a coffee and get Kevin some food.

Looking around the place he felt the same, familiar pressures. He had a good life here. The house was a new four-bedroom detached 'villa', part of a development that included security gates and CCTV cameras. From the kitchen window he could see to the end of their long rear garden, backed by an eight-feet wall mounted with razor wire. They had a gardener who came once a week to tidy things, repair the lawn where Kev had kicked it up, trim the roses. For the house they had a cleaner who did the equivalent but came more regularly. It was a nice life. Maria had a horse which she stabled near Heywood. Kev went to a nursery that was within walking distance. They had all the usual appliances, two cars, took holidays abroad three times a year, had two ungrateful cats that came in and out at will via a catflap, as if *they* owned the place. It was comfortable.

But it was precarious. Maria didn't realize how precarious. Everything he had depended upon him maintaining his position with Raheesh Khan. If Khan decided he couldn't trust him then it wouldn't just mean the end of the house, the cars and the cats.

He frowned, struggling to open the lid on a new jar of coffee. It was a sealed, vacuum-packed tin with a ring pull, which, for some reason, wouldn't work. He yanked at it and it came off in his hands, leaving the seal intact. He cursed and put it down on the side. He looked at his hands, holding them out in front of him. They were shaking.

Aidan Kershaw and Ian Whitfield had brought this shit on him.

'Fuck you, Kershaw,' he said quietly, careful that Kevin wouldn't hear. 'Fuck your whole fucking family.'

42

Ronnie knew the stress was getting to him when his hands began to shake. He pulled the car over and cut the engine. It had never been *this* bad before. He tried to remember how many coffees he had drunk in the last twenty-four hours and lost track after eight. That was probably it, then.

He looked around. He was on the B-road out to Steve Fleming's place, surrounded by fields. Fleming wasn't going to be there – he was still in hospital and would be for some time yet – but Ronnie had awoken with a nagging feeling that he should go back out there and look at the scene again while the house was empty and there was no one to disturb his thoughts. Maybe it would help with what he was going to do that afternoon.

He had arranged to speak to Fleming at 2 p.m. and wasn't looking forward to it. He had discussed it with the SIO and got agreement to co-opt Karen for this one task. He wanted her, not Debbie Moor, to take the lead. She hadn't answered her mobile so he had left a message explaining things, asking her to meet him there. He had no idea how to approach Fleming, or even what to ask him. On the basis of a hunch he was going to pressurize an injured man who had just lost his wife and unborn child, in the vague hope that he could force him to disclose information he wasn't even sure he was withholding in the first place. Karen would know how to handle it.

His suspicions were probably all nonsense anyway. Perhaps he should have let Riggs charge Myers instead of bailing him. Or go for Akil Al-Talehi. But Al-Talehi had said nothing to the interviewers for Scythe, and if he repeated that pattern once they had him in Killingbeck then there would be no evidence against him at all.

He held his hands out in front of him and watched them trembling. Caffeine had never done that to him before. It had to be stress. Nobody thought he got stressed about these things; they thought he was calm, detached, professional. But it was true what he had said to Karen – he often felt like a duck, and had been paddling frantically ever since this case had started.

He turned the key in the ignition and set off again.

He got about fifty yards before his whole body began to shake. He pulled over again quickly. Lucky he was on a deserted country road. This time he cut the engine and got out. He could take a little walk, he thought, exercise his legs, get some fresh air into his lungs. He wished he had a bottle of water with him. He felt thirsty.

He stepped onto the gravel by the side of the road, left the car door open, and looked around him. It was still early, just after 7.45 a.m. The rising sun was about 45 degrees above the horizon, a huge crimson orb suspended high over a field of flaming wheat, everything tinged red. He couldn't help but stare at it. But as he stood there, gawking, his legs felt suddenly weak, like he might be going to faint. He sat back down quickly, legs out of the car, then bent forward and held his head between his legs. No more coffee today.

When was the last time he had fainted? When he was thirteen years old, in a PE class at school. So why would it be happening again now? He waited until the sensation had passed then sat up straight. About 300 yards in front of him a flock of birds, startled by something, rose all at once from a copse at the edge of the field. They spiralled in the air, growing in numbers. Were they starlings, come here all the way from Russia? he wondered. Migration never ceased to amaze him. How could they travel so far, year after year? It wasn't just the navigational feat, but that they actually had the strength to do it, to fly thousands of miles. He smiled, imagining it. He could hear them calling to each other, a frantic crescendo of raucous noise.

For a moment he forgot about his trembling limbs. For the first time in many years, thoughts of Sharon came to him, absurdly coloured with a kind of nostalgia for her – or for those times, when he had been young and in love with her. Laura's mother. Sharon had loved nature. She had loved animals and birds, loved watching them and listening to them. She had felt the wonder of it and shared it with him. He remembered that.

But he felt sick now. His thoughts veered swiftly from the stress theory to food poisoning. What had he eaten yesterday? He couldn't recall. Come to think of it, what *day* was it today? He took his mobile out and fumbled to see the buttons. He couldn't see them properly. Deep breaths. He would have to call Laura, ask her what she thought. He managed to get her mobile number up and pressed dial.

'Laura?'

'Hello?'

'Hello, love. Sorry to bother you. I'm just calling to—'

'I'm in a faculty meeting. I can't talk.'

Did they have faculty meetings this early? 'Sorry, love,' he said. 'I thought you'd be at home still.'

'That's OK.'

The line went dead. Had she hung up on him? She had sounded tetchy, annoyed to be disturbed by her dad, no doubt. He would have to apologize later.

He looked up from the phone and realized he couldn't see the field. Not clearly. It was as if there was a grey film smeared across his eyes. He rubbed them and immediately felt dizzy. He took a deep breath and tried to stand up.

Something happened. The ground twisted underneath him. He didn't manage to get to his feet, but felt himself slumping forwards, out of the door. A second later he was lying on the ground.

He sighed, knowledge of what was happening suddenly infusing him with calm. It wasn't stress or food poisoning. It was something worse than that. But he didn't feel panicked or frightened. He closed his eyes and waited. He couldn't move at all. He couldn't even hear properly.

Time slipped over him like a sludge. He tried to relax about it, but had little choice anyway. There was no pain. Just a slow series of distorted sensations. At least he didn't feel dizzy, now that he was flat out.

After a short time (or was it a long time?) he heard noises, then people talking. Someone was asking him a question – a male. *Was he in pain?* There was no pain, but he couldn't tell the man that. He couldn't move his tongue at all. But he didn't mind that. It was quite restful, just lying here, not caring about anything. *Que sera, sera.* That was where he was now.

He felt people moving him, changing his position, lifting him. Then he was lying on his back and he could feel warmth on his face. The sun? He tried to enjoy it, then began to think about Laura. She would be embarrassed if she could see him, flat out and helpless. Maybe he had peed himself too. *What was going on?*

He could hear himself breathing, feel his heart still beating. That was good. He had not had a heart attack. Heart attacks were painful. What was it, then? A panic attack of some sort? The idea was ridiculous. *But what, then?*

He was thinking about it as his vision began to clear. Then, for a moment, he thought he was only waking up from a dream. He began to smile. It had been a nightmare of sorts – though a relatively peaceful one. But still only a nightmare. He was alive, at least. He could feel movement under his body, rocking him, and a noise he recognized. He listened to it, trying to identify it. It was a siren.

He could see a man leaning over him now. Someone dressed in green, holding something with a plastic tube running out of it, talking softly to him. So it wasn't a dream. His eyes shifted away from the man and he saw the low ceiling of a vehicle above him. He recognized that he was in an ambulance and felt relief. How long had he been lying there?

'You with me?' the man asked. 'Can you hear me now?'

Ronnie smiled at him. He tried to say something as well, but no words came out.

'That's good,' the man said. 'Don't try to talk. Just keep focused on what I'm saying. Don't leave me. OK?'

43

Karen sat in Powell's office drinking strong coffee, waiting for her nerves to settle. The scene with Pete, the disruption of sleep, the encounter with Caroline – it was all affecting her. She needed to collapse into bed and crash out for hours, purge her brain of it all. Powell was trying to help – making her coffee, talking with interest about her home life and Mairead – while looking through his emails. But her home life was the last thing she wanted to focus on. Luckily, his interest didn't last long. He was back only a few minutes before someone brought him a fax with the DNA results.

They were positive. Al-Talehi was their man. Powell looked as if he couldn't believe it.

'You think it's OK even with the witnesses' descriptions not matching?' she asked reluctantly. She felt none of his relief.

'I couldn't care less about that,' Powell said. He stood up. 'Witnesses make errors; DNA doesn't.'

'What about the gibberish?' Karen said. 'Al-Talehi speaks good English.'

'And Arabic,' Powell said. 'Caroline wouldn't know the difference between gibberish and Arabic.'

She could see his spirits beginning to soar. And this was just the start of it. They'd do an interview, get a briefing going, tell everyone. Then there'd be congratulations and back-slapping all the way to the pub, for lunch. Meanwhile, Caroline would still be rotting in the hospital bed, hacked up, tongueless, no nearer to understanding why this had happened to her.

'We should interview him,' she said. 'We need to know why he did it.'

'We don't *need* anything more than we've already got,' he replied.

'But you're right.' He nodded. He was pacing up and down behind her, unable to keep still. 'We have to put this to him.'

'Let me do it.'

He came round to his side of the desk again and frowned at her. 'I don't think it would be a good idea to change personnel now.' A DS called Jeff Neve had so far done all the interviews with Al-Talehi.

'But this is about women,' she said. 'About his reaction to them. If I'm in there with Jeff it might provoke things.'

'We can't provoke anything, Karen. He's a sick man. He has to be assessed before each interview and there's a psychiatric nurse in on everything as an Appropriate Adult. We've already got two reports that say he's mentally ill. Provoking him is out of the question.'

'But we have to know why he did it – for Caroline, so I have something to tell her. Let me try – just to see if it works.'

He looked uncertain. 'We have to be careful,' he said. 'We don't want to fuck everything by giving the defence the chance to claim oppression.'

'I *will* be careful. I know what I'm doing.'

He sat down, thinking about it. 'A confession would top it off,' he admitted. He smiled slightly. 'And you could be right. A woman might just do it.'

It took them almost an hour and a half to set up the interview. Al-Talehi was examined by the police surgeon and certified fit for both continued detention and interview. The Appropriate Adult said he could be there immediately, as did the interpreter. But the solicitor was in court when they paged him. Meanwhile Powell tried to trace Jeff Neve, who was on a rest day, without success. He decided to do the interview himself, with Karen sitting in, on condition she said nothing unless he specifically asked her to.

The solicitor was called Mark Simmons, a local man well known to Karen from other cases. About thirty-five years old, he was competent, fair and shrewd – not the kind to advise his clients to say nothing automatically, though that was precisely how he had advised Al-Talehi in previous interviews. As soon as he arrived Karen took him to the interview room and spent fifteen minutes disclosing the new evidence to him. She switched the tape machine on so that everything that passed between them was recorded.

'So DNA taken from blood traces found under Caroline Philips's fingernails matches my client's DNA, already held on the database,' Simmons summed up when she had finished. He sipped calmly from the coffee she had made him. He didn't look surprised.

Karen nodded. It couldn't get much more incriminating. 'Akil has to account for this now,' she said. 'He has to come up with some kind of explanation.'

Simmons shook his head doubtfully. 'I'm not even sure he will understand what it means,' he said. 'If he's anything like yesterday I would have to say that I don't think you should be interviewing him at all.'

'He's back on the medication now. The doctor examined him this morning and found him fit. He's lucid.'

Al-Talehi had been prescribed an anti-psychotic drug for over six months, but had stopped taking it weeks ago. Now that he was in custody they had started dosing him again. Still, Simmons didn't look convinced. 'I'll need to speak to him before we start,' he said. 'But I wouldn't get your hopes up. If he's as confused as yesterday my advice to him will be the same.'

'To say nothing? His only way of defending this is to tell us how his blood could innocently be there. You have to tell him to talk, Mark. We need his explanation. We need to …' She caught herself. She sounded far too desperate. Desperation wouldn't make Simmons change his mind. She took a breath and rubbed her eyes. Her skin felt rubbery, stretched. Her eyes were stinging. The idea of interviewing Al-Talehi had injected adrenalin into her, but beneath that she was at exhaustion point. She needed to be cautious.

'You don't need anything,' Simmons said, echoing Powell. 'Not with the DNA evidence. What's the point of disturbing him further? The poor man was suicidal yesterday.'

Karen bit her lip. *The poor man.* Simmons felt pity for Al-Talehi even though he now knew what he had done.

'I'm thinking of the victim,' Karen said, giving it one last try, keeping her voice even. 'We both know he did this to her. If we could explain to the victim *why* he did it, that might help her. It would help with his sentence, too. You know that.'

Simmons shrugged hopelessly. 'I'll see what he's like,' he said. 'But I don't think anything is going to help the victim now.'

*

With six of them squeezed into the interview room the air very quickly became stale, stuffy and too hot.

Al-Talehi sat directly opposite Powell across a small table. The Appropriate Adult – a psychiatric nurse called Dave Spenceley – sat to one side of him, with the interpreter on his other side. Both Powell and Karen thought Al-Talehi spoke English well enough, but Simmons had insisted, so they didn't have a choice. The interpreter was an elderly man with white hair and beard. He was Pakistani, but had lived and worked in Saudi. Simmons sat at the end of the table, next to Karen. The table was so small Al-Talehi could easily make contact with them across it, but Powell didn't look worried about that.

With good cause. The man they brought in from the cells was a confused, weepy, hunched-up and shuffling individual, dressed in the standard detention overalls, handcuffed behind his back until the custody sergeant sat him down and removed the cuffs. He looked at the ground until he was seated, then stared at the surface of the table.

When the custody sergeant had gone, the tape machine was switched on, the introductions were made and the caution was read out and relayed in Arabic. Then they ran into their first problem.

'I'm sorry, but it's the same thing as yesterday,' Spenceley said. 'I'm not sure Akil is capable of understanding the caution.'

'In any event, I've strongly advised my client to exercise his right to silence,' Simmons chipped in, while the interpreter was still repeating to Al-Talehi what Spenceley had said. 'It's my opinion that he shouldn't be interviewed at all.'

Powell sighed. 'Can we hear from Akil on that?' he asked, speaking to Spenceley. 'If you're right then we'll stop. But I want to hear from Akil whether he understands the caution.'

'I've told him to say nothing,' Simmons said. 'That's the only thing I could advise him in this condition.'

'I understand that. But I still want to ask my questions.'

'He won't answer you.'

'So he understood *your* advice well enough?' Karen couldn't help making the point.

Powell didn't say anything to reprove her. 'If he understood his solicitor's advice to remain silent, he must be able to understand the caution,' he said instead, looking at Spenceley.

Spenceley looked at Al-Talehi, sitting beside him. The interpreter was still whispering to him, translating it all. Al-Talehi appeared to be shivering slightly. His arms were crossed over his chest, and he looked wide-eyed, frightened. His eyes had been described as 'bulbous' or 'staring' by witnesses. She wondered whether that had been an effect of the lack of medication. His eyes were large, dark and worried, but not bulbous. And he wasn't staring at anyone. He looked too scared even to make eye contact with his own solicitor.

Karen knew he was twenty-nine years old from the information they had on him already. When they had brought him in yesterday he had been clean-shaven. Already this morning he had a thick, black stubble. The hair on his head was tousled and dirty, but normal length. She thought he looked much shorter than any of the descriptions given of him, and slighter. But then Caroline wasn't a strong woman. It wouldn't have taken much to knock her over and pin her down.

'Did you understand the caution the man just gave you, Akil?' Spenceley asked him. Al-Talehi looked quickly at him, then looked away again. He was confused, even Karen could see that. Probably Simmons was right – they shouldn't be doing this.

'Maybe if you explain the caution in ordinary words?' Spenceley suggested.

Powell cleared his throat. 'Akil. Can you listen to me, please?' He waited to see if Al-Talehi would look at him, but he didn't. He was starting to rock slightly now, from side to side. Karen could see blood encrusted up his nose, and one of his cheeks was bruised. He had been like that when they brought him in (they had carefully photographed each injury) – the result of an unexplained fight with Ahmed Ibrahim, one of the builders who had renovated the Flemings' place. Neither Ibrahim nor Al-Talehi would say anything about the altercation. Ibrahim had been arrested and bailed by the Bulldog squad who wanted to arrest and interview Al-Talehi once they were finished with him here.

'The caution I read out to you means that you are free to say nothing at all to me,' Powell said. 'Do you understand that? You don't have to say *anything*.'

The interpreter leaned into Al-Talehi and spoke in Arabic. Al-Talehi risked a quick, furtive glance in Powell's direction, then, unexpectedly, said something very quickly to the interpreter.

'He understands that,' the interpreter said.

'OK.' Powell looked visibly relieved. 'But the other part of it is this: if you choose to say nothing to me, then later on, if we go to court, the judge and the jury might think it means you are guilty. Do you understand that?'

Al-Talehi nodded this time, before the interpreter could speak.

'He understands that, too,' the interpreter said.

'Good. Do you know what the truth is, Akil?'

Karen sat back. Because he was a mental health case and there was an Appropriate Adult in, Powell had to go through a series of formal questions to find out whether Al-Talehi knew the difference between truth and falsehood. But at least Al-Talehi seemed to be listening now. As Powell asked the questions he either responded with nods, or in Arabic, to the interpreter. Only when Powell had finished and was speaking again to Spenceley – trying to get him to agree that they could proceed – did Al-Talehi sneak a look in her direction. She met his eyes and he looked away at once. She saw no hatred of women in his expression. He was frightened of her, as he was frightened of everyone else in the room. He looked like someone who had woken up to find that he was in a different century, on a different planet, surrounded by aliens. He had ruined Caroline Philips's life, but in this room he looked ill, in need of treatment. It was hard to put the two things together.

'First I'm going to start going over items of evidence we've already mentioned in other interviews,' Powell said. 'What we're trying to discover here is what part you might have played in the stabbing of a young woman called Caroline Philips.'

The minute Caroline's name was mentioned, Al-Talehi started to cry. Powell paused, to see if he would stop, but instead Al-Talehi continued weeping and started to mutter, in English. It was hard to make out what he was saying. Karen thought he might have been saying he was sick, and that he was sorry. It wasn't clear.

Before Powell could get him to clarify, Simmons jumped in, reminding Al-Talehi of his advice. 'I've told you that I think it's best if you say nothing, Akil. You remember that? You don't have to say anything at all.'

Al-Talehi stopped speaking, but the tears were still running out of his eyes.

'He's not fit to be interviewed,' Simmons said.

'The doctor says he is,' Powell replied. 'Do you want a break, Akil?' he asked.

'That might be best,' Spenceley said. 'Then I can have another word with him.'

'*You* can speak to him in here,' Powell said. 'You're not his solicitor, you're the Appropriate Adult.'

'No break,' Al-Talehi said, quite clearly, interrupting them. He shook his head vigorously. 'You tell me what I have done. You tell me.'

'I want to tell you what has happened,' Powell said, carefully. 'Then I want *you* to tell me what you have done.'

'Once again, Akil, my advice to you is to say nothing—'

'You've given your advice, Mr Simmons,' Powell said, cutting him off, annoyed. 'You can't repeat it throughout this interview.' He turned to Spenceley. 'Has Akil understood his solicitor's advice?' he asked.

'I understand,' Akil said. 'Tell me what I have done.'

Spenceley shrugged. 'I think he understands,' he said.

Powell took a deep breath, then started to go through the evidence they had. There wasn't that much of it. They had a sighting of him at a newsagent's on Harrison Road at 6.30 p.m., then Colin Norton's evidence placing him at the top of King Cross. In between he could easily have walked to the attack site and committed the crime. Al-Talehi listened to it all with his head down, shaking, tears dripping from the tip of his nose on to the desk. When asked whether he had been in the newsagent's on Harrison Road he nodded. Asked if he had been at King Cross, with blood on his T-shirt, three-quarters of an hour later, he looked up with panic in his eyes.

'I don't know. I don't know any of it. I can't remember anything.'

Simmons sighed theatrically, and Powell gave him a cautionary glance.

'This young girl was very brutally attacked, Akil,' Powell said. 'Her life has been ruined. Someone pinned her down and stabbed her repeatedly, in the mouth. Could that have been you?'

Al-Talehi started to sob, rocking backwards and forwards on the seat. 'It is not me ...' he said. 'It is not me.'

'Is that a denial?' Powell asked, speaking very gently.

'I don't say anything. My solicitor say me that. I don't say anything. Because I not remember ...' He sounded desperate, miserable, bewildered.

'So you're not denying it?' Karen asked him softly. Powell looked over at her this time. She kept her eyes on Al-Talehi. He looked at her, then looked away again.

'You're saying you don't remember, Akil? Is that right?' she asked.

'I can't deny it. I don't remember anything. When these things happen it is like I am not there. I am not there. It is another man, inside me. Not me.'

'When which things happen?' Powell asked.

'Terrible things. Terrible things.' He brought his hands up and tried to wipe his face. But his arms were moving clumsily, like a baby's hands. He almost managed to hit Spenceley instead. He was very agitated.

'Caroline had blood under her fingernails,' Powell said. 'We think she scratched her attacker. You have scratches on your chest. Do you understand that? Could Caroline have scratched you?'

Al-Talehi was crying aloud now. Karen wasn't even sure he could hear Powell.

'I think you should just put your new evidence and we should call a halt to this,' Simmons said.

'We should stop it now,' Spenceley said. 'I'm very worried about him.'

Powell looked over to Karen, as if asking her what to do. She shrugged. 'It's a waste of time,' she said. 'He's sick. Put the DNA to him because we have to. But he's already given us enough.'

Al-Talehi had carried out the attack. He couldn't remember it because he should have been taking medication and wasn't.

She listened as Powell told him about the DNA evidence. Al-Talehi was crying so loud she expected the custody sergeant to arrive any minute. Spenceley looked very uncomfortable.

'That means it's your blood under her nails,' Powell said, finishing. 'Have you anything to say to that?'

'He can't even hear you,' Spenceley said, talking above the noise. 'We need to stop this and call a doctor.'

'Can you hear me, Akil?' Powell repeated, speaking louder. 'It's your blood. Caroline scratched *you*. That's what I'm saying.'

Karen turned her eyes away from Al-Talehi, disgusted with it. She had hoped to feel rage against him, a desire to strike him. But he was genuinely distressed and confused. He really could not remember what he had done, but knew it was something horrific. If she felt anything for him it could only be a kind of pity. This was what happened in life. Some people were healthy, some people were sick. It didn't make it any easier to cope with or understand, but it wasn't Al-Talehi's fault. Not *this* Al-Talehi, the man sitting weeping about it. He was as distraught as they were.

The interpreter started to speak, relaying what Al-Talehi was now muttering feverishly in his own language. 'He is apologizing,' he said. 'He is apologizing over and over again for what he has done. He does not remember, but he is sorry. That is what he says.'

44

Richard Powell asked her to pass the news to Caroline. She didn't want to, but couldn't say no. She had been keen to interview Al-Talehi for exactly this reason – to have something to tell Caroline, to be able to explain it to her. She could hardly refuse to speak to her because what they had learned was distressing and useless.

So she drove to the hospital again and sat in the same room she had been in four hours earlier, by the same bed, holding Caroline's hand. The atmosphere felt like a suffocating blanket of misery, wrapped tightly around her. It was so oppressive she had to concentrate on regulating her breathing, to make it seem like she was functioning normally.

'The man we are holding will be charged later today,' she told her. She kept her eyes on Caroline's as she spoke. 'The evidence is strong. We're sure it was him.'

Almost anything else would have been easier, she thought. A rape attempt, a robbery, a grudge of some sort. Something that held within it a germ of hatred for Caroline to hang on to, to respond to. But instead she had to tell her that she was the victim of a random attack by a sad, sick man who couldn't even remember what he had done or why. A man who was devastated and confused by his actions, who had repeatedly and abjectly apologized for something he could barely be held to blame for. Probably there wasn't even a 'why' that made sense to anyone but him at the time. He had failed to take his drugs and he had seen Caroline on a path. A random connection on Saville Park. *Nothing* personal about it. *Nothing* that had anything to do with Caroline. Under other circumstances he might have focused the same savage attentions on something inanimate – a tree, or a car. Caroline had ended up where she was because she was an anonymous placeholder in a dysfunctional mental scheme.

'He's a man with an illness,' Karen said, as if that explained everything. 'He has mental health problems.'

She placed a pad in Caroline's hands and asked her if she had any questions. But there were no questions. Caroline stared at her, unblinking, no readable expression in her eyes at all.

Back at the station Karen ate a late breakfast, alone, in the canteen. The canteen staff tried to chat to her, but she gave them monosyllabic replies. There was a knot of pressure, right where the pain in her chest should have been. She felt her mental state to be more precarious than at any point in the last few years.

When she went back through to the CID room the atmosphere was buoyant. All nine detectives were in now, talking and laughing about Al-Talehi. She gathered the CPS had already agreed a charge against him, but first he was wanted at Killingbeck, where he was now a possible suspect in Bulldog too, despite the lack of DNA evidence against him for that case. No one spoke to her. She had an odd feeling that they were wary of her, that they were avoiding eye contact. She sat down at her desk and looked at the pile of work that had accumulated over the last two weeks.

After a while someone sat at the desk opposite her. She looked up. It was Dick Nuttall, the other Halifax DI. Close up his face was covered with tiny red marks, like spots, or insect bites. He nodded at her. He looked grim, but that wasn't unusual.

'There's someone in with Richard,' he said. 'Richard' meant Richard Powell. They always called Powell 'Richard' and Nuttall 'Dick', to distinguish between them. 'He was looking for you,' he continued, speaking very quietly. In her peripheral vision she could see that some of the excitement had abated now, and a couple of the others were watching to see what they were talking about.

'Who is it?' she asked.

'A superintendent from Discipline and Complaints – Franklin. Do you know him?'

She bit her lip. He was the bastard who had tried to pin Stijn's death on to her. He had spent four months hounding her, and had twice arrested and interviewed her. She had been suspended for the entire time.

'What does he want?' she asked.

'I don't know,' Nuttall said. He smiled sympathetically. 'I just thought I should warn you.'

She nodded, and he stood up and left her. She waited for a second then looked over to Powell's office. There was a window into it, but Powell had positioned a big whiteboard in front of it, so she couldn't see what was going on. She realized she had started to sweat.

What were the options? Wait and see? Or get up and leave? That was easy. She stood to leave, but only as Powell's door began to open. Too slow. She paused, saw Powell put his head round the door and check her desk. She caught his eyes. For a moment she thought he might simply look through her, then close the door and pretend she wasn't there. He looked as if that was what he wanted to do. But instead he brought a hand up and summonsed her, a quick, discreet gesture. She nodded and began to walk over to him. She could see Franklin now, pacing the restricted space inside Powell's office; she remembered that big, balding head and stocky, aggressive frame.

'Can you just step inside?' Powell said quietly, when she had almost reached him. His face was drawn, serious. Whatever it was, it wasn't going to be good.

She stepped in and Powell closed the door on them all. The office was small and the day was hot. The atmosphere was stuffy. She could smell male sweat.

'Hello, Karen,' Franklin said. 'Please sit down.' A business-like tone to his voice. Unpleasant work, but somebody had to do it.

'DC Sharpe to you,' she said. She remained standing, by the door.

Franklin shrugged. 'As you wish.' He was dressed in a normal grey suit, but he looked forbiddingly official.

Powell sat down at his desk, behind Franklin, then cleared his throat nervously. Karen saw him gesturing frantically to her, making some kind of motion with his hand, across his head.

'Someone has made a serious allegation about you,' Franklin said.

She could see he was enjoying it, behind the mask of official disinterest. He waited in vain for her to reply. She gritted her teeth and stared at him.

'I have been asked to investigate it,' he said.

'Don't I get representation?' she asked.

'Not yet,' he said, smiling sadly. 'I'm just here to notify you and arrange a suitable time for an interview.'

'An interview?'

'Yes. Sometime today.'

'What's the allegation?'

'A man called Brian Johnson has accused you of theft.'

It was all she could do to keep her face blank. So that was what Powell had been gesturing to her – a combing movement. But it was impossible that Johnson would *know* she had taken his comb. He had seen nothing, so if he had complained then it was nothing but an assumption. There could be no evidence.

'Do you have anything to say to that?'

'That's hardly an allegation. Theft of what? When? Don't you know your job? You're meant to serve me with proper notification, in documentary form.'

'This isn't a disciplinary matter. It's more serious. I'm conducting this as a criminal inquiry.'

'Of course you fucking are. If I scratched my head in public you'd treat it as criminal.'

'Do not speak to me in that way. Kindly remember your rank.' He raised his voice slightly, biting, then caught himself and took a breath. 'Try to do yourself a favour,' he said. 'It doesn't always pay to be aggressive.'

From behind the desk Powell coughed, nervously. She looked over at him, clasping her hands behind her back. 'Brian Johnson alleges you took a comb belonging to him,' Powell said.

Now was the time to frown in disbelief. She did.

Franklin looked down at Powell, smirking slightly. 'Please leave this to me, Dick,' he said.

Powell shrugged. 'OK. But she's right about the paperwork. If not, we should have a fed rep in here—'

'I have the paperwork,' Franklin said. He shifted on his feet, jutting his chin out. He had a nerve to talk about aggression.

'You're going to serve me over a *comb*?' she asked. It was ridiculous.

'Theft is theft, officer,' Franklin said, pompously. He bent down to the briefcase at his feet and opened it. 'Besides, there may be other aspects to this theft. It may have been an attempt to obtain evidence illegally.'

'I can't do an interview today,' she said. 'I've been on all night.'

'You will have to.'

'Or what? You arrest me – for an allegation about a fucking comb?'

'Don't use language like that.'

'You find it offensive, right?' She felt a violent urge to step over and kick him. Take his legs out from under him.

He straightened up, face red, hand clutching a sheaf of papers.

'I'm sure a mutually convenient time can be arranged,' Powell said. He cleared his throat again. 'Tomorrow maybe,' he suggested. 'Karen has been on all night and did valuable work with—'

'If that's what you want,' Franklin interrupted. 'But you'll have to have this anyway.' He sorted through the paperwork and pulled out a pink sheet. He held it towards her. She didn't take it.

'Please don't be childish,' he said.

She didn't move.

He took his arm back, then scratched his head, as if he were only now recalling what it was like to deal with her. 'It makes no difference,' he said. 'I can tell you just the same.' He looked up at her. 'It's a formal notice of suspension,' he said. 'You're suspended as of this moment.'

45

It was just after midday as she came down into Manningham, in heavy traffic. She crawled along Toller Lane with all the other drivers, watching their nerves fraying. Her brain felt dead.

She was suspended again. At the moment she was finding it hard to take that in, to compute what it might mean for her. She could ask Ronnie what he thought she should do. He would know. But before she could see him she had to sleep, and before she could sleep she had to take Mairead over to Pete's parents' place. On the way she had to tell her what was going on. Could she do that, then just dump her on the mother and father of the man she was going to leave? Mairead had known Pete for a long time. She was going to be very distressed about it. Another dose of issues from her mother.

At 11.20 a.m. she pulled the car on to the driveway at Pete's house just as the postman was walking to the door with the second delivery. She nodded at him through the open car window.

'Lovely morning,' he said to her.

'Is it?'

He frowned, handing her a bundle of letters. 'Nice weather, I mean,' he said.

'I'm glad you like it,' she said.

She got out and walked over to the house, not even wanting to go in. Pete's car was on the drive, so he was there, waiting for her, no doubt. She fished in her bag and found her mobile. She had switched it off after getting back to Halifax that morning, too stressed to answer the thing. She switched it on now and saw four voice messages, one from Ronnie, three from Pete. There would be time for them later.

But she had only got as far as turning her key in the front door lock before the phone began to ring. She paused on the doorstep and pulled the door closed a little, then turned her back on it and answered the phone, standing on the step, in the porch. Above her the sunlight was fierce, making her squint uncomfortably.

'Hello?' She hadn't recognized the number that came up.

'Karen?'

'Yes. Who is it?'

'It's Tim Thorne, Karen.'

Why would *he* call her? She sensed something from his tone immediately. 'What is it?'

'Where are you?' he asked.

'Why? What's up?'

'You're not driving?'

'No. I'm at home. Why are you calling?'

'I've got some bad news, I'm afraid. I thought someone ought to tell you.'

Mairead, she thought. But that was stupid. Why would Tim Thorne call her if something had happened to Mairead? Besides, he sounded upset. 'What is it?' she asked again.

'It's about Ronnie.'

'What about him?'

'He was driving out to the Fleming place this morning. He had some kind of episode—'

'Episode?'

'Yes. We're not sure yet what it was. They found him collapsed at the roadside, beside his car.'

'Is he OK?'

Silence.

She bit her lip. 'Is he OK?'

'He's dead, Karen. He died in the ambulance.'

It was as if she had stepped off a ledge and was tumbling through the air, in freefall. She wanted to ask him if it was a joke, but knew it wasn't. She couldn't take it in, couldn't say anything. She leaned back against the wall of the porch, her legs shaking.

'Karen? Did you hear me?'

'Yes,' she said. She could hardly get the word out. Her tongue felt like a thick stump, stuck in her mouth. She sat down suddenly, frightened she might actually fall.

'I thought somebody should tell you,' he said again.

'Yes. Thank you.'

'I knew about you two ...'

He stopped speaking. She sat staring at the ground, her breath fast now. She tried to think of something to say, some way to react to it. But it didn't seem true. How *could* it be true?

'Is it certain?' she asked, uselessly.

'I've been there,' he said. 'I've been to the hospital, seen Laura—'

'Why? Why did he die?'

He mistook the question for something rational. 'They don't know yet,' he said. 'They say maybe an aneurysm.'

'Yes. But *why*?'

A long silence.

'I don't know, Karen. I don't know why. I'm sorry.'

She placed the phone on the ground and looked down the driveway, trying to make the thought slot into place, connect it with something. But it wouldn't work. Ronnie couldn't be dead, not just like that. All around her, the day was continuing as if nothing had happened. She could still see the same things, the same objects and colours. She felt sick.

She could hear Thorne's voice speaking to her still, from the abandoned handset. She picked it up and cut the connection. From behind her the front door opened. She looked over her shoulder. Pete was standing there, frowning at her.

'Are you coming in or what?' he snapped. 'I've been trying to reach you all fucking morning. Mairead was meant to be gone an hour ago. Why isn't your mobile switched on?'

She stared at him, not understanding. She saw his expression change as he registered her own. His features relaxed. 'Is something wrong?' he asked.

The knowledge of it lurched inside her, as if it were alive. She wanted to throw up. She gasped and leaned back against the wall. Then she knelt down and started to cry, big sobs that stuck in her throat. He bent down beside her at once.

'Karen, has something happened?' he asked again. He put his hand on her shoulder. She brought a hand up and took hold of it. 'What's the matter?' he asked.

She didn't know what to say. She was taking gasps of breath now. He squatted down beside her, in the porch.

'Has something happened to you?' he asked again.

She shook her head. 'Not to me. Someone died.' She looked towards him, still clutching his hand.

'Who?' he asked gently, voice full of worry now. 'Who died?'

'Ronnie Shepherd,' she said. 'He collapsed and died this morning.'

He frowned. 'Ronnie Shepherd? The DI?'

She nodded.

'Shit,' he said. Then she saw him asking himself the question: *Why is she so upset about that?*

'He was deputy SIO on Bulldog, right?' he asked, carefully.

She nodded again, trying to control her breathing. She saw Pete look away from her, stare at the ground, then nod twice, to himself. He sat back, taking his hand from hers. He looked at her as if she were something disgusting.

'It was him, then,' he said. 'It was Shepherd you were seeing.'

SATURDAY, 7 JULY

46

Tim Thorne sat behind Riggs's desk, leaning his elbows on the cheap Formica surface and resting his face in his hands. He closed his eyes. His brain was full of confusion. It had been like that since Wednesday, when he had been peremptorily informed that he was now deputy SIO on the Bulldog inquiry. Ronnie Shepherd had keeled over, Tom Joyce had gone off on stress leave (no one was sure whether Ronnie's death was the cause or not), and, for some reason, David Riggs had picked him to act up.

'Are you OK, sir?'

He nodded, keeping his head in the same position. It was a DC called Clare Isles who had spoken. She had come in to tell him something about Ian Whitfield. It had been non-stop like this for almost fifty hours. One decision after another with no help from Riggs at all. Riggs was totally fucking useless.

He wasn't sure he could take much more of it. If he had been able to sleep even a little it would be different. But normal sleep patterns had been out of the question since Wednesday. Even Riggs had called him in the night, at 2 a.m., asking for an update on Akil Al-Talehi. They were holding Al-Talehi on a warrant of further detention. So far he had blanked all their questions in repeated interviews. Without more there wasn't going to be a charge against him in relation to Enisa Fleming. And getting more wasn't proving easy.

Shepherd's death had shocked him – but only in the way of all unexpected deaths. It hadn't sunk in at an emotional level, and why should it? Yes he had worked more than once with Ronnie, was familiar with his working habits, and, because of Laura, knew him personally a little better than some others, but Ronnie wasn't a friend.

That attitude had changed at the hospital. Laura had been so distraught and dishevelled he had barely been able to recognize her. She had looked mad. It had taken three nurses to calm her. As Tim arrived she had been howling at the top of her voice, pulling at her hair, slamming her fists off the wall. He had tried to intervene at once, to help her, but she had flailed at him with her nails as if *he* were to blame. He had livid scratches down both arms.

'Shall I continue?' Clare Isles asked. He nodded again, still not looking at her. He wished she would go away. Maybe if he ignored her for long enough she would. He needed time to be alone, he thought, not to have to deal with a thousand queries each day. A thousand decisions that he alone seemed to be responsible for. He brought his hands away from his face and looked at Clare Isles.

'Sorry, Clare,' he said. 'I haven't had much sleep lately. What did you want to say?'

'Ian Whitfield, sir. I went round to his girlfriend's place some time ago, where he lives, and she told me he was abroad, working in Holland. She said he had left on the first of June ...'

He had heard all this at a briefing weeks ago. He let her go on. He had always half-fancied Clare Isles. One of the things he liked about her was that she was more bulky than the women he was usually attracted to. (Laura was as thin as a rake.) Clare was almost plump, but she had a way of moving and looking at you that made her very sexy. Rumour was that a few months ago she had started on the Atkins diet. She was losing the kilos too rapidly now, he thought. It made her look older.

'Then this week I got details from the aircraft manifests,' she continued. 'They show that Whitfield did fly out to Amsterdam on the first of June, but on a fixed return ticket. He returned five days later. So he has no alibi for the night of the eighth, and either Nadine Askwith is lying when she says she hasn't heard from him, or he's gone AWOL on her.'

'Nadine Askwith is the girlfriend?'

'Yes.'

'Whitfield,' he said, thinking aloud. 'The guy from the removal company.' He thought about it. 'Didn't we already upgrade the action to locate him?'

'Yes. Mr Shepherd upgraded it once we found out he had no alibi, on Tuesday night ...' The night before he died. A little coloration came to her cheeks as she mentioned Ronnie. Very attractive. 'He's still outstanding,' she said.

'Is that why you're here?'

'No. Not quite. Over the last few days I did a few more checks on Whitfield,' she said. 'I know he doesn't fit the profile. I know there's no discoverable personal link between Whitfield and the Flemings, so everything I'm doing goes back to the burglary line really ...'

'That doesn't matter. Tell me what you've done.'

'Well, I thought it might be useful to find out the addresses Whitfield had worked while with the removal company. I got them to give me a list for the six months prior to him leaving their employment. Then I tried to correlate those addresses to burglary reports from the same period.'

He rubbed his eyes and looked at her. 'That sounds interesting,' he said. It also sounded like a lot of work.

'There wasn't much of a correlation,' she said. 'The figures looked normal. In six months Whitfield was involved in sixty-five removals in West Yorkshire. Of the premises involved – so far as I have been able to match them – only five were burgled within roughly the same period.'

'Sounds average.'

'Yes. But then I ran a check on the values of the properties. That took a little more time. The most expensive five properties from the list were the same properties that were burgled.'

That *was* impressive. 'So you think Whitfield might have been a property scout – scouting out high-value properties for associates to target?'

'It's possible.'

He sat back in the seat and thought about it. It was good, hard, detailed work that she had done. If it were true, then it would account for the lack of any other signs of scouting or preparation. Whoever had carried out the burglary wouldn't have needed to do any scouting because Ian Whitfield had already done it for them. If he had moved the Flemings in he would have known about their valuables, their lack of alarm system, the best entry and exit points.

'But they took nothing,' he said.

'They were disturbed. Things went wrong.'

He nodded in agreement. 'It's worth a closer look,' he said. 'Good work, Clare. Good initiative.'

She coloured again, then smiled, more pleased with his praise than he expected.

'But I don't know what else we can do,' he said. 'Finding Whitfield is a priority action already.'

'That's why I came to see you, sir. I think he will show up at Askwith's sooner or later. I was wondering if we could get cover for the premises.'

'Proper cover, you mean? From the FTT? No way. Not today.'

The Force Tactical Team – along with nearly half the officers on duty county-wide (including fifteen detectives from his teams) – had all been drafted in to assist with pre-emptive public order duties. The BNP and the 'anti-fascist league' were both planning to hold demonstrations in central Bradford that afternoon. The BNP march had been banned and the Force had put a lot of intelligence-gathering activity into identifying extreme right-wing racists who might want to turn things into a riot. Throughout the day those suspects were going to be arrested or monitored. There was no chance of them getting the FTT today.

'I just thought a couple of our own people,' Isles said. 'I would do most of it, if you authorize the overtime.'

She was keen, but why not? 'OK,' he said. 'Take three others and set up a proper rota. Run it through till Monday, then we'll take stock if there's no result. This race riot fuss will have quietened down by then.'

47

This all came back to Stijn and what he had done to her.

She saw it as if she were watching it happen to someone else. Every time she thought of it, it was like that – something brutal, inflicted upon somebody else, which she was being forced to watch. She could see the woman, down there in the narrow storeroom, flat out on the floor, she could see the things that were happening to her, but she could not feel them as if she were that woman, looking out at the world with her eyes and her senses. She was floating above it all, an invisible spectator. But at every moment she knew the woman was herself and the young girl with her, snivelling and distraught, covered in blood, was Mairead.

It made it worse that it came to her like this. It wracked her with impotent anguish, flooded her with pity for the woman. It made her stuff her fist into her mouth, forcing back the tears, as her whole body burned and shook with fear and rage. To see it acted out in front of her, over and over again, while she could do nothing but watch the woman suffer, somehow made it more horrific. As if it were not simply an appalling memory that, with time, would fade.

She couldn't escape the reality of it. It was like documentary footage, each time as real as the last. She could not believe human beings could be this cruel to each other. She could see the pain and terror in the woman's eyes. She could *see* her trying to stifle her cries to spare her daughter from hearing them. She could see the man pinning her down, his hand between her shoulder blades, his immense tattooed body grinding her into the ground, so heavy the woman was suffocating, gasping for air. She could see him pushing his thick, massive, erect penis inside her, forcing her legs apart with his knees. And all the time, in the room next door, listening, she could see her daughter, weeping hysterically, restrained by the other man, who held a gun against her head.

Stijn had raped her as her daughter was forced to listen. Karen had known what he was going to do and had tried to fight him off. He had struck her so hard she had been reduced to a quivering wreck without motor reflexes, something he could tear the clothes from, slap, punch, kick and stamp on. He had arranged her on the ground beneath him like a ragdoll. When he first started penetrating her she had been so badly concussed she had been only half-conscious of it.

Before that, both men had struck Mairead as well, without any concern for her age – at that time, one and a half years ago, she had been only eleven. But they had set out deliberately to terrify her, to use her to shock and frighten her mother. They had beaten and punched them both, held guns to their heads, threatened them over and over with the prospect of their own deaths. Karen had thought for certain that she would die that day. She had found out since then that Mairead had feared the same.

And these images were a fraction of the whole. She had hours of it in her head, squirming and teeming like a destructive parasite, each image leading to others, one after the other, mounting up and rising in concentrated terror until the whole thing was like a deafening, relentless scream tearing her head apart.

She sat in the car and screwed her eyes shut against it, her hands holding tightly on to her hair. She banged her head off the steering wheel, trying to force an alternative pain into her brain. She kept going until her nose started to bleed. The blood brought some kind of relief, a chink of light shining through the asphyxiating fog of memories and images.

It was over, in her past. A year and a half ago. She had killed Stijn for what he had done. There was nothing more that could be done except to forget him. Yet try as she might, that would not happen: *We all have a past. The trick is to survive it, move on, keep going.* Ronnie Shepherd's words. But he was dead.

She let the tears come. Tears for Ronnie were better than this compressed coil of internal panic. Or the crippling guilt she felt on account of Mairead and everything she had subjected her to. She wanted desperately to see Mairead now – to put her arms around her and hug her, to look at her and see that she was alive and well and unscathed by it all.

But Mairead wasn't unscathed. What she had seen and suffered would mark her for the rest of her life. There was no going back now.

What was done was irreparable. You got one chance with children. She had wasted hers.

She looked around, taking in her surroundings for the first time. She was on the hard shoulder of the M1, just inside West Yorkshire. Three days ago she had got into this car with Mairead and driven her to Pete Bains's parents' house near Harrogate. During the journey she had tried to hold herself together, for Mairead's sake, but Mairead was far from stupid. She had known something was wrong. She had even refused to hug Karen when they parted. She didn't do that unless she was really distressed. Pete's parents were visibly worried also. Karen had tried uselessly to reassure them, but by then she had felt as if she were running a fever. She could hardly speak without her teeth chattering. The priority had been to get away from them, to get away from everyone.

So she had got back into the car and kept going. She had driven aimlessly until long after dark and then pulled in to a service area somewhere. At the time she had no idea where it was and hadn't cared. Now she knew she had ended up just north of Glasgow. She took a room in the motel there and, during the subsequent three nights, left it only twice – to pay and to demand that she not be disturbed (an instruction they had ignored twice), and to buy alcohol from the shop in the service area. She had selected a litre of cheap whisky, intending to down the whole bottle. But that hadn't happened. She had taken barely a sip before exhaustion had laid her out.

She could remember little of the hours between then and now. It was as if she had taken a drug, her vision affected so that everything was a muddy grey. Time had washed and eddied around her, and mostly she had lain on the bed, too tired to think clearly, too tired even to move. At some point she had found herself in the tiny en suite toilet, staring at her face in the mirror. On the floor at her feet were bits of credit card (cut in two), the remains of her police ID (cut into many pieces), shreds of papers from her purse and pockets, all of it lying spread across the bathroom floor. She had destroyed anything that could identify her as Karen Sharpe.

When sleep came it was disturbed and shallow, and each time she woke she felt only more fatigued, more dejected. She wanted desperately to snap herself out of it. She didn't want this to end up like the other times. She had enough of a survival instinct kicking inside her to know she couldn't let that happen again.

In 1988, after Mairead was born, it had been so bad she could not remember anything about the birth. She had told Ronnie that. It was because she had been like this that she had walked out on her own daughter. The depression had been so overwhelming she had wanted to end it by killing herself.

It had taken three months in a psychiatric hospital to put her back together. After that they had given her the name Karen Sharpe and sent her north, to start a 'new life' – without her daughter.

But it hadn't worked.

She looked at the traffic streaming past her. She had woken up four hours ago determined to see Mairead, even if she had to pick her up early from Pete's parents. That was why she was here. But now that she had covered the distance she knew she couldn't see Mairead in this condition. If she could calm herself sufficiently to speak without sobbing, then maybe she could call her. But that was all.

She fumbled for the mobile in her bag and looked for Mairead's number. Pete had left countless messages since Wednesday, apologizing, asking her to return, worrying, yet all she had sent him was a one-line text telling him she wanted to be alone. Now, alongside his messages, she saw again the message from Ronnie. She had already listened to it many times, but she listened again now. It was the last thing he had said to her:

'Karen, it's Ronnie. Sorry to call so early, but I want you to come up to the hospital this afternoon. At two, if possible. I know you're off the squad, but I'd still like you to handle something for me. I've cleared it with Riggs. I want you to talk to Steve Fleming again. I think he's not been giving us everything. I need to have him pushed a bit, just so we know for sure. I think you would be best to handle that. Let me know if there's a problem. I'll explain more when I see you ... OK, bye then.'

There was a short pause before the 'OK, bye then', as if he had been considering saying something more personal, then thought better of it. Who knows who might have access to her mobile? At least, that's what she hoped had been going on in his mind. A futile hope now.

She needed to keep her consciousness full, busy, teeming with external detail. It was the only way she knew to deal with what was happening to her. *Keep busy. Keep going. Work.* It had taken her nearly three days to get this far, determined to get out of the bed and function. But she had a chink of light now, a glimpse of clarity.

The build-up to this fall had taken months to grow inside her. She could see that now. Her reactions had only gradually become extreme, out of proportion, because she had let things mount up inside, swamping her. She had not known Ronnie Shepherd long enough to react so hysterically to his death. His death was a blow, it was terrible, but it shouldn't have toppled her like it did. The truth was that Stijn had done that, many, many months before – the delayed fuse planted in her brain. Then there were the problems with Pete, and all the wounded, sad people thrown in her path to keep the lesion alive and festering. Jana Fleming had started the process, Caroline Philips had accelerated it. She could hardly close her eyes now without seeing images of Caroline's butchered mouth. Random destruction, thrown at her from the other side of that thin divide, from the world she was rapidly slipping into. Caroline was there already, sinking in a vortex of horror, everything she had once believed destroyed in the space of moments. Ronnie was just the last straw, dying suddenly for no good reason. Another random trigger.

Taken together it was too much to control. She needed to give herself time to take each set-back separately, in context, to absorb it. She needed Mairead. But she couldn't be selfish. The last thing Mairead wanted was another visitation from her mad mother, face streaked with tears, eyes red and sore, limbs trembling with the fear of all the things she had wreaked upon her, all the things she was powerless to protect her from.

If she could occupy herself just a little longer, get herself back to normal by tomorrow, then pick up Mairead as planned, in a normal, stable condition, that would be best. Better than showing up distressed and disrupting all her plans. She had to put Mairead first.

But how was she supposed to stay busy? They had suspended her. She wasn't even supposed to work.

Ronnie had asked her to visit Steve Fleming. That was something she could do as a civilian, an ordinary person. She had met the man, developed a relationship with him. She knew his daughter and his in-laws. There was nothing to stop her paying him a private visit, in a private capacity. Even Franklin couldn't stop her doing that.

She sat with her nose dripping blood into her lap and struggled to think of the things Fleming needed to be asked. What was it that Ronnie had in mind? She could do it. She could *make* herself think about it all, force so much work into her brain that there was no room for the grief, the misery, the depression.

All she had to do was start thinking about Fleming, and keep going. *Keep going.*

What *could* he be hiding? And why? The man who had forgotten his roots. The phrase appeared in her mind without warning.

Where had that come from? Anyway, it wasn't accurate. Fleming didn't want much to do with his drunk of a father, but that didn't mean he had forgotten his roots.

So why had she thought that? Then it came to her: Colin Norton. That was where the phrase had come from.

She couldn't have been more wrong about Norton. She had questioned him about a witness statement she had been certain was false. She had thought him a liar – read all the signs of lying in his words and gestures – yet he had been telling her the truth. But now she remembered him looking at a picture of Fleming on the TV. He had made a remark and she hadn't really listened. Now she recalled it. '*He's forgotten his past.*' That was what he had said.

She started the engine. Why hadn't she thought more carefully about that? She had heard Norton mutter but had paid it little attention. She had taken it as a comment about Fleming forgetting his roots because he was white and had married a Muslim, but Norton hadn't said that. What he had said implied something else. How would Colin Norton know that Steve Fleming had forgotten his past? How did he even know who Steve Fleming was?

Visit Colin Norton again. Ask him about it, she thought. *Keep going.*

48

Michael Rawson got to Altrincham by midday and drove through the security gates at Khan's place without hindrance. Khan had a mansion off Arley Road – a real mansion, with a striking red clock tower, two distinct wings, a gatehouse and a half-mile driveway flanked by sycamore trees and security cameras. Normally Michael enjoyed coming to the place. In the last four years – since he had stopped managing Khan's security – he had only ever been here on pleasure trips.

Khan threw extravagant parties. Minor celebrities were often guests. Maria loved it. And Khan had always treated them well. He managed to give the impression that they were as important as the other guests, even the famous ones. He probably did that with everyone – it was a gift he had – but Michael appreciated it nevertheless, for Maria's sake.

This time was different. This time he had been summonsed. That made him very uneasy. He watched the cameras at the gate swivel to zoom on his face while other cameras comprehensively covered a perimeter around his car, and, as the gates slid back, knew that someone in the cellar security room in the main building must surely have recognized him to open them so quickly. Probably either Phil Malone or Bobby Singh. He had interviewed them both for their jobs. He had installed the entire security system (in all twenty-seven rooms and throughout the 17-acre grounds) and knew exactly how it worked. Khan kept a twenty-four hour presence on the premises, usually consisting of four men with differing roles. But there were always two men in the CCTV suite.

He left the car on the huge gravel crescent outside the front entrance and then walked two hundred yards around the side of the building, down a short flight of steps leading to the 'tradesman's entrance'. There was a stone-carved sign above the low wooden door which said just that – 'Tradesman's Entrance' – next to another CCTV camera. He rang the silent bell. The door opened almost at once and he found himself staring up at Suresh Venkatsami, Khan's personal assistant.

Venkatsami was tall, gaunt, angular, always clean-shaven, always smartly dressed in suits, shirts and ties. He looked like an expensive city PA, and had perfected the art of looking down on everyone else with undisguised disdain. Michael – in his usual jeans, shirt and battered Barbour – felt scruffy beside him. Exactly like a tradesman. But he knew the full list of Venkatsami's duties, so aside from considerations of rational fear, he had never had much time for Venkatsami's attitude.

Venkatsami didn't smile, didn't greet him. But that was no different from normal. 'You're late,' he said, instead. 'You had an appointment for midday.'

Michael checked his wristwatch. It was five past twelve. He felt a little trickle of sweat down his back. 'Yeah,' he said. 'Looks that way.'

'I'll apologize to Mr Khan for you.'

Inside, he was thoroughly searched by a smaller Asian man he didn't recognize, relieved of his clasp knife and sent along to the library. He knew the way. He sat in the two-storey room (it was a proper library, with ladders to access the higher shelves) and wondered if Venkatsami already knew what was going on.

He had a long wait. That *was* different. Plenty of time to consider his position – exactly what Khan wanted him to do, presumably. He went over again in his mind the things it would be impossible to tell Khan. He didn't want to slip up.

From his time working here he knew of at least four men who had come here 'on business' and not got out again. They had left, of course, literally – because nothing, *nothing*, ever happened within these premises (that was an absolute rule) – but they had driven out through the gates as good as dead men. It was that simple. He had nothing to do with the arrangements – that was down to Suresh – but he knew what had happened to them.

He wasn't personally frightened, because he had never suffered those kinds of fears. That was what had marked him out as different at school, and it was why – despite his average build and height – other men were normally afraid of him. He knew that 99 per cent of the ability to successfully use violence came down to fear, the anticipation of damage. For one reason or another – maybe the sheer number of scrapes he had been in before he was fifteen years old – he had never felt a fear of personal harm or pain. Not ever. Every fight he had gone into – including those in the boxing ring – he hadn't given a damn about what kind of damage might be done to his body. He had been in severe pain several times in his life, but had learned very early on that pain was one type of stimuli, like many others – something that could be focused on, brooded about, or ignored. With concentration, it was possible to ignore almost any pain.

So what Khan might decide to do to him *personally* meant very little (and Khan knew that). But it was Maria and the kids he was frightened for. It was what Khan might do to them that gnawed at his gut and made him hunch over himself with anxiety. Like himself, Khan was a 'family man', which meant that his *own* family was everything to him. All other priorities and considerations fell into line behind that.

The door opened eventually, but it wasn't Khan who came in. Instead a small, traditionally dressed Asian woman shuffled in with a tea-tray bearing a teapot and two cups. She placed it on a small round table opposite Michael, at the other side of the library. She didn't look at him.

Khan appeared a few minutes later, closing the door behind him and walking quickly across to the tea-tray. He was nothing special to look at. Average height, well groomed (finely clipped, thin beard and moustache) with swept-back grey hair, about fifty-five years old. Like the tea lady, he didn't look at Michael. Michael stood up to greet him, but was ignored. That made him a little afraid. Not too much, but enough so Khan would notice. Khan had a nose for fear.

'Will you have tea, Michael?' Khan asked, already pouring a cup. His voice was smooth, accented with both Manchester and Pakistani inflections, but full of the presumptions of wealth. He was dressed in a dark-grey suit, but with a Pakistani cut to the jacket, which buttoned all the way up to his throat. He looked like a successful businessman with an abundance of connections, which he was, to most people round here.

'No thanks,' Michael said. He didn't drink tea. Khan knew that and probably remembered it. He had an impressive memory, and Michael had worked for him for the better part of the last ten years, closely. They knew a lot about each other, but never once, in all that period, had Michael had a summons of this kind.

Khan straightened up, gripping a china teacup quite delicately. He took a sip from it, slurping noisily.

'I had hoped never to have to meet you like this, Michael,' he said. He still wasn't looking at him. He was about ten feet away. The chair Michael had sat on – hard, black leather – was one of two easy chairs, both of which were at Michael's side of the room. He stood awkwardly by the chair, wondering whether to go over towards Khan. They normally shook hands.

'It's not very good for business to have to meet like this,' Khan added. He meant his personal involvement. That was what Suresh – and others like him – were for; to take that risk. On Wednesday it had been Mohammed Raj that Michael had spoken to, Khan's present security 'consultant'. Raj had then spoken to Khan and got back to him. Michael's request had been that Khan help him get Ian Whitfield out of the country. But Khan's response had been unexpected. Not only was he not prepared to help get Whitfield out, he wanted Michael to make sure Whitfield did *not* get out. He wanted Whitfield dead. Things had gone into seriously fucked-up mode after that.

Michael had been careful to conceal his own role when giving Raj the story. The story he had sold Raj was one of family ties gone wrong. Whitfield was Kershaw's cousin; he had screwed up and come to Kershaw for help. Kershaw, in turn, had asked Michael to approach Khan. In fact, Kershaw had no idea he was contacting Khan. He had hoped Khan would go for it without asking too many questions. It rang true enough, and putting the blame squarely on Kershaw and Whitfield was hardly a lie, given that it was Kershaw who had dragged him into this and Whitfield who had fucked everything up.

But when Raj responded he had clearly communicated Khan's anger with Michael. The implication was that he was holding Michael *personally* responsible, and if Michael didn't sort the matter then he would. Khan wanted the thing tidied quickly, before anyone got ideas and started looking in his direction. Aidan Kershaw was a part of Khan's set-up. Everyone knew that. So if the police started looking at him, it represented a threat to Raheesh Khan. That Kershaw had acted alone, without authorization from Khan – that Khan, in fact, had nothing whatsoever to do with the incident – was irrelevant. The connection was there through the personnel. That was the threat, and Khan didn't tolerate threats.

'I'm sorry it's all working out like this,' Michael said, clearing his throat, standing by the chair. Khan took another sip of tea. He *still* hadn't looked in Michael's direction. 'But I'm sure it will all be sorted soon.'

'It's not sorted already?' Khan raised his eyebrows. 'I thought you might be able to tell me it was already resolved, this issue. Then we could all get back to normal. That's why I asked you to come here.'

'It's complicated to resolve—' He started to explain, but Khan shook his head, silencing him.

'I don't want to know why. You know better than that. I just want a solution.' He turned from the table and put his back to Michael. He appeared to be inspecting the books.

Michael had been in this room with him several times and had never once seen him take a book from the shelves. Raj had told him Khan had purchased the entire library from the estate of some English lord. It was a show, for decoration only – like all the other trappings with which Khan painstakingly and expensively surrounded himself, including his many lucrative and legitimate business interests. When you were shipping the quantities of 'product' that Khan was shipping you needed a lot of straight outlets to clean the proceeds. Washing the money was a more time-consuming job than making it. Nearly all of Khan's big projects – the things that really immersed him – were in fact laundering and layering operations. *Making* money was easy by comparison.

'You wouldn't believe the amount I spend to make sure I am accepted in this country,' Khan said, with that unerring ability to say things that followed on from your private thoughts. 'It's a very expensive task. It's not easy to be accepted in English society. No matter how much money you have. There's too much racism. I don't tolerate racism.' He spoke calmly, gently even, no trace of threat in his voice. But the threat was there. Everything about his manner was screaming it to Michael. Was it because Enisa Fleming had been Asian – was that the extra dimension?

'You know that,' Khan continued. 'Racism is bad for business. This difficulty you are experiencing now has racist overtones, I believe.'

Michael opened his mouth to object – to tell him that Enisa Fleming's ethnic origin had nothing to do with the cock-up – but Khan just kept talking, back still turned.

'The problem with extreme actions is that they attract extreme responses,' he said. 'Police responses, press responses. That is why I *insist* that no such things should happen without my permission. My personal permission. You understand that, Michael?'

'Yes, Mr Khan. I do understand. What happened was—'

'What happened was unforgivable.' Khan placed his cup back on the table and stared at his feet. 'It will never be forgiven or forgotten. I expected better from you, Michael.'

He had already been through this with Raj. Michael shifted uncomfortably on his feet. Had he made a serious mistake coming here in person?

'This sort of thing is precisely what makes people want to turn the spotlight on. It makes them want to pry. They *have* to look, they *have* to ask their questions. It's a very uncomfortable position for everyone. It's the sort of position that makes me wish to cut my ties with the personnel who produced the problem. Sometimes that is all I *can* do in this kind of circumstance. And why shouldn't I? I gave no one permission to do this. I knew nothing about it.' He turned towards the bookshelves again, then reached a hand out and ran it along the spine of a volume. Michael felt a shiver run up his own spine. 'You realize how serious the position is, Michael?'

'I do, Mr Khan.' He was starting to sweat quite heavily now.

'You realize the affection I have for you?'

He didn't answer that one. Khan had affection for none but his own.

'This is all very distasteful,' Khan said. 'We have worked together for such a very long time. We know so much about each other. You know where your loyalties lie, Michael? You are fully aware of your responsibilities to me?'

'I am.'

'Your loyalty is not owed to Aidan Kershaw. He thinks he is your boss, but we know better. Aidan isn't even from these parts.'

What did that have to do with it? Aidan was from Yorkshire, originally. It wasn't far from 'these parts.' Closer than Pakistan.

'If there are things you need to say about Aidan, about his involvement in this affair, then you should speak to Suresh or Mohammed. You know that?'

'Yes.'

If only. The problem with giving Khan the complete truth – trying to offload it *all* on Kershaw – was the extent to which it would incriminate himself. Like it or not, he couldn't completely turn his back on Kershaw now. He was implicated.

Khan picked up the teapot and poured more tea. 'You weren't personally involved, Michael? You can guarantee me that?'

'I can guarantee you that, sir.' No choice but to lie. He hated lying to Khan, because he knew the penalties for being caught out.

'I hope so. I do hope so.' Khan sipped again at the tea, once again slurping. 'I think I can give you twenty-four hours,' he said. 'But after that I will have to ask Mohammed to deal with things. You understand my position?'

'Of course, Mr Khan. It will be sorted. You have my word.'

'Within twenty-four hours.'

'Yes.'

'I'll see you back here tomorrow, then. Bring Aidan Kershaw with you. You can go now. You know your way out.'

Michael thought about trying to say something else. But grovelling was useless. The result was what mattered now. He heaved an audible sigh of relief instead. Khan didn't react. Michael muttered goodbye and walked over to the door. As he stepped through it he looked back. Khan was still at the table, his back to him. He hadn't looked at him once.

49

It was nearly midday by the time Karen reached Mixenden. Outside Colin Norton's house she sat in the car and took deep breaths. Then she inspected her face in the mirror. There was blood clotted up both nostrils and she looked as if she had spent three days in tears. That's what Mairead would have seen if she'd picked her up early. She got out before she could dwell on that and walked straight up to Norton's front door.

It was a woman who opened the door. She was around 5ft 4in, thirty years old, and was wearing the blue skirt and jacket suit Karen recognized as the uniform for the Halifax building society. She was carrying the six-year-old Karen had seen previously, and looked as if she were struggling to hold him up. The kid had some kind of dried food smeared across his face. As before, Karen could hear the noise from the TV.

'Mrs Norton?'

The woman looked her up and down, frowning. 'Yes. Who are you?'

'Police . . .' She had no ID, she realized. That was in pieces in the bin of some cheap motel in Scotland. 'Is Colin in?'

The woman looked to be about to argue with her, or ask for ID, but the kid in her arms was struggling. She was hassled. She stepped back from the door and shouted for her husband instead.

There followed a kind of argument, with Colin senior shouting from upstairs that she should 'just close the fucking door and tell them to fuck off', and his wife telling him to do it himself. Then, without saying more to her, the woman walked through the door Karen knew led to the TV room and closed it after her. Karen was left standing on the doorstep. She waited, trying to maintain a normal level of patience, but she felt wound up inside, her legs and hands twitching with irritability, her breathing too quick.

After a moment Colin Norton's head peered from the landing above, looking down the stairs to see who was at the door.

'Can I speak to you, Colin?' Karen called out. Her voice sounded flaky.

He started to come down the stairs, cursing and swearing under his breath. Once again, he was naked from the waist up, wearing only a pair of jeans, his feet bare. 'You come to nick me, then?' he asked, once he was at the door. He stood right on the step, right in front of her, deliberately trying to intimidate. ''Cos it'll take more than you.'

'I haven't, Colin, no.'

'How many white boys you going to pull then – just to let a few students have their fucking march?'

'Sorry?' She didn't understand what he was saying at all.

'I've heard all about it. Three of my mates were arrested this morning. You know what I'm talking about ...' He looked her up and down. He was so close to her he had to step back a pace to do it. She saw him frown, doubt coming into his eyes. 'You been in a fight?' he asked. 'You look fucked.'

She looked down at herself. Her shirt and trousers were spotted with blood, crumpled, probably smelly. She had taken no change of clothes with her.

'I had a nosebleed,' she said.

He smirked at that, as if she were lying.

'I'm not here to arrest you,' she said. 'I don't know what you're talking about. I'm here to ask you about Steve Fleming.'

That puzzled him, but he didn't change his stance. He was *trying* to be aggressive with her. Did he *want* to be arrested?

'Last time I was here,' she said. 'You saw Steve Fleming on the TV. You said something about him which made me think you might have known him.'

He laughed at her. 'That why you're here?'

'Yes.'

He was relaxing now, figuring it out.

'So you don't want to nick me?'

'No.' She was revolted just looking at him. With his chest bare she could see too much of him. Including the tattoos. He had reminded her of Stijn last time she was here. Now it was even worse. 'Do you know Steve Fleming?'

'No, I don't. I've never met the man.' He was smirking at her, as if

287

already he knew what piece of knowledge she was looking for.

'When you saw him on TV you said he had forgotten his past,' she said. 'What did you mean by that?'

She expected him to say something about Fleming having married a 'paki'. But he didn't. 'You should ask *him* about that,' he said, instead.

'About him forgetting his past?'

'Yeah.' He leaned against the side of the door and extracted a packet of cigarettes from the rear pocket of his jeans.

'Why?' She could smell a kind of raw, male odour coming off his skin. If he didn't tell her quickly she was going to faint, she thought.

'Because he used to be best mates with Aidan Kershaw, as I remember it.'

'Aidan Kershaw?' She had no idea who he was, but she had been right about Norton knowing more.

'Yeah. When he lived up in Holme Wood. They were thick as thieves. This was when Fleming was a kid.' He put a cigarette in his mouth and lit it.

'You said you had never met him.'

'I haven't. But I knew of him. I was brought up in Cutler Heights. We were in gangs. Rivals.' He exhaled a long stream of smoke to the side of her. 'Kids stuff. You know.'

'Steve Fleming was in a gang?'

'A *racist* gang,' he said. 'Kershaw ran it. Racist. Like you accused me of being last time you were here.' He was enjoying it now, enjoying having the knowledge she didn't, enjoying pricking some imaginary bubble around Steve Fleming. 'And then Fleming went south and married a Pakistani,' he said. 'So he certainly did forget his past.'

50

An hour later Karen walked through the corridors of Killingbeck feeling as if she were on ice. Thin ice. But frozen enough for the chill to have risen up through her legs and into her chest. A cold compress seemed to be gripping her heart. But numbness was better than emotional incontinence. It was a step forward. She went to the toilets first and splashed water on her clothes, trying to get the blood out with paper towels. That left a huge wet stain over her crotch, as though she had wet herself. She cleaned her nostrils carefully, not wanting to start the bleed again.

They had let her in at the front counter because they recognized her. Not that she was banned from entering police stations. This was the fifth time she had been suspended; she knew the rules.

The station seemed empty. She found a computer in the room where the caseworkers would usually be – far from anything operational, or where she might bump into people she knew. She logged on with her own ID and password, both still functional.

The only Aidan Kershaw she could find was a thirty-two-year-old Manchester nominal, a middle-range drug-dealer who had spent three short spells in prison. There was a mugshot of him on the system, but not much current detail because he was active in Manchester, not Yorkshire. Even neighbouring police forces generally didn't share much more then skeleton intelligence info on a systematic basis, unless there was significant cross-border activity for a subject. Consequently, there were no up-to-date lists of aliases or associates, no intelligence on his present status. She could try logging onto the GMP system for that, but the information there probably wouldn't help with whether this Aidan Kershaw had grown up on the Holme Wood estate in Bradford.

His criminal convictions went back to 1980, when he was twelve years old. All the convictions prior to 1987 were from Bradford Magistrates

Court, which meant it was at least possible he came from Holme Wood. By 1988 he had apparently moved to Manchester, though, because the convictions started coming from Manchester Crown Court. He was first imprisoned for a 'Class A with intent to supply' offence in 1990, for eighteen months. Two other periods inside followed during the nineties, both of similar length.

Only two offences were not drug-related and both were from his youth. They were minor public order offences, but there were no details listed. If the convictions came from that far back it was hard to find out whether he had been prosecuted for racially aggravated offences, because those hadn't existed in the early eighties. But racial incidents usually ended up being public order offences, so that was a possible match as well. Possible. There was nothing on the system to suggest Kershaw had led a racist gang, and nothing matching him to Steve Fleming. Steve Fleming had already been checked out and was, naturally, clean. He was a prosecutor.

It was possible there was more information on Kershaw, if she could get into the Local Intelligence Office at Dudley Hill, but she doubted it – not from that far back. She couldn't bring herself to contact Pete Bains's skinhead squad and ask them. She might end up getting Pete himself. She didn't want to speak to him just yet.

She walked slowly up to the Bulldog incident room. As she neared it she passed the open door of Riggs's office, where she had first met Ronnie, three weeks ago, to the day. There was no one in there. She leaned against the door frame, biting her lip, looking at the chair in which he had been sitting. In the car afterwards she had been so close to him that she had been able to smell his aftershave. All gone now. His body, his clothes, the scent on his skin.

She walked along the corridor. The whole floor felt deserted, as if she were the only person in the station. Where was everybody?

The Bulldog incident room was silent, empty. She sat down at a HOLMES terminal and tried to use her log-on ID to search for Kershaw. The ID was invalid. That didn't surprise her. It didn't mean that someone had acted on her suspension, just that she was off the squad and the password had expired. She stood up and began to look around the office instead, checking the whiteboards, leafing through paperwork on desks, searching without much hope through the manual collections of actions stored in the cabinets behind the indexers' terminals.

Surprisingly, she stumbled across something. On 15 June there had been very low-grade information forwarded from Greater Manchester Police suggesting that a local Rochdale nominal might have had something to do with the killing of Enisa Fleming. The nominal was Aidan Kershaw. But the information – graded E4 – was classified as very unreliable and from an unknown source. She doubted there had been a follow-up.

She kept looking. On the series of photos pinned to the incident room walls, showing every suspect so far in the inquiry, with brief notes as to how they connected, she came across Kershaw's name again – but not under a photo of him, as a suspect. Instead, he was listed under a photo of Ian Whitfield, as an associate. Whitfield, she recalled then, was one of the two DNA hits from the actual crime scene, one of the men from the removal company who had transferred the Flemings from London.

It turned out that Whitfield was a relative of Aidan Kershaw, a cousin on his mother's side. There was intelligence that Whitfield had occasionally run drugs for him. There was also a note about a correlation between high-value premises visited by Whitfield in his capacity as a furniture remover and burglaries of the same premises. Whitfield had no known alibi for the night of 8 June and was still wanted.

Karen sat down and tried to get her brain to focus on it. There was a series of connections, but so far they didn't amount to much. Enough to ask Steve Fleming about, though. Since she couldn't source any more information about Kershaw today, the only way she would find out if Norton was telling the truth would be to ask Fleming about it directly.

51

Tim Thorne sat on the very edge of the bed in Laura Shepherd's bedroom and felt uneasy. He had arrived half an hour ago. Laura had answered the door in pyjamas and dressing gown, though it was well past midday. At first he had been shocked by her appearance, but that had quickly given way to concern.

Laura had deep, dark rings under her eyes, and the eyes themselves had a glazed, bloodshot aspect, which he had most often seen in drug users just beginning to come down. Her hair had clearly neither been washed nor brushed since Ronnie's death, her skin was white and bloodless and, most of all, he could not believe how much weight she had lost. The pyjamas were hanging off her. She had the look of someone who was starving, and he suspected she had eaten nothing since he had seen her in the hospital three days ago.

At first she had stared without recognizing him, then had stepped back away from the door, silently, to let him enter. 'I'll just get dressed,' she had muttered, leaving him alone.

For half an hour he had tiptoed nervously through the house, scrutinizing the debris left behind. Somehow everything had looked shorn of meaning. When he had last visited here he had not realized how much of the junk in the place belonged to Ronnie. Now all he could see were Ronnie's objects – his sailing books, boat pictures, chandlery ornaments – all touched by him and still in place, as if he would walk in at any moment and resume where he had left off. Everything looked neglected, forlorn, like objects in a very old person's house or a bric-à-brac shop, where they would perhaps end up – things from another century. Whatever they had meant to Ronnie, whatever memories they held, was gone for ever. The place made Tim shudder. It seemed as if Laura didn't live there at all, as if her slight, receding presence was not enough to give the place energy. It was something he hadn't noticed while Ronnie had been alive.

Eventually he had walked through to her bedroom and knocked lightly on the door. She hadn't answered, so he had pushed the door open gently and looked in. She was on the bed, curled up in a ball like a baby, totally naked, the pyjamas and dressing gown at her feet. She wasn't crying, wasn't moving at all, in fact. He whispered her name, and she rolled slightly to look at him, exposing a breast without appearing to notice. The expression in her eyes was not what he had expected. He had thought he would see pain; instead he saw fear. 'It's only me,' he said quietly. But she wasn't frightened of him.

'I don't know what to do,' she mumbled. 'I don't know what to do.'

He sat now on the very edge of the bed, at a distance from her. But he could not stop himself from looking at her, or from filling his nose with the scent of her – a bed scent, devoid of artificial perfumes, just Laura; the smell he could recall from beneath the commercial fragrances, when he had last been in this bed with her.

Where her legs were pulled up against her sunken belly (her back to him) he could see hairs in a thick stubble, where she had not shaved for three days. And her pubic hair. Even the hairs in the crack between her buttocks, the shape of her labia, her anus. He cleared his throat slightly and felt like a voyeur. A flush of blood came to his cheeks, but she wasn't looking at him now, was barely even aware of him. She had curled up again, withdrawn from it all.

'I came to see how you are,' he said, not knowing what he should say. 'And to tell you what's been happening.'

She didn't react.

'Laura? Do you want to know what's been happening?' Anything to get her out of this.

She moved a little. 'Happening where? Why are you here?'

'Happening with the inquiry,' he said. 'Ronnie's inquiry. I'm standing in for him ...' He hesitated and stopped. That sounded bad. How could he stand in for him? Ronnie wasn't coming back. Besides, she didn't want to know about Bulldog. And that wasn't why he had come here.

She stretched a leg out and raised her head, peering around the room, looking for him.

'I'm over here,' he said. He resisted an urge to reach out a hand, to touch her. Why *had* he come here? Hoping for something he knew he couldn't have?

She turned on to her back and looked at him. He had a view now straight between her legs, up across her stomach to her breasts. She had so many freckles it looked like a stain. She was frowning at him, again as if she didn't recognize him.

'Are you OK, Laura?' he asked gently.

'Tim Thorne?'

'Yes. That's me.'

She propped herself up on her elbows. 'What are you doing here?' She looked perplexed.

'I came to see you,' he said. He watched her eyes gradually take in her own nakedness. 'Your pyjamas are there,' he said, pointing. But instead she pulled at the quilt on the bed, dragging a corner over herself, then sitting up. The quilt only covered her to her waist. 'Can I cook you something?' he asked. 'You should eat.'

'I don't want anything.'

'Have you been eating? You look thin, Laura.' His eyes kept straying to her breasts now. She didn't reply. She was looking at him like he was something from another world.

He felt the gloom getting to him. He shouldn't have come here. Not just because it was useless, but also because he was wanted elsewhere. They had already taken nearly all his squad and put them on Operation Wheel – that was the name they were giving to the public order situation in Bradford. There were marches and counter-marches in the city centre, but that wasn't the real worry. The intelligence was pointing to levels of organization in the background – not amongst the whites, the neo-fascists they had been concentrating on – but amongst the Asians. The intelligence was predicting that the Asians were going to start something big. They could burn Manningham to the ground for all he cared, as long as he wasn't involved. But he was involved. He had got the call an hour ago, as he was driving over here. He was expected at The Tyrls by four o'clock.

He stood up. He had to do something to get her out of here. 'If you get ready I can take you out to eat,' he said. 'We can go somewhere more cheerful.' *Cheerful.* The word sounded wrong as he said it. Her father was lying in a box in a funeral parlour somewhere in Whitby, not even buried. The funeral was scheduled for Tuesday. She wasn't going to be cheerful, no matter what he did. 'We can get some fresh air, at least,' he added.

She stared at him as if he were mad. 'With *you?*' she asked. She even laughed a little, at the absurdity of it. 'I have enough trouble getting rid of that dizzy blonde they gave me as a liaison officer.'

She sank back into the pillows, legs wide apart and sticking out from beneath the quilt. He let his eyes roam furtively over her flesh and was surprised that the hairiness, the smell, the loss of weight, didn't bother him at all, when it came to it. Her nipples looked hard, standing on end, for some reason. He felt himself beginning to react, inside his trousers. She rolled on to her side and he could see the mole halfway down her back that he had advised her to have removed once upon a time.

Was he meant to touch her? Is that what someone in his position would do, if there had not been the intimacy between them?

Her chest was shaking now. She was crying, silently, without tears. He knelt on the bed and leaned over her. In his head he had an image of them coupling here, the sweat, the stickiness, the heat. She had made strange little whimpering noises as he had licked her.

He could put his arms round her now, he thought. He *wanted* to put his arms round her, to console her somehow. It was embarrassing that he found her so attractive, that even now, when she was this disabled with grief, he was still getting aroused looking at her. He straightened up, away from her. He didn't dare touch her.

'What can I do, Laura?' he asked. His voice sounded slightly high-pitched.

'Get out,' she said, blubbering the words. 'Get out. Go away.'

52

Steve Fleming had been moved from intensive care to a private room. When Karen arrived, just before three o'clock, he was alone in the bed, sitting up and drinking something, watching the television mounted on the wall in front of him. She knocked and entered.

'Hello, Steve,' she said. He was frowning at her. 'Karen Sharpe. Remember?'

'I remember.' He didn't look pleased to see her. 'Nobody told me you were coming.'

'No.' She shrugged. 'Sorry about that. Is it OK to stay for a while?'

He moved a hand listlessly, as if he didn't have the energy to object. She pulled up a chair and sat down.

His voice was much stronger now. There were fewer tubes going into him and fewer machines ranged about the bed. He was breathing unaided, without the tortured, rasping sound she had heard last time she had been here. She guessed the punctured, collapsed lung was healing. The machine draining his chest cavity (through a tube inserted through his side) was still beside the bed, making a rhythmic, aspirating sound. The bottle it emptied into was full of a thin yellow fluid, streaked with blood.

He still looked like someone who was living in hell. The eyes had a deep, sunken, frightened appearance, the face stripped of fat, the cheekbones sticking out painfully. His head above his left eye was without bandages now, revealing a four-inch-long ragged scar, still thick with knotted stitches, purple and black around the edges, like something from a Frankenstein movie. The second shot had probably been aimed at his head, but had instead hit the wall behind him. Splinters of brickwork had sliced his head open above the left eye. On the cover of the bed his wrists looked thin and fragile. He looked to be on the edge of an emotional precipice.

'You seem better,' she said, working to keep her thoughts under control. She was standing on that precipice herself.

From behind her the TV was distracting. They were saying something about public disorder in Bradford.

'What happened to you?' he asked. He was looking at her shirt and trousers. The water stains had dried, leaving the blood stains more or less as they had been before.

'Nothing,' she said. 'An accident.'

'Shouldn't you be there?' he asked, nodding towards the TV.

She turned and looked quickly at it. There were pictures of Centenary Square, with large crowds hemmed in by police lines. Some kind of public demonstration. She turned back to him.

'How have you been coping?' she asked.

He shrugged. She could see he wasn't gong to give her more than that.

'Has Jana been today?'

'They come in the evening.'

'Good. She's a beautiful, bright girl.'

'Yes. They told me you spoke to her. I didn't want that.'

'I asked Varisha,' she said.

'Varisha isn't her parent. You should have asked me.'

'You were very poorly, Steve. That's all.'

'I don't want her to suffer any more. Christ. She saw her mother bleeding to death ...' He broke off and choked a sob. She waited for him to recover himself, but he didn't. He started to cry instead. Just sitting there in the bed, looking vacantly at his hands, chest moving only slightly, copious tears running down his cheeks. She leaned forward on to the bed and put her face in her hands. Could she do this?

She sat with her eyes closed listening to him. The coverage on the TV continued. Her head felt heavy; her neck and back were stiff and sore. For three days she had had a headache, which varied in intensity from being so bad she felt nauseous and dizzy, to a mild, constant irritation. But it never went away. Her eyes were red and painful; she felt completely dried out. At Killingbeck she had made an effort to sink a litre of water, worried that she was dehydrated. It made no difference. Sleep was what she needed. But if she gave in to that the nightmares would return; Enisa Fleming bleeding to death, the visions of Caroline's sliced-up face and mouth. There were the usual nightmares about Mairead, too. If she let sleep take her she would wake up with the weight pulling her down again, the fog wrapped round her. *Keep going.*

When it didn't seem as if Fleming was going to stop crying she straightened up. She wasn't even meant to be here. She would have to think of something else to do to occupy herself. She started to stand up.

'I'm sorry,' he mumbled. 'I must stop this. I'm sorry.'

'That's all right, Steve. I understand. Do you want me to call a nurse?'

'No, I'm OK.' He wiped at his face with the sleeve of the pyjamas, then picked up the remote for the TV and switched it off. 'Please sit down. Don't go. I can talk. It's OK.'

She sighed, then sat down again.

'What did you want?' he asked.

His face was pumped with blood now, from the effort of crying. The skin looked livid, blotchy, like a baby after a tantrum. She looked at him for a long while, wondering whether to go on, so long he became uncomfortable and looked away.

'What did you want to say?' he asked again.

'I was just visiting,' she said. 'To see how you were coping.'

'Really?' He seemed sceptical.

'There was something I wanted to ask about, but it can wait.'

'Ask it. I'll try to help.'

She nodded, thoughtfully. OK. *Here we go.*

'A link came up,' she said. 'A link between the builder whose DNA was recovered from your house – Ian Whitfield – and someone else.' She saw him react to Whitfield's name, his eyes blinking rapidly, his facial muscles tightening. She expected him to launch into a frustrated rant about how Whitfield was bound to have been there because he had moved them. That was what had apparently happened last time he was asked about Whitfield.

'A link to who?' he asked, instead.

'A man called Aidan Kershaw.'

The effect was as dramatic as if she had slapped him. His head actually snapped back, away from her.

'I take it you have heard of him,' she said, surprised.

He was staring intensely at her, his lips moving as if he wanted to say something, his eyes wide.

The blood was draining from his skin as she watched.

'I was told you knew him when you were a kid,' she tried.

He took a long gasp of air, his eyes still on her.

'Is that true?'

He said nothing. He looked terrified.

'It's OK, Steve,' she said, gently. 'You don't have to worry about it. This is just a routine kind of background follow-up. If the questions upset you—'

'Who?'

'Sorry?'

'Who?' The word was a strangled noise in his throat. 'Who told you I knew Kershaw?'

She shrugged. So he did know him. 'I don't remember. It was on the system. A background check—'

'Kershaw. Fucking Kershaw …' He looked away from her and started to breathe very rapidly, as though he were struggling to fill his lungs. 'I have to tell you,' he stuttered. 'Now I have to tell you …' The breathing caught up with him and he began to heave at the air, each movement causing him obvious pain.

'I'll call a nurse,' she said.

'No! No! Wait.' He held a hand up to stop her. 'Please wait.' He began to sob again, looking away from her. But this time it was worse. The sobs were huge, each one pulled from deep within his damaged lung, creasing his face with pain. It became so bad she thought he might pass out.

She stood up.

'I'll have to get a nurse, Steve—'

He shook his head. 'No. I have things to say to you. You can't—'

She hesitated and he swallowed furiously, gulping back the emotion. 'I knew,' he said. 'I knew it all the time …' She stepped forward and tried to take one of his hands, to reassure him, but he wouldn't let her. 'I should have said. I should have told you. But I was afraid.' He wiped the tears away impatiently. 'I was too afraid to say. So I lied.'

'Afraid of what? Lied about what?'

'Afraid of Kershaw. He tried to kill me. He stabbed Enisa to death. I couldn't say anything, though. I couldn't tell the truth. I lied in my statements because I was too scared he would come back for Jana. I couldn't—'

That stopped her. It wasn't true, because Aidan Kershaw was on the DNA database, so it definitely wasn't him who had wielded the knife against Enisa. Probably he hadn't been there at all. It was virtually impossible to enter premises and shoot or stab someone without leaving traces of your DNA. And none of the samples came back as a match to Aidan Kershaw or any of his known aliases.

'It can't have been Aidan Kershaw,' she said. 'We have DNA from—'

'Not him personally. Not there.' He took a huge breath and settled back in the pillows. There was an expression of abject misery in his eyes. 'I don't know who it was. But they spoke of Kershaw. They spoke of him ...'

She sat down quickly, keeping her face blank. Jesus Christ, she thought, Ronnie had been right. Fleming *had* been holding out on them.

'You heard the men mention Kershaw?' she asked.

He was still crying as he spoke. 'I heard one of them say Kershaw had told them to burgle the place ...'

'Kershaw? Or Aidan Kershaw?' There could be thousands of Kershaws.

'They said Kershaw. But it's him. I know it. The other said Kershaw had told him to shoot me. That might have been Whitfield, the man with the removal company ...'

'Ian Whitfield? You told the inquiry it wasn't him.'

'Again, I lied. I had to. To protect Jana.'

'Would you recognize him?'

He shook his head. 'No. No. No. I'm guessing. I didn't see them properly. I'm going on his voice. It might have been him ...'

'You're talking about the one who shot you?'

'I don't know. I don't know who did what. They were out in the garden with Enisa. I tried to get to them but I couldn't ...'

He broke down completely then, bawling and crying at the top of his voice. She looked towards the door nervously. Surely someone would hear him – or see the signs on one of the monitoring machines. She didn't want anyone to come now. She wanted him to get control of himself and tell her more.

She reached forward and began to stroke his hand. 'It's OK, Steve,' she said. 'It's OK.' She kept saying it over and over again, trying to get the stimulus into his brain. It would work eventually. Eventually he would have to stop crying. 'None of this was your fault,' she tried. 'You must know that.'

'It was *all* my fault,' he blurted out. 'Everything that has happened is my fault.' He sucked at the air then pushed himself right back into the pillows. She let go of his hand. The tears were still running out of his eyes. 'I couldn't say anything because of Jana,' he said again. 'This was a warning. Even the date was almost the same. He will come for Jana now. If he finds out I have told you he will come for Jana ...'

'No one is going to harm Jana. Jana is safe ...' What did he mean by the date being the same?

'No one is safe. They came into my home to kill me. They could take Jana at any time.'

'Jana is with Varisha. I can have a police guard outside the premises within minutes.' Not quite true.

'That won't work. Nothing will work.' He shook his head vigorously.

'I promise we can protect you,' she said. 'We can protect you and Jana. That is not an issue. But you have to tell me why you think Aidan Kershaw would send men to kill you.'

'I *have* to tell someone. I have to ...' The sobs came in a renewed wave, doubling him up. 'But you won't be able to protect us. It's useless ...'

She had to calm him somehow. She started making soothing noises, as she would to a baby, but it only seemed to irritate him.

'You can tell no one what I tell you,' he said. His eyes fixed her with desperation. 'Promise me you will tell no one unless I tell you that you can.'

'I promise. Of course, I promise.'

'I can never give evidence against him. You don't understand what he is capable of.'

Aidan Kershaw was just a middle-range drug-dealer. She doubted he was capable of a murder like this.

'Why do you think it's Kershaw?' she asked. 'Why would Kershaw want to kill you?'

He wiped at his eyes again and then closed them, head back. Had he changed his mind? It looked as if he was deliberately stopping himself from continuing, holding his breath. Or maybe he was just too exhausted.

'Why do you think Kershaw would want to kill you, Steve?' she asked again, almost whispering.

He held up a hand. 'Wait.'

She waited.

He kept his head back, eyes now focused on the ceiling. She could see him struggling to control himself, to get on top of it. It took him nearly five minutes to do it, to regulate his breathing so that it didn't cause pain, to get the tears out of his eyes, the constriction out of his throat so that he could speak properly. Then he began to tell her.

He was breathless all the time he was speaking. Sometimes he had to stop and gulp for air. Twice he broke down and started crying again, and she had to wait minutes before he could continue. But in the end he got it all out. As he spoke, she took out her pocketbook and wrote it all down, as if she were taking notes for a statement.

53

*I was brought up on the same estate as Aidan Kershaw. Holme Wood, up
by Dudley Hill. He was two years older than me and always in trouble. I'd
known him since I was little, but it wasn't until I was about twelve that
I got to know him better. Everyone up there thought he was mad. I'm sure
he was mad. But he wasn't afraid of anything. I was afraid of everything
and everyone back then.*

*My dad was an out-of-work drunk that people used to laugh at. He was
racist – he thought the Asians had put him out of work. Throughout my
life he called them 'pakis', wanting them all sent 'back home'. That's what
I grew up with. He didn't beat me – no more than other kids were beaten,
anyway – but he didn't like me. My mother used to like me, I think, before
she started drinking as well.*

*I was a little kid, always shorter than everyone else. I couldn't fight.
Even if I could have got angry enough I didn't have the size for it, the
weight. I tried at first. I can remember the first fight I had. Someone forced
me up against a tall kid at school. He took offence. We arranged to settle it
after school, at the bus stop. He was there before me, with his mates. You
were meant to take your jacket off before you started, but I jumped him
as he was in the middle of getting his off. I punched him in the face, but
he hardly blinked. Then he took his jacket off, closed me down and pulled
my jacket over my head, dragging me forward. Then he just kneed me in
the face until he'd had enough. I still have the chipped front tooth from
that.*

*I learned that fighting wasn't for me. That meant I had to find people
to protect me. If you couldn't fight – or didn't have someone to fight for you
– then you were picked on all the time. All the little kids were bullied. I
found Aidan Kershaw to protect me. It's a standard story. He was two years
older than me but he was stupid. He had missed a year because he had
been in some kind of trouble, and then was forced to start in our year for*

some other reason. He was the oldest kid in our year, and the most stupid. I was bright, though nobody had bothered to notice that. I could do his homework for him. I laughed at his jokes, tried to get on his good side. At first he picked on me as well, but eventually he got to depend upon me. That's how it started.

By the time I was twelve you would have said we were friends. I can't believe now that I could have made a friend of someone like that. I can't even think what we had to talk about. But we used to talk. When I think back now it seems like any other friendship a kid might have. At least in the early years. It had started because I wanted protection, but as we got older it wasn't like that any more. I think it was a real friendship.

I didn't just see him at school. I saw him after school, around the estate. By the time he was fifteen he had already been to prison, on remand, for something he didn't do, he said. But the police knew about him. They would come looking for him whenever someone got their car broken into. Once I saw a couple of officers put him against a wall and beat him senseless. He deserved it, I'm sure. But I didn't think that way then.

He had a gang – a group of kids who used to fight with other kids from the same estate or neighbouring estates. I couldn't fight, but he still let me into the gang. He used to say I was the brains. The organizer. I did organize things – all sorts of petty, nuisance crimes and fights. But I never took part. My parents didn't have a clue what I was up to. I would come home from school, eat if my mother was sober enough to cook, then go out. If there wasn't food at mine I could go round to Aidan's place and eat there. His father was a night watchman on building sites and a bit of a bastard. He was rough with Aidan. But Aidan's mother was a nice woman. She worked in the Seabrook's crisp factory and smelled of old frying oil. She doted on Aidan.

After we'd eaten we would be out all night on the estates, 'playing'. But it was hardly play. From about thirteen years old Aidan knew how to break into cars, steal them, drive them. He used to barrel a car from the estate and then drive us all over Bradford. One night, when I was about twelve, he drove us down to Sheffield and we hopped a train back.

I was sometimes out until long after midnight. At school my grades slumped – so nobody ended up noticing that I was clever. I'm not blaming anybody. It was weakness that kept me with Kershaw, and that's down to me. I looked up to him, hero-worshipped him. He seemed to know what he was doing, was never afraid of anything. Now I realize that he had a screw loose. I knew that then, but things appear differently when you're a teenager. Things he would do that were bad just seemed courageous to me. I wished I could do the things he could.

In the mid-eighties it started getting worse, though. Aidan became like a more active version of my dad. He hated Afro-Caribbeans, Asians, Poles, Italians. The only ethnic minority he had respect for was the Chinese. There weren't many Chinese in Bradford back then, but those there were he wouldn't get mixed up with. I have no idea why. Probably he had watched something on TV about triads.

He started a gang called the White Protection Committee. It was never very big. It never got up to very much, either. There were five of us in it by the time I was fifteen. It was all petty stuff, but it was racist. I went along with it. I feel sick thinking about it now. I shouldn't have gone along with any of it – not even the smallest things they did. If I had objected to the smaller things then maybe it wouldn't have progressed to something worse. I had some influence over Aidan. He used to listen to me.

During the summer of 1986 things started to get out of hand. Aidan was getting obsessed with it all. I found out he was talking to people from Combat 18 – some real headcases – who weren't keen to let him in. He wanted to prove to them that he had what they needed. So we started a little 'anti-paki' campaign in Manningham. Aidan was nearly eighteen then. He had a clapped-out car. We used to drive down there and target Asian businesses. Then come back and plan the attack. Mostly they were stupid things. Once we had a phase where we would drop dogshit through their letterboxes. The worst it got was spraying insults on the paving outside the shop, or across the windows.

I always used to sit in the car and watch. I never did anything. Sometimes the others would kick against this, wanting me to take part. But Aidan had this thing about it. He never expected me to take part, never wanted me to. He just wanted me to be there. I know now what was going on. I think he used to look up to me because I was brainy. He needed my praise, my approval. When it started getting more serious he used to go out by himself and do things, then come back and tell me about them later. I think he might have been homosexual. I'm not sure. If he was it would have been something he could never admit to.

By the age of fifteen I was sensing all these things and wanting to pull away from it. But it was all I knew back then, so that was difficult. I could see other kids around me who went to school regularly, did the work, got the grades. I knew where they were headed. I knew they would be sitting on good jobs in five years' time and I would be still traipsing around after

*Aidan Kershaw, like his little poodle. And I knew I was as intelligent as
these other kids. I don't know what would have happened if things hadn't
come to a head. Maybe I would have got away from him. Maybe not.
Maybe I'd be in prison now. But at least Enisa would still be alive.*

*The night things changed was 12 June 1986. The proximity between the
two dates – the date of my wife's death and the date this all happened in
1986 – is not accidental. The attack on 8 June was designed to warn me.*

*On 12 June 1986, in the evening, we went out together, just me and
Aidan. The plan was to go to Manningham and start some trouble. Each
time we went there things were getting more serious. This night Aidan
was in a foul mood and talking openly about bashing somebody properly.
There was a bunch of Asian kids who hung out by their cars on Toller
Lane – just a little further down from the police station – and each time
we passed them there would be name-calling, threats. Sometimes they even
followed us. One of them waved a gun at us once, but we were sure it was
fake. Aidan had it in for this kid and wanted to 'scout' him. That's what
he called it when he checked out a place or a person as a target. He wanted
to find that kid, follow him home, find out where he lived, so that he could
jump him. I didn't like the sound of that at all. But I got in the car with
him. I always got in the car with him.*

*We stopped at a cigarette shop halfway down Leeds Road. It was run by
a white guy who was racist. It was the only shop on that bit of Leeds Road
that Aidan would use. While Aidan was in there a little Asian kid went in
after him. I don't know what happened in the shop, but Aidan came out
saying the kid had 'lipped' him, meaning he said something which showed
a lack of respect.*

*I tried to talk him out of it but he wasn't having it. When the kid came
out of the shop, Aidan watched him walk away then drove the car after
him. This was about seven o'clock in the evening – a bright, clear day,
people out on the streets. The kid didn't seem to know what was going
on because he never once looked round when we were following him. He
turned off down a long snicket that leads past the school up there and
Aidan just stopped the car, got out and went after him. I was left sitting
in the car.*

*He was gone a long time. Long enough for me to worry that something
serious was happening. But I didn't worry. Since then, I've obsessed about
what I was doing, just sitting there, letting it happen. I've tried to remember
what I was thinking about, what was going through my mind. I couldn't
see down the snicket, because there was a bend in it, but I suppose I must*

have thought, even then, that Aidan would catch up with him, because he was fast on his feet and the boy wasn't even aware that he was coming after him. I don't think I thought about it as something real. How could I? If I had seen it as something real I wouldn't have just sat there. Aidan hadn't asked me to be lookout or anything like that. So I wasn't watching out to see if anybody else followed him. I think I just sat there and waited for him to come back. Here we go again, I thought. Aidan was used to fighting. I had seen him in many fights, even fights where they had picked up sticks and used them. But they were more evenly matched. Aidan was tall, gangly. This Asian kid was tiny. He must have been about fourteen, I think, two years younger than me. I was old enough to have known what was going on, old enough to have done something about it.

When he came back to the car Aidan looked mad. Different from other times. He was panting, out of breath, and there were flecks of blood on his face. Just tiny spots of it. The sort you might get if you punch someone in the nose when their nose is already bleeding. He wanted to get away quickly. He wouldn't talk to me at first, then just started laughing really loud, as we got going up the Leeds Road. He was laughing like a lunatic.

We didn't continue to Manningham but went straight back up to Holme Wood, so then I knew something had happened. I went to bed that night worried about it. The next day I saw the newspaper and TV reports. The kid was a thirteen-year-old called Feroz Khan. He was visiting relatives in Bradford, so he wasn't even from there. The reports said he had been set upon by a gang of white racists and beaten unconscious. He was in intensive care and probably had brain damage. The police were calling it a 'frenzied attack', an attempted murder.

I cried all day when I found out about it. I was terrified. From the very beginning I knew I was responsible. Aidan actually came round to see me that evening, as if everything were normal, but I wouldn't go out with him. I told him that to his face and he looked hurt by it. It was the first time I had refused to go out with him, ever. I haven't seen him since.

I thought the police would find me within days. I thought there must have been witnesses. It was broad daylight, in an alleyway in full view of many houses. They had both been into a shop just minutes before.

But nothing happened. Weeks passed and I grew sick with worry about it – literally sick, so that I couldn't get out of bed. But still no one knocked at the door. And each night Aidan kept coming round and trying to get me to go out with him. As if nothing had happened. I sent my mother or father to the door to refuse. They knew I was in some kind of trouble that *involved him. I heard him shouting at my mother once. He was very angry that I wouldn't see him, but couldn't do anything because he had to keep his head down. I listened to him and knew I had to get away from him, that I was frightened of him.*

After three weeks I ran away to London. We had a relative down there. I went to stay with her and didn't come back until six months ago. From London I found out that the boy didn't die, but had suffered serious injuries and would be in a wheelchair for the rest of his life.

I put him in that wheelchair. That's the way it seemed to me then. That's the way it seems now. I didn't swing a punch, or pick up a rock like Aidan did. I didn't stamp on his head (they had the footprint of a shoe from the boy's face, but still didn't arrest Aidan). But I could have stopped it. There were so many ways I could have stopped it.

When I think back now it seems like a nightmare. I cannot imagine being the person I was then. I can hardly believe that I was that person. I don't have a racist bone in my body. Yet I went around stuffing dogshit through letterboxes. I sat peacefully in a car waiting as a 'friend' beat a poor little Asian boy to within inches of his life. Was that me? Was it really me?

I cared afterwards, when I found out what had happened, but at the time it was like I was in a daze. I think of it and it is as if I am thinking about someone else. When I came back here I couldn't bring myself to think it had all been real. I was married to Enisa. I had Asian relatives, an Anglo-Asian child. I almost had a nervous breakdown thinking about it.

I went back to the place and looked at it, saw where I had just sat in the car and waited. I went to the library and found the newspaper stories from the time. Feroz Khan had been visiting from Cheshire, it said. One of the stories gave his address. I drove over there and found the place. I don't know what I was going to do. I wanted to see him, I think, just to know that it was real. It was going round and round in my head, driving me crazy. I had some mad idea that I could atone for it, that I could help him. But the address was a mansion, a huge place at the end of Arley Road, in Altrincham. It had a long driveway, a tall, redbrick clock tower, security gates. I waited outside the gates until a security guy came and asked me what I was doing. I asked him if Feroz Khan still lived there but he wouldn't tell me. I didn't dare do anything else. Even if he lived there I reckoned he didn't need my help. I went back home and started to try to put it behind me, to get it into perspective.

Then in May I saw Kershaw in Leeds Crown Court. He wasn't the defendant. He was there with someone he knew who was charged with drugs offences. I think Kershaw was a defence witness. He recognized me at once. I was across the other side of the waiting area. I tried to ignore him but he caught my eye. He put his hand up and pointed it at me, like it was a gun, then mouthed something. I don't know what he said. It was a threat, though. It might have been 'I know where you are.' Something like that. I knew as soon as I saw him that he would feel threatened. I was working for the police, as he saw it. He must have feared I would just tell them about him, about what he had done.

I didn't think he would take it further, but on 8 June it caught up with me. I've known all my life it would catch up with me. I just wish they had killed me instead of Enisa. Enisa hurt no one.

54

As Karen stepped outside the hospital and squinted into the bright afternoon sunlight her mobile started to ring. She checked the number and saw it was Tim Thorne. For once she wanted to speak to him.

'Is that Karen Sharpe?'

'Yes. I need to speak to you, Tim—'

'And I need to speak to you. Right now. Where are you?'

'At Leeds Royal Infirmary. I've just been to see Steve Fleming.'

That caused a long pause. As she was listening to it she recalled that she was meant to be suspended. For a moment she had completely forgotten.

'I thought so,' he said eventually. 'I can be at Milgarth in five minutes. Meet me there.'

'OK, but you should listen—'

He cut the line on her. Again.

He was waiting for her at the front counter, dressed in uniform for some reason, though it didn't look as if he had worn it for a long time. Both the shirt and trousers were full of creases. He looked a mess. As she walked through the front entrance he pushed himself off the counter and looked at her with a stony face. He didn't greet her.

'We'll go to an interview room,' he said, pointing. The interview rooms he meant were on the public side of the station. They were used for speaking to ordinary members of the public.

'I can go into the station,' she said. 'That's not prohibited.'

He stopped and turned on her. 'You're suspended,' he said, voice tight, low. 'You're fucking suspended.'

'I know I'm suspended. And I know the rules—'

'You don't. Not if you think you can walk into any station, access computer information, move about as if you were on duty ...' He was angry.

'The rules state that—'

'You are permitted into your home station under certain circumstances. Killingbeck is not your home station. Nor is Milgarth.' So that was what was getting to him; someone had told him she had been at Killingbeck, in the incident room. He was controlling his temper, but she thought he wanted to scream at her. She looked back to where the counter staff were looking on with obvious embarrassment. 'Have it your way, then,' she said.

She followed him into one of the tiny interview rooms. As soon as the door was closed he started to speak, almost shouting, demanding an explanation for something. She tried to focus on his words, but her brain had a tendency to switch off when she was being shouted at. Maybe he was asking her if it was true she had been to see Steve Fleming. But she had already told him that. She sat down on one of the chairs, placing her bag on the table in front of her. She could hear a buzzing noise in her ears, feel her pulse increasing. She didn't want to be in here if it was going to be like this. She resisted an urge to shout back at him, to tell him to shut up. Instead, she took the statement out and handed it to him.

'I took a statement from Fleming,' she said. 'You can read what he said to me.'

She had got statement sheets from the casualty office, then transferred her notes on to them. Then she had gone back into Fleming and tried to read it back, hoping he would sign. But he had been irate with her, terrified she would broadcast the information. She had tried to reassure him, but he had fallen into a coughing fit. She had got halfway through her notes before he had pressed the buzzer for the nurse. Then she had to leave. As she walked through the doors he was gulping water, trying to stop coughing, desperately reminding her of her promise. Maybe he had called Thorne afterwards and complained.

'You took a statement from Steve Fleming,' Thorne said. He looked stunned. 'You're suspended ...'

'I think you should read it. Before you say anything you should read it.'

He slammed a hand on the table in front of her, making her jump. '*I should put it in the fucking bin and forget it ever happened.*' He was speaking through gritted teeth. '*What did you think you were doing?*

What did you think you could achieve?' He started to pace up and down in front of her.

'Just read it.' She turned away from him. If he was going to continue like this she should leave quickly. She could feel the adrenalin in her system now. Technically he was right to be annoyed, but he only had to read and consider the statement to realize how important it was. She had unearthed crucial new information for his inquiry.

He took a breath, seeing she wasn't listening, then glanced at the sheets of paper, turning through them quickly, not reading properly. She watched him out of the corner of her eye.

'Did you invent all this?' he demanded, when he was finished.

'Invent it?'

'Yes. Have you invented all this?' His voice was overexcited.

'Of course not—'

'That's what a lawyer will ask. Because you are presently suspended on suspicion of fabricating evidence.'

'Forget that. That's nothing to do with this.'

'I cannot forget it.'

'You know I didn't invent that. That's what Fleming told me—'

'There's no signature.'

'He wouldn't sign.'

'So what use is it?'

'It's a start.'

'It's nothing. Does he even know what he is talking about? Do you realize what kind of concoction of sedative drugs he is living on? The man is half insane with grief. I was told only yesterday that they feared he was suicidal—'

'*This* is why. He blames himself.'

'Is it? I thought it was because his wife was stabbed to death three weeks ago.' He leaned over the table and jabbed a finger against his temple. 'Use your fucking head, Sharpe.' His face was bright red.

'What I have written is what he said.' She stood up. There was no point in being here. 'It's up to you whether you do something about it.'

'I'll do something about it on Monday. I'll send an officer who has not been suspended to speak to him. To find out whether he said anything like what you have written.'

'He will deny it. He made me promise I wouldn't tell anyone.'

'It's all hearsay anyway—'

'You would do better to try to locate Feroz Khan. Or Ian Whitfield. There's a chance Fleming will recognize Whitfield's voice.'

'I thought you said he wouldn't give evidence?'

'We need to change his mind. Now we know what his evidence would be.'

'And set up a "voice parade" for Ian Whitfield? Are you fucking serious, Sharpe? After Fleming has already told us countless times that it *wasn't* Whitfield?'

'If we had Whitfield in custody he might think differently.'

'Finding Whitfield is already a priority.'

'Hardly. You have two detectives assigned to sit outside his house and wait for him.'

'Two detectives are all I've got. And you can only know that because you have been accessing information that you are not permitted to access.' He almost stamped his foot. 'You're suspended, Sharpe. You're out of the loop. You don't have a clue what is going on here today. The whole Force is being drafted to Bradford to cope with a fucking riot. I came here only to make sure you are fully aware of what will happen if you go anywhere near my inquiry again.'

She frowned at him. He was standing far too close to her, trying to threaten her with his physical proximity. The urge to throttle him was almost overpowering. He was standing with his eyes inches from her face. He was making assumptions, because she was a woman. But he was much shorter than her. She could take hold of him by the neck, push him back against the wall, choke the fucker. She could watch his stupid, acne-ridden face turn blue, watch him splutter for real.

She placed her hands firmly at her side, turned away from him, opened the door and walked out.

55

It took her nearly two hours to reach Altrincham.

On the way over, on the M62, she considered what she already knew. There was a possible scenario that fitted, but it had problems. It went like this:

Aidan Kershaw, a middle-tier dealer from Manchester, finds out that his childhood friend Steve Fleming has returned north from London. He gets nervous. Steve Fleming is the only person alive who can give evidence about a racist attack carried out by Kershaw in 1986. Kershaw sends men to Fleming's property, possibly including Ian Whitfield. The intention is to seriously injure Fleming in order to warn him to keep his mouth shut. Things go wrong. Fleming and his daughter survive, but his wife is brutally killed.

There were at least three things wrong with it. Firstly, Kershaw could only have found out that Fleming had returned by chance – either because Whitfield helped move the Flemings, or because Kershaw saw Fleming in court, or on the TV. Maybe Whitfield was using his job to scout high-value burglaries for Kershaw and Kershaw realized one of them was the property belonging to Fleming. One way or another, it had to be chance that started the ball rolling. She didn't like that.

Secondly, the date didn't work for her. As a sign meant to convey the meaning of the attack it was useless. Why not attack Fleming on 12 June, if that was the intention? Fleming had to be wrong about that. More likely the date was irrelevant and the intention from the outset was to kill Fleming, not warn him. No need to communicate reasons to a man you intend to kill.

But if that was the case – if Kershaw wanted Fleming dead – then she couldn't understand it at all. It was hardly plausible that a hardened Manchester criminal, with many previous convictions and time in jail, would be *that* frightened of a witness to a crime from fifteen years ago.

Even if there was a fear that Fleming would, for some reason, suddenly decide to take his conscience to the police, an experienced criminal like Kershaw would know that the odds of anything coming of that were very slim. Different if the old case had been a murder, perhaps – but not a beating. That was the reality of it. Corroborative evidence would not be available at this distance from the event, and Fleming's evidence alone would hardly be something to set the lawyers on fire. Besides, he was as implicated as Kershaw. She could see the CPS saying no to it. Even if they didn't, without corroboration Kershaw could probably just dig in and deny it. A jury would have difficulty convicting him on the evidence of a lone accomplice.

So, thirdly, as against the perceived possible risk to Kershaw, sending armed men to shoot or kill Fleming was too massive a response. It didn't work. She was assuming that Kershaw was capable of a level of logical appraisal, that he hadn't just seen Fleming in court and panicked. Or, indeed, that he wasn't just some kind of mindless psychotic, for whom all this reasoning would mean nothing.

Was Thorne right? Was Fleming making connections where none existed? Perhaps Whitfield's presence at the scene (and subsequent disappearance) *was* mere coincidence. The case had been full of false starts from the outset. And why prefer one species of chance over another?

Finding out whether Feroz Khan existed (and, if so, could identify his attackers from fifteen years previously) wasn't going to help prove a motive against Kershaw – unless Khan *could* ID his attackers, and Kershaw, somehow, knew this in advance. But verifying Fleming's account was the logical place to start. There wasn't much else she *could* do. It was unlikely Feroz Khan still lived where he had lived fifteen years before so she reckoned tracking him down – assuming he wasn't a figment of Fleming's brain – might take some time. That was good. She had to do something and if it wasn't this she couldn't think what else it might be.

The place Fleming had described – at the end of Arley Road in Altrincham – was not difficult to find. Though there were many residences of similar scale in the area, none of them had a clock tower, clearly visible through the electronic entrance gates that barred the half-mile drive to the front of the house. From the gates, the building looked like a converted equestrian centre. There was a central section at the end of the driveway, with an arch leading to a courtyard and the clock tower above the arch, then two wings on either side of the tower, presumably turning back to enclose the courtyard. All set in expansive lawns, dotted with sycamore, ringed by a twelve-foot wall with security cameras and razor wire.

She pulled up to a security intercom, which looked like the ticket machine for a car park, and watched three CCTV cameras swivel to scrutinize her car. Another was mounted inside the intercom box, pointed directly at her face. She wound the window down and pressed the buzzer beneath it.

'Can I help you, madam?' A male voice speaking from a grille beside the camera.

'I'm trying to find Feroz Khan. Is this the right place?'

'And you are?'

The question surprised her. She had expected an immediate negative.

'Your name, madam?' he asked again.

Her name? If things went further than asking questions at a gate post she didn't want them to be able to trace her to West Yorkshire Police.

'Helen Young,' she said, then immediately thought of Ronnie. She felt a shiver in her spine. It was who she really was, but this was the first time she had called herself Helen Young since she was eighteen years old. The words felt strange in her mouth.

'Is this the place?' she asked again. She didn't want to speak to Khan, just find out where he was. She would be surprised and disappointed if this did turn out to be his residence. She looked at her watch. What would she do with the rest of the day?

'Are you from the *Manchester Evening News*?' the voice asked her.

'It's a private matter,' she said, puzzled.

Whoever it was didn't hear, though – he was already speaking over her. 'You're half an hour early,' he said. 'We expected you at seven.' Immediately the gates started to open.

She leaned towards the microphone to repeat her question and correct him. He still hadn't told her whether Feroz Khan actually lived there. Then she thought better of it. If they were letting her in she could ask in person.

She drove slowly up a driveway crossed by speed humps, flanked by trees. There were more security cameras in some of the trees. At the large gravel semicircle in front of the main building she parked the car and walked up to the front entrance. There was somebody standing inside an elegant stone porch, waiting for her. As she neared he stepped towards her, hand extended, a smile on his face.

'Suresh Venkatsami,' he said. 'I'm Mr Khan's personal assistant.'

So this *was* the place. She shook his hand. He was tall and strong-looking, but he had a limp grip. She opened her mouth to ask him her questions but he was already leading her inside. 'Come this way, please,' he said. 'Feroz will see you straight away.'

He took her through a massive marble atrium with a complex glass ceiling decorated with stained glass. They passed through two smaller reception rooms with plush carpeting and antique furnishings, then into a two-storey room with floor-to-ceiling bookshelves, a gallery and very high windows – a library.

In the middle of the room, gathered around a small coffee table and two leather sofas, were three people: a woman and two men. One of the men – the younger of the two – was in a wheelchair. Both men were Asian. The woman was white, and looked to be in her late twenties, at most. She was standing behind the man in the wheelchair, holding it. The other man – a bearded Asian in his mid-fifties – was standing a little in front of the other two. He stepped forward to greet her as she walked towards them.

'Helen Young?' His hand was held out. She shook it. Another limp grip. 'I'm Raheesh Khan,' he said. 'I'm delighted you could come.' He met her eyes and smiled. She guessed he must be the father of the man in the wheelchair. 'This is my son Feroz,' he said.

Feroz was already looking at her, but his expression was vacant. He didn't hold a hand out. He was a very frail man, perhaps thirty years old, though it was difficult to tell because his face was so hollow. He sat slumped in the wheelchair, a trickle of saliva dribbling from the side of his mouth. Karen felt the same crushing sense of horror she had felt looking at Caroline Philips. A few minutes of mindless brutality. This was what Steve Fleming had told her about, what he had hidden throughout his life. She placed a hand on her stomach and swallowed the bile rising in her throat. She felt a flush of heat pricking at her face. She was staring at the man and he was staring back at her, but there was no real comprehension in his eyes.

'Hello, Feroz,' she said. 'It's really nice to meet you.'

He didn't react.

His father was pushing something into her hand. She looked down at it. It was a glossy press release. Her eyes scanned through it as Kahn senior talked to her, offering her tea, then launching into an invective about the lack of wheelchair access in public buildings. The press release was about a 'substantial' donation that the Feroz Khan Foundation was making to a charity called All Access UK.

She looked up at Raheesh Khan and felt confused and guilty. They thought she was a local journalist, come here to get the story on the donation. She hadn't said she was, but nobody had bothered to ask her properly or seek ID. They had made assumptions because she had showed up roughly when they had expected a young, single female to show up. The PA was standing just behind the father, not saying anything. The father was telling her all about the gift, a slightly desperate tone to his voice as he explained how the donation had been selected by his son, not himself. Feroz Khan didn't look capable of making any such choices. She wondered if he could even speak. As she looked at him she could feel the emotion swelling inside her. Her mouth was dry, her throat sore, her legs beginning to feel shaky. She looked around for somewhere to sit. There was only the spare sofa in front of Feroz, beside the table. She noticed cups and a teapot on a small silver tray. She sat down, sensing that the movement took the father by surprise.

The woman behind Feroz poured her a tea. She hadn't been introduced. Karen assumed she was a private nurse. Beside her, still standing, Raheesh Khan had started upon the lack of government funding for disabilities. And all the while his son sat in the wheelchair, immobile, mute, staring at her with black, uncomprehending eyes.

She cleared her throat. What was she doing here? And why? She had to get out. She had what she had come for. She had investigated the whereabouts of Feroz Khan as far as she dared, given she was suspended. The squad would have to do the rest. She had to tell them there was a mistake.

'I'm sorry,' she started. Her voice was hoarse. Raheesh Khan stopped talking. She picked up the tea the woman had poured for her and took a sip. It was too hot and she burned her tongue. She cleared her throat again. 'I'm sorry, but I think there's been a mistake,' she said.

The father frowned at her. 'What kind of mistake?'

She stood up. She didn't know how much Feroz was capable of understanding, but she didn't want to take the risk. 'Can we talk very briefly somewhere private, Mr Khan?'

He looked puzzled. 'This *is* private,' he said.

'Just you and me, I mean.'

He took her to a room adjoining the library. It seemed to be an office, with a huge mahogany desk, a meeting table, several functional chairs. He sat behind the desk and she sat in front of it. There were files and folders arranged on the desk in neat piles, all at right angles to each other. She was still holding the press release he had given her.

'Are you all right?' he asked her. 'You look as if you've taken a bad turn.'

She shook her head. 'It's just seeing your son,' she said. 'I'm sorry. But I know how he came to be disabled. I find it upsetting, that's all. I'm very sorry.'

His face clouded.

'In fact, that's actually what I came here to ask about,' she said. She saw that he didn't understand. 'I came to ask about the events of fifteen years ago,' she explained. 'I'm sorry if there was a misunderstanding ...'

'What events of fifteen years ago? What on earth do you mean?' His voice had hardened suddenly.

For a moment she thought she might have got it wrong. Maybe it was another Feroz Khan.

'I'm sorry. I thought Feroz was injured in a racist attack fifteen years ago. On the twelfth of June nineteen eighty-six ...' His face stiffened into a mask of tension, so obvious she stopped speaking at once.

'*How do you know that?*' He hissed the words at her. '*Who told you?*' He jumped forward suddenly and so violently that she started backwards in the chair. He looked as if he might lean over and hit her. He swept an arm across the surface of the desk, scattering objects and papers across the floor. '*We do not talk about that in here! We do not talk about it!*' He shouted the words into her face.

She froze. He looked insane. His eyes were burning, his muscles taut, his fists clenched. He had looked normal back in the library, but had flipped in an instant. The change was so sudden she had no time to react. She gripped the sides of her chair and kept her mouth closed.

'*How did you find out about these things?*' he demanded. '*How did you find out?*' His voice was still raised, but that wasn't the worst of it. The way he spoke loaded every word with menace. From behind her she

319

heard a knock at the door. He looked up to it, yelled a command in Urdu, then looked back at her. Whoever had been there didn't knock again.

She kept her eyes away from him. She wanted him to calm down. She actually felt physically threatened. If she could she would get up and leave now, but he would chase her, she thought. The man was off the edge. His body language was radiating the threat of explosive violence. She didn't understand it at all.

He took a breath, then moved his body back slightly. She glanced at him. A dribble of saliva had wet his chin. He wiped it away with irritation and swept a hand across his head. Then groaned quietly – a low, guttural, wounded sound, from deep within his chest.

'I'm sorry,' he said. 'I apologize. Of course you would know about that. You are a journalist.'

She didn't dare correct him now.

He sat down heavily and rested his head on his arms, on top of the desk.

'My son can remember nothing of that evening,' he said, speaking into his arms, without moving his head. His voice was muffled, as if he were crying. 'His memory is very short-term. They beat him so badly that ...' She saw him clenching up again. He raised his head and stared at her, teeth gritted. There were no tears. 'Those racist white *fuckers*,' he said. 'If you had seen my son before you would not believe it was the same person.' He sat back quickly, with a jerk. 'What do you want to know about it? Why?' He was suspicious now.

'I was going to do a feature on racism,' she said. Her voice sounded false, forced. 'I thought it would be an appropriate time. Something to run alongside the article about the donation ...'

Why was she lying? Because she was frightened of him? Or frightened of hurting him. Either way she didn't want to have to sit there and explain that she was a suspended police officer digging her nose in where she shouldn't have been. Best to lie, make excuses, get out quick. She could tell Thorne that she had checked the address and found Feroz Khan. Then someone from GMP could come and do a proper job.

'Of course,' he said. 'I am so sorry I shouted at you. But you do not know how much pain this thing still causes me ...' He held a clenched fist over his heart. 'I am a very wealthy man,' he said. 'But I would give it all away to have my son healthy again.'

'I understand.'

'Or to find the bastards that did that to him. If you write an article you can say how disgusted I am with the police. They did nothing. Back then they did nothing. I spent thousands trying to find the perpetrators ...' He paused. 'If I had identified them they would be dead now.'

He meant it. There was no embarrassment about the outburst, no indication that he had spoken rashly. He meant it and he had the money to do it. Best not to say anything about Kershaw and Fleming, then. Best not to say anything at all.

'Perhaps it would be insensitive to do the feature,' she said. 'Perhaps it's best if I don't write about this at all.'

He nodded grimly. 'I would appreciate that.'

She looked at her watch. They thought she was a journalist who was due to arrive within fifteen minutes. She didn't want to be here when that happened. 'I'd better leave,' she said. 'Thanks for this.' She held up the press release. 'It is all I need really.' She stood up.

He looked surprised. He didn't stand up with her. 'What? You will leave already?'

'I have enough,' she said. 'Besides, I feel a little shaky ...'

He coloured and looked at the floor. 'I have frightened you,' he said.

She nodded meekly. 'A little. But it's OK. I understand. I'm sorry I caused you to remember things you were trying to forget.'

'Not forget. I will *never* forget.' He slammed a clenched fist on to the top of the table, making her start again. It was like Jekyll and Hyde.

'I will call for Suresh,' he said. 'He will see you out.' He pressed a button on an intercom system on the desk and spoke quickly in Urdu. Then he sat back and put a fist in his mouth. He looked as if he wanted to scream. She waited uncomfortably. She hoped 'Suresh' wouldn't take too long.

'This has been unfortunate,' he said. 'An unfortunate misunderstanding.'

'Yes.'

Still no Suresh. The silence made her want to panic. He was refusing to look at her now. She didn't know why she felt so uneasy about it, or so threatened. She felt the need to say something to fill the silence, but didn't dare in case she put her foot in it again.

The door opened and Suresh stepped inside.

Khan didn't look at either of them. 'Miss Young is leaving now,' he said. 'Could you show her the rear exit, so she doesn't need to go through the library again?'

56

Michael Rawson could hear Kershaw as he came through the doors from the service entrance – the dull sound of blows punctuated by Kershaw's cries of frustration and rage. He started to run at once, down the short corridor to the door that led to the basement. The door wasn't even locked. He pushed it open and stood on the threshold.

Kershaw was across the other side of the room, next to the sauna, stripped to the waist, sweating, his face and chest spotted with blood. In front of him Ian Whitfield was tied to a chair and slumped over himself, hanging by the ropes, completely motionless.

'Jesus fucking Christ,' Michael hissed. 'I can hear you from the service entrance.' He closed the door, locked it and moved quickly across the room. The atmosphere was poisonous, reminding him of other rooms in other places, each of them hot and humid, all with this same combination of odours – blood, sweat and fear. He had it caught up his nose before he got halfway across the room.

Kershaw was panting heavily, bent over double, trying to catch his breath. He was holding a short metal bar. He looked dangerous, but unless you were tied to a chair and incapacitated, it was all show. In his mid-thirties, slightly taller than Michael, with the exaggerated muscle definition of an obedient ex-con, a shaved head and a lop-sided face (one eye noticeably lower than the other) – Michael knew that when it came to it he was useless, a coward. Kershaw didn't like being hit, which meant the muscles counted for nothing. He enjoyed violence, but only when it was like this.

Michael wrenched the bar off him. 'You stupid fucker. I told you to wait for me.' He looked down at Whitfield. 'Have you killed him?' He brandished the bar in front of Kershaw's crazed eyes. 'I told you never to use a fucking weapon. I told you.' He threw the bar across the floor. Kershaw watched it clatter against the wall then looked up at him, still catching his breath. His eyes had that half-drugged look he only got by hitting people. Michael wanted to walk out on him every time he saw it.

'*Never* use a weapon for interrogations,' he said, struggling to keep his temper. He had learned that in the military. Bare fists were more precise: you could feel what you were doing, measure the damage accurately. With a metal bar or a shank of wood it was impossible to tell when bones were breaking. Men could die accidentally like that, and accidental deaths made Michael cringe. But Kershaw wanted to lose himself in it, go berserk, indiscriminately crush and gouge. He was like some kind of fucking animal. Michael looked again at the figure on the chair and felt sickened. Whitfield was Kershaw's flesh and blood, his cousin, yet he had done this to him. 'You achieve nothing like this,' Michael told him. Then he wondered if Kershaw had achieved exactly what he wanted.

'The fucker just kept saying the same things, over and over ...' Kershaw gasped. 'What else could I do?' His eyes changed expression. 'Where did you go?'

Michael stepped back and took a deep breath. The urge to lash out at him was strong. 'If anyone heard you we're fucked,' he said, ignoring the question. 'You hadn't even locked the door.'

They were in the Grange Golf and Country Club, a sports complex with saunas, swimming pools, squash and indoor tennis courts, practice ranges, gyms, and pitches for rugby and football, besides two eighteen-hole golf courses. The place was in the countryside, between Rochdale and Heywood, north of Manchester. It was a front. Raheesh Khan owned the place and Kershaw pretended to manage it for him. But Khan rarely visited and, thank God, had no idea they were here now.

From above him Michael could hear the grunts, gasps, exclamations and stamping collisions of two people dashing around a squash court. The short, percussive crack as the ball struck the walls was not unlike the sound made by a small-calibre weapon being discharged – or the impact of a hard implement on flesh and bone. The sound was a regular part of his nightmares. Down here, in the bowels of the complex, it was muted. Sounds going from here up to the courts would be similarly dulled, but not completely. And though the punters might at first mistake the violence for another game of squash, it wouldn't be long before somebody came down to investigate.

'Where have you been?' Kershaw asked again. 'You were gone over an hour and a half.'

Michael ignored him again. 'I told you not to touch him till I got back.' He was angry about it. He had wanted to question Whitfield, to pressure him carefully.

'You were away over an hour and a half,' Kershaw repeated. 'I had to start. Where have you been?'

Kershaw suspected something – he always did. The relationship between them was complicated. The business, the *real* business, was Kershaw's, not Michael's, but Kershaw was in control only because Raheesh Khan kept him there. And Khan had put Michael in beneath him for a reason. Kershaw knew that, and knew also that Khan's ties with Michael were closer.

'Have you been to see Khan?' Kershaw demanded. He straightened up, eyes hardening. 'I already told you about that. I warned you.'

Michael looked at him contemptuously. 'You don't tell me what to do. You know better than that.'

Kershaw stared at him. His jaw muscle was grinding now. 'Have you been to see Khan?' he asked again, barely opening his mouth.

'Of course I fucking have.'

Kershaw began to ball his fists, quickly closing and opening his fingers. 'I told you. I don't want him involved.'

'You told me. So what?' Michael stared carelessly at him, waiting for Kershaw to register pecking-order reality. It was like watching an ape in the zoo.

'I asked you, Michael,' he said finally, breaking eye-contact. 'I asked you not to go to him.'

'He was going to find out sooner or later.'

Kershaw dropped his eyes to the floor. 'Is something going on?' he asked, lips tight. 'Why didn't you tell me you were going?' A little trace of fear now.

'I was going to ask you that question,' Michael replied. 'What's the big problem with Khan knowing?'

Kershaw shifted from one foot to the other, still staring at the floor. 'No problem. We just didn't need to bother him.'

A lie. But what was he lying about?

'That's not how you usually play it when there's a problem. Usually you're begging him to help at the first sign of trouble.'

There was a moment's silence while Kershaw chewed at his jaw and thought about that. 'We're too dependent on him,' he said eventually. 'We should handle our own dirt.'

'And that's it? That's why you didn't want him told?'

Kershaw looked up. Reacting so strongly had given something away, but his expression was guarded now. 'That's it,' he said. 'What else would there be?'

Michael shrugged. That was what he had wanted to ask Whitfield about.

'So what did he say?' Kershaw asked. He tried to make the question sound casual.

'Not much.'

That Khan wanted Whitfield dead would be music to Kershaw's ears. But Michael was still looking for a way to avoid that.

'What did you tell him?' Kershaw tried.

'I told him Whitfield screwed up.'

'You left me out of it?'

'More or less. I said Whitfield was your cousin and he asked for help.'

Kershaw nodded. 'You sure about that, Micky? You sure I can trust you on that?' The tone was more pleading than threatening.

'Call him and ask.'

A strange shiver ran through Kershaw, as if he were cold. But the temperature in the place was tropical. 'No need,' he said. 'I trust you, Michael. If you had to tell him, you had to tell him.'

Michael pointed at Whitfield. 'Did he say *anything* before you did this to him?'

'The same shit,' Kershaw said quietly, his eyes shifting away again. 'He says he's told no one. That's all he would say to me.'

'That wasn't all I needed to speak to him about.'

But Kershaw knew that already.

When Michael had first brought Whitfield here, right after the incident, Whitfield had told him that Kershaw had *told* him to use the gun, that Kershaw had *instructed* him to kill Fleming. That had been his defence. Straight off, no time to think about it or fabricate. Michael had put it to Kershaw and he had denied it, but the look in his eyes had been evasive.

'How did Khan take it?' Kershaw asked, panic creeping back into his voice.

'He said he wants nothing to do with it.'

Kershaw's relief was visible. His shoulders slumped and he took a breath. 'Thank Christ for that.'

'He wants it tidied quick. We have to go to him tomorrow and tell him it's sorted. Both of us.'

'We can do that. We can handle it.'

'Like you already have, you mean?'

Michael took hold of Whitfield's hair and pulled the head back. The face was unrecognizable. Even his own mother wouldn't know him. Everything was twisted, squashed, swollen monstrously, lathered with bright running blood. There was a two-metre square puddle of it on the tiles beneath the chair. The boy (how old was he – nineteen?) was still breathing, but in fits and starts. Michael couldn't tell whether his eyes were damaged; they were so puffed up they wouldn't open for weeks. Was he going to die right now? Maybe not, but it wouldn't take much to finish him.

Michael sucked the rancid air into his lungs. 'He's useless to us like this,' he said bitterly. 'He can't tell us anything now.' He let the head drop. 'Did you do this to silence him?'

'Silence him? I was asking him questions. That's what you wanted.'

'That's right. I wanted to do the asking, though.'

'So chuck him in the cooler. He'll come round.'

'The cooler will kill him.'

The room they were in was little more than a large storeroom filled with old broken tables and chairs, planks of wood, tins of paint. There were some benches and lockers, a shower and a toilet, all lit by long strips of neon lights. The smell of the place was like a cross between a mechanic's garage and a fitness club. The sauna was built into the corner. It was meant to be down here for the staff to use, though that had never happened. This area was strictly off-limits.

The 'cooler' was Kershaw's favourite way of breaking people down. Shackle them in the sauna and leave them to sweat. If the temperature was kept below 38C then they could live for almost a week, without food or water, slowly drying up. Ian Whitfield had already been in there for a day.

'Maybe we should kill him now,' Kershaw said. 'I can do it.'

To Michael's knowledge Kershaw hadn't killed before, not personally. There were one or two beatings he had ordered that had gone too far, but that was from way back, from before Michael had anything to do with him. 'Shut up, Aidan,' he said quietly. 'I have to think about this. That's why I told you not to start until I got back.'

Michael had wanted nothing more than to kill Whitfield from the moment he had got him here. But life wasn't so simple. Whitfield had criminal convictions, so his DNA was on some database – which meant the police were going to come for him pretty quickly. Michael had no police record, so his DNA was nowhere but inside his body. Which meant he was safe, if he could only contain things, prevent leaks and do something about Whitfield. But killing him was no easy matter, whatever Raheesh Khan might want.

For one, Whitfield had a girlfriend. To buy time, Michael had visited her and told her Ian was in trouble and they were trying to help him. The police would come to her, he knew, so he told her to tell them Whitfield was working abroad. Whitfield had actually done a Dutch run for them about a week before the fuck-up, so there would be some evidence to back that up, providing no one looked too closely.

But if they killed Whitfield, then sooner or later his girlfriend was going to kick up a fuss. They couldn't just get rid of her, too. She would be missed straight away. Unlike Whitfield, she had family who cared about her. And where would it end, if they started on that road? The best thing would have been to disappear Whitfield somewhere foreign, keep him happy for a while. That was why he had gone to Khan for help. So much for that.

Then there was the issue of leaks. Michael was fairly sure Kershaw would have kept his mouth shut, but who else had Whitfield talked to? So far as Michael was aware, Fleming's address had come to Kershaw's attention through the usual route – Whitfield had worked a removal there as part of his day job. Whitfield was a kid, a stupid kid. He had a cheeky mouth and an adolescent brain. He didn't know how to keep a secret to save his life. Michael had repeatedly told Kershaw not to use him. Michael guessed Whitfield had told half the world about the impending job at the Flemings'. That was another reason Michael had wanted to question him personally. He looked around for something to wipe his hands on. 'What a fu cking mess,' he muttered. 'What a stupid fucking mess.'

57

On the ring road around Manchester Karen called up Linda Parish's number on her mobile. Linda worked for GMP on their Drug Squad. Many years ago they had done a couple of cross-border drugs cases and got to know each other. As was the way, the cases had ended and they hadn't spoken for years, until Karen had needed help on a fraud case a couple of months ago. As it happened, the suspect had been connected to a small-scale Manchester supplier, so Karen had asked Linda for help locating him. It hadn't worked out, but it had re-established the link to Linda. She was the only officer in GMP that Karen knew well enough to call.

She rang her on instinct, because Khan had been strange and she knew nothing about him, not because she suspected him of anything. She just wanted to make sure there were no gaps in her knowledge. Linda surprised her.

'Raheesh Khan is the biggest heroin supplier in the north-west,' she said. 'Ships large-scale, bulk, from Afghanistan, Pakistan, Turkey. He's probably supplying an area from Scotland down to Nottingham.'

Karen pulled into the slow lane and crawled, phone glued to her ear. 'You have to be kidding me?'

'Straight up. Don't fuck with him.'

'Shit. I tried to enlist his son as a witness ...'

'Did he agree to see you?'

'He didn't know I was police. Are you sure we're talking about the same guy? Big house at the end of Arley Road, in Altrincham?'

'There's only one Raheesh Khan out there.'

'He has a son in a wheelchair?'

'Feroz Khan.'

'I don't believe it.'

'You spoke to him?'

'He thought I was a journalist come to interview him about a charitable donation.' She told Linda about Khan's fit of temper.

'If you've annoyed him, watch your back,' Linda said. 'Although he won't touch you if he knows you're police. He knows what he's doing. But he runs a big set-up. Lots of money involved, lots to lose. Be careful ...'

'You're looking at him?'

'Not us. He's way above us. You know how it is.'

'*Someone* is looking at him?'

'Twenty-four seven, I assume. But we wouldn't know about it.'

'What about Aidan Kershaw?'

She knew him, too. Kershaw was a part of Khan's distribution network.

'How fucking stupid can I be?' Karen said aloud.

She ended the call and felt a buzz of adrenalin in her veins. *Now* it was beginning to work. Aidan Kershaw wasn't frightened of a prosecution. He was worried about his boss finding out that he had crippled his son fifteen years ago. *That* was why he would try to silence Steve Fleming. If Khan knew what Kershaw had done he would kill him.

She called Thorne at once. However annoyed he was, he needed to know about this immediately.

But he wasn't on his office number, or anywhere in Killingbeck. He didn't answer his mobile, either. She left a message asking him to call her urgently.

58

Pete Bains stood by himself in the top-floor canteen in Bradford Central Police Station and stared through the windows at the pall of smoke hanging in the evening sky above Manningham. He felt a panicky sickliness in his stomach, the sort of feeling he had long ago learned to recognize as a substitute for fear. On the table behind him were his overalls and helmet. It was too hot to wear them for prolonged periods indoors, though that was what he was meant to do, so that he was ready to jump into action at a moment's notice.

He knew the procedures because there was an emergency plan for this kind of incident, and it wasn't that long since he had been trained on it. But he had been standing around for half the day now, either in briefings at Wakefield or here, waiting for the call that would get him out and into it. He felt nervous when he thought about it, but his impatience was far greater. Stuck in here he felt useless and bad-tempered, unable to keep his thoughts off Karen.

They had given him EGT 6, an evidence gathering team of four men (including himself), consisting of two full-kit heavies (shields and batons) and a camera operator. There were five such units deployed – out there, already in the thick of it. But he had been given the reserve team. They were on stand-by so that the SIO could direct them to hot spots.

As the day progressed, and the threat of full-scale riot increased, they had appointed an SIO to work alongside the Silver Commander. The Silver Commander was Phil Read, a superintendent from Bradford North. He was in control of the public order operation. The SIO was John Munro. He was tasked with treating the night as a major inquiry before it was even over. If there were going to be arrests and prosecutions then they had to start focusing on that now, filming the ringleaders, getting footage to identify them. All the evidence gathering teams were working to the SIO.

They had been driven here in a convoy of other officers, and had arrived to find a town centre that looked like the aftermath of an invasion. It had taken them nearly an hour to get from the edges of town to within walking distance of Bradford Central. Everywhere they tried there were big blue buses and assorted coaches parked on the verges of the main routes leading into town, causing massive tailbacks and delays. They were already bussing in re-enforcements from as far north as Northumberland.

Bradford had erupted. The long-feared racial fuse had finally touched off an explosion. In the space of a few hours the town centre had been transformed into a seething cauldron of urban destruction on an unprecedented scale. Public order had ceased to exist in a wide area, from the city centre up White Abbey Road and into Manningham. Though all he could see from here was the smoke, Pete had been briefed as to what was going on at ground level.

A crowd of over two thousand exultant, enraged youths, mainly Asian, were torching and plundering at will, attacking the police with a ferocity that had taken everybody by surprise. They had already set fire to six or seven properties, all 'white owned'. Cars were being hijacked and set alight, then rolled into police lines. Neither the Fire Brigade nor the ambulance services could get anywhere near the flash points, so parts of Bradford were burning unchecked.

He had seen some of it on the TV here, when they had first arrived. The room was deserted now, but two hours earlier it had been filled with hundreds of uniformed officers from Lancashire, Manchester, Cleveland, North Yorkshire and Northumberland, all being kitted out in full riot gear, with shields, helmets, long truncheons and fire retardant overalls, while, at the same time, hasty briefings were shouted out by West Yorkshire liaison officers. The station had been electrified with excitement and fear. He had felt it like a charge in the air the moment he had stepped through the rear doors.

He had waited downstairs with his own team for over two hours, after they had transferred here from Wakefield. Then he had left them to come up here and stare anxiously at the view. The others had been more relaxed, sitting around chatting, playing cards. Maybe they didn't have a home on the edges of this thing; maybe their emotional life wasn't falling apart.

He had called his parents once – to make sure Mairead and Prem weren't headed for a day trip in Bradford. Mairead was in the garden and had to be called to the phone. Pete chatted to her as casually as he could, asking what she was doing with Prem, what they had planned and suchlike. During yesterday's call he had tried to get out of her what Karen had been like on the trip over, but without much success. Mairead didn't like to get between them, and she usually knew when there was something wrong. She hadn't asked for Karen and so he hadn't told her that Karen had disappeared God knew where. He didn't want to worry her before there was definitely something to worry about. He gathered from Mairead's comments that her mother hadn't called her, either.

He looked away from the view and checked his mobile again. Two days ago he had been on the point of reporting Karen as a missing person, then she had sent him a single, short text, asking to be left alone. He checked now for further messages. On Wednesday – when she had more or less admitted to having a relationship with someone else – he had been steaming with anger and hurt. But then she had left with Mairead and the anger had evaporated at once into fear.

The truth was he didn't really care who Karen had been shagging. If it was Ronnie Shepherd, as she seemed to suggest, then he was dead and out of it. Fuck him. The betrayal was nothing compared to the risk of losing both Karen and Mairead again.

Mairead was a daughter to him now. Not *like* a daughter. She *was* his daughter. That was how he thought of her. She was his responsibility. After Karen had taken her to his parents, he had pondered at length the awful prospect of Karen removing Mairead and herself from his life once again. He had to try to find a way to stop that. Right now, that meant letting her have her time away. He had texted her apologies for his reaction and couldn't do much more. At least there was a good side to her suspension – it meant he was sure she wasn't in the front line getting pelted with petrol bombs. But if this riot didn't reach some kind of natural conclusion it was going to spill over the back edge of Manningham. Then maybe none of them would have a home to go back to.

He checked his watch again. He had told the camera operator that he was up here, and had given him the number. He didn't want to miss the summons. He couldn't understand why they were being held back in the first place. Judging by the gathering cloud of smoke, there were already more than enough hot spots.

The trouble had started with an 'anti-fascist' demonstration in the city square right outside Bradford Central Police Station. There had been a strong turn-out – a crowd of more than three thousand, all peaceful for most of the day, all worried at rumours that white, right-wing thugs were about to descend on the Asian areas of Bradford. But his squad – the skinhead squad, as they called it – had effectively put a stop to that. For the last twenty-four hours they had been actioning the intelligence gathered painstakingly over two months. There had been arrests across the county. At road blocks they had stopped buses of youths and turned them back with public order warnings. Only a handful had got through, but in two bars in the main shopping area fights had broken out, one with a near-fatal stabbing.

After that the day had spun out of control. It became a stand-off between lines of riot police and a huge, swelling crowd of hostile young men, nearly all Muslim, all flooding down to the town centre from the Manningham area, where they mostly lived. Some officers spoke of a co-ordinated attack on the police, with ring leaders clearly using mobile phones to whip up support.

'Inspector Bains?'

He looked round. A small, uniformed woman was standing at the door to the room.

'Sergeant,' he said. 'Detective Sergeant Bains.'

'I'm sorry. Sergeant Bains. I've been sent to bring you to Mr Munro. I couldn't find you in the stand-by area.' She looked annoyed that she had had to hunt him out up here. 'Can you come now, please? It's urgent.'

She had a car parked at the back of the station. He sat in the front with her, and the other three members of his team were crammed un-ceremoniously into the back, with the shields, overalls and camera gear thrown into the boot. He was wondering how she would get through the lines of public order vans and trapped traffic, but she revealed that soon enough.

She was the most aggressive, vocal driver he had ever come across. She put the siren and lights on, wound down the windows and yelled at anyone that got in her way. She drove at dangerously fast speeds through scattering crowds of civilians, up through town and out, always heading uphill, towards the smoke. He strapped himself in and closed his eyes. Any minute he was expecting a brick to come crashing through the windscreen.

But once out of the centre of town the crowds thinned out. They drove along the edges of the disorder, climbing the hills to the north-west of the city. Driving up parallel to Manningham, on the Thornton Road, everyone seemed to be hurrying somewhere, head down. To his right there was a continual wail of sirens and high columns of smoke in the darkening sky. He tried to get information from the driver as to the limits of the riot, but she didn't have a clue.

The street she took him to was less than a twenty-minute walk from his home, but he tried not to think about that. It was cordoned off and riot vans were lined up along its length. She pulled up beside an incident control van.

'Mr Munro is in there,' she said. She pointed.

As they spilled out he thought that it was *possible* Karen was at home and in danger, but it seemed unlikely. His guess was that she would pick Mairead up tomorrow, as planned, then come back. Only then would he find out what was going on between them.

Up here they were close to the centre of it. Up here he could *feel* it, something quivering in the air, supercharging it with tension. From past the houses at the end of the street he could hear the roar of the crowd, only streets away, like a football match.

'What the fuck is happening over there?' he said. He felt nervous now that he was near it.

She glanced at him. 'It's a riot, sir,' she said, her face deadpan. 'The Asians are burning their own part of town and we're trying to stop them.'

He nodded. Was she trying to provoke him, because he too was Asian and this was his part of town, too? Even as she spoke, a thunder-ous, thrilling roar went up, as if someone had scored a goal. 'They've taken somebody out,' she said. 'They shout like that when someone gets hit and falls.'

He turned his back on her and walked up to the IC van. There was a single uniformed officer standing at the rear doors. He called back into the interior as Pete approached. Almost at once John Munro came out to meet him.

'Pete Bains,' he said. They had met before. Munro, a very tall man, was frowning intensely, kitted out like everyone else in black public order overalls. Behind them, two marked vans accelerated down the street, sirens blaring.

'Did you get through all right?' Munro asked him. His eyes followed the two vans.

'No problem,' Bains said. 'You want us to stand-by up here?' He looked around. An ordinary Bradford street. The juxtaposition of relative normality – here, only streets from the disorder – and what he knew was going on *just over there*, was surreal. At the bottom of the street, vans were discharging heavily clad officers in the hundreds, instructions shouted out to them by sergeants and inspectors. Another roar went up from the crowd, followed quickly by the sound of explosives detonating.

'Fireworks and petrol bombs,' Munro said. 'There's going to be some heads cracked tonight. They've been waiting to kick off like this for years.'

Pete wasn't sure whether he meant the rioters or the police; either way, he had to be one of 'them'. 'Where do you want us?' he asked again.

Munro was gazing towards a new column of smoke rising above the houses at the end of the street. 'It's getting nearer,' he said. He turned to Pete and shook his head. 'They took us by surprise,' he said. *They, the Asians.* 'The casualties are mounting too quickly. There are already over a hundred and fifty officers down. Just over there.' He pointed. 'They can't get the ambulances through to pick them up.'

One hundred and fifty casualties, and it was only eight-thirty in the evening, still daylight above the town. The worst was surely yet to come.

'Don't you live over there?' Munro asked.

'A bit further over,' Pete said.

'The posh bit of Manningham?'

'Heaton.'

Munro shook his head. 'I hope we can contain it, Pete. I hope for your sake we can contain it.'

'Do you want us to wait here, sir?' Pete asked again. At the rear of the car that had brought them up, his team were in their overalls, waiting.

'I want you over there, Pete,' Munro said, nodding at the smoke. 'I want you right where it's happening.'

59

It caught up with her again outside Whitfield's address. Exhaustion and something else, a blackness that made her want to put her head in her hands and cry. At Khan's it had been obscured by curiosity and fear, but it hadn't gone away. Calling herself 'Helen Young' and thinking about Ronnie started it off again. Every time she thought about him she felt lost. It was stupid beyond comprehension. She hadn't known him long enough to feel this much. The horror and guilt, what had happened with Stijn, Jana's confusion, Caroline – they were all magnifying it into something greater. She knew that, but still couldn't stop the emotions swelling inside.

She leaned her head against the car window and closed her eyes. There were brightly coloured lights flashing behind her eyelids. She tried to ignore them and let her breathing slow. She wanted to sleep. Even if the nightmares came, she wanted to sleep.

But sleep wouldn't come even if she tried now. Her brain was racing, connecting things that shouldn't be connected. She sat up straight, wound the window down and took a long breath of cooling evening air. The street outside was quiet. She looked for signs of the officers Thorne had posted to watch the address, but could see nobody. Her plan had been to tell them about Whitfield, since she couldn't get Thorne. That was why she had come here.

She got out of the car and walked the length of the street, checking cars on both sides. There was nobody watching Whitfield's place. Maybe they were inside. Maybe the girlfriend was co-operating. She walked up and rang the bell.

It was answered by an overweight woman with an unfriendly face. 'Nadine Askwith?' Karen asked her. She looked to be in her late twenties, and wore a suspicious expression.

'Are you police?' she asked.

Karen sighed. That meant they weren't inside. She thought about it for a moment. Turn away and leave it, or push just a little bit more? If she turned away now the night would resolve itself into checking into some cheap motel and drinking. Or driving back and facing Pete. She didn't relish either option.

'*Are* you police?' the woman asked again.

She made a decision. 'No,' she said. 'My name is Helen Young. I'm looking for Ian. Are you Nadine Askwith?'

'Yes.' She was still holding the door half-closed. 'Who are you, if you're not police?'

'I'm here privately,' she said.

'Privately? You mean you're a bailiff?'

'No. Not a bailiff.' What to tell her? What would open her up? 'I have something important to tell you about Ian.'

'Like what?'

'I'm looking for him. I want to interview him.'

'But you're not police?'

'I'm a journalist.' Why not? She was Helen Young and she was a journalist. Maybe Helen Young *would* have ended up as a journalist, if she hadn't taken so many wrong turns. She waited for a more promising response from Askwith, but it didn't come. She showed no inclination to open the door further, even less to invite her in.

'Ian may be in great danger,' Karen tried.

That brought a change of expression. Askwith was frowning now. 'In danger from who?'

Karen glanced around her. She was the only person on the street. 'From a man called Aidan Kershaw,' she said, lowering her voice. 'His cousin.' It was at least theoretically possible. After all, Whitfield wasn't only a key suspect, he was probably a key witness.

She watched Askwith closely as she mentioned Kershaw. She recognized the name. The frown deepened. She tried to work out what it meant. She couldn't. But it was enough information to make her step back and hold the door open. 'You'd better come in.'

Karen stepped into the hallway and closed the front door behind her. She followed Askwith into a small front room, the TV room. Askwith produced a packet of cigarettes and offered her one.

'What's this about Aidan?' she asked. She was taking it seriously.

Karen waved the cigarette away. 'You know him?'

'Of course. Like you said, he's Ian's cousin. Why is Ian in danger?'

'Do you know where he is?' She was trying to listen for other sounds from the house.

'Not here. Are you going to tell me what you mean?' She put a cigarette in her mouth and lit it. Karen thought she heard a noise from the floor above. Askwith saw her eyes move to it. 'It's the baby,' she said. 'He's asleep. Tell me what you meant when you said Ian was in danger.'

'Whether he's in danger depends upon where he is. Do you know where he is?'

'He's abroad. Working.'

The same answer she had given previously to the inquiry. 'You sure about that?'

'No. I'm never sure about anything when it comes to Ian. But that's all I know. That's what he told me.'

'When was the last time he contacted you?'

'Tell me why he's in danger.'

Karen rubbed her face. 'It's possible he knows something about Aidan,' she said. That also was true. 'Something Aidan might not want to get out.'

Askwith shook her head, puzzled. 'Like what?'

'Something about an assault.'

'What assault?'

'An assault many years ago. An attack on a boy called Feroz Khan.'

'I've never heard of him.'

'He's the son of Raheesh Khan.'

'I've never heard of him, either.' Her expression said it was the truth. 'This isn't about the murder of that Asian women, then? The one that was stabbed to death?'

'It might be about that as well. These things might be linked.'

Askwith folded her arms and stuck her jaw out. 'I don't get it,' she said. 'How does all that make Ian in danger? And what's it got to do with you?' She exhaled smoke in Karen's direction.

Karen stepped sideways. 'I work for the *Yorkshire Evening Post*,' she said. 'I do investigative journalism. I'm looking at a link between the two cases.' She sat down on the seat nearest her. She wasn't going to get anything out of this woman. The truth was she didn't know how to begin. Her brain wasn't up to it.

'Who did you say you were?' Askwith asked again. She was sceptical now.

'Helen Young.'

'Not police?'

'No.' She was going to have to give her more. 'It's possible Aidan Kershaw is connected to both attacks. That's what I'm looking into. I write the crime column.'

'Shouldn't you be speaking to the police, then?'

'I have. They think Ian might be a witness. That's why he could be in danger.'

'From Aidan?' She was thinking about it.

'Yes. From Aidan. Do you know where Ian is? That would be the easiest way to make sure he's safe.'

'Aidan wouldn't hurt Ian.' She didn't sound convinced, though.

'*Can* he hurt Ian? Does Aidan know where Ian is?'

'How would I know?' She pulled a mobile from her back pocket and stared at it, as if thinking about whether to use it. There was a trace of panic about her movements now.

'If you know where Ian is then you should tell me,' Karen said. 'So we can make sure no harm comes to him.'

'We? Who is we?'

'Me and you.'

'I'll ask Michael,' Askwith said suddenly.

'Michael?'

'He's a friend of Ian's. He knows where Ian is working.'

Karen watched her bring up a number and ring it. She waited.

'Micky? It's Nadine.' Silence while Micky said something. Then, 'No. That's not it. There's a woman here looking for Ian.' She broke off. 'What did you say your name was?' she asked Karen.

'Helen Young.'

'She says she's called Helen Young.' A long pause there. Was Micky speaking? Karen couldn't hear. 'She's a journalist,' Askwith said. 'What? No. I don't know. She says Ian might be in danger.'

Karen listened carefully. She had the feeling that Askwith was lying to her somehow, that she was concealing something as she spoke to the man. There was something about the tone of voice that communicated a different meaning to the words used.

'She says Ian is in danger from Aidan,' Askwith said, as if *asking* him: *is Ian in danger from Aidan*? 'Aidan,' she repeated. 'Yes. Aidan Kershaw. No. I don't think so. She wants to know where Ian is.'

She was asking for his permission, it seemed. Asking his permission to say where Ian was. Or permission to talk to her at all.

'He wants to talk to you,' Askwith said suddenly, holding the phone out towards her.

Karen took it. 'Yes?'

'Who did you say you were?' Male voice, Manchester accent.

'Helen Young.'

'You're a journalist?'

'With the *Yorkshire Evening Post*.'

'And you want to find Ian Whitfield?'

'Yes. Do you know where he is?'

A pause. 'Can Nadine hear us?'

Karen glanced over at Nadine. She was sitting on a chair opposite her now. 'I doubt it,' she said.

'Good. So don't tell her I said this. I know where Ian is. I can help you.'

Alarm bells went off in her head.

'Do you want to know where he is?' he asked.

'Yes.'

'Well, here's the trick. It'll cost you.'

'I see.' So that was it. Maybe not so alarming after all.

'I want a hundred.'

Cheap. 'I'm sure that can be arranged.'

'You give me one hundred and I'll tell you where he is.'

'I need more information up front.'

'Not up front. You'll get more if you pay. Give the phone back to Nadine.'

She sighed and handed it back to her. She heard Nadine listening to him. Was it fear that was in her eyes now?

'He wants to meet you now,' Nadine said, as she cut the line.

'Now?'

'In a pub near Bury. Do you know Bury?'

'Not well.'

'I'll give you directions.'

341

60

The street lighting had come on and it was getting steadily darker as she reached the place. It was an Irish pub, north of Bury, on the way out towards Ramsbottom and the moors. The Shamrock and Harp, it said on the sign swinging above the lit entrance, but Nadine Askwith had referred to it as 'the Sham'. Karen had never heard of it.

She parked in the car park and sat for a while trying to think. Her mind felt weary, her reactions and thoughts lagging. But beneath that were the first signs of improvement. She felt marginally better. She was achieving something. She had kept herself busy, worked through the worst of it. If she kept her thoughts away from Stijn, away from Ronnie and Pete, then there was a good chance she would even sleep tonight. That would work wonders. Then Mairead tomorrow. Things would be fine after that. She could begin to see a perspective on it all. She just needed to rest, think about things carefully, work out what she really wanted to do. Let herself recover.

So what was she doing here? Was she being stupid?

She had come here on autopilot, because the chance had presented itself. She doubted anything was going to come of it, though. Michael Rawson – Askwith had given her his full name – had sounded as if he had sniffed a chance for quick cash. Probably he had no idea where Whitfield was.

She scrutinized the location. The place looked harmless enough. It was a white-washed stone building on the edge of sloping fields, surrounded by hawthorn and elm. You turned off the road and took a lane to the back of the place to park. It was darker in the car park than out on the main road, because the lighting was poor. The car park was full of cars, though. The place was out in the sticks, but it was busy.

There was another building, a farmhouse, adjacent to the place (no sign of life, all lights off), but not many other houses nearby. In the

342

distance, she could see the lights of Bury. A warm summer evening. It threatened to remind her of London, of standing on the hotel balcony looking out across Ealing Common as the daylight faded, Ronnie hugging her from behind. She steered her thoughts clear of it and got out her mobile instead. She could call Mairead now. She was calm enough.

Then her eyes found the time on the dashboard. She was late and she needed to try Thorne again before going into this place. Mairead wouldn't want to speak for long, of course – she would be busy with Prem – but Karen didn't want it to be rushed from *her* side. She made a quick decision: call Thorne, meet Rawson – if he shows – get the info, *then* call Mairead when she was done and had as much time as she wanted. After that, call it a day and get some sleep somewhere.

She got Thorne's answering service again. This time she left a full message. She took her time and told him everything – the visit to Khan, the urgent need to find Whitfield, the visit to Asquith and then the meeting here. She gave Rawson's name, though it wasn't much use without a date of birth. She had asked Askwith his age (mid-thirties, she'd said) and had tried to run a check herself. After six attempts to get the Control Room she had finally got through and given the operator the details. The answer came back that there were thirty-five possible matches. The operator demanded to know whether the enquiry was urgent. Obviously they were busy with something else. She gave up.

Why was she worrying about it at all? Even if she was misjudging everything, nothing was going to happen in a place like this, with so many witnesses. She got out of the car. Immediately, from within the pub, she could hear music, voices. The place sounded packed, lively. Behind her, in stark contrast, the evening was filled with the silent warmth of country lanes in summertime. An owl was hooting from high up in one of the elms – the only sound she could detect outside the pub. The night air was cool and refreshing. She waited for a while, savouring it. A bottle of pure oxygen would probably do the trick, she thought. She realized with some shame that she had been wearing the same clothing since Wednesday. Maybe the shame was a good sign.

She walked up the lane leading back to the road. There was a view along the side wall of the pub to the road and fields beyond, a telegraph pole leaning slightly at the end of the lane.

Inside the entrance hall there were doors to the bar on one side, the lounge on the other. A man was standing in the space between the two doors. He looked like a bouncer. He nodded at her. 'Evening,' he said.

She nodded back at him. There was a sign on the lounge doors, 'Private Function', but she could hear nothing from within. All the noise seemed to be coming from the bar. The bouncer pushed the bar door open for her and a wash of noise surged out. She stepped in.

Saturday night. The room was small, dense with people. She let the doors close behind her and moved towards a quiz machine that was beside a TV set mounted on the wall, just inside. Then leaned back against the wall and scanned the crowd. At the far end she could hear musicians playing jigs and reels on harmonica, guitar, keyboards. Celebrating happy little Ireland. There was a notice pinned to the wall beside the door: 'Brendan Power Trio: Irish Session, 7 July 2001. The Sham, Bury.' But she couldn't see the musicians for the crowd. Most people had their back to her. A mixed bunch of men and women, mainly young, everyone with drinks in hand. Presumably they were all going to drive home afterwards.

Over by the bar she could see a tall man in a black shirt staring at her, as was the barman. Could black shirt be Rawson? Askwith had refused to describe him, except to say he had a moustache. *He* would find *her* had been the attitude. In any case, the man in the black shirt was clean-shaven.

The air was thick with cigarette smoke, the ceiling a dirty brown colour from years of it. Beside her, a young woman in a short skirt was playing the quiz machine, cursing and exclaiming as she got the answers wrong. Finally she gave up and walked off.

Karen looked up at the TV. No one was watching it and the sound was off. There were images of cars on fire, police vans racing through dark streets. Then lines of policemen with riot shields in front of a huge crowd of missile-throwing protestors. She saw three petrol bombs lobbed behind the police lines; one of them exploded across the back of an officer, swallowing him in flames. She assumed it was Portadown, Garvaghy Road – the usual build-up to marching season. It was 7 July, so only five days to go.

Suddenly she realized what the caption said: 'Bradford, West Yorkshire: LIVE.' She felt a momentary shock, then realized this was why she couldn't get hold of Tim Thorne. Her thoughts raced to Mairead again. Was she safe? She was at Pete's parents, miles away. But Pete could be caught up in it. Her heart leapt with sudden, unexpected fear for him, and she took her mobile out to call him.

The door opened and a man stepped through. He was of average height and looks, slightly overweight, dressed in a crumpled green Barbour. He had a moustache. He looked harmless, but she knew it was Rawson before he even approached her. She put the phone away.

'Helen Young?' he asked quietly.

'Michael Rawson?'

'That's me.' He looked over at the man in the black shirt and they exchanged nods of recognition. The barman did the same. Obviously he was well known here.

'You like the music?' he asked, cheerfully.

She ignored the question. She didn't have the energy for small talk. 'What can you tell me about Ian Whitfield?' She had to raise her voice to be heard.

'We can't talk here,' he said. 'It's too loud. Come out to my car.'

'Here is fine.' She was almost shouting, but nobody would be able to hear. 'Just tell me what you know.'

'I don't want people to hear us. We can go out to my car. It's just out the back.' He took the Barbour off and held it under his arm. He had powerful, developed upper arms and shoulders. She looked at his hands. The knuckles were chewed up and misaligned – a fighter's knuckles. 'It's too hot in here,' he said, catching her look.

She heard the alarm bells again, but didn't know why. His face looked normal. The nose had been broken, like her own, but he wasn't covered in lumps and scars. She let her eyes skim over the rest of him. He was wearing a blue T-shirt. Her gaze fixed on his forearms. There were three sets of long parallel lines, like welts, running down the left arm as far as the hand. Were they recently healed scratch marks?

'Do you know where Whitfield is?' she asked. 'Or were you fucking with me?'

He looked away from her, then at his feet, then across the floor. He was embarrassed. 'I know someone who knows where he is,' he said finally. He changed his stance a bit. He looked uncomfortable.

'So you were bullshitting me?'

'No. I know he's here, in this country – not in Holland like Nadine thinks. I just don't know where. If you give me the amount we agreed, and double that to this other fella, then you'll get your information.'

'You didn't say that on the phone.'

'I thought you wouldn't come if I told you about the other guy.'

'Who is the other guy?'

He shrugged, as if the name didn't matter. 'Another friend of Ian's. I can take you to him.'

She didn't like it. She glanced past him. A few people had turned now and were watching them instead of the musicians. Did they realize something she didn't? They looked nervous.

'I haven't got three hundred pounds,' she said. 'My deal was with you only.'

'You could get the extra cash,' he said. 'You could go to a cash-point.'

Was that it? Did he intend to rob her? She looked carefully at him, trying to box him, fit him into a bracket she could risk assess.

He smiled sheepishly at her. 'Maybe you could talk him down,' he said. 'Or go, if you don't like it.' He shrugged again. 'It's no shit on me.' He seemed genuine about that.

'OK. Let's take it one stage at a time,' she said, sighing. 'Where is this other guy?'

'In another pub. About half a mile up the road. That's why I got you to meet me here.'

She stared at Rawson for a moment then nodded.

'You want me to take you to him?' he asked.

She nodded again. Something *was* going on. But she couldn't work out what. A simple scam, to get cash off her, when they actually knew nothing? 'OK,' she said. 'Take me to him. But I don't pay you anything until after he's given me the information.'

'However you want to play it,' he said.

61

Rawson went through the door first, into the entrance hall between the two bars. The bouncer had vanished. She followed him into the lounge, asking at the same time why they were going in here, instead of outside. 'It's just a short cut to the car park,' he said, without turning. He seemed casual, relaxed. He even said something about the weather.

The lounge bar was empty – a large, dark, cold room, full of empty tables, with drapes across the windows, like a pub function room. She hesitated. Rawson realized she had stopped and turned back to her. Suddenly her legs felt so weak she had to put out a hand to steady herself, leaning against the wall.

'It's just through here,' he said. 'What's up?'

She felt threatened, in a position of extreme vulnerability. And yet there was nothing happening. She had to get a grip on it, be rational. She *knew* nothing to suggest this man was really a danger to her. It was a feeling only. But her feelings were the last thing she should trust right now. Even if there was something he was keeping from her she was sure the knowledge of her real identity – as a police officer – would control things. He didn't look the sort to want to step over that line.

'I'm fine,' she said. Her voice sounded faint in her ears. She pushed herself off the wall. 'Let's go.'

But everything was slowing down. She moved three paces behind Rawson, walking slowly, the sounds muted, her vision narrowed. She could feel the adrenalin release, part of her brain desperately telling her she was in danger – but only the part that had been systematically distorted over the last few days. She refused to process the information. She could see herself following him as if she were compelled, see each new step in slow motion, but she forced herself to ignore the sensation and continue.

Still, as they passed through the lounge she dared not take her eyes from his back. He was saying something else to her, speaking over his shoulder. They reached the far end of the room and Rawson opened a small metal door. Artificial light streamed into the room from the street lights outside. She stepped after him, following him through the door, disorientated, uncertain. What was going on?

They walked up the long wall by the side of the pub, cars parked beside it. She looked past the cars, out on to the main road. No traffic. He was leading her towards a battered, blue Citroën ZX, an old model, normal enough in its day, a family car. The reflection from the street lights stopped her seeing into it. She kept following him. He reached it, opened a rear door for her, then stood aside. She saw now that it wasn't the street lights that were the problem: the windows were tinted. That wasn't normal.

If she got into the car she was on his territory. She had to know what she was going to do. She had to decide. Why did he have tinted windows? Did that mean anything?

She paused about two yards from the open door, hesitating. She tried to see inside the vehicle, but couldn't. 'You get in first,' she told him.

'I can't,' he said. 'I'm driving.' He laughed softly, as if she had said something ridiculous.

She stepped closer and looked around him. She could just see the edge of the nearest seat, through the gap. There was a child's toy lying there, some kind of model airplane. So he had children. She felt herself relax slightly.

She took a breath and her vision cleared, providing a brief moment of objective clarity. She was being ridiculous. There was nothing here to be afraid of. He was even smiling at her now. She stepped past the open door and placed a foot inside the car. At the same time she bent her head down and looked into the interior. There was a man in the furthest back seat.

She felt astonished. Rawson had said nothing about there being someone else there. His presence changed everything. Frozen in the doorway – half in and half out – she hadn't a clue what to do. Too late.

She felt Rawson's big hands on her back, thrusting her forward. She pushed back violently, but was already off balance. Her body twisted, one foot in the vehicle, one foot out. Then the other man's hands were on her, dragging her in. Rawson pushed again and she fell head first across the back seat, the model airplane breaking beneath her. She kicked out behind her and tried to get her head up. Someone was pinning her down, someone else shouting something. She opened her mouth to scream and felt a huge, jarring blow to the back of her head.

She closed her mouth. Collapsed. Everything slowed down.

She struggled to pull herself upright. There was no pain, but her balance was gone. She was gasping for breath. In front of her everything was spinning. Rough hands held her upright, then pushed her back in the seat. She could feel wetness on her face, a fierce throbbing in the back of her scalp. In front of her someone was shouting things. At her? She couldn't hear properly.

They had struck her head with something, scrambling her reflexes. She had been here before. There was no point in fighting it. It would clear. But she had to wait for it to clear. Until then she was helpless. She couldn't even speak. Either they would kill her now or it would continue. But she couldn't do anything about it.

She let go, sagging inside herself, letting it overwhelm her. The disorder was too much. All her motor reactions were shot, her vision, her hearing. She had to try not to panic.

She twisted her head sideways, away from where she thought Rawson would be, towards the window of the vehicle. She could feel the motion of the car jolting her. Rawson must be driving. She had made a massive error over him, missed something huge: she should have gone with her feelings. Too late now.

They were moving already. Her stomach turned, wanting to throw everything up. She let it come, retching miserably, head hanging forward. She hadn't eaten since that morning so there was nothing but bile. She brought a hand up and wiped her eyes clumsily, then saw the view through the car window, still unclear, shifting and moving with its own life as if she were savagely drunk. A road, a hedge, street lighting. She tried to control her breathing.

All her life she had suffered a fear of helplessness, of being held at the mercy of others. It was her most common recurring nightmare. Not dying, not even the pain of being tortured, beaten, stabbed, shot (all those things had happened to her and she had survived) – but the helplessness. Being bound, held, immobilized, arms and legs spread out on a table somewhere, shackled and waiting, unable to do anything to help herself, to stop it. That was what Stijn had done to her. Was it going to happen again?

She turned her head slowly, looking for Rawson. Who was he? What had she missed? She couldn't see him now, or hear him. She had to wait for her voice to come back, then tell him who she was. She tried to say it now; *I am police*. She said it over and over again, trying to get her mouth to open properly, her tongue to move, but the sound that came out was unclear. Could they even hear her?

Suddenly she realized that the other man – the one sitting beside her – had a silenced gun in his lap, pointed at her, a complacent smile on his face. He was saying nothing. Where had she seen his face before? A photograph somewhere. She stopped trying to speak. If they had guns she had to be more careful. She had stepped into the deep end. She had to work out what they had done and what level they were at before she started saying she was police. Telling the wrong people you were police could get you killed. She felt an instant of relief when she remembered she was carrying nothing to identify herself.

Through the window behind the man the road was visible, speeding past in the darkness, the intermittent illumination from the street lights strobing across the tinted glass, lighting his face orange, then black. Orange, then black.

She had an instant of terrible, racing mental lucidity. Everything she had done in the last three weeks had been an aberration, a species of private insanity. Even Ronnie. She had been mentally ill because Stijn had raped her in front of her child. It was that simple. She had let it get to her and it had brought her here. Into this world.

62

Pete Bains had seen nothing like it. It was like a scene from hell, everything lit with a flickering orange glow. Everywhere he looked there were fires blazing, filling the air with drifting black smoke. Burning, gutted cars, a pub alight, somebody's house. He wore a riot helmet with the visor down. The inside was covered with sweat and condensation, the visor chipped and scratched so that his visibility was restricted, everything stained orange and red. He was crouched on one knee, frozen in the action of pointing out something to the camera operator, also crouched, beside him. In front of them their guards – two strapping officers with full-length perspex riot shields held up above their heads – kept glancing back nervously, waiting for the signal to cut and run.

The crowd was like a beast. It had a collective life, a unified roar so loud it almost drowned out the continual scream of sirens, the crackle of radio traffic, the furious activity of vans, ambulances and marked cars, that were approaching and leaving, picking up and disgorging ranks of heavily encumbered men.

The mob. He could see it through the legs of the double lines of officers ten yards in front of him. The police line stretched from one side of the road to the other, close-linked, shields at head height to form a barrier. The task looked hopeless. Reaching far back into Manningham where the road led uphill, he could see thousands of youths, masked, jumping, chanting, leaping about like excited apes, moving and swelling, filling the street like a vast, squirming monster, lashing out indiscriminately with fire and destruction. Petrol bomb after petrol bomb exploded amongst the black overalls and glinting helmets, scattering men and women across the street.

Minutes before it had been worse. They had been further back then, filming from a safe distance as multiple lines of police slowly retreated beneath a barrage of projectiles so dense that the air looked black. He could not believe so many missiles could be held in the air at once, for so long. The effect was like a cloud of insects, swirling above the cowering lines of officers. Except each tiny speck was a stone, a stick, a bottle, or half-brick, torn from the road or the walls of houses and properties nearby. Waves of lethal objects hurtled down on the shields, without pause, so fierce and continuous that it had sounded like hundreds of machine-guns, a massed, repetitive series of percussive impacts.

He had watched rows of frightened officers creeping backwards then, men and women dropping like dead weight as bricks crashed through the defences and took them down. The images had looked bizarre, back-lit in fiery orange and red by the blazing cars and buildings. It was hardly possible to believe it was happening, here, on what had, only hours before, been a normal English street.

Then the supply of stonework had dried up. The attack had withered. The beast had moved, shifted, settled back on itself, shrunk away. In the pause, the order had come through to storm it, to take out the front line of ringleaders.

So the vans had tried to get up from the rear, laden with reinforcements. But they were moving up a road that had already been fought over. The surface was layered with broken stones and bricks. It no longer even looked like a road, more a dry river bed, strewn with rocks. The vans had foundered at once, tyres blowing. They had been forced to dismount the men from way back and send them forward in columns. By then the beast had recovered. The onslaught was beginning again, the stones crashing down afresh on the front line of shields. And once again they were creeping backwards.

It had been like that all night. Backwards and forwards, all the way up the hill from the city centre. He didn't even know what the plan was – if there was one. Keep pushing them back into Manningham? Nearer to his home. Why? Doing it this way the rioters had the advantage of significantly higher ground. He couldn't understand it. The latest reports said more than three hundred officers had been injured.

He saw one officer fall about three feet in front of their protection. He had been crouching behind a shield and a brick glanced off the top of it, hitting his helmet. He fell to the ground, pole-axed, and lay still. More objects fell around him. A stick bounced off his back. He didn't move. A trickle of blood spread away from his face, across the paving. Then suddenly he was surrounded by other officers, the helmet peeled off quickly but carefully. Pete recognized the bloodied face. It was a DS called Tim Thorne, someone Karen had worked with recently. He was being picked up by the arms, dragged away.

'*Officer down! Officer down!*' they were yelling as they hauled him back.

'We should fall back,' the camera operator shouted.

'I want to get closer,' Pete shouted back. 'I want the ringleaders' faces.'

'It's too dangerous—'

'It's dangerous for everybody. Let's do it.' He stood and tapped the guard nearest him, then gestured frantically forward with his fingers. The man shook his head, his shield dropping slightly. 'This is far enough,' he shouted. From the corner of his eye Pete saw something loop brightly into the air, over the front line of shields. It curled lazily upwards, then started to drop towards them – a Molotov. He grabbed the man's arm and pulled at him, shouting a warning. The bottle struck the ground right in front of him, broke, then exploded into running flames that flowed under the shield and shot up the man's body. Pete moved back, stumbling, automatically bringing a hand up to protect his eyes. Then tripped and landed on his back. He felt a rush of heat around his head, then someone stumbling over him.

'*Fall back!*'

There was screaming and shouting all around him.

The front line had caved in and rioters were running at them with sticks raised. Officers closed them down from both sides and a fierce pitched battle started. Pete looked for his camera operator and saw him sprawled on the ground just ahead of the fight. He stood up and ran towards him, but something struck his left knee, taking his leg away and spinning him across the ground. He came back to a sitting position and howled in agony, clutching at his leg.

The camera operator started to move. Pete crawled forward and grabbed his foot, shouting at him to fall back. He could hear the clatter of the helicopter above them. He looked quickly up, towards the front line. The crowd had broken through again and was charging forward, screaming and yelling. He staggered to his feet and started to run.

63

Michael felt sick thinking about it. It wasn't that he had a problem with hitting women (you hit who you had to); the problem was when they were pretty. And she *was* pretty. Although maybe that was the wrong word. 'Pretty' meant soft, feminine, defenceless – not the sort of thing he would go for at all. Up close, this one – Helen Young – was exactly what he would go for. Not unlike Maria. Except Maria wasn't as tall. Or as well proportioned, confident and clever. Helen Young was a good five inches taller than him, he reckoned, and probably more intelligent than him as well – when she was doing things she knew about. Coming to Bury to meet a total stranger in a pub had been foolish. A godsend for them, though.

She didn't look very attractive now, slumped over herself, blood running down her face, vomit on her clothing, out of her depth and sinking fast. They had to find out why she had been prying and who she had been prying *for*. They had to find out what she knew and who had told her. But Kershaw could be a bastard with women – sadistic. He *liked* to ruin their faces, *especially* when they were pretty. So he would have to keep Kershaw off her. If he let Kershaw loose on her she would end up like Whitfield, no use for anything.

Up until an hour ago – when Nadine Askwith had called – Michael's plan had been to try again with Whitfield, if possible without Kershaw being present. Askwith's call had changed everything. Now it was all damage limitation. For as long as the danger was simply that Whitfield had blabbed to his friends about a burglary the problem was containable. It was containable even if – for reasons unknown – Aidan Kershaw had set him up to do something he wouldn't otherwise have got involved with, sending Whitfield along with instructions to shoot Fleming (as Whitfield claimed) without telling Michael what was really happening. But what Askwith said turned the situation on its head.

As soon as Young had left her, Askwith had called Michael again with the full story. Young was not only making connections between Whitfield, Kershaw and Fleming, but had actually accused Kershaw of attacking Raheesh Khan's son. That suggestion came out of the blue like a hand grenade.

What Michael knew about Khan's son was that he had been crippled in a racist attack fifteen years ago. That was why Khan was like he was, they said. He had been wealthy already – before the attack – but then had gone bitter. The drugs business was the result. It sounded like good PR to Michael, but Khan himself had told him he would kill anyone connected to his son's attack, and Michael believed that. Khan had killed people for much less. Michael had rung off and immediately confronted Kershaw with the accusation.

'Questions about *what*?' Kershaw had asked, his face draining of colour. 'What was she asking questions about?'

'A journalist told Askwith there was a connection between our mess here,' he had nodded down at Whitfield's slumped body, 'and what happened to Khan's kid fifteen years ago.'

The information might have sounded absurd if he hadn't already had his suspicions about Kershaw. But as he had watched his face, he was sure it was far from absurd. Kershaw went rigid.

'You're fucking lying,' he said. His voice was high-pitched with fright. 'You have to be fucking lying.'

'Why would I lie about it? This journalist said there was a connection. Is there?'

'Jesus. I don't believe it …' Kershaw backed away from him. 'Helen Young! Who the fuck is Helen Young?'

'That doesn't matter. Is there a connection? If there's a connection you need to tell me, Aidan. You need to tell me now.' He had taken a step towards him then, intending to grab hold of him, shake him, whatever was necessary to get it through to him, but Kershaw had squatted down suddenly, his face ashen.

'I feel sick,' he said. 'I feel fucking sick, Micky …' He started to retch.

Michael squatted down on the floor beside him. Kershaw was bent over double, bile dribbling on to his shoes. 'I'm with you on this one, Kershaw,' he said. 'I'm with you because I'm loyal. But there are limits to everything. If you want my help on this you have to square with me. You have to tell me what's going on.'

Kershaw looked up and wiped the spit from his mouth. He looked like death. 'I don't know what's going on,' he said. 'I know as much as you.'

Michael held his gaze. The eyes were wide, fearful, but unflinching. Difficult to tell where the lie was. 'Is there a connection between Khan's son and this?' he asked.

'What? What kind of connection?'

'You tell me. *Is* there a connection?'

'I have no idea, Micky. We need to find the journalist. We need to ask *her*.'

'We'll get the chance to do that soon. But I want *you* to tell me, Aidan.'

'Oh, Jesus, Micky. Jesus Christ. If he finds out he'll fucking kill us.'

Michael had stood up then, knowing he wasn't going to get it out of him. 'I know he'll fucking kill us,' he said. He had sounded calm, but he was very far from it.

At the end of the day he had no illusions about it. You tried your best to keep things clean, but if you couldn't get them clean enough, you hit the road. That was where he was now. He had to decide in the next few hours whether he was going to see Raheesh Khan to turn Kershaw over to him, or whether he was going back to Maria and the kids and baling out tonight. All of them. Into a car and off to Heathrow. On to a plane and away. It was that desperate.

64

Kershaw had wanted to start on her in the back of the car, as Michael was driving, so once they got away from the Sham Michael had stopped and changed places with him. He wasn't looking forward to the hours ahead. He had to smash her up, make her squeal, reduce her from a tall, elegant, confident woman to a snivelling, terrified wreck that would give him the information he wanted. And then, depending on the answers, he might have to put one in her head. It was such a fucking waste. It made him grind his teeth to think about the cock-ups Kershaw had foisted on him in the last month. He was in it up to his neck now, one killing after another.

The car pulled through the big gates to the country club. There were lights on up in the bar and in the reception area. The place was meant to close at 11 p.m., but they normally let people stay on and drink until much later. Tonight they would need to turn them all out, just in case.

Kershaw took the car round the back and down the ramp to the service entrance. Michael watched the woman as the automatic doors rolled up and the car slipped into the shadows inside. She was trying to see out of the windows, he thought, squinting, wiping the blood from her eyes. But her head was rolling around as if she were drunk. Kershaw had brought the butt of his pistol on to the back of her head. Not a good idea. He was lucky the thing hadn't gone off and killed him. He hadn't struck her that hard, but then she was a woman. In his experience, no matter what women said about being able to put up with pain (Maria went on and on about the birth of Kevin), they couldn't hack it when it came to the real thing.

After they had changed places Kershaw had driven silently for the entire journey. He was chewing away at himself, keen to get at her. He would take some controlling.

'You go up and clear the punters,' Kershaw said, once they had stopped.

'You're the manager,' Michael said. '*You* clear the punters. I'll get her in.'

Kershaw gave him a dirty look in the mirror. 'I'll tell Luke to clear the punters,' he said. Luke was the guy who actually ran the place, as a job. 'We need to work fast, Micky. We haven't long.'

'Don't worry about it.'

'*I am fucking worried about it*!' He started shouting. '*Don't tell me not to fucking worry! Christ! If we don't sort this we're dead*!' He slammed his hands off the steering wheel.

Michael waited for him to calm, but instead Kershaw kicked his door open and got out. He stalked off towards the basement.

Michael searched through the cloth bag Helen Young had with her. Later he would have to go back to the Sham and retrieve her car. The bag was full of rubbish – women's things. No means of identifying her. She didn't even have any credit cards. Her mobile phone was locked, and not with an obvious sequence of numbers.

He held the gun up and opened the door next to her. 'No fucking around, Helen,' he said to her. She twisted her head to look in his direction, frowning, as if she had only just realized he was there. 'We're getting out here,' he said. 'You have to walk. If you don't walk we drag you.'

She walked very unsteadily, propped against his arm, the gun pressed against her head, just in case. She wasn't going to try anything, though. She needed a hospital. He took her through to the basement and saw that Kershaw was already in there, busy dragging Whitfield from the sauna. Whitfield looked dead.

'Tie her to that chair,' Kershaw said, pointing to the high-backed chair they had used to restrain Whitfield.

'She doesn't need tying,' Michael said. 'She's already out of it.'

'Don't argue with me, Micky. Not now.' Kershaw was overstepping himself. Michael could see things getting out of hand very quickly.

'You tie her,' he said. Maybe that would be enough to keep him happy for a while.

He sat her on the chair and bent down to check Whitfield. Kershaw had left him on the floor in front of the chair, on his stomach. He was naked, covered in sweat, his breathing very shallow, his eyes closed up with bruising. His entire body looked black and blue, and he stank.

Michael could find a pulse at his neck, but it wasn't strong. His skin felt scorched.

'He's going to die soon,' he said to Kershaw. 'If we want to keep him alive we should—'

'Forget that fucker. Get some water on *her*. Wake her up.' He pointed at Young.

'She's not asleep,' Michael said. 'She's concussed.'

Michael watched as Kershaw fixed her to the chair by tying her hands behind it, looping the rope through the bars and pulling it cruelly tight. Then he backed the chair against the sauna wall. He hadn't bound her feet. She was panting, taking deep, panicked breaths, straining against the ropes, looking around her. But saying nothing.

'Wake her up,' Kershaw said again. 'I want her head clear. I want her to hear me.' He was speaking in short, tense sentences. Michael thought he might explode at any point.

Michael fetched a bucket of water from the shower and tipped it slowly over Young's head, washing away the blood, forcing her to shake her head and gasp for breath. Then he stepped back. Kershaw walked in front of her, between Whitfield's motionless body and the chair. His jaw muscles were working away, grinding his teeth together. 'Who are you?' he asked her. '*Who the fuck are you?*'

She flinched as he screamed at her. 'Helen Young,' she said. She spoke slowly, slurring the words. Michael thought she was starting to cry.

'Hit her, Micky,' Kershaw said. 'Break her fucking jaw.'

Michael sighed. 'Her name doesn't matter,' he said. 'Who she works for is what we need.'

Before meeting her he had called the *Yorkshire Evening Post* and asked to speak to Helen Young, one of their journalists. It hadn't taken them long to inform him that no one called Helen Young worked there. That didn't mean she wasn't a journalist, but it was a complication. If she was a journalist, why would she have lied about which paper she worked for?

'You don't want to hit her?' Kershaw wasn't looking at him. He was staring at the floor, cracking his fingers, packed with energy. 'You don't want to obey my instructions?'

'It's a lot of effort, Aidan,' he said. 'We should hit her if we *need* to.'

'*You fucking puff!*' He took a step closer to Michael. He was so frightened he was forgetting his place. 'You fancy her? Is that it?'

Michael took out his packet of cigarettes. He smoked three a day, at most. He wasn't even sure he enjoyed them. It kept him calm, though. He placed a cigarette in his mouth. The temptation was to remind Kershaw forcibly who he was speaking to, but now wasn't the time. Now he just had to try to keep a lid on things.

'*You* hit her, Aidan,' he said, keeping his voice calm. He lit the cigarette. 'If you want to mess her up, *you* do it. I don't want to mess her up. I want to get information from her. If you fuck her up she won't be able to answer anything. She'll be as useless to us as Whitfield.' He kicked Whitfield's inert form with the toe of his shoe.

Kershaw cursed and stepped away from him. He took two steps towards her and, for a moment, it looked as if he *would* strike her. Then he relaxed a fraction and stepped back.

'I *am* Helen Young,' the woman said. 'You have to believe that.'

'I don't have to believe anything,' Kershaw said, raising his voice again. 'You have to *convince* me. Why were you looking for Ian Whitfield?'

'It's my job.'

Michael pulled a chair from the wall and sat on it, leaning on the backrest, placing the gun on the floor beside him. Kershaw was going to work himself into a fury, lose his temper and damage her. At some point he would have to intervene, but first he had to let Kershaw run free. It was like dealing with a child.

'Why are you trying to fuck me over?' Kershaw demanded of her. 'What have I done to you?'

She shook her head, slowly, painfully. She *was* crying now.

'Do I know you?' Kershaw went on. When he was agitated he was never any good at this kind of thing. 'Do I know Helen Young?'

'I don't know you,' she murmured.

'So who sent you to look for Whitfield? Who sent you to rake shit against me?'

She shook her head again, then bit her lip and sobbed.

'Who paid you?'

'I'm a journalist. I work for the *Yorkshire Evening Post*—'

Kershaw stepped towards her. 'You're a lying bitch.' He raised his hand to shoulder height.

'It's the truth.'

His hand lashed into her face. Michael grimaced. The blow was strong, snapping her head viciously sideways. She screamed something. Kershaw swung again, bringing the back hand across the other side of her face. The chair rocked, but stayed upright.

'We called the *Post*,' Kershaw shouted. 'They don't have a Helen Young working for them. So someone must have sent you. Who sent you?'

Young tried to shake her head.

'You told Nadine Askwith that I was going to kill Whitfield. Who gave you that information?'

'I didn't say that …' She was sobbing uncontrollably.

'Don't try to fucking deny it! You told her I attacked Feroz Khan.'

'No one said that.'

'She has told us you said that.'

'I just get an assignment,' she said. Her lips were split, bleeding. 'I get paid and I get given an assignment.'

She was sticking to the story. That was worrying. Kershaw had frightened and damaged her enough for someone normal to give in and spill the truth. Most people would already be too terrified to lie further. So either she *was* a journalist or she wasn't a normal punter. But what, then? Police? That thought brought a shiver to Michael's spine. She had muttered something about the police in the back of the car. But she had no ID on her. Could she be undercover? Even if she was, it was too late now.

Kershaw clenched his fists. '*Tell me who told you I attacked Feroz Khan!*' He was standing right in front of her, bent over her, yelling the words. '*Tell me who told you that lie!*'

'I don't know.' She was looking up at him, eyes wide, tears all over her face. 'I can't tell you what I don't know. It was in the paperwork they gave me—'

He swung his fist towards her face, a low, underarm blow that she ducked just in time. His knuckles hit the top of her head and he pulled back to try again. Michael stood up then, dropping the cigarette to the tiles. It would go too far now. 'That's enough, Kershaw,' he said. 'You don't know what you're doing.'

But Kershaw had snapped. His body was shaking, his voice piercing, mad. He swung both fists at her in quick succession, hitting her head, then her chest. Then again, catching her face, her jaw, her teeth. She started to shout out, trying frantically to avoid the blows.

'*I'll show you what happens to liars!*' Kershaw yelled. '*I'll show you what we fucking do in here ...*' He bent lower and began to punch into her stomach and breasts.

Michael stepped forwards and tried to pull him away.

'*Get your fucking hands off me*!' Kershaw yelled. He was still going at her. 'I'll fucking kill her. She's trying to fuck me over. I'll kill her ...'

Michael locked both arms around him, from behind. He pulled back, dragging him away from her. Kershaw twisted from his grip and staggered backwards, almost tripping over Whitfield's prone form. His eyes were wild. 'Give me your gun, Micky,' he shouted.

'You're not killing her now, Aidan. We have to know what she was doing—'

'*Give me your fucking gun*!' He barged past him and stooped to pick it up.

Michael stepped quickly in front of the woman, blocking his aim. 'We don't kill her until we know the answers,' he said. He held both hands up. Kershaw pulled the slide back on the gun. His face was wet with sweat. 'You can't kill her, Aidan,' Michael said to him again. He tried to sound calm, but he felt exposed. Kershaw was a lunatic. 'If you kill her we're dead. We'll go to Khan's tomorrow without knowing what's going on. We have to find out *why* she's saying these things.'

He saw Kershaw slow for a second, thinking about it. But not for long. 'Get out of the way, Micky,' he said. 'I'm not going to kill *her*. I've only just started with her.' He placed one leg astride Whitfield, then stooped and gripped his hair. '*You see this*!' he shouted. He was staring past Michael, at Young. 'You see what happens to fucking liars.' He pulled back Whitfield's head by the hair, bringing his bloody face up so that she could see it, then placed the gun against the side of his head.

'Don't do that, Aidan ...' Michael started. He saw Kershaw screw his eyes shut, and realized that he wasn't faking. '*Aidan*!' he yelled. '*Do not fucking*—'

The gun made a short, percussive crack, recoiling sharply. Whitfield's head jerked sideways, then erupted in a spray of fragmented bone, blood and brain. The gun was so close to his face the blast blew half his head across the floor. Kershaw was left standing with a clump of something in his fist – a piece of hair or scalp. He unbalanced and fell backwards on to the floor.

For a fraction of a second there was silence.

Michael stared at the mess. The tiles were drenched with it, as if someone had sloshed a bucket of steaming liquid all over. The material was spattered up the wall near the door, almost twenty feet away. Kershaw's face, clothing and hair were splashed with big gouts of crimson and black. He started to flail around on the floor, unable to see for the mess in his eyes.

At his feet Whitfield's body was kicking at the floor, suddenly coming back to life. Michael stepped quickly over it and removed the gun from Kershaw's fingers. The grips were warm and slippery.

'You stupid fuck, Kershaw,' he said between clenched teeth. 'You shouldn't have done that in here.' It was a forensic nightmare. He looked back towards Young. Her eyes were open and she had seen everything. She had seen Kershaw kill someone. Whoever she was, they couldn't let her go now. 'That was stupid, Kershaw,' Michael said. 'Really fucking stupid.'

Kershaw wiped blood from his eyes, then pulled himself to his feet. He was sucking air through his nostrils, hyperventilating.

'He was a shit,' he said, voice trembling. 'A shit who didn't do what I told him to do. He deserved it ...' He looked down at Whitfield's twitching body and pulled a disgusted face. 'He's like a fucking chicken.'

It was enough. Michael stepped close to him and grabbed his T-shirt at the neck. Kershaw's fists came up automatically, ready to lash out. But he saw the gun.

'What didn't he do, Kershaw?' Michael hissed the question into his face. His mouth was inches from Kershaw's eyes. 'What didn't he do that you told him to do?'

'I didn't mean it like that.'

'Don't lie to me.' He shook him violently, walking him backwards with the gun pushed against his chest. 'No more fucking lies! *What didn't Whitfield do?*'

'Christ, Micky! Take the fucking gun away—'

'I'll shoot you with the fucking gun. I'll put you down, right here, right now. Enough of this shit. You tell me what is going on!'

'OK. OK. I'll tell you.'

'You knew Fleming before you sent us there. Right?'

'OK. I knew him.'

'Was it personal?'

Kershaw nodded. 'I had to warn him,' he said. 'It was a warning.'

'Fuck! I knew it!' Michael broke away from him and walked into the middle of the room. He had guessed, but that wasn't the same as being told. 'You stupid bastard,' he said. 'You stupid fucking bastard.'

'I didn't tell this fucker to kill him,' Kershaw said. 'I told him to warn him.'

'By shooting him?'

'No. To burgle him, to frighten him.'

'You sent me along with a fucking juvenile lunatic without telling me what was going on.'

'I thought you would control him.'

Michael rounded on him. '*He* told me you had instructed him to shoot Fleming.' He pointed at Whitfield's body. 'I believe *him*. Why the fuck should I believe you?'

'You're over-reacting, Micky. It was a simple job if this little shit hadn't screwed it—'

'What did Fleming need warning about?' He stepped over Whitfield's body and strode back towards Kershaw. Kershaw raised his hands at once, backing off. 'What did Fleming need warning about?'

'Don't lose it, Micky. We're in this together. We need each other to clean this—'

Michael stood in front of him and pointed the gun at his crotch. 'What did you need to warn him about? *Did* you fuck up Khan's son?'

Kershaw shook his head, eyes on the gun.

'Did you do that? Did you fuck up his son?'

'I didn't do it. This has nothing to do with that—'

'So what's the link?'

'That's what we need to find out from this bitch.'

'What did you need to warn Fleming about?'

'The fucker jailed me.'

'*That* lawyer? Steve Fleming? That's what this is about?' He didn't believe it.

'He jailed me, four years ago. I didn't want him killing. I just wanted to warn him.'

'I don't believe you.'

'It's the truth.'

'You sent us to burgle a lawyer because he put you away? You expect me to believe that? I should walk out on you now. You fucked Khan's kid, didn't you? That's what this is about.'

'You can't walk out—'

364

'Why should I help you? Why should I even speak to you? You lying little shit-head.'

'You're in this as much as I am. You stabbed the woman, Micky.'

'I stabbed her because she saw your fuck of a cousin shoot her husband, because she recognized him as the removal man.'

'You knifed her thirty-four times, Micky. What the fuck were you doing?'

Michael spun away from him, seeing the images all over again. Not just Enisa Fleming. That had been a necessity. She had struggled and Whitfield had got in the way, tried to prevent it. They were outside so it had to be quiet, but if she had kept still, if both his hands had been free, it would have been quicker. He had already started on her by the time she started yelling about being pregnant. Too late by then. That was bad enough. But the images filling his head were worse than that even. Things for which there had been no justification. The same memories that leeched into his nightmares every night.

He walked over to the furthest wall of the room and leaned against it. His breathing was laboured. If it got bad he would have an asthma attack. He couldn't let that happen. Behind him Kershaw was still talking, still going on about it.

'Shut up, Kershaw,' he said. 'Shut the fuck up.' Kershaw wasn't going to tell him the truth. He would have to get that out of the woman.

He turned and looked at her. Her head was down and she was breathing heavily. But she was listening to everything. Without a doubt. He was going to have to silence her now. That was certain.

Michael looked at Kershaw. He had a nerve asking him what he had been doing. The man who got an erection by breaking people's bones. Why had he ended up working with filth like this? He felt soiled thinking about it. He wanted to scream and shout at the man, throttle him.

'Let's calm down,' he said, instead. He took another very deep breath. 'Let's all just calm down.'

He shook himself and stepped back. He had to get his head clear and work a way through this.

'I'm calm,' Kershaw said. 'I'm calm.'

'Let's try to get a plan together.'

Kershaw was looking down at himself, arms held out to either side, as if seeing the mess for the first time. 'Look at the fucking state of me.'

'You have to clean that off,' Michael said. 'You have to clean it off carefully.'

'I want to find out who *she* is,' Kershaw said. 'We have to find out who told her all this. Then I can clean them *both* off me.'

'I'll find out how she knows,' Michael said. 'Leave her to me.'

Kershaw looked dazed now, as if he were struggling to take in what he had done. He looked around himself, frowning. Was it the first time he had killed anyone?

'You need to clean yourself, Kershaw,' Michael said again. 'You need to clean up and calm yourself. I know how to handle this.'

'Put her in the cooler,' Kershaw said. 'Work her over then leave her in there on full blast. Then we can start again. I want to be here when you speak to her.'

Michael nodded. Of course he did. He wanted to control it, make sure nothing slipped out that would incriminate him.

'OK,' he said. He looked at Helen Young. He had to soften her up, get her to believe her life depended upon telling them everything, but without going too far. It was a precise skill, not to be done in anger. So he had to calm down. So far she had given them nothing. She had cried, but she was tougher than he had assumed. The sauna would work by itself, if they had the time to wait. But they didn't. So he would have to work on her first.

'I'll shower then go up to the bar,' Kershaw said. 'I need a drink.'

'You do that. I'll come for you when she's ready.'

Kershaw shrugged. 'I trust you, Micky.' He smiled, a crooked, insane smile, his face flecked with blood. 'You come and get me before you speak to her, right?'

Michael nodded.

'We can work this out,' Kershaw said. 'We can find a way through it.'

Out of the corner of his eye Michael could still see Whitfield's body twitching. 'Just go, Aidan,' he said. 'I'll see you in the bar.'

Kershaw nodded, turned and strutted out, wiping the blood from his hands on his trousers. Michael waited for him to disappear, then sat down on the chair and took a deep breath. He checked his watch. Almost half past eleven. When would this be over? It was like a continuous nightmare. He looked up at the woman. Her head was up now. She was sitting watching him, shaking from head to foot, blood dribbling from her hairline, mouth, nose.

'What are you going to do to me?' she asked. Her voice was a whimper. He stood up and took off his jacket. He placed it on the back of the chair and unbuttoned his shirt. This would make him sweat.

'What are you going to do to me?' she asked again.

'I'm sorry,' he said quietly. 'I don't like this, either.' He took off his shirt and folded it carefully. 'But at the end of the day I look after my own,' he said. 'That's what we all do.' He looked into her eyes. 'I don't like hurting attractive women.'

'Please don't hurt me ...'

'I'll try to keep off your face,' he said.

65

She wanted to curl into a ball and give in to it. Her senses were over-
whelmed. She could not cry out because the effort of taking enough
breath to shout sent a knifing pain through her chest and left her
breathless. She had to concentrate just to get enough air into her
lungs.

She was drifting in and out of consciousness, with just sufficient
awareness to know the pain as a blinding saturation, wracking her
body. She ground her teeth, every muscle contracted. Her percep-
tion of individual injuries was blurred, her entire body twisted into a
devastating, nauseating cramp.

She could not remember anything like it. But it was easy to forget
past pain. She knew she *had* felt this before, had suffered these injuries
– and worse – and had survived. It would pass. She had to find a way
to hang on, to get herself through it. But finding the mental space to
think was difficult. Every moment of lucidity had to be wrenched from
the vice.

He had tried to flood her with pain. He had done it carefully, clin-
ically, telling her exactly what he was doing. He used deliberate blows,
measured force, sufficient to bruise, but not to break anything. That
had been his intention. He had decided that he didn't need to break
anything. Breaks were dangerous – life-threatening if they were big
enough. He needed her alive and able to speak. Because she was a
woman she would crack quickly anyway. That was the way he spoke
about it. But it was an error. Long ago they had trained her how to deal
with this, how to soak it up. What he had done to her was controllable.
She had suffered at the hands of worse men. Stijn had almost killed
her. And she had survived that.

She would survive this.

He had untied her to do it, moving her off the chair. As soon as her hands were free she had thought to try something, but he had been too quick. The first punch was to the back of her head, to the place already injured by the gun butt. It had brought the shutters down at once. She had been so concussed she could do nothing then.

He had punched her slowly, methodically, turning her round and working his way down her spine and her ribs, finding her kidneys, probing for the areas he could bruise and inflame. She had felt three ribs crack. He had continued, rolling her like a sack of sand, punching into her stomach and chest. He had even prised her legs apart and punched her there.

He had wanted her helpless, incapable of resistance. But she could fight it. She was not *just* this physical thing, overcome with traumatic sensation. She was *inside* the swollen casing of flesh and bones and nerves and muscle. She could find the part of her that was untouched by it.

She gritted her teeth and forced herself to *focus* on the pain. To focus on it, not to run from it. It was a physical fact. Nothing more. Something she could concentrate on, or not. She had to get it to that point – where she had the choice. Where she could switch it off.

She felt the shivering increase rapidly, but at the same time the pain was changing, becoming a scorching heat that radiated through her. She let it swell and subside, her knees pulled up to her stomach, her limbs writhing automatically with every new spasm. She started to count, feverishly, as she had been taught to, driving her attention towards the numbers, each number filling her mind, competing with the pain.

When she could feel the surface she was lying on, when she could hear her breathing, the moaning in her throat, she opened her eyes.

Darkness.

He had dragged her into a sauna. Before he had shut the door she had caught an instantaneous yet unclear image of the room, illuminated by the light behind his shoulders. She had seen fixed wooden benches, a metallic sauna heater, a blood-stained floor. Her eyes had been open and working because he had avoided her face. Another mistake.

The immediate agony would pass. Tomorrow it would return and she would not be able to move. The pain would be like a swollen strait-jacket encasing her. But that was tomorrow. She had to get there first.

She kept telling herself what she knew about injuries like this: how-ever bad they felt now, they would heal. Superficial trauma, extensive contusions, a few hairline fractures. That was what a doctor would write. She had to see it like that and not be afraid. Fear bred shock and shock could kill.

Meanwhile there was adrenalin. The adrenalin would *really* kick in soon, rescuing her. For an hour after it started she would be high with it. That was also when people died of shock. For her it would be a window, a way out of this.

With every minute that passed the pain changed into something duller. She could cope with a dull ache. If the level became consistent enough she could master it and function. It was the sudden, razor-sharp blades of it that swamped her, cutting through her body from top to bottom.

Not yet, she thought. *Not yet*. She held her position, closing her eyes again. She had to give herself time. She was not going to die. Not like this. She was going to get out of here and phone Mairead. All she wanted to do was phone Mairead. She kept bringing her mind back to that.

She had to conserve her strength, let the pain drop back, wait for the moment. It would come. Rawson had dragged her gagging and half-conscious to this place without even bothering to tie her again. His third mistake. If she could hold herself together long enough she would be able to get up and move around, find a way out.

Rawson had weaknesses. Why had he not wanted to damage her face? Because she was attractive? Yet he had stabbed Enisa Fleming thirty-four times. He was the man with the moustache, described by six-year-old Jana. He had killed her mother, but spared Jana. Weakness. He seemed the more calculating of the two men, but he was equally unbalanced. Kershaw was more volatile, unable to control himself. But Rawson was still the one to fear, with or without the weaknesses.

She had known the other was Aidan Kershaw before Rawson had called him that. She had seen his mugshot in Killingbeck.

Before Kershaw had shot Whitfield her aim had been to convince them she was nobody, a helpless journalist who had been given a story to follow. She needed them to believe they could kidnap her, beat her up and leave her so terrified that she wasn't worth killing – because she was too scared to report it. It was her only chance to stay alive. To have told them she was police would have been a major error.

But then Kershaw had killed Whitfield in front of her. That changed everything. Now they were going to have to kill her. She was a witness. So there were no options. She had to recover and do something.

Kershaw had gone off to clean himself, Rawson to make phone calls about her. He had asked her if she was police as he was thumping her, so he had those suspicions, too. He would be trying to check that now, phoning to see if anyone had heard of DC Helen Young. It made no difference now what she was. Police, journalist, whatever. She had seen too much.

It was always the same with blows to the head. Unless they started to bleed into the brain – and she had suffered that before – they cleared if you could switch off and wait long enough. But that wasn't possible in a sauna. Already her clothes were drenched with sweat. She guessed the temperature was up to about 40C, and rising. If they left her in here for long enough she wouldn't have the energy to do anything.

She opened her eyes again and tried to move her legs. He had hardly touched her limbs, but there was still pain as she moved. The way he had aimed carefully at her torso made her think he must have boxed professionally. Another weakness. If he had been more brutal – if he had used a weapon – she would be past help now. He was banking on being able to question her. She waited, taking deep breaths, then pushed herself into a sitting position.

The heat in the place hit her like a wall. How long could she stay alive in here without water? She stifled the panic and began to feel her way around herself. He had done very little damage to her fingers or her hands. He had been trained to do it that way, she thought, to aim at the trunk, bruise only the parts normally hidden by clothing. That rang bells from her past – from professional interrogators she had run into.

It took her less than ten minutes to work out that the place was big enough for about six people, with two sets of fixed benches, in tiers. In a corner there was a sauna stove, boiling to the touch. The walls were thick and strong, not mere panels; the door did not even move as she pushed at it. She suffered a wave of despair and sank back against the wooden bench, sucking the thick, stagnant air into her lungs. The pain throbbed suddenly across her back, reaching into her kidneys with needle fingers, doubling her up. What had he done to her kidneys?

She slid to the floor and lay in a shivering ball again. The heat was overpowering. If they didn't come for her soon she would pass out. But when they came it would be to kill her. If she had not the strength now to stand up and kick the door down, how would she be able to fight an uninjured man?

She felt the tears starting again. Then, behind them, the panic, the blind fear of death. She had fucked it up. She wasn't going to get out of this alive.

She needed a weapon. She felt around with her fingers. The wooden benches above her were made from struts of wood and she tried to loosen them. Then she found a strut from the very back of the bench was already loose. She started to work at it. The action was exhausting, filled with halts and frustration as the pain in her back and chest shot through her again and again. But she managed to work it loose, then pull it off. There were nails jutting from one end of it. She felt stronger at once. The adrenalin was taking over.

She could probably kick the sauna heater from the wall. Would that start a fire, or electrocute her? Probably just jarring it enough would smash the elements. But they would see that at once, as soon as they opened the door. When they came for her she didn't want them to think she had moved an inch. So she left it, left the heat pouring out of it, gambling, hoping she could hold on. She lay on the floor where he had left her, trying to get the position exact, her right arm outstretched and lying under the wooden bench, the strut of wood just touching her fingertips, within reach.

She didn't have to wait long. There was movement from the room outside. Her heart leaped into overdrive, filling her brain with blood, sending more adrenalin through her. Had they given her enough time? For what she was about to do she needed strength, coordination. She lay still on the floor, breathing slowly, shutting out the pain, trying to hold the energy in, to conserve it. She had to think herself into it, ignore everything else. She began to breathe more slowly. The pain in her head was the worst now – a huge, bone-splitting headache, affecting her eyes and face, right down to her mouth. It wasn't just where they had hit her. It was dehydration. How long had she been in here? She guessed maybe thirty minutes, maybe a little more. Not long enough to kill her. She could do it. *Concentrate. Focus. Wait for the moment.*

She heard the lock in the door turning. She squinted through her eyes. The door began to open. She started to breathe with exaggerated effect, screwing her eyes against the light, but keeping still, not moving a muscle except for her chest. She heaved her chest up and down, gasping through her mouth. The pain in her side – where he had broken the ribs – was intense.

Someone stepped inside the cabin, standing over her. She heard him say something – it was Rawson. He was stooping over her, inspecting her.

'What a fucking mess,' she heard him mutter, so close his mouth must have been inches from her face.

Not yet, she thought. *Wait for the moment*. She felt him move backwards. Was he alone?

'Helen Young,' she heard him say. He was speaking quietly. He leaned over, closer to her. She saw his right hand place something on the bench to the side of her. A gun? He had not noticed the missing spar of wood. 'Can you hear me, Helen?' he asked. He must be alone. 'I've been sent down here to finish it.'

She let the words float over her, focusing all her concentration on his position in front of her.

'But first I need you to speak to me,' Rawson said. She saw his hand move and bring something to her lips. She felt something cool on them. Water. *He was giving her a drink*. He was squatting over her, almost sitting beside her. She could hardly believe he had made so many mistakes. She let the water run into her mouth and swallowed it.

'That's good,' he said. She had a leaping surge of emotion, an ecstatic, giddy happiness that almost brought a smile to her lips. *He thought she was half-dead*. He had put the gun down and was crouching over her. All she needed now was to pull her strength together, to gather it. She started taking deep breaths.

'It's over for you,' he said. 'But you can take Kershaw with you. You can tell me about Kershaw before you go. Did Kershaw attack Feroz Khan?'

She was almost there. She murmured unintelligibly to him, squinting at him through nearly closed eyes.

'Can you hear me, Helen?' he asked again.

Her hand closed around the wood, gripping it tightly.

'Do you know whether Kershaw attacked Khan's son?'

She rolled quickly away from him, the pain ripping through her chest. Then back, the strut out from under the bench. She saw surprise in his eyes, but already she was swinging. She whipped the strut in a long low arc above her head, forcing all her strength into the blow, screaming and exhaling all at once. He was reaching out a hand towards the bench when she struck him. His head bounced sideways, then wobbled, the hand slipped from the bench and he fell to his knees. She scrambled backwards, dragging herself to her feet, still shouting as the pain tore through her. The first blow had struck his left temple, a clean, heavy impact. This time she raised the stick above her head until it was touching the sauna ceiling. She drove it down on to the back of his head.

He fell forward then reared back, crying with pain and confusion. She thought he was going to stand, but he fell instead, tumbling into the sauna heater. She heard a singeing hiss, a scream of agony and came at him again. This time she smashed the strut into his forehead. He rolled on to his hands and knees, his eyes screwed shut. She dropped the strut and grabbed his shirt at the shoulders, from behind, trying to pull him backwards, to bang his forehead into the metal heater, but he was too heavy. She looped an arm around his throat instead and pulled him to her. He began to struggle, but without coordination.

It was a lock she had used before, but a long time ago. She tried to get the right grip, holding him to her, concentrating on his movements, blanking out the pain in her torso. Her arm was slipping because he was bleeding somewhere. She couldn't get a tight enough lock. She forced him to the floor and got her knee into his back. Then she had it. She cupped his chin and twisted his head sharply, trying to break the neck against the lock.

He realized what she was doing and began to thrash, throwing her off him at once. She lurched backwards and found his gun. He was making a noise like an animal, growling in his throat, sucking at the air. When she stood back from him he collapsed to the floor and didn't get up again. She had his gun in her hand but she didn't want to use it. It would be like sounding an alarm. She didn't know how far away Kershaw was.

He was trying to push himself to his knees but couldn't. She had injured him somehow. She had to have another try, now, before he got his strength back. She put the gun down and rested both knees against his back, pushing him into the floor. He started to writhe again, but there was less strength now. She could control him; he couldn't throw her off. She passed her arm under his throat and searched for a good, strong hold. He was trying to say something, but his voicebox sounded crushed. He started to cough and splutter. She pulled his head back and hooked one arm behind the other, bracing herself. He was making a gargling noise in his throat. As his head came back she was looking into his eyes. His face was smashed up, but he could see her. She saw that he could see her. She took a deep breath and wrenched back on his head.

It didn't work. She let his head sink forward and lay on top of him, gasping for breath, trying to ignore the pain, trying to recover herself. Could she leave him alive? What had she done to weaken him? If it was only the blows to the head he would recover. She couldn't take that risk. She had to try again.

'One more time, Michael,' she said to him, gritting her teeth. She pulled back again, this time getting a good twist to his head. A strangled, sputtering noise came out of his mouth. If she held him for long enough like this he would suffocate. But she didn't have the stamina for that. She took a deep breath, feeling the pain slice through her. His handiwork.

'One last go, Michael. Here it comes ...' She counted it down in her head. *One. Two. Three.* She screamed with the effort, putting her whole body into the snapping, backwards motion.

Crack. She felt the neck go, the noise like a stone whacking off the bottom of a car. She collapsed forward, sprawling across him, wheezing for air. Beneath her she could feel his body twitching and jumping. She rolled off him and lay on her back, chest bursting at the seams.

66

No time. She had to move. She forced herself to her feet and stood above him. His head was twisted almost 180 degrees, the eyes wide open, the mouth drooling. The chest was still moving, but he was gone. There was a large scalp wound, she saw now, where she had hit him the first time. She remembered the nails sticking through the wood.

She picked up his gun again and stepped out of the sauna cabin, supporting herself against the wall, the gun held out in front of her. Whitfield's body was still lying there in the pool of blood. The room was a basement of some sort. There was no one else there.

She went back into the sauna and found a mobile phone on Rawson's body. Not her own. Where was her own? She tried to call the emergency number but there was no signal, so she put the phone in her pocket and went back into the basement. The effort was sapping her rapidly now, the adrenalin wearing off. Within fifteen minutes she would be collapsed into a heap. She had to find Kershaw before that happened. She checked the gun. It was a Sig, unsilenced, not the weapon he had been holding earlier. The safety was on and he hadn't even chambered a round. She popped the catch and slid the magazine out, checking for rounds, then fitted it back together and drew the slide back.

She staggered into a corridor beyond the basement, then found the garage where the car was. There was a fire notice on an electrical cabinet near the automatic doors which gave the address of the place. It was a Golf and Country Club near Heywood.

She made her way to the public areas on the first floor – deserted, dark – and looked for signs to the bar. When she had worked out where it was she took out the mobile again and dialled 999. She gave them the address and told them she was police in need of urgent assistance. She gave her number and rank, then cut the line.

It took nearly ten minutes, gasping her way through the corridors, to find the bar. It was on the top floor, with big panoramic windows on to a floodlit driving range. She looked through the porthole glass in the doors and could see him in there. He was at the furthest end of the room, cleaned up, clothing changed, kitted out in a suit and shiny shoes. He was standing by the windows with a group of four others, all in suits, shirts with unbuttoned collars, ties removed, all with beer glasses in their hands. They were laughing at something, seemed drunk. He didn't look worried about anything. A mental case.

The room was narrow, with twenty or thirty round tables – all empty now – a long bar with shutters down, subdued lighting and a wall of high sloping windows. As she shouldered the double doors open she could already hear the sirens outside. Kershaw was on his mobile as she came in, probably trying to find out why sirens were headed his way. They all turned casually as she entered, then saw her, stumbling across the room towards them, blood all over her features, a gun in her hand.

Two dropped their glasses at once and dived for the floor; the other two ran in opposite directions, one still holding his beer. Kershaw dropped the mobile and reached inside the jacket he was wearing. She held the gun up with both hands and stood still, holding her breath, aiming carefully. She fired twice. The first shot missed, punching a hole in the huge window behind him, shattering the glass into a thousand fragments. The second struck his right shoulder, driving him backwards against the window sill. She took a step forward and shouted, 'Keep still, Kershaw. Keep your hands in the open!' The words came out cracked, stressed by the effort of shouting against the pain.

A look of horror transfixed his face as he realized he was hit. He slipped sideways along the window sill, clutching at his shoulder, a terrified snivelling noise issuing from his lips. But he couldn't take his eyes off the gun. She began to walk towards him. Did he have a gun inside his jacket? His hand had moved away from there.

'Do you have a gun?' she hissed. 'Are you armed?'

In her peripheral vision she could see the two who had bolted sideways waiting for her to pass them, then running full flight for the door. The two who had dived were curled in trembling protective balls near her feet, hands over their heads. She stepped past them, gun still pointed at Kershaw. He hadn't answered.

'Do you have a gun, Kershaw?' she asked again. She was almost on him now.

He shook his head frantically then began to stumble backwards, crashing through the chairs and tables, trying to get away from her.

'Stay there!' she insisted. 'Stay where you are!'

He tripped on a couch and toppled across a table. The table top slid from the base, depositing him on the floor. She took two quick steps over to him, stooped and pushed the gun into his face. 'Stay still!' She ran her hand over his clothing. He had a pistol in a holster, under his armpit. She took it out and placed it on the window ledge. Every move she made he flinched, jerking away from her. Where she had shot him the blood was pouring through his sleeve.

She stood back from him and looked at his convulsing face. Had he ever been this afraid before? Had he ever experienced *this*? The impulse to put the gun against his forehead and pull the trigger was overwhelming. He began to howl hysterically, pleading and begging with her to leave him. She felt like spitting on him.

'Aidan Kershaw, I'm arresting you for the murder of Ian Whitfield,' she said. 'Do you understand?' The words didn't get through to him, so she repeated them.

'You fucking shot me,' he whimpered. 'Jesus Christ. You shot me ...'

SUNDAY, 8 JULY

67

Until she saw the pictures on TV Mairead hadn't worried about her mum at all. She had been too angry for that.

On Wednesday, before she had been brought out here, something had happened with Pete, and she had heard her mum crying outside the house. Pete's voice had been raised, shouting. Another argument, though her mum didn't usually cry when they argued. Normally she was doing the shouting. Mairead couldn't remember the last time she had heard Pete yelling. He was always calm, kind, careful.

She stayed in her room and waited for it to be over.

Her mum had come up and hugged her after a while, her face red, her eyes full of tears. She had barely been able to speak without crying. Mairead had asked what was wrong but she wouldn't tell her. Her mum had wanted sympathy, but Mairead had only felt irritated with her. She had been here before. She knew what was happening.

Since they had started living together again (that was how she described it if anyone asked) her mum had been with four men, including Pete. They had lived with all of them. The men had either moved in with them or they had moved in with the men. From there on it was always the same. Things were good for a while; her mum was happy, Mairead started to like the men, and then her mother went off them. They began to argue. Her mum found someone else. They moved out.

They had already done that with Pete once before.

In between there had been something too horrible to think about.

She assumed it was all happening again. For Pete to end up shouting could only mean her mother had been with someone else. She didn't know what was wrong with her; why did she always do this? She liked Pete and she liked living with him. Of all the men her mum had known, Pete was easily the nicest, the most normal. She had heard him shouting and could tell that he was upset and hurt. She had felt sorry for him. She didn't feel sorry for her mum at all; she brought misery upon herself, because she couldn't follow her own advice. 'You have to find happiness in what you've got,' she was always saying to her. 'If you are always wanting something else, something more, something different, then you'll be miserable your whole life.' *Like me*, she should have added.

Mairead liked Pete's parents too – where she was now. Manny and Jas treated her with respect. They didn't pry or ask hostile questions about her friends, or her school. They didn't just walk into her room like her mum did. They made a fuss of her if she wanted it, but they left her alone, too. They treated her like an adult. Her visits here with Prem, during school holidays, were always things to look forward to. Prem was the closest friend she had ever had.

Her mum didn't have parents – or, at least, not parents she spoke to. Mairead had never even met her real grandmother. She had met her dad's parents – her real dad's parents – but that was a long time ago now and she didn't like to think about it. She had been happy with her dad. She could remember nothing bad about the first eight years of her life. Unlike now.

Sometimes she still missed her real dad.

She told Prem things she told nobody else, not even Pete. (She tried not to tell her mother *anything*.) She had told Prem about her dad and how he had gone to prison, about the time her mum had lived with a lawyer called Neil, how she had been kidnapped (that was the first time she had seen someone dead), about poor, sad Nicholas Hanley (who had been killed in front of her, because he had tried to help her), and about the horrible man her mum had stabbed to death in a shower cubicle (though her mum had made her swear never to mention that to anyone).

It hadn't seemed so awful, telling Prem about it, because Prem thought it was all fantastic, like an adventure story. At night, when they went to bed and switched the lights off, Prem would ask her about things and she would start talking, telling her the stories. Prem listened as if it were a real story, something made up. Sometimes she would talk to Prem until two or three o'clock in the morning.

'You're not making it up?' Prem would ask. 'You're not lying to me?'

'I'm not making any of it up,' she would reply. She never invented details because she didn't have to.

Prem was the first person who had ever made her feel she was special because these things had happened to her. Instead of freaky. Her mum had never said she was freaky, but she had never talked to her about it, either. She couldn't talk about it because as soon as she tried she started blubbing.

Prem imagined it all like a movie, which wasn't how it had been. It made her shake to remember some of the details. Prem thought Mairead was courageous, strong, clever. Nobody else that they knew had been through anything like it. 'I can't believe I know you,' Prem had said once. 'I don't know anyone else who knows as much as you do. You must feel like everyone else is stupid.' Which was exactly what she felt about most of the kids at school.

She had never really had a friendship like the one she had with Prem. If her mum left Pete then she wouldn't see Prem again. It would be like all the other times she had started to get to know someone. Just when things were beginning to work, her mum started to behave like this. Then they packed up and moved on.

She had been moving all her life. From one house to another, one parent to another, one of her mum's boyfriends to another, one school to another, one friend to another. She was sick of it. For once she wanted to stay where she was, with the people she knew.

So when her mum had dropped her here on Wednesday she hadn't really cared that she was leaving in tears. Her mum had cried on and off in the car all the way over, but that hadn't bothered her, either. She was determined *not* to be bothered with it, because it was her mum's fault. Because she did this all the time.

'Just ignore her,' she had said to Manny, who had been worried about her. 'She gets like that.'

But she had felt horrible then. Her mum had wanted a long hug before she left, but she had pushed herself away and walked off instead.

She *had* been upset over the last few days, but she was sure it wasn't about her mum. The week before, Alexia had called Pete a 'paki'. She had said other cruel things, too, about all of them – about her mum, Pete and herself. Mairead had not seen Alexia since then. She had told Prem about it yesterday and ended up crying, without really knowing why. She had sobbed so much it had surprised her. It had started with just a few tears and then she had not been able to stop. Every time she had tried to control herself it just got worse. In the end she had no idea why she was so distressed. But it had been horrible. Poor Prem! She had been so nice to her, trying to hug her, trying to get her to think about other things.

Then the TV pictures had changed everything. She had seen them on the TV in her room first. 'Race Riot in Bradford' the captions said. It had all looked mildly interesting at first, until she realized what was going on. There were pictures of police officers on fire. In another scene a group of boys beat a police officer with sticks, and he or she was left looking dead, not moving. Later, the pictures made it there was a war going on.

'Do you think Pete is in that?' Prem had asked from the other bed.

But Mairead wasn't even thinking about Pete. 'My mum might be there,' she had said quietly.

At ten Pete had called. He told Manny he had been slightly injured, but was safe. He was at a casualty station and would be home as usual in the morning. Mairead spoke to him.

'Don't worry about your mum,' he said. 'She's not involved.'

'Is she on duty?'

'No. Don't worry about her. We're both safe.'

He had been in a hurry, hassled, but she had sensed he was lying. If her mother wasn't involved then why hadn't *she* called her to say that? The more she thought about it the more convinced she became that her mother was there, that one of the police officers she was looking at on the news coverage *was* her mum, dressed up in riot gear so she couldn't recognize her, being pelted with stones and petrol bombs, cowering for her life. From the moment she realized how serious it was all she could think about was her mum.

By midnight she was really panicking about it. She had gone downstairs and spoken to Manny, telling him she wanted to go home, that she needed to see her mum. Manny had been lovely to her, but said that Pete had told him she was to wait there until she was collected tomorrow. It was too dangerous for her to go back to Manningham.

That had made her worse. What if her mum wasn't involved, but was sitting at home and the house was petrol-bombed? She had started getting hysterical then, crying on Manny, waking up Jas and Prem. In the end they had all sat around downstairs, trying to console her. She couldn't remember ever wanting to be with her mum so much.

Just after midnight she had tried to call her, on her mobile. On the news they were saying that the worst of it was over, so she thought it might be safe to try. But there was no answer. She had gone upstairs to make the call, by herself. Afterwards she had sat on her bed and wept again. The only reason she could think of that her mum would not answer was that something was wrong.

Prem had come in and sat beside her, not saying anything.

'I think she's going to leave me again,' she had said to Prem. 'I'm frightened she's going to leave me.'

It had gone on like that all night. She had not slept at all. It was the longest night she could remember. Manny and Jas had phoned Pete again at some point. But he couldn't get away. He hadn't even been able to speak to her.

At six in the morning he had called and told her that her mum was in hospital. By that point the news hadn't surprised her.

'She's OK,' Pete had said. 'She's going to call you as soon as she can.'

Manny was to drive her back to Manningham. Then they would go and see her mum.

She had washed and waited for Manny to get ready, all her attention focused on her mobile, waiting for it to ring. Pete had not told her what had happened to her mum or why she was in hospital. So she had worked herself into a state about that as well. 'I knew it. I knew it,' she kept saying to herself, even when Prem was standing watching her. 'I knew he was lying.' As she brushed her teeth her hands were shaking.

She was ready long before Manny, pacing up and down outside with her bag. They tried to give her breakfast but she didn't want any. The only thing she wanted was to speak to her mum.

Once they got to Bradford, Manny had to take many detours to get her up through Manningham. Coming down into Bradford she saw columns of smoke still rising from somewhere up near Lister's Mill. Police in full riot gear stopped them at three different road blocks. They were so aggressive with Manny it was scary, but he answered their questions calmly, unbothered. He kept telling her not to worry. The police told him the whole of Manningham was a 'crime scene'.

As they passed the bottom of White Abbey Road, by Cemetery Fields, she got a glimpse up the hill, where she had watched it all happening the night before on the news. There were stalled police vans and ambulances stuck in the middle of the road, tyres flat, windows smashed out. The road looked like something out of a disaster film, so thickly strewn with half-bricks and stones she could not see the tarmac beneath. All along the sides of the road were burned-out or boarded-up buildings, glass fragments everywhere. She thought about her mum, caught up in the middle of it, fighting for her life. She felt frightened just imagining it.

Higher up the hill there were men standing around the wrecks of charred cars. It looked as though the place had been bombed. Some of the houses that had been on fire were still smoking. At school they had shown her old films of London in the Blitz. It looked like that. Manny gazed silently at it all as they threaded their way through the police cordons and diversions, then, once they were through, tutted softly to himself, shaking his head.

They were almost home when her mobile finally rang. She scrambled frantically to get it out of her pocket, her heart racing. It was a strange number, one she didn't recognize. She placed it to her ear and said hello, then listened to the voice on the other end. Her eyes began to swim at once.

'Hello, Mum,' she said.